Dead Calm

Also by Level Best Books

Thin Ice

Quarry

Deadfall

Still Waters

Seasmoke

Windchill

Riptide

Undertow

Cover photograph by Kristen Daynard.

Kristen recently graduated from the University of New Hampshire at Manchester. She works as an Assistant Librarian and enjoys taking photographs.

Best New England Crime Stories

Dead Calm

Edited by

Mark Ammons
Katherine Fast
Barbara Ross
Leslie Wheeler

Level Best Books
Somerville, Massachusetts 02144

Level Best Books
411A Highland Avenue #371
Somerville, Massachusetts 02144
www.levelbestbooks.com

text composition/design by Katherine Fast
cover photo © 2011 by Kristen Daynard
Printed in the USA
ISBN 978-0-9838780-0-1
Library of Congress Catalog Card Data available.
First Edition
10 9 8 7 6 5 4 3 2 1

Dead Calm

Contents

Introduction

In August 2010 when we became the editors of Level Best Books, our primary goal was to produce a book. Of course, we wanted it to be the best book it could be, but with three months until release, our major focus was to have *a* book. We didn't have time to think about what would happen after we published.

What happened after was—to our delight, reviews were great, sales were brisk, and then came the nominations. Judith Green's incomparable "A Good, Safe Place" was nominated for an Edgar® award. Sheila Connolly's superb "Size Matters" was nominated for an Agatha award and Kathy Chencharik's chilling "The Book Signing" won a Derringer for Best Flash Fiction. We felt like we'd been hit over the head with the Lucky Stick.

So this year, our goals are high, and we're sure our readers' expectations are as well. We think *Dead Calm* is our best anthology yet.

As always, we begin with the Al Blanchard award-winning story. Among many things, Al Blanchard was President of the New England Chapter of Mystery Writers of America and a co-founder of the New England Crime Bake, which celebrates its tenth anniversary this year. We believe Al would have loved Lee Robertson's moody and powerful winning story, "Prom Shoe on Nantasket Beach," about a child who discovers something that changes his world.

Children also make discoveries in Judith Green's "Let Dead Bones Lie," and Janice Law's "The Armies of the Night," although that's where the similarities end.

If you've spent the recession dreaming about retribution against some of the institutions that got us here, we recommend Woody Hanstein's "Endgame," and Dashiell Crowe's "Clamming Up." For revenge of a more personal nature, try "All that Glitters," Kate Flora's prequel to her tale in last year's anthology, and Mary E. Stibal's "Sisters in Black."

The eternal battle between husband and wife is represented here by Louisa Clerici's delicious "The Rose Collection," and Ruth M. McCarty's tension-filled "Skye Farm Standoff." The *Kama Sutra* and banana peels somehow both figure in Leslie Wheeler's flash story, "Klutz."

Nothing is what it seems in Peggy McFarland's "The Red Door," and Tom Sweeney's "Cold-Blooded Killer." Characters take matters into their own hands in J.A. Hennrikus' "Her Wish," Sharon Daynard's, "A Fortune To Be Had," and Katherine Fast's "The Black Dog."

Finding exciting new voices is a part of Level Best's mission, and we believe we've succeeded this year with Adam Renn Olenn's funny and surprising "Coronation," C.A. Johmann's flash fiction "Death by Deletion," Daniel Moses Luft's "Boxed" and John Bubar's "Ambushed."

An unsolved murder hangs over the story in Steve Liskow's "Sweet Hitchhiker," while a school teacher is tormented in Pat Remick's "The Lesson." A memorable protagonist struggles with anger management in Nancy Gardner's "Count to Ten."

Joe Ricker's "The Fallen," and Cheryl Marceau's "Nameless," are darkly gripping. If your taste runs to the lighter side, we recommend, Michael Nethercott's hilarious bank robbery gone awry, "Plain Vanilla," Barbara Ross' cautionary tale about drunk emailing "In the Rip," and Mark Ammons' exclamation point on the whole collection, "Repose."

Photo contest winner Kristen Daynard supplies the eerily appropriate image for our cover.

We offer grateful thanks to everyone who has helped us: the former editors, the booksellers and librarians, Sisters in Crime, Mystery Writers of America, The Short Mystery Fiction Society, The New England Crime Bake. And especially the writers, "old" and new who have trusted us with their stories. We will do our level best to continue to earn that trust.

Mark Ammons
Katherine Fast
Barbara Ross
Leslie Wheeler

Prom Shoe on Nantasket Beach

Lee Robertson

On that electric-blue day of my youth I found the shoe. It was wedged between two rocks, its heel broken. I pulled it out and saw it was all dented and crushed in. When I turned it, foamy water trickled out that just stunk. "Rotten eggs" didn't even do it justice. Not even close.

The toe was pointy and despite the debris, I could tell the shoe had once been white, or ivory. A velvety material. It was a classy kind of shoe. A wedding or prom shoe. Kicked off in honeymoon throes? Cast aside before a post-prom skinny-dip under a Hull moon? In the black and undulating sea. That unforgiving sea.

I held the shoe in my palm, its peeling sole glistening in the sun, and decided it had been an expensive shoe. No girl, or woman, would leave a shoe like that, I thought—the shoe weighing in my hand, light and somehow human in its twisted, dented, fragile way.

My sister Honor ran up to see what I'd discovered and promptly covered her nose and went, "Eww. Where did you find *that*?"

"Between the rocks. Over there. See."

"Where's the other one?"

"There is no other one."

Our brother Gil joined us and snatched the shoe from my hand. He stuck one of his little club feet in it, sang, "I'm a lady!" in broken falsetto with a swing of his hips, and took off down the beach in sand-

1

spraying staggers, the shoe flying from his foot and flop-landing in the widening ocean spit, sandpipers darting around the strange ivory intruder.

I ran over and scooped it up, the water rushing in, the sand draining around my ankles.

□ □ □

We were staying with my Aunt Jackie, a chain-smoker, in her small, gray, weathered house on stilts: looked like a "walker" straight out of *Star Wars*. But it was right across the street from Nantasket Beach and right down the street from Paragon Park—a glittering, blinking, loud and stinky amusement park. A true paradise for children. For all ages.

Behind the Penny Arcade, the red strip, loomed the pristine curve of the Giant Coaster, my personal favorite. Its white spokes gleamed in the sun like an intricately woven shawl, creating shawl-pattern shadows on the asphalt. Its ticking could be heard all day—more slender yet somehow more threatening than the junior Galaxi's raucous clatter. From below, the Giant Coaster's fall sounded like a soaring; but when you were on it, it sounded like coals rumbling in your ears.

I didn't mind staying with Aunt Jackie. She liked to collect sea glass and had a gravelly cough. She was a pushover and often pulled me aside and ran a hand over my hair, giving me a side part I disliked and ruffled away once she was finished.

"Danny, you're gorgeous," she'd rasp and mom would smile and say my head was big enough.

Dad sat on Jackie's front porch and fooled around with his fishing gear. He'd ask me to join, but I'd almost always decline.

□ □ □

For breakfast we had donuts and cereal, sugary stuff that stuck to the roofs of our mouths before scratching down. Honor, Gil, and I ate breakfast at the table with our cousin John. Aunt Jackie occasionally stuck her head in: "Everything okay, kids?"

Honor and Gil would scamper off, the screen door slapping behind them. Outside, wild thrashing green and lemon Hull light. A gust of salty sea air would coast in. John and I talked. Guy talk. He was fourteen, like me, but smaller. He had thin blond hair and blue eyes, buck teeth that made him look even younger. We made secret plans. Things we wanted to steal. Places we wanted to sneak into. Fried stuff we could eat. John said he could get his hands on some yellow tickets for Paragon Park. He'd tell me how, when the time was right.

One morning he handed me the newspaper, clotted with red donut jelly.

"Check out this broad, Dan."

I pressed out the paper before me and followed suit.

Above her, the big black letters "Missing Girl." I skimmed over where she was from, Pennsylvania, and how long she'd been missing, blah, blah, fuzzy little print as though too heavy on ink, and focused in on her picture. She was the prettiest girl I'd ever seen. One of the prettiest girls, for sure.

Most of all, I liked her smile. It was a coy smile. I liked the line of her jaw, her pretty hair all sprayed up like a wave and out at the sides. I wasn't sure about her eye color but it seemed a deep, melting, ocean blue. But it could also have been green. A swampy, murky green. It was hard to tell on a newspaper page.

"She's *really* cute," John said, pointing a determined finger at the person beside the girl, with big furry hair, little shorts and a bare midriff.

"She?" I looked at John incredulously. "John, that's a dude."

"No!"

"It is!"

I fluttered the paper at him and told him to look for himself. He gasped.

"It's her brother, look below," I told him and he gasped again. "He just has muscles so it looks like he has tits. Little ones."

"Oh man," John said, covering his mouth. "I coulda sworn that was a girl."

"Well, it isn't."

There was a mild newspaper-tug-of-war at the end of breakfast but I won and put the folded picture of the pretty girl in my sports bag, right beside the shoe.

◻ ◻ ◻

"Where the hell did you learn how to catch?"

Most of my father's remarks to me started with "Where the hell." Possible alternatives: "What the hell . . ." and "Why the hell . . ." and "Who the hell do you think you are?"

The Frisbee struck my hand with such force, it burned. I was not a sissy but the blow smarted and I squinted down into my palm at a red mean streak.

I whipped the Frisbee back with an anger that made it turn sideways and slide through the air like an impotent blade. He caught it between his strong fingers and held it before his hairy stomach.

"What the hell kind of a throw was that? How old are you? Six?"

He wasn't really my father and hadn't been around when I was six. He was a later accessory of mom's, like a belching handbag or a scowling scarf.

As laughter echoed in all directions across Nantasket Beach with its stone-studded, olive sand; as the carousel chimed, and the Giant Coaster roared behind me, followed by screams—I wished I could be anywhere but there, with him.

◻ ◻ ◻

She followed me.

Everywhere I went.

At the Playland Penny Arcade with its blooping noises and mechanical laughter. At the Kooky Kastle—a peaked-green Frankenstein chasing a girl. On the Round-Up with Honor, our hands gripping the white bars, our backs pressed hard against the white cage. Even on the Tea Cups with nutty little Gil. Her face followed me. That smile. That face. That jaw line. Those eyes.

Had she been here? She must have. Had she been swallowed in the crowd? Lost amid thick swabs of cotton candy and competitive calls: *"Win one for the girl!"*

Maybe she took off with one of those guys. Those guys with mustaches and tattoos.

I couldn't shake the feeling she was dead. At the water slide that snaked down beside Paragon Park, I climbed the endless, not-so-sturdy stairs with countless others. Not racing like the other kids, the carpets pulsing water with their footprints. I climbed ponderously, with a new weight. Where was she? *Where are you, Missing Girl?*

At the top of the slide I could look out and see thin white seams rippling in. Endless Atlantic beyond. My skin burned in the wind; my arms covered with goose bumps. From below I could hear Taco's synthetic "Puttin' on the Ritz"; or maybe it was Prince's hyper "Delirious" or Survivor's punching, jog-paced "Eye of the Tiger." Memory clouds detail. But I know I looked out and thought the world had lost one pretty girl.

□　□　□

Little did I know that Paragon Park itself would soon be lost to the world. Our last summer on the magical premises. Its rides would no longer race and turn, its lights no longer flash. No more child cries would reach into the heavens. Paragon Park would be sold and condominiums would take its place.

My Giant Coaster would be sold to Six Flags and rechristened "The Wild One."

But I didn't know this yet that summer. Cousin John mentioned the threat of a sale but I thought he was just full of shit. Lying as usual. Paragon Park sold? Never!

We had just bought ice creams and were passing Fascination. Girls in fluorescent-orange bikinis with brown baked-in bellies and wispy hair fluttered by and John gaped back at them. As if he had a chance. He was telling me one of his tall tales, no doubt, when we both spotted the "Missing" announcement taped to the glass. The girl.

It gave her age, her name, and a description. So her eyes were green. I'd been wrong. Could have sworn they were blue.

In the close-up, her face beamed with the friendly insouciance of adolescence. A playful scattering of freckles across her nose won my heart. Hadn't seen those in the paper.

Then there was a second picture, full body: a pink shirt with monstrous shoulder pads; beautiful breasts; jean shorts with raggedy ends; and at the end of her tapered, tan legs—white, high-heeled shoes. Fancy shoes.

I hadn't told John about the shoe and so I held my bursting tongue.

Was it the same one? Had she drowned?

The craziest scenarios whirled in my mind from drown to shark to murder to kidnapping.

I sat down on the wide ramp leading to Nantasket Beach and searched the sea for an answer. The beach took on a cold and widowed edge. The sea could be dangerous. It could swallow you up and spew out your shoe.

At night I tried to look at her picture, John snoring in the bed across from me, our window open to soft wafts of sea air, the curtains blowing in gently. It was hard to see her without light, but I thought I could make out the approximate glow of her face. My imagination made out her eyes, and they threw a desperate, horrified look.

□ □ □

Around noon the parking lot at Nantasket Beach blazed, an inferno for the soles. We kids stepped quickly, towels flung over our butler arms. Don't know why we didn't just put on our sandals.

Mom I could spot a mile away, her white purple-webbed legs parked in front of her, her dark sunglasses on her complacent face, a fluttering blue umbrella behind her. Once a day she walked to the water and entered slowly, her thighs plump and dimpled, the water droplets on them iridescent. She walked in an inch at a time, eventually submerging her shoulders for commencement of her doggie-paddle: chin stiff and raised, hairdo unmarred.

Our "father" remained on his blanket, his face unreadable behind the sunglasses. I was pretty sure he was checking out girls: girls in tiny lime bikinis; girls slapping on Hawaiian Tropic; girls smoking and reading *Seventeen*—Billy Idol's "Hot in the City" sizzling from their radios. Some girls looked back at him.

Must have been his hairy stomach.

Maybe they thought he was older and wiser. More mature.

Once in a while he pulled himself up, straightened his shorts, and took off for a leisurely walk down the beach, a lion on the prowl. Nantasket Beach was long and we often lost sight of him.

Later when he returned, his throat was beef red with protruding veins. He'd clap his hands with a cheerfulness that made us kids falter, because the cheerfulness was so rare. He'd suggest we go out for cheeseburgers. Yeah! We'd like that, wouldn't we? Kids? And onion rings. Hell, yeah.

His cheer only ever lasted till it was time to pay the bill. Then his face got tense. By the time we were back at Jackie's, his face was stony again as he sat before the murmuring television. Mom and Jackie gossiped quietly in the kitchen. We kids reluctantly played Parcheesi. Moths whirled around the lamps and hit them.

☐ ☐ ☐

At night, Nantasket Beach settled down in violet and charcoal hues. The red sun hung heavy and portentous on the horizon. As the beach grew darker and darker, the high sea wall—barely able to hold back the tide in stormy times—became a kind of Babylon where couples leaned and kissed, and shadowy figures hid.

John hurried up and grabbed my arm. He whispered, "I got a lead!"

"Who?" I asked, Paragon Park's colorful glitter lights flashing above our heads. "What?"

"Follow me!"

I ran after him up the beach ramp, past smoking young people and more couples kissing. "John? What?"

The sea air was especially salty that night and my breathing seemed heavier. We stopped under a streetlamp and John grabbed my shoulders, his blond hair white under the glow.

"Dan. I know who killed her."

"*Who?*"

He impatiently beckoned and we crossed the street. A stout woman with a glittery scarf on her head sat by the curb with a sign promising "Your Future: For Five Dollars."

"Oh, you don't mean *her*, do ya?" I said, tearing my arm from his grip.

"No, of course not!" he said with rigid jaw. "Think I'm stupid?"

He drew me to a restaurant window, red-checkered tablecloths inside. A corpulent waiter with a twisty moustache carried a platter of spaghetti and settled it grandly on the customers' little table. I gave John a questioning look and he said with brow raised,

"The girl. She worked here."

"She did?"

"Yeah."

"How do you know?"

"'Cause I found out. She was working here for the summer. Wanted to earn some cash for college. And have a good time."

I looked in at the restaurant again, into its pinkish glow: girl-ponytails swinging, receipts tearing; the fat guy busying around, wiping his forehead with a cloth. I could imagine her working here. It fit.

"Yeah and so?" I asked. I watched the fat waiter spin around again and deliver another huge platter, this time something creamy. Fish? "Well, you don't think that guy did it, do ya?"

John threw me a sepulchral look. "No. Not *that* guy. But maybe the other one." He nodded. "Look at the guy at the end of the bar, Dan."

I looked and saw a strange guy dressed in black. He was wearing something around his neck that resembled a black tooth. He drank some kind of orange-red concoction. He looked shady, sure. But it didn't make him a killer.

"He's weird," I told John. "But I seriously doubt he'd stick around here in Hull after murdering a girl. Don't ya reckon?"

John said, "He might. If he was *nuts*."

The weird guy drained his drink, slapped dollar bills on the counter and slowly headed for the door. John and I turned and hurried toward the gate to Paragon Park.

"We should go home," I said, blinding gold lights behind me. "We're supposed to be back."

"Nonsense," said John. "My mom never cares when I come home."

The weird guy approached, even pausing beside us to light a cigarette. He was so close, I could smell his leather jacket. He passed and John gestured we should follow him.

I passed jeans-clad masses—clouds of cigarette smoke, ride smoke, jacket leather and sticky-sweet candy aromas. Screams rose and fell, turned inside out. Girls laughed hysterically; some cackled like witches. I saw teddy bears, sneakers everywhere. The Giant Coaster had a spectral quality at night; its ticking and notches resounded, then the soaring . . . The relentless climb, the deadly fall. You wild one.

The cool salty smell of the sea, the mechanical grease of the rides, and the warm wild odors of humanity having fun made for a powerful mix: one you couldn't forget. Fetid was the odor of the Bermuda Triangle, its little log-boats crashing in with boisterous regularity, splashing all over the place. A blonde girl screamed who'd been splashed.

"Dan, c'mon!" John scowled.

We followed our suspect all the way to Kooky Kastle, the scary ride, where we abruptly lost him.

John flapped his arms like a turkey. "Shit!" But I was calm. I didn't believe that our "killer" was truly the one. No, indeed. Our suspect had been a wild card, a wild one. I was more suspicious of the "normal" guys passing by in abundance: crew cuts and plain looks, muscle shirts; bellied fathers and old lonely-looking souls with clawed hands and greedy eyes. They were the ones I wondered about.

Though I pressed to go home, John insisted we take a ride on the Sizzler. For John it was all a game. A sleuth experiment. For me it was no game. For I'd started to fall in love with this girl. At least, with her newspaper picture. How could I enjoy myself when she was God knows where?

We were whipped around, John's elbow in my rib, his legs crushing mine. The greasy long-haired guy at the controls looked bored. He taunted: Did we want to go faster? Faces began to whiz, metal parts groaned. John yelled and laughed, and crushed me even more. All became a haze: the red lights, the endless crowds, the burning bulbs. I let the wind paralyze me in my seat. My face turned to stone. I felt no fascination. Just that icy oceanic chill.

□   □   □

I never did show John the shoe.

The summer passed and it remained in my sports bag, wrapped several times in my purple sweatshirt. A couple of times I took it out. Stolen moments. Its rotten-egg smell had subsided, replaced by a faint but definite smell of sea. Little wisps of seaweed on it had dried to the consistency of the flowers mom pressed in her books—a hobby I never understood. If you really loved flowers, why would you squish them between pages? When I blew on the shoe, one brown piece fluttered away like a dead moth.

Why I didn't bring the shoe to the Hull police? I'll never know. I should have. Parents were searching for their daughter. Police were searching for answers. Tourists were uneasy.

We look back, see past behavior, and can't understand it.

Why didn't I say anything?

I think I would say . . . I feared for my life.

On that silver day, we left Nantasket Beach. We left Aunt Jackie and John and their weathered gray house. We left Hull and Paragon Park. We gave the beach a last goodbye. Mom, Honor, and Gil took a last trip to the beach bathroom, with squeaky talk and careful steps. "Dad" looked up with his sunglasses and guessed the traffic on our long ride home. I nodded and mumbled, and crossed my arms. He began to clear crap out of our trunk, his arms swiping and tossing. He piled a bunch of it in my arms and told me to throw it away. I trudged to the next waste container and tennis balls, badminton birdies, hamburger wrappers, paper cups, plastic forks and innumerable paper towels spilled from my grip.

I returned to the trunk just in time to see him reach in deep and extract it—like a white tooth from a cavity, its heel spearing out. He nonchalantly wrapped it in a towel, but I'd seen it. A flash of clean white, of ivory. The perfect twin. *He might. If he was nuts.* Something wrenched in my stomach. Beach light can play with you, especially on an overcast day like that one. But I'd seen what I'd seen. He shoved the towel in my arms. "What the hell are you waiting for? Throw it the hell away."

I looked toward the restrooms, then back at the beach ramp.

"What the hell are you waiting for!"

I walked over to the dumpster, clutched the towel a last time. I told him, "But I like this towel." He barreled over, ripped it out of my arms and threw it away. He pushed me back to the car by my shoulder and opened the back door. I turned around to say something, my face turned up, my hands open, but he cut me off.

"Get in the car."

△   △   △

2011 Al Blanchard Award Winner **Lee Robertson's** *fiction has appeared in* Thuglit *("Pink Champagne")*, Absent Willow Review *("Emma Bovary")*, Yellow Mama *("Doppelganger")*, Powder Burn Flash *("Only the Lonely") and* Boston Literary Magazine *("Special"). She is working on her novels and has a blog, "Only Time Will Tell," at www.writerleerobertson.wordpress.com.*

Plain Vanilla

Michael Nethercott

All poor Tinker craved was a taste of fireworks with that lanky, brown-curled sweetie. Just a little release after all the taut-wire activity of the last few weeks. Not much to ask, really. But then the gal started in with all her crazy hoodoo patter, holding Tinker's wallet to her forehead and saying she could see his past, oh yes, his recent troubled past. And what she saw then was this: blood on the snow. Hot red on cool white. And damned if that didn't douse young Tinker's passion quick as bullets. Because, of course, it was true.

But maybe I'm outracing myself here. To understand Tinker's distress, you'd really have to go back to that night in Dorchester at Charlie Kepp's place. We were squeezed into Charlie's living room with a small mob of miniature savages running underfoot as Charlie bellowed at Angie to scoop up his spawn and all their cousins and their cousins' cousins because, damn it, didn't she see he was about to have a business meeting? Once Angie had vanished with the devil brood, Charlie shoved a beer into each of our hands (excepting Lionel who was pure in all things) and told us to plant our backsides on his ratty furniture. He threw something smooth on the hi-fi (Perry Como it was) so as to cover up our talk. With his hosting responsibilities all met, Charlie lit up a cheapo cigar and dropped his own wide load into a beat-up easy chair. Then he got down to the niceties of the plan.

"It's a plain vanilla heist," he told the three of us. "No frills, no thrills."

Charlie droned on concerning all the particulars about timetables and bank tellers and Tinker's finagling with the alarm system. He went on about a lot of things, but to be gospel with you, most of it sailed right past me. I mean, I perked up whenever my part in the merriment was mentioned, but a lot of the other nuts and bolts stuff was more than I needed to worry on. Especially whenever guns were brought up. No lie, I've never been one for gunplay. Sure, I did my soldier-boy stint in Korea, but even then I managed to stay fairly clear of firearms, both ours and theirs. As luck would have it, I landed an assignment as a driver for the brass; and since those majors and colonels seemed eager enough to avoid the front lines, then, golly gosh, I was more than happy to keep us as far from the nastiness as possible. Of course, every now and again we'd run into some mischief, errant mortar fire or whatnot, and I'd have to earn my beans by squealing like a drag racer around snake bends that would wear down a gazelle. After one of those little Sunday drives, more than a few valiant officers required a change of trousers, I can guarantee you.

That's all worth mentioning because you could say it led me to my civilian career as a wheelman. I'll get back to the job and all that in a sec, but to dwell a little more on my mama's only son, I want to put it down here that I am one good Joe, born and bred in Quincy, Massachoo, and as American as suspenders. A swell guy—hail, well-met and all that—and anyone who's a straight shooter will tell you as such. Good guyness is apropos for a wheelman, at least according to most of the movies I've caught down at the Bijou when I couldn't scrounge up a date and actually went to see the blasted motion picture and not grope some dolly. In those heist flicks, the driver is usually a nice regular chap who, through immense social pressures, throws his lot in with a bunch of unsavory types. Pretty much my story. When I finished my stint overseas, I came back, had a run of putrid luck and fell in with hard hombres like Charlie Kepp. Maybe Charlie wasn't Dillinger, but he had done a couple years for pummeling a pawnbroker in Dorchester and had his fat fingers in a lot of dubious pastry. I'd performed a few chores for the man, had taken the wheel for a couple gas station knock-offs, and had backed him in several other minor league antics.

Now Charlie was aiming a few notches higher: an honest-to-Jesse-James bank job. For experience, he pulled in one Lionel Witherspukk, a cat as odd as his name. Short, skinny and sour-pussed, Lionel didn't drink, didn't smoke, didn't use spicy vocabulary. In fact he hardly spoke at all except, rumor had it, on Saturday nights when he'd pay certain painted ladies to stand stitchless before him while he sat on a stool reciting the Gettysburg Address. Sure, I know I can't prove that, but can you blame me for wanting it to be true? Anyway, despite his quirks, Lionel had a couple armed robberies on his résumé, so Charlie signed him on. Me, as I said, I'd proven myself a reliable getaway man; and Tinker—a blushing, fidgety kid who looked like a dumbfounded angel—was recruited for his electronics chops.

"No frills, no thrills." That's what Charlie Kepp wanted. And on that night in his rundown apartment with Como crooning and our noses stuffed with the smoke from Charlie's miserable stogie, I'm sure, to a man, that's what we all wanted, as well.

Fat chance we'd get it. But to be fair, you'd have to say that we did our homework over those next couple months. Charlie ran us through the drills roughly a quillion times, fine-tuning as we went. For a big sloppy palooka like Kepp, he sure could be all finicky and fastidious when a bankroll was on the line. We were aiming for an early winter's day—whenever the first hefty snowstorm hit. Mastermind that he was, Charlie had worked up his own dazzling theory about police and precipitation.

"The city coppers drive real crappy in the snow," he insisted.

"And why is that, Charlie?" I just had to ask.

"Dunno. But it's the way things are."

"What makes you so certain?"

"I got a feeling for stuff like that. Like how gin tastes better if you drink it on a Wednesday. Or how dames spit as good as guys, but they never do it in front of you."

"Sounds like you've got a real gift, Charlie."

He grunted and scratched his belly all contentedly, like some big, unkempt orangutan digesting bananas. God love him, this was our leader.

Though Charlie wanted a snowstorm to botch up the cops, he never bothered to ask me about my own skills on a slick wintry street. Maybe I just reeked of self-confidence and he assumed I was aces on all terrains. And you know what? I am. Finally, first week in January, a big snow front comes rolling into town and Charlie gives us the thumbs up. I gotta say I was feeling downright chipper as we cruised towards the Grand Boston Savings Bank. I could damn near smell the small fortune of greenbacks that our little field trip would net us. Beside me in the passenger seat, Charlie looked grim and determined, all business. In the backseat, Lionel looked indecipherable, and Tinker . . . well, Tinker sported his usual wide-eyed gape, which you could compare to a mouse about to be swallowed whole by a snake. We had masks, guns, Tinker's tool kit and canvas bags to be filled by gobs and gobs of sweet casharino.

Now, I'm an upbeat sort. I don't like to dwell on past mistakes, because that kind of pondering can get you what the head docs call an obsession. Here's my motto: Give it your best shot, don't cry over spilt milk and loose lips sink ships. If that's too heady, then you can just boil it down to if you screw up, shut up. So I pretty much will, except to say that nobody could have figured on a pair of off-duty lawmen shopping next door at the ladies apparel shop. They were picking out something silky and naughty for some lady friends when they got wind of the commotion we were causing. Well, next thing you know, I'm tearing down the side streets, snow slapping across the windshield, with Tinker who's bawling and Charlie who's bleeding— from four bullet holes in his chest and gut. As for Lionel Gettysburg, we'd been separated in all the confusion and he had fled somewhere on foot. All this troublesomeness and not a single greenback to show for it.

If that wasn't gloomy enough, turns out Charlie was also mistaken in the matter of the cop's prowess on snow. They were keeping up with us pretty smartly, sirens shrieking bloody murder, and it took all my best moves to outrace them. But outrace them I did, and before long I was pulling into the alley behind Charlie's apartment building and getting Tinker to stop blubbering and help me haul our riddled bossman out of the car. That's when the blood on the snow happened. As we were holding Charlie up between us, some big red drops began falling onto the white ground and Tinker and I just sort of paused and stared down, fascinated really, watching as each drop landed. It was like seeing some crazy work of art being painted right before our eyes. You know, like that oddball modern goop the snooty highbrows are always cooing over. Bright red on bright white. Sickly beautiful in its way. Then Charlie started buckling, so we dragged him to the building's back entrance and somehow got him up the five flights to his apartment.

I'd brought him there because, frankly, I didn't know what the hell else to do with him. Luckily Angie and the kids were out of town at her sister's, so we didn't have to worry about any upsetting encounters. We plopped poor Charlie into his old easy chair and I found a towel to stick over him, to soak up his oozing life, as it were. He was breathing real slow and I wasn't entertaining any optimistic notions, though, as I say, I'm generally very upbeat. He looked up at us through half-closed eyes and I knew he didn't have any notions, either. Just before Tinker and I vamoosed, I slipped the Perry Como album onto the hi-fi, so as to make Charlie's final moments pleasant. I'll admit it, I'm a sentimentalist.

We laid low that night. Next morning the papers were brimming with word of our desperado deeds. Turns out that while Lionel was escaping on foot he had traded shots with those off-duty cops, drilling one guy through the shoulder. Nothing fatal, but enough to get his brother officers real frothy to nail us bad eggs. Of course, we'd all been masked during the job, but somehow that didn't completely settle our nerves.

"The police have ways," Tinker sputtered. "They've got tricks and detections and all that tricky stuff. Jesus, they took down Charlie! Maybe we should get out and go somewhere else. Like Indiana."

We were holed up in my own dumpy rented room, playing cards half-heartedly, just trying to keep ourselves calm and distracted. "Why Indiana?" I asked Tinker.

"'Cause they say it's real flat there." His eyes bulged. "Flat's good because you can see for miles and no one can sneak up on you when you see for miles."

I nodded. "You got a point, Tinker. Flat is good. But let's not panic here. It was a sadsack heist after all. We didn't get away with a dime, so they might as well find some more well-to-do badmen to chase."

"But that wounded cop—"

"Wounded, not dead. Everything's on the mend, kid. Just stop being so twitchy, okay?"

I was talking a good game, but truth be told, I was a tad twitched out my own self. I couldn't quite black out the image of poor perforated Charlie sinking into his easy chair and the sunset. No way I wanted to go out like that.

Lionel Gettysburg showed up later that afternoon. We told him right off how happy we were to see him so alive and unincarcerated. Instead of stating his own pleasure at seeing Tinker and me, he merely snorted at us. Then he asked about Charlie.

"We've got some bad news regarding Charlie." I laid it all out.

Lionel didn't bat an eye. "So it goes. But without Kepp around to corral you two . . . well, you'd just better keep your jaws riveted shut from here on out. If you talk to anyone about anything, I'll know. And, trust me, you don't want me to know."

It was the most conversation I'd ever heard slip out of his thin, grim gob. I tried to assure him with my motto about milk and lips and ships, but he didn't seem too comforted.

"If I hear either of you messes up, you'd just better pray the cops find you first." Then the mean little bastard made his exit.

Tinker was raining sweat. "He's serious, yeah?"

"Oh, forget that headcase," I said. "Isn't it lousy enough that the job went bad and we ended up penniless and our boss got shellacked? We've got to take heat from that runt Lionel, too? The hell with him. We'll be just peachy, honest."

A couple weeks passed and no news was good news. Charlie had a nice low-key funeral, which Tinker and I thought prudent to miss. Good ol' Angie had somehow handled things so that her husband's lead-filled cadaver drew no undue interest from the authorities. I knew a guy who knew a guy who had a cop cousin, and the word was that the police trail had gone nicely chilly. I started to breathe a little easier, figuring we were finally out of the woods.

Then one afternoon at a malt joint, Tinker met the afore-mentioned lanky brown-curled sweetie and things went balooey. Not that I begrudge the kid his infatuation. Millie was a certified doll, no arguments, who did full justice to a pink argyle sweater. And God knows poor Tinker was ripe for a little feminine sensibility after dwelling in my grubby male habitat for the past two weeks. As a matter of fact, I was with him when he first set his googly eyes on the girl. I even encouraged him to go sit beside her at the counter, buy her an egg cream and commence with the conversing. Myself, I laid low in a booth sipping coffee and reading a Roy Rogers and Trigger comic book. From time to time, I'd glance up to find out if Cupid was seeing to business. And damned if he wasn't. After a half hour of chitchat, it was hello young lovers and the pair of 'em was off to catch a matinee and make with the back row squeezings.

From there on out, their perky little romance went full throttle. Inside of a couple days, they dispensed with the pretext of film appreciation and trotted their sweaty young bodies straight to

Millie's west side apartment. With all the recent melodrama, Tinker definitely had some tensions he needed released, and Millie, bless her, seemed up to the task. Of course, I reminded him not to moan out any professional secrets while he was rumpling the bedspread. He assured me it would never happen. For a week or so, the kissy kids kept the bees and the birds plenty busy. Me, I managed to get my face slapped silly by a beauteous bar waitress who didn't approve of what I wanted to order. So, situation normal.

About a week and a half into their courtship, Millie trots out her heebie-jeebie act for poor smitten Tinker. As he told it to me later, they were perched on her sofa one night after he had Romeoed her Juliet or visa-versa, just shooting the bull, when Millie informs him that she's got these here dark powers on account of her ma and her ma's ma having had them, too. All she needs is to handle an object that has a close connection to a person and she gets these bona fide spooky vibrations.

So, like a dope, Tinker gives her his wallet of all things. Maybe he chose that because it was so close to his rear end, same as his sappy brain. As I said, what a glorious dope. Anyway, Millie holds the wallet to her forehead and, vavoom, she gets the image of blood dripping on snow. Hearing this, Tinker panics, says he's gotta go and makes a beeline for my place. Turns out I'm not there, so he heads instead to a local gin palace, drinks himself even stupider and winds up blathering about red snowflakes to a roomful of intrigued barflies. Swell.

Tinker finds me home the next morning and he's a royal mess from the mix of booze and hocus pocus. He barely gets his story out when the door swings open and there stands Lionel, short and silent and malignant.

Rather graciously, I thought, I plucked a bottle of soda pop from the icebox and offered it to my newest guest. Ignoring me, Witherspukk stared at Tinker for a solid minute before closing the door behind himself and pulling out a big ugly revolver. He waved it at the kid's nose.

"I told you I'd find out if you talked," he hissed. "Not that it was much of a challenge, the way you blabbed to half the town last night."

Tinker went white. "I didn't say anything about the heist, I swear. I just mentioned to some people about blood and snow and that stuff."

"Oh, is that all?" Lionel almost smiled. Almost. Then his look turned hard as granite. "I'll do you both now. Then I'll do the punk's little dame. Then I'll sleep better." He leveled his gun.

Now, I don't know where my next move came from. It was either genius or battiness, probably both. What I did was gasp real loud, point at the thin air behind Lionel and cry out, "Jesus, it's Charlie!"

Sure, I knew that Charlie was presently fertilizing six feet of topsoil. I knew it and I knew that Lionel knew it. And what I was pulling was a stunt straight outta the chintziest B-picture from a fifty-cent double feature. It was a corny ploy, simple-minded and rather embarrassing, really. But damned if it didn't work. When I yelled "It's Charlie!" Lionel actually glanced over his shoulder, giving me the split second I needed to hurl the pop bottle at his head. The gun went off, but thankfully the bullet missed Tinker and me by a nifty couple inches. Lionel staggered against a wall as we bolted past him out the door, plunging ourselves down the stairs and into the street.

We must have sprinted for a good half-hour before we ducked into a dingy diner and burrowed ourselves into a back booth.

Tinker was quaking something awful. "We gotta get to Millie's before Lionel."

"Aw, Lionel doesn't even know where Millie lives."

"He'll find out. You know that."

I did. But I didn't want to. I didn't want to clean up after Tinker's big reeking mess and go save his witchy beloved and give Lunatic Lionel another sporting chance to stuff my coffin. It just wasn't in my best interest. I much preferred to stay right there in that grungy eatery, order myself a BLT and peruse the daily news. I'd leisurely take note of President Eisenhower's latest speech, bone up on the major league box scores, and check the obituaries to make good and sure I wasn't in them.

But Tinker wouldn't let up. "You gotta help me! Millie's a good kid, you said so yourself. We can't let that mad dog Lionel get at her."

Mush-hearted sucker that I am, twenty minutes later I had exited a taxi with Tinker and was pounding up a staircase towards his girl's apartment.

When we reached the third-floor landing, I grabbed Tinker roughly by the arm. "Apartment 3-B, right? Do you hear that? There's a man's voice in there."

He listened and agreed. "He must have beat us here! What are we gonna do now?"

I leaned against the banister and shut my eyes tight. We were too late. It was a lousy thing, no denying, but there it was. Neither Tinker nor me were packing gats, and even if we had been, we clearly weren't the sort of fellas who could outgun a steely character like Witherspukk.

"Plain vanilla," I said to nobody.

"What?" Tinker choked on his own whisper. "What are you talking about?"

I opened my eyes and stared at Millie's locked door. "Charlie promised it would all be plain vanilla." I was feeling kind of dreamy. "I like plain vanilla. But everything's been the wrong flavor, hasn't it? Like Neapolitan ice cream—just too many stupid damned flavors."

"Have you gone nuts?" Tinker inquired. "You're jabbering about ice cream while poor Millie's in there—"

"Right. Millie," I said and lunged at the door, shoulder first. I was going to die for love. The ludicrous part being that it wasn't even my love, but some other goofball's. Impulse, that's what they call it. I was having a hair-brained, fatal impulse.

The door busted in nicely, we heard a woman scream, and Tinker and I rushed into the room.

There lay sweet Millie, eyes wide, sprawled over a big plush sofa and appearing mighty fetching in a wispy black nightgown. And sharing that sofa with her was the man whose voice we had heard through the door. A man who sure wasn't Lionel. No, this bub weighed in at roughly twice Lionel's size and was pretty much made of muscle (which you could see plain as day on account of his being stripped to the waist.) The guy had a couple old scars curving across his face like train tracks and a sneer that would wilt a garden.

"What the hell!" he shouted as he leapt to his feet and shoved Tinker and me back against a wall. His right hand turned into a huge gnarly fist, which he now drew back—the better to ram it straight through my pearly whites.

Millie screamed again. "Don't, Ace! I know these guys."

I grabbed hold of my fleeing wits. "Yeah, we're her friends."

"Friends? Friends?" Ace repeated the word as if he'd never heard of such a notion. "These two bozos?" He dropped his fist and took a step back, eyeing us like we were something he needed to scrape off his shoe.

Nobody said anything for way too long. Finally, Tinker puffed up his narrow chest and declared, "Millie's my girl."

Ace snickered. "Is that a fact?"

"Yes," Tinker informed the half-naked caveman looming over us. "We're sweet on each other."

This statement damn well delighted big Ace. He called out merrily, "Hey, doll, is that right? Is this schoolboy your honey?"

Millie finally peeled herself off the sofa and came to stand beside Ace. I couldn't help but notice how she wrapped her arms around his beefy bicep. Tinker couldn't, either. My poor partner looked suddenly all pale and queasy. I pegged it for motion sickness, due to the ride he was getting from ol' Millie.

Avoiding Tinker's eyes, Millie sighed and squeezed closer to Mister Neanderthal. "Gee, I'm sorry, Tink," she said. "You're a nice kid, but Ace here just does it for me. He's got charisma."

I'm no bookworm, but if charisma means having pectorals like

Old Ironsides and a personality like arsenic, well, then Ace was just dripping with the stuff.

Obviously in a state of shock, Tinker tried to sputter out something, "But, Millie . . . You and me . . . We . . . And Lionel . . ."

Ace stepped forward and grabbed a handful of Tinker's shirt. "That's enough, sonny. You heard what the lady said."

I wanted to ask Ace who the hell wrote his lines, but, deciding to retain my teeth, I merely said, "Let's go, Tinker."

"No," said Tinker. He sure was choosing one crummy time to discover manhood.

Ace, with an admirable show of composure, didn't rip his prey's head off right there and then. Instead, he unhanded Tinker and walked calmly over to a nearby chair with a jacket draped over it. From a side pocket, he slid out something which he promptly pointed at Tinker's brains. I tell you, I was getting awful sick of revolvers, especially when they were aimed in my general direction.

Not bothering with adieus, I yanked Tinker out of there and bustled him down to the sidewalk. I'd just started to drag him down the avenue when a taxi pulled up to Millie's apartment building and out steps Lionel. Luckily, we were far enough away that he didn't notice us. He vanished into the building and for a hefty moment we just stood there staring.

Then Tinker starts whining, "We've got to go back! We've got to—"

"Oh no," I groaned. "I've used up my brave deeds quota. And so have you."

We got into a tussle, with Tinker trying to pursue Lionel and me trying to subdue Tinker. In the midst of our disagreement, several loud gunshots echoed from above. We stopped dead and looked up towards Millie's. A second later, as if on cue, the glass exploded and someone was half hanging out the window, very bloody and very still. Ace.

A couple more seconds passed and out into the winter street

burst Millie, still garbed in her peek-a-boo nightgown. Not seeing us, she raced like a madwoman up the avenue, then vanished around a corner. Finally, as the third act so to speak, out staggered Lionel, clutching his gun to his stomach and looking none too healthy. He slowly made his way down the street in our direction, leaving a little trail of blood drops in the snow. Familiar. He saw us, opened his mouth (to, no doubt, offer a kind word), then crumpled to the ground. There were certain working girls who would now be needing a new client come Saturday night. The show over, Tinker and I skedaddled straightaway.

And that was that. In my opinion, it had all worked out real snugly. Big Ace and Little Gettysburg had gone on to whatever accommodations the good Lord had booked for them, and Tinker and myself had dodged a bullet—in the most actual, painful sense of the term. Not long afterwards, we heard through the grapevine that Millie had snagged a bus to Detroit or Chicago or some other oasis of bright lights. Wisely, Tinker didn't even think to follow his lost love. He seemed content to chalk up their spoiled romance as one of those character-building growing experiences that separate the men from the dinosaurs. Or something along those lines. By early spring, Tinker himself had left the city for a new, much flatter life. Indiana.

That pretty much ties it all up, except for one unfortunate P.S. concerning yours truly. While I was never fingered for my part in the bank job, Lady Luck must still have harbored a grudge against me. A few months back I got pulled over with a trunk full of slightly stolen wristwatches. And, boy oh boy, didn't that make the arresting officer's day. To sum it up then, I'm presently not behind the wheel where I belong, but behind fat iron bars where I'm not doing anybody a damned bit of good.

But, you know, at least I'm not stewing in hell or Indiana like my former associates. So, as I've no doubt mentioned before, I try to stay upbeat.

△ △ △

Michael Nethercott *has published stories and plays in* Alfred Hitchcock Mystery Magazine, The Magazine of Fantasy and Science Fiction; Crimestalkers Casebook; Plays, the Drama Magazine; *and various anthologies including* Best Crime and Mystery Stories of the Year, Thin Ice, Dead Promises, *and* Gods and Monsters. *He is a past recipient of the Black Orchid Novella Award for traditional mystery writing.*

Klutz

Leslie Wheeler

Tom Ferron awoke as he often did—to sounds of destruction. His wife Helen was a world-class klutz. Glasses shattered in her hands. Ladders tottered the moment she came near. Books cascaded from the shelf when she reached for one. She bumped into people, knocked things over, got tangled in electrical cords and dog leashes, and tripped over everything in her path. In twenty-two years of marriage, she'd left behind a trail of wreckage. My "Angel of Devastation" Tom called her. "Helen-proof your home before we come over," he advised friends. "Remove all breakables, and serve the food on paper plates." Cracks like this drew laughter from everyone, except Helen.

Now what? It was trash day, and the noise seemed to come from outside. Perhaps she'd dropped the garbage bags down the fourteen steep stone steps that gave the entry to the house an imposing look. Too bad she hadn't gone down with them. But, despite cuts, scrapes and the occasional broken bone, Helen always managed to escape serious injury.

At first, he'd found her clumsiness endearing. His chest swelled with manly pride when he fixed things she broke and cleaned up her messes. Not anymore. Helen's awkwardness soon became annoying, and finally, now that he'd had enough, convenient. All he had to do was arrange for a fatal accident, and no one would question it.

Divorce was out of the question. She'd never agree. Probably knew she couldn't manage without him. Even more important, she was his cash cow. Her money kept the little Rooskie gymnast he saw on the sly happy. Olga was young and beautiful. She was also an avid student of the Kama Sutra and an amazing contortionist, able to twist her lithe body into positions he'd never dreamed possible. What would they do tonight? Mardi—whatever the Indian word for Crushing Spices was? Or maybe Churning Curds, or the Knee Elbow position?

But business before pleasure. How to off Helen? Should he arrange for the heavy crystal chandelier in the dining room to crash down on her as she changed a bulb? Fix it so she strangled herself with the extra long cord on their old wall phone? Toss a hair dryer into the bathtub with her? No. Too ordinary. He was a smart man. He should be able to think of something more creative. Lately, he'd started following the Darwin Awards, so he knew about all the stupid ways you could kill yourself. Like playing catch with a rattlesnake. Or trying to tip a free soda from a half-ton machine only to have the machine topple over on you.

But Helen was clumsy, not stupid. People would become suspicious if he did anything too outlandish. Best to keep it simple.

In the shower, Tom was careful not to slip on the soap Helen had knocked off the shelf. He dressed and descended the stairs into a cloud of smoke.

Helen's harried face poked out the kitchen door. "I burned the toast and the eggs and bacon."

Tom fought the urge to yell at her. Instead he replied gently, "Don't worry, my little Angel of You-Know-What. I'll grab a bite on the way to work. Everything else okay?"

Helen's mouth quivered as if she were about to cry. "A garbage bag broke when I was taking it down. There's gunk all over the front steps."

Again, Tom resisted the urge to explode. "I'll take care of it on my way out."

"What a sweetheart you are! Don't know what I'd do without you."

No, but I'll manage fine without you. Very fine indeed.

"There's . . . um . . . something else."

Tom groaned inwardly. "Yes, dear?"

"I dropped the remote when I was trying to turn on the TV this morning. I think it's busted."

"I'll look at it when I get home. I'll be late again tonight. I'm going to the gym after work. Gotta keep in shape, you know."

"Yes, darling. Have a nice day."

"You, too." Might as well enjoy yourself. Could be your last day on earth.

Tom grabbed his briefcase and gave Helen a quick kiss. On the front porch he surveyed the damage from the broken garbage bag. The steep stone steps were littered with banana peels, chicken bones and skin, and the slimy remains of wilted vegetables. Ugh!

Dodging a recycle bin filled with cans and bottles, and two newspaper-stuffed paper bags, Tom seized the second, half-empty garbage bag Helen had left on the porch. He'd use it to collect the debris.

He'd just bent to pick up a piece of cucumber on the top step when a blast of noise from the house nearly sent him flying. "What the—?" Tom turned around and saw a shamefaced Helen at the front door.

"Sorry. This works after all." She held up the remote.

Tom pressed a hand against his pounding heart. "You gave me a real scare. Don't do that again."

"You poor thing." Helen rushed over. "I'll clean up the mess later. But please take these down with you now." She thrust the two bulging paper bags of newspapers at him. Still rattled by the blast of noise, Tom struggled to get his arms around the awkward load. He extended a foot into the air behind him, hoping to find purchase on the first step. Instead, he slipped on something squishy and teetered precariously, trying to regain his balance.

"This, too!" Helen rammed the heavy recycle bin into his chest.

Tom plummeted backwards in a hail of cans and bottles, bones snapping, skull cracking against each granite step before slamming into the pavement below. In the dimming light, he glimpsed an angel hovering over him. The angel smiled and shook her head. As he drew his last breath, Tom heard her say, "No more grinding spices for you, hon."

△ △ △

Leslie Wheeler *is the author of three Miranda Lewis "living history" mysteries, including* Murder at Spouters Point, *published in 2010. She is delighted to be entering her second year as a co-editor at Level Best Books, where her short stories have appeared in five previous anthologies.*

Coronation

Adam Renn Olenn

I checked myself in the rear-view mirror to make sure I wasn't going to show up with bird shit on me or anything. I got out of the car and locked it, then chuckled—like anybody'd steal it out here. A path led through the weeds up to the house, and I knocked, but too softly. I knocked again, louder. Too loud? I didn't want to sound rude. *Oh, for Chrissakes, stop worrying about the tone of your knock.*

There was no answer, so I looked around the corner of the house and saw a small cabin. "Hello?" I called as I stepped through the overgrown yard. Maybe he forgot?

I heard a voice from inside say, "Come in!" and I startled when his face appeared in the doorway.

My God, it's really him. "Hello sir, I—"

"Oh please," he said as he turned away, "hang up that 'sir' shit. Call me Steve, Stephen, Stevie, four-eyes, whatever."

Inside a lamp and a laptop sat on a small desk. The walls were hidden by bookcases, and two fabric easy chairs sat at the edges of a ratty woven rug. He folded himself onto the desk chair, slow and lanky as a giraffe, and gestured to the easy chairs.

"Can I offer you a Coke or something?" he said. "I'd offer you a beer, but I just ran out twenty years ago." He laughed awkwardly.

"Do you have any water?" I asked. "The drive was pretty long."

He handed me a bottle of water from a mini-fridge and I took a long pull.

"Sorry to drag you out back of beyond," he said, "but I don't like driving back and forth to Bangor when it's cookin'."

I wiped my mouth. "Are you kidding? I'd meet you in Red Square if you liked. I'm just thrilled to have a chance to talk to you."

He waved this away like there were gnats in the air. "Thanks, but I hope you didn't come all this way just to kiss my ass."

"No, sir. You said you'd like to talk about my book."

"Oh right, of course!" He crossed the rug, and as he passed me he made a short diversion, as though stepping around a hole in the floor.

He pulled a thick stack of papers from the bookcase behind me and sat back down in his chair. He flipped through it, pausing at the pages where he'd turned down the corners. I tried to pretend I was just resting after a long drive instead of following his every movement.

Finally he spoke. "It's good. I think you got a little bogged down in the second act, but not terribly so. And at times the purple prose strayed to aubergine when lavender would do." He shot me a 'gotcha' smile. "Nervous?" he asked.

"No . . . well, yeah. I mean, of course, a little . . . If you don't mind, I was hoping to ask you a few questions about your process," I said.

"Shoot."

"One of the things I love most about your work is that it's never about what it's about. For instance, your first book isn't really about telekinesis and revenge, it's about defining one's morality. Your plague story was actually about repentance and redemption. When you set about a book, do you have the underlying story—the *human* story—in mind, or are you focused on the surface layer?"

He clasped his hands together behind his head and took a deep breath, letting it out slowly. His gaze shifted above and somewhere behind me. "Whaddaya think, Albert?" he asked aloud.

"What?"

"Oh, that's just something I say when I'm thinking," he said with a queer smile, and continued, "Well, I mostly concentrate on the task at hand, but human nature interests me. It's one of the four subjects: human nature, the nature of God, the nature of reality, and the unknown. What else is there that's worth talking about?"

I scribbled fast, trying to catch it all before the words could flit away like bats.

"You write with conviction," I said. "The worlds you create feel so real to the reader that they must feel real to you. It would be easy to wonder how someone could stay sane when forcing his mind to dwell in such dark places."

"Well, I don't force it, that's for sure."

"It makes me curious," I continued, "do you believe in monsters, or is it an elaborate self-deception? Are you just playing the role of someone who believes in those things when you sit down to write?"

His eyes narrowed. "I wouldn't be able to do what I do if I didn't believe it on some level. But your idea is an interesting one: what if I'm putting myself on, going into a creative trance? Hypnotizing myself into thinking I'm the kind of person who really sees monsters, then describing what that person sees? No way to know, I guess, unless there's somebody to corroborate the story, or debunk it." He fell silent for a moment. "Debunk it. Wouldn't that be neat? Or maybe that'd be even scarier, knowing it was all in my head."

"Stephen," I said, "I know you've been asked this hundreds of times, but I don't intend it in the usual fan-at-a-book-signing way: where do you get your ideas? Is there a routine you use to dig in the depths of your imagination?"

He'd been drifting off a little, as though following some narrow trail in his mind, but when I asked the question his attention was on me like a searchlight. "What was that?" he snapped.

I knew he'd heard me, but he's the king, so I tried again. "Why do your stories revolve around fear? Are you dealing with old fears, or are there things in the present that make you afraid?" He looked at me for a long time. My palms felt damp.

"Basically," he said slowly, "you want to know if I write about monsters because I think they're real." He paused. "Do you think I'm crazy?"

I had the sense that what I said next was important. "Not at all. As you said in your book on writing, good writing is just well-ordered thinking set down on paper. Your thinking is too well-ordered to come from a mind that isn't fully under your control—unless you've got one hell of an editor," I joked, trying to break the chill that had settled on our conversation.

He didn't laugh. "You really want to know, don't you?" he said.

I sat up in my chair. "Well, yeah. That's why I asked."

"No, I mean you *really* want to know."

He was starting to weird me out. "Yes," I said, "I do."

He swiveled around in his desk chair, and from behind some paperbacks on the far bookshelf he pulled out a wooden box, maybe a foot long. It looked old, and it had an uneven shine to the outside as though the wood had been polished by the oil of many hands. He put it on the table next to me and sat down. "There's your answer," he said, "if you want it."

I looked at the box. It didn't have a clasp, but there were two small hinges on the back. The top had a crack running from one end, and the sides had a slight concavity as though the years of handling had worn it down like a saddle-backed old stair.

"You're sure?" he said, and fixed me with a serious look.

I nodded and picked it up; it was lighter than I expected. It gave a slight tremor, and I was surprised to see that my hands were shaking. I opened it. Inside was a pale stick with feathers wrapped around one end. I took it out of the box, and felt its dryness against my damp palm. I felt like it was drawing my sweat into itself. It was then that I noticed the gentle curve along the length of the stick and the nubs at the end.

"This is a bone, isn't it?" I asked.

He nodded.

"Human?"

He nodded again.

"Where did you get it?"

"Well, it came down through the Penobscot shamans, but I promised the person who gave it to me that I wouldn't tell."

"Oh." I grasped the bone by its shaft and swished the feathers through the air. I jabbed it at him. He flinched.

"Quit screwing around. It's not a toy."

"Sorry. I thought maybe you were putting me on."

"Hardly."

"What do you do with it?"

"You don't do anything. Just hang on to it."

"Wait, you mean this is for me to keep?"

He nodded.

"Thanks. It's really cool."

"Believe me, the pleasure is all mine. But I give it to you on two conditions: the first is that you never reveal where you got it, and the second is that you may only give it to someone who really wants to receive it. You'll know who that person is when you meet them."

I looked at him sideways. "Uh, OK."

"Good," he said, "that's done." He rubbed his hands on his blue jeans.

"So, getting back to my question, I was wondering—"

He held up a hand. "I've answered your question. You just haven't understood the answer yet."

His cryptic-kung-fu-master routine was getting a little irritating, though I didn't want to admit being irritated by the man I'd waited decades to meet. I put the Indian thing back in the box and shifted in my chair. Outside, the last colors of sunset were draining away.

"So tell me," he said, "where do you get *your* ideas?"

That threw me a little. "I don't know. I just think of people and places I know and try to imagine how they'd behave in different contexts."

He smiled. "Write what you know. Works like a charm."

"Yeah. That's why I've always been so fascinated by your writing. You're able to talk so convincingly about things that there's no way anybody could know."

He chuckled and took a Coke from the mini-fridge. "Want one?" he asked.

"Sure," I said, and he tossed it over. I caught it and noticed he was staring at the bookshelf behind me. "What is it?"

"Nothing," he said. "Nothing at all." He was grinning a dopey grin, and I was starting to wonder if maybe he'd been lying about the beer.

I turned around to see what he was staring at. In the corner next to the bookshelf, there was a man. His skin was gray and the front of him was gone—you could see his heart and lungs behind the ragged battens of his ribs. His liver sagged out, threatening to fall on the floor.

I jumped out of the chair, knocking over the table, and the lamp tumbled over. The lightbulb flashed with a blue pop and I screamed.

"What is it?" Stephen asked, a twinkle in his eye.

I stood against the wall, breathing in shallow bursts. My legs felt unsteady, and I went down. I don't remember hitting the floor.

□   □   □

It was dark and my head was killing me. I shifted it on the pillow. Sleeping? A dream? I didn't remember going to bed; my memory felt loose and watery. I'd driven up to Maine—or was that the dream? The bed felt hard and I rolled over to check the clock, but instead of glowing numbers, all I saw was the wood floor of the cabin. I could hear the flat tap of something dripping.

"Are you OK?" gurgled a voice in the dark. For a moment, I felt the tingle of anxiety that comes with waking up disoriented, but it was replaced by a terrible awareness. I'd driven up here and met him, all right; he'd given me some old Indian bone; and then there was that guy.

I groped for my cell phone and turned it around, sweeping its blue glow across the room like a weak flashlight. Something was sleeping on the floor—a dog, maybe? Couldn't be, not with that rhinoceros-like skin.

"I wouldn't wake it, if I were you," said the voice.

I aimed the phone at the voice and saw him standing in the corner, the man with the excavated chest. Something glinted in the light, and I saw blood dripping from a dangling bit of intestines. It waggled slightly with his breathing.

"I'm Albert," he said. He pointed to the thing on the floor. "I'm sure that thing has a name, too. I just don't know what it is, and that it's mean."

"But h-how are you h-h-here?" I said. I hadn't stuttered since the eighth grade, but my mouth had that mealy, twitchy feeling again, and I fought to control it.

"Here? I live here. Well, maybe that's the wrong word . . . I had a house up the other side of the field."

"But your chest?"

"I had the cover off the harvester to fix a jam. I normally woulda shut her down first, but the light was fading so I just figured I'd do it quick and be extra careful. It worked, too, but the digger arm got stuck on a rock. I thought it was still jammed and leaned in to free her up, but that shifted things enough so the digger come free. Went in my stomach and out the top of my chest, and kept everything in between for the good earth."

I swallowed loudly and felt embarrassed. I looked out the window and saw that a stain of color had splashed the eastern shore of the sky.

"Am I dead?" I asked.

"Don't look dead," said Albert. "You feel dead?"

I shook my head.

"Me," he said, "I feel dead. No doubt about it. It's like when you break a bone, you can just tell you're not gettin' off with a sprain. It's got its own feeling. As soon as that digger come through me, I knew. Been here ever since." He pointed to the floor at his feet.

"I thought you said it happened out in the field?"

"Oh, this cabin wasn't built 'til forty years ago. For the mother-in-law. She hated it."

"Because of you?"

"No, she couldn't see me. I think she could feel me, though. Like when you're alone but you feel there's somebody there?"

"Uh-huh?"

"That's 'cause there is. World's a crowded place. But I suppose I don't have to tell you, now's you can see."

The light outside was getting brighter, and the birds started up. I heard gravel crunching and feet on the wooden porch. He opened the door.

"Oh good, you're alive," he said. "How're you feeling?"

I looked from him to the corner.

"Did you meet Albert? Tall guy, had an accident with a harvester?"

"You mean him?" I said, pointing to the mangled man in the corner.

Stephen looked where I was pointing. "All I see is a bookcase."

I shielded my eyes from the sunrise and looked up at him.

"That's Albert. And there's probably some horrible dog-like thing sleeping on the floor over there, right?" He waved at the area where it snoozed in the early light.

I nodded.

"I would advise you to take pains not to wake it up," he said. "But perhaps all this would be better discussed over breakfast. Do you think you could keep it down?"

I nodded again.

"Good. There's a restaurant in town you'll enjoy. At least, it won't be upsetting."

We took his rusty pickup down the sweeping, forested roads into town. It was beautiful, except for a blood-soaked boy sitting in a tree.

"Yeesh," I muttered.

"Kid in a tree?"

"Mm-hm."

"Car accident, nineteen sixty-one."

He drove around the town square and parked in front of a diner. I started walking towards it.

"Hunh-uh," said Stephen. "The diner's good, but it's got things'll put you off your eggs." He jerked his head for me to follow him to a Bavarian restaurant with amber-tinted diamond windows. It was dark and uninviting. "Trust me," he said, "this is your best option." Inside was a bar and restaurant that looked like they hadn't made breakfast in years, unless you count the kind that comes in a bottle.

"Hey, Ken," said Stephen as he led me to a table, "brought a friend."

The paunchy bartender came over with coffees. "What'll you have?"

"I think today calls for an omelette, pancakes, and a pitcher," said Stephen.

"Give you two outta three. I'll not have Tabby after me."

"Just testing you," Stephen said with a smile.

I looked around for a menu.

"Order whatever you want," said Stephen, "I have an arrangement here."

"I'll have waffles, please," I said, "and a side of bacon."

"You want bacon, Steve?"

"Sure, why not? It's a day to celebrate."

"Somebody's birthday?"

"I suppose in a way."

Ken shrugged and waddled off to the kitchen.

Stephen turned his mug of coffee so the handle was going the right way and took a sip. "You're probably wondering what in the sweet fuck is going on."

I nodded and stirred one of the little tubs of cream into my coffee.

"Well," he said, "I wish I could tell you what it is or how it works, but I can't. All I can tell you is that I was in my early twenties when he gave it to me, and I've been living with the thing ever since. Until last night, that is."

"When who gave it to you?"

He held up a long finger. "Ah-ah. Remember the two promises you made. I've been led to believe that those promises confer some degree of protection from the things you are now seeing. I was never inclined to test that assertion."

"What are they?" I asked.

In the kitchen, the skillet hissed like an angry cat.

"Well, as you probably learned from Albert, the people are just people. Or were. The other things . . ."

"Like that dog-thing?"

He nodded. "Like that. Those are . . ." He studied the oily surface of his coffee. "Those are things that live on the other side."

"Are there a lot of . . . things?"

"Oh, tons. They're everywhere. That's one of the reasons I never moved down to Boston or New York. It's hard to find a building that doesn't have someone or something in it."

"Does everybody, you know, hang around like Albert?"

"No, not hardly. Most folks go . . . I don't know . . . to heaven, hell, the Great A&P in the sky? Who knows? Only a small fraction get stuck, but they pile up over time. Like luggage."

The door to the kitchen swung open and Ken brought our plates. For a while the only sound was the clatter of silverware. Once we'd pushed our plates away and had our coffees topped up, I asked him some questions about writing. I was sick of talking about monsters.

I reached for my wallet.

"That won't be necessary," he said.

"Stephen, please. It's the least I can do."

"First, as I told you before, Ken and I have an arrangement. I pay for every day whether I eat here or not, and he doesn't itemize. Second, and far more important, is the fact that I went to my studio today and was confronted by nothing scarier than a haggard-looking author. No monsters on the floor, no chest wounds in the corner."

He took a sip of coffee. "If your experience is like mine," he said, "you'll go through stages. You'll spend the first year or two scared blind. Then once you get a sense for what's dangerous and what's not, you'll start to see the humor in it; you may even find it boring. Eventually it'll grate on you, the fact that you can't go to the movies without seeing some guy who had a heart attack, or giant crows with goat heads at your kid's soccer game. It gets old. But at some point someone will come along to relieve you. I spent a lot of nights doubting that, but it's true." He took another sip of coffee. "You're living proof."

A terrifying thought occurred to me. "What if I die before I pass it on?"

He shrugged. "Beats me. You can tell the answer to whoever finds the bone."

Ken cleared our cups and we thanked him. Stephen held the door as I stepped out into the morning sunshine. It wasn't even ten and the day was already hot. He drove up the sun-dappled roads, and the gravel crunched under us in the driveway. We got out and shook hands.

"Thanks, I think," I said.

"Well, you're welcome. I hope you're able to put it to some use. If I wasn't a writer, I probably would've killed myself. Then again, I guess I almost did." He looked out over the field. "Before you go," he said, "could I ask you a favor?"

"Sure."

"Would you say goodbye to Albert for me?"

I nodded and whisked through the tall grass to the cabin. Bees glowed in the morning sun, tending to their flowers. Inside, the dog-thing snoozed on the rug, a puddle of drool beside its misshapen snout.

"Hi, Albert," I said.

He tipped his head in an acknowledging nod.

"I'm heading home now."

"Ayuh," said Albert, "I suppose."

"Stephen wanted me to say goodbye for him."

"He leaving too?"

"No, but since last night, he can't see you any more."

Albert thought on this. "Well, tell him I've enjoyed his company."

"I'll do that, sir."

I left the cabin and walked back to my car. Stephen was waiting. I delivered Albert's message and Stephen looked away. I dug out my car keys.

"Thank you," he said.

"For what?"

"For taking it, for talking to Albert. For a nice visit."

"Sure." I didn't know what else to say.

I took my briefcase and the wooden box to the back of the car and popped the trunk. Inside, a middle-aged man in a gray suit lay there staring upwards, peppered with bullet holes. I jumped back.

"Something in there?" asked Stephen.

I glared at him.

"My advice?" he said, "Buy new. Used cars have too many surprises."

△ △ △

Adam Renn Olenn *was born in Providence, Rhode Island and figured out how to read by the time he was three. He studied English at the University of Virginia and music composition at the Boston Conservatory, and lives near Boston, Massachusetts with his wife and children. This is his first publication.*

Let Dead Bones Lie

Judith Green

Margery Easton felt a breeze. A tiny, beckoning finger of air. She looked up from her book. In this drafty old farmhouse, breezes sneaked in through window frames, beneath doors—but this was more. As if a door were standing open.

She'd been getting some of the reading done for her American Lit course while the children napped, but now she stood up, walked quickly to their bedroom and peeked in.

Jenny lay in her crib, cheeks flushed, pacifier clamped in place under her tiny nose. Melanie had fallen asleep on the rug, her favorite storybook still clutched in her hand.

Margery's eyes moved to Tommy's bed. Empty.

Margery raced across the living room and into the tiny kitchen. The kitchen door stood ajar, just wide enough to let a three-year-old slide through.

She jammed her feet into her barn boots and dashed out into the dooryard. "Tommy?" she called. She scanned the dooryard, the driveway, the back pasture, the barn, listening for his call, or for the r-r-r-r of a little voice making the motor noise for a toy truck.

But all she could hear was the rush of the brook. During the heavy rains of the last few days, the brook had roared like Niagara, spilling over its banks into the pasture. Now it had abated, but still . . .

Heart pounding, she ran across the pasture toward the brook. And there he was! She saw him below her as soon as she reached

43

the edge of the banking. He crouched by the water's edge, running his bright yellow matchbox car into a smooth, round hole in the dirt.

"Tommy!" Margery scrambled down to snatch the boy into her arms. "Oh, Tommy, you scared me, disappearing like that." Holding him tight, she tried to climb back up to the pasture, but slid back as loose dirt gave way beneath her feet, where a whole section of the banking had newly washed away.

"My car!" Tommy squirmed out of her grasp and squatted down to r-r-r-r-r the car out of the hole.

"Come on, sweetheart," Margery said. "The baby will wake up."

"I want my garage!" With one pudgy hand, Tommy rubbed away some of the mud. What he'd been playing with now gleamed smooth, off-white. "Kin I bring home my garage?"

"Okay, okay." Margery bent down and stuck a finger into the hole, jiggling the object to loosen it from the mud. As she yanked on it, another dark hole appeared beside the first. Staring out at her were the empty sockets of a human skull.

☐ ☐ ☐

The deputy sheriff arrived in just over an hour. "Afternoon, Margery. I understand you've found something?"

He clambered over the banking, took a long, solemn look, then called in a report on his radio, after which he got busy with a great deal of yellow crime scene tape. "Please leave the area undisturbed until the coroner and the crime lab people get here," he said, climbed back into his patrol car and pulled out of the driveway.

Margery watched him go, the baby on her hip, Melanie clinging to the leg of her bluejeans. "Thanks a lot, Eric," she muttered, and snagged Tommy as he made a beeline for the fluttering yellow tape.

☐ ☐ ☐

The promised coroner, a middle-aged man in rumpled grey trousers and Bean boots, didn't show up until the next afternoon. "From the sound of things, the body'd been there a while. I figured we didn't need to bust a gut getting here."

He and the two young men he'd brought with him disappeared over the banking with shovels and cases of equipment. Margery could hear them working: the *shenk* of the shovels sliding into the mud, murmured conversation. Someone from the Lewiston paper arrived to take pictures. Neighbors began to drift in and stand around in the driveway; cars went by on the road, slowly. Word had got out.

Margery was dying of curiosity. The moment her husband got home from the high school, she corralled a neighbor to watch the children and dragged him with her toward the brook.

The men had excavated quite an area of the banking. On a piece of sheeting lay the skull, jawless, as well as shards of bone, teeth, a handful of shirt buttons, part of a shoe. One of the young men was making notes on a clipboard. The coroner stood staring into the hole, smoking a cigarette.

"So what've we got?" Tom asked.

The coroner squinted up at them. "Well, we're pretty sure he's dead."

Tom just nodded. "He? It's a man, then?"

"Probably. A young man is my guess. Lab'll give us a more definite answer."

"Do you know—um, how long he's been there?" Margery asked.

"Hard to tell. Thirty years?"

"Thirty years?" Margery's hand went to her mouth. "I thought it had been there for centuries. You know, an Indian burial or something."

"Oh, no. Could be forty years, maybe fifty. A hundred, tops. The soil around here is pretty acidic. Bones don't last long."

"We just bought this place last summer," Tom offered. "I didn't know we'd bought a family cemetery, too."

"I don't think this was a cemetery. We haven't found anything beyond this one set of bones. With so little left, it's gonna be hard to pin down a cause of death. There is a mark on the skull." He put a hand to the back of his own head. "Could be a fracture, but the bone's pretty far gone. Hard to tell. Lab may be able to give us more, but I doubt it."

"Well, let us know if you need anything. Coffee or whatever." Tom put his arm around Margery's shoulders and turned her toward the house. "C'mon. Let's go see if our little monsters have tied Millie up in knots yet."

"But, Tom," Margery said, "who do you think it was? How will they ever find out?"

Tom shrugged. "They'll look at death records, I guess. Maybe even missing persons reports. But I still think it was someone who lived here. A family member."

"In an unmarked grave?" Margery shuddered.

She dragged Tom to a halt, and they stood staring at their home. Plain and straightforward—and in need of paint—the house stood where it had for almost two hundred years, patiently facing the road. The big barn loomed next to it, and beyond that the green wall that was the edge of the woods.

"When I was a kid," Margery said, "this was the Wetherell place. The Wetherells were pretty old, and Mrs. Wetherell couldn't walk very well. Polio, maybe? I don't know who had the house before them, but—"

"Margery—" Tom's voice held a note of warning. "I don't think we should get involved in this—this body. Everyone is related to everyone around here. You never know what you're stirring up."

"But, Tom—" Margery had to trot to keep up with Tom's long legs as he headed again for the house. "We are involved. We live here. And I've been meaning to do a little research on the house anyway. The very early days," she added quickly, "way back. Wouldn't it be fun to know when it was built, and how many cattle they kept in the barn—and I've got that paper to write for my American Lit course." She grimaced. "Oh, why did I ever think I could raise a family and go to college at the same time?"

"Mm," Tom said.

□   □   □

The house had been built in 1802 by Ezekial Gage, from Rowley, Massachusetts. He and his wife had five children, of whom three lived to adulthood. The farm passed to the second son, Ethan, who . . .

Using her elbow to pin open the fat volume of the town history, Margery dutifully took notes for her paper—and to show to Tom. But this was all far too early. By the time the body had been buried next to the brook, the Gages would have been long gone.

"Mama! Tommy's stomping on my teddy bear!"

"Tommy, stop it," Margery said without looking up.

"But the bear is biting me!" Tommy cried. "Rowrrr!"

In the bassinet at Margery's feet, the baby's eyes flew open, and she began to wail.

"Oh, now see what you've done." Margery let the book fall shut and reached for the baby.

□   □   □

Tom had promised: just as soon as school let out in June, he'd start on the new kitchen. The first step would be to gain floor space by tearing out the partition between the kitchen and the pantry.

And today was the day. Margery packed up the food and dishes and all the other bits and pieces she kept in the pantry, gave Tom a big kiss, and loaded the children into the car to get them out of his way for the morning.

The perfect time for a trip to the old cemetery.

With the baby in a backpack, and a child by each hand, Margery walked through newly mown grass, studying the narrow, lichen-covered gravestones. She found Ezekial Gage's stone, shared with his "beloved wife" Sarah, and two heart-breakingly tiny stones nearby for their babies. Just down the hill was their son Ethan, with three wives all in a row: he seemed to wear them out early.

According to the town history, the older brother, Caleb, had been lost at sea. Hmm. Maybe the family noised that about, then buried him by the brook? No, no, too long ago. And what had Caleb ever done to them?

Okay. Now what?

The house had stayed in the Gage family until 1910, she knew, when Ethan's son sold it to the Wetherells. Margery remembered when old Mr. Wetherell died, and his wife went to live with their daughter out in Ohio or Indiana somewhere. There had never been any other children. Because of the polio?

After that, the house became a summer place. It was owned by a series of out-of-staters—and more and more run-down—until she and Tom bought it as a "fixer-upper."

With the children trailing after her like ducklings, Margery walked over to poke around among the newer headstones. She found Mr. Wetherell's. Presumably he was under it.

In the backpack, the baby started to fuss. Anyway, Margery was running out of ideas. Time to go home and see how Tom was getting along.

□   □   □

Tom was standing at the kitchen sink sipping at a mug of coffee when Margery and the children trooped into the house. "Hi, ho," he called. "Where've you all been?"

"We've been to the simmiterry!" Melanie crowed. "Where they put dead people!"

Tom's pale blue eyes met Margery's over the rim of his mug. "Sweetheart, I wish you'd leave this thing alone."

"How's the demolition going?" she countered. "Look! You haven't even started!"

Tom jerked his chin at a crowbar lying across the kitchen table. "I have started. See? I found that!"

"Good! Now use it!"

"Okay, okay." Tom set down his coffee mug and disappeared into the pantry. "Boy, I don't know what's been holding this wall up all these years," he called. "There's a huge crack in the plaster, up in back of the top shelf."

Margery stood in the doorway, watching, as he jammed the crowbar under the shelf. With a rending shriek, the shelf split away from the wall, followed by a cascade of broken plaster and a billow of white dust. "Blech!" Tom shouted. "This is going to be lots of fun!"

He let the shelf drop to the floor, then started on the one above it. More plaster fell away from the ancient pine lath. He leaned on the crowbar, sneezing as the dust engulfed his face.

"Wait! There's something in there!" Margery called. "It must've slipped through that crack and down into the wall." She slid under Tom's arm and tugged a bit of paper out from behind the broken plaster. "Oh, it's a recipe, all in that spidery old handwriting. Fried salt pork with milk gravy."

"I can just feel my arteries hardening." Tom peeked into the crack, then drew out another slip of paper. "Mrs. W's rhubarb punch," he announced.

"Old Mrs. Wetherell!" Margery said.

"Drinking rhubarb punch would make you old!" Tom attacked the upper shelf again. "Here's something else," he said as the plaster tumbled down. "It's got a ribbon tied around it."

Margery snatched it out of his hand. "The handwriting's different. This one's a letter addressed to someone named Maud Lovitch. Who on earth is that?"

"Well, open it," Tom said.

Carefully, Margery lifted the brittle flap of the envelope and slid out a sheet of paper covered in a strong, angular handwriting. "It's dated Fort Williams, Portland. 22nd October, 1918," Margery said. "Oh, Tom, someone was going off to war!"

"No, he wasn't," Tom assured her. "The Armistice was less than two weeks off. The guy missed out."

"Okay. Anyway, he says: "Dear Maud, Thank you for your several letters, the most recent having found me at Fort Wms, where, as I have passed my physical examination quite handily, I have joined several hundred other fellows drafted this month for training. Soon we will leave to do battle with the Hun. I must say—"

"I wonder if he was disappointed not to be sent over," Tom said.

"Well, he's way better off not going," Margery said, as if the fellow were getting into uniform at that very moment. "He says, 'Your news, dear little Maud, was quite surprising.'"

"What news?"

"He doesn't say. He just goes on, 'I ask that you wish me well, as if God grants that I survive on the battlefield, I am to be married upon my homecoming to Miss Amelia Greene, of Scarborough. I trust that this finds you and young Randall quite well. I enclose a small amount of assistance. I wish it could be more. I remain Yrs truly, Stephen.'"

Margery gazed down at the letter as if she could will it to talk to her. "This Maud Lovitch must be related to the Wetherells. She probably put the letter and the recipes up on the shelf for safekeeping, and they slid through the crack, and she couldn't get them back without tearing out the wall. Poor thing. I wish we knew about the surprising news. And I wonder who young Randall was. Oh, honey, you don't suppose—"

"Suppose what?"

"That Randall was the . . . the body? Or maybe it was this Stephen who wrote the letter?"

"Margery—"

"Well, I can't get a thing out of the coroner's office! They're not even trying to identify him! And here he was buried right in our back yard."

"Margery—" Tom jammed the crowbar into another crack in the plaster.

"Wait! There's got to be more letters!" Margery stood on tiptoe, trying to see into the broken section of the wall. "I'll bet the ribbon was tied around a whole bundle of them."

Tom leaned on the crowbar. "I don't know if I'm participating in a séance with departed spirits," he grunted, "or a soap opera. Please, sweetie, would you get the kids out of here? Go visit your mother or something. I promise: if I find anything else, I'll save it for you."

□ □ □

"Got the whole gang along, I see." Erlon Nesbitt eyed the baby in Margery's arms, then leaned over the counter to examine Melanie and Tommy.

"We're off to my mother's," Margery said as she set a loaf of bread and a jar of peanut butter on the counter, "so I've got to bring something the kids will eat. By the way, do you remember the Wetherells? They lived in our house, back along."

Now Erlon peered at Margery, his eyes as bright and piercing as a crow's. "You think the Wetherells had something to do with that dead body in your back yard?"

Margery felt a flush rising to her face. "No, of course not. Besides, it was way out in the pasture. I was just trying to remember—Didn't Mrs. Wetherell have some kind of problem? Was it polio?"

"Not polio." Erlon took off his glasses and rubbed them against his shirtfront, then lifted them to the light. "My grandfather said it was a motor car accident. Way back. I guess it busted her up wicked, and she never healed right. Did you need anything else? Some cookies for the kiddies?"

"Uh—yes. Let's have two of the chocolate chip." Margery pointed into the bakery case. "The Wetherells had a daughter, didn't they? What was her name? It wasn't Maud, was it?"

Erlon shook his head. "Gladys." He slid open the back of the bakery case and slipped two cookies into a tiny paper bag. "She must've been just a tyke when Mrs. Wetherell got hurt."

"Oh, dear. Poor Mrs. Wetherell, raising a little one in that condition."

"I think they had someone living in." He shook out a larger bag and elaborately loaded Margery's three purchases. "You want this on the slip?"

"Yes, thanks. 'Bye." Margery scooped up the bag and herded the children out into the sunshine.

If Erlon hadn't been watching, she would have done a dance step right there on the steps. They had someone living in. Why hadn't she thought to talk to Erlon sooner? In a Maine village, the storekeeper knew everything!

"Mama," Melanie said, "you forgot Daddy's newspaper."

Margery looked into the bag. So she had.

☐　☐　☐

"Why, hello, Margery. Oh, you've got the baby!" The librarian peeked into the sling where the baby slept tucked under Margery's chin. "This is your newest, isn't it? What's his name?"

"Her name is Jennifer," Margery said. "I parked the other two with my mother, so I'm in a bit of a hurry—I'm researching the history of our house, the old Wetherell place. I'd like to look at the Weekly Standard, from about the time of World War I."

The librarian put her fists on her hips. "They never did identify that body they found on your property, did they?" Margery felt her cheeks grow warm again, but the librarian was already digging in a cabinet, unloading small, square cardboard boxes. "Those issues from way back are all on microfilm."

The close, dark type of the ancient newspapers ghosted through the balky microfilm reader. Margery estimated Gladys' age, then searched, week by week, for the announcement of her birth. At last she found it, on February 10, 1918: "A blessed arrival . . ."

She pushed forward until she came to the accident, the following April. The description was succinct: "Mr. and Mrs. Edward Wetherell met with an accident in their new motorcar near to Back Pond. Mrs. Wetherell was severely injured, and was transported to the hospital in Portland." Nothing else. What had caused the accident? Had the baby been with them?

Focus. Stay focused. Margery cranked the pages through the viewer, week after week, until at the end of June she hit pay dirt. "Mrs. Edward Wetherwell has returned home, following her injuries in a motorcar accident last April. Assisting her during her convalescence is Maud Lovitch, of Brownfield."

Bingo.

Margery let the microfilm screech through the mechanism until she came to October. The newspaper hardly mentioned the Great War—a weekly column called "Among the Farmers" took the whole front page—but on the fourth page, there it was: a list of twelve young men sent for their physicals. Included in the group were Stephen Bard, and Stephen McAllister.

In the front pack, the baby whimpered. Pretty soon she would be bellowing. Margery returned the microfilm to the front desk and headed out of the library.

Two Stephens. Darn!

□ □ □

The next morning, Margery was struggling to feed breakfast to her family in what was left of her kitchen when she heard the crunch of gravel in the driveway. She peeked out the window as a small car, black and immaculate, pulled to a stop.

An elderly man climbed out. He wore a blue sports jacket, its plaid lining sagging below the hem in the back, and a striped necktie. He looked about him—at the house, the barn, the vegetable garden already in need of weeding—and then walked toward the kitchen doorstep.

Margery had the door open before he had a chance to knock. "Hello?"

"You're Mrs. Easton?" the man asked. "I happened to speak to Erlon Nesbitt, down to the store, and he said you were asking about my mother." He smiled up at her. "I should introduce myself. I'm Randall Lovitch."

Margery stared down at him, at the ring of gray hair around his shiny bald patch, at the badly tied necktie, at the car door still standing open. The first thing that came to her mind was: Funny, I'd always pictured Randall as a baby.

"My mother and I lived here for several years when I was

a youngster," the old man was saying. "Mother took care of Mrs. Wetherell, and little Gladys."

"Oh, my," Margery said. She looked back toward the table, where Tom was calmly pouring Cheerios onto the baby's high chair tray. The kitchen, with its ragged hole into the pantry, looked as if it had been bombed. "Do come in, Mr. Lovitch. Please excuse the mess. We're doing a bit of remodeling." She grabbed a dishtowel and wiped plaster dust off a chair. "Please, sit down. We're very interested in the history of our house."

"Well, I don't remember it all that well." The old man creaked into the chair. "I was quite young. My mother took the position with the Wetherells after my father was killed."

Margery gasped. "Killed?"

"He died in the trenches in World War I, before I was born. I don't think my mother ever got over his death. She didn't talk about him very much, or any of her family, really. She was all alone in the world, except for me."

"But I thought—You see, we found a let—"

"Margery!" Tom cut her off. "Why don't I show Mr. Lovitch around the place, while you stay right here and give the children their breakfast?"

□ □ □

When he'd seen the old man safely back to his car and out of the driveway, Tom stalked back into the kitchen. "Margery, you were going to tell Mr. Lovitch about that letter? What were you thinking?"

"Well, we have in our possession something belonging to his mother," Margery said. "And it was most probably written by his long-lost father. So wouldn't you say it should go to that poor old lonely gentleman?"

"His mother told him that his father was killed in the trenches! You want him to trade his war hero father for a love-'em-and-leave-'em jerk?"

"But he has a right to the truth!" Margery cried.

"No." Tom's voice was gentle now. "He has a right to believe the story his mother told him." He put his arm around Margery's shoulders. "I know this is your home town, not mine. I'm just an out-of-stater—"

"Oh, I don't think—"

"—but I've lived here long enough to know that the past is never really gone. It lives on for generations."

Margery gazed down at the floorboards, scuffed with footprints in the plaster dust. She let her shoulders sag pitiably. "You're right. But, Tom—"

In her seat, the baby chirruped. Tom scooped her up and held her high in the air, eliciting squeals of joy. "Who's Daddy's little princess? Eh?"

□ □ □

A firefly flashed against the windowpane. As Margery lay in bed watching it, downstairs in the living room the clock began to strike. On and on. Ten, eleven, twelve.

Midnight.

The firefly whisked away into the night.

Tom's voice was sudden in the darkness. "She didn't do it, you know."

"Wha—?" Margery tried to sound sleepy. "Who?"

"Maud Lovitch. She wasn't responsible for the—the remains down by the brook. Even if this Stephen person got her pregnant and then abandoned her, well, it's an old story. Too bad, but not a case for murder."

"I suppose."

"So let's forget about the whole thing. Okay?"

Margery snuggled against him. "Okay."

But as soon as his breathing slowed into sleep, she sat up, listening to the brook as it chortled through the pasture out there in the dark.

Tom was right, of course. Maud had loved Stephen enough to

risk getting in the family way. So why would she want to bump him off and stuff him into an unmarked grave? Besides, Stephen was out of the picture, living in that rose-covered cottage in Scarborough with his little wifey.

Then why had Tom suddenly started talking about the dead body again? It meant he knew something. He'd found something.

Margery slipped out of bed and tiptoed out into the hall, carefully avoiding the floorboard that squeaked. She paused outside the children's open door, listening to the sweet music of their breathing. Then she tiptoed downstairs to the kitchen.

After he took down the pantry wall, Tom had loaded the debris into cardboard boxes and hauled them out to the barn. He'd also taken away the garbage from the step-on trashcan in the kitchen. He'd even put in a new garbage bag.

Tom never emptied the kitchen trashcan.

Grabbing a flashlight from the kitchen drawer, Margery stole out the back door and scurried across the dew-wet gravel of the driveway to the barn. She looked into the trash barrel: no bag of kitchen trash. Then she spotted the bag under the boxes of broken plaster. Tom had tried to hide it!

She hauled the boxes off and ripped open the bag. Inside, among grocery packaging and a few scrunched paper napkins, and slightly damp with coffee grounds, was another envelope addressed to Maud Lovitch. Heart thumping, Margery drew out the letter and tipped the flashlight over it.

Yes, the writing was in Stephen's angular style. "12th May, 1921. Scarborough. Dear Maud, It has been several years, I know, since last I wrote. I address you at the Wetherells, as I have heard from my mother that you still reside there. The Lord has not seen fit to bless my wife and me with a child, and as we can provide a far better future for young Randall, we have decided it will be best to have him come to live with us, and visit you for several weeks each summer. I will arrive Monday next, late in the forenoon, to bring him away. I remain

Yrs Truly, Stephen."

Margery stood there, mosquitoes whining around her head, and read the letter again. And again.

Randall was all that Maud Lovitch had in the world. And now Stephen wanted to take him away—

"Margery?" Tom's voice called from the house. "Margery, are you out there?"

She stabbed the flashlight button and stood there in the inky darkness, holding her breath and feeling like a total idiot.

He shuffled into the barn doorway, a dark, rumpled shape against the faint starlight. "You found the other letter." He sighed. "I knew it would bother you, so I threw it away. But, Margery, he didn't take the baby away. Mr. Lovitch was raised by his mother. Now for God's sweet sake, come to bed."

□　□　□

It was two days later, after lunch, that the black car pulled slowly into the driveway again, and Mr. Lovitch climbed out. Tom came in from the garden to greet him, leaning his shovel against the house next to the back door and wiping his hands on his shirtfront before shaking hands.

As Margery came out onto the doorstep with the baby on her hip, Mr. Lovitch slipped a photograph out of the inner pocket of his suit jacket and handed it up to her. "I plumb forgot to show you this last time I was here. I thought you might like to see a picture of my mother, how she looked when she lived here. This was taken when she was nineteen, the year after I was born."

Margery gazed at Maud Lovitch, at her dark eyes and the soft drift of curls across her forehead and her young, resolute chin. And then she looked down at Maud's son, now already stooped with age.

Inches from her hand, the shovel leaned against the clapboards on the side of the house. How easy it would be from here, she thought, to grab that shovel. To swing it. If someone threatened your child, you could swing that shovel from up here, as he stood down there, swing it down on his head—And you could drag his body across the pasture, and use the shovel to dig—

Stephen Bard or Stephen McAllister. Whichever one it was. Had his wife come looking for him when he didn't come home to Scarborough? What had Maud told her?

"Your mother was very beautiful, Mr. Lovitch," Margery said. "You must remember her with great fondness." She passed the photograph to Tom. "Won't you come in for a glass of lemonade? Give me just a moment—I've got to change the baby—"

She stepped into the house, the air cool after the bright sunshine outside, and carried the baby through the kitchen and into the living room. She pulled open a drawer in the battered mahogany desk that had come with the house, and extracted the two letters, tied together again in their dusty blue ribbon.

She crossed the room and dropped them onto the hearth. Quickly, before she could change her mind, she took a match from the box on the mantelpiece, struck it, and bent to touch it to the corner of the uppermost letter. Then, holding the baby tightly against her, she watched the letters burn.

△ △ △

Judith Green *is a sixth-generation resident of a village in Maine's western mountains, with the seventh and eighth generations living nearby. She served for many years as director of adult education for her eleven-town school district, and has published twenty-five high-interest/low-level books for adult new readers. This is her ninth story for Level Best Books, the most recent of which, "A Good, Safe Place," published in* Thin Ice: Crime Stories by New England Writers, *was nominated for an Edgar® award.*

The Black Dog

Katherine Fast

I arrived at the first watercolor class a little early and a lot nervous. Half an hour later, three older women struggled into the room pulling carts laden with art paraphernalia.

The short one wearing a pink cap frowned at the brushes, paints, and Arches watercolor paper spread out before me. "I'm Amie. This is the Advanced Artists Workshop."

"I'm Cat. Pleased to meet you."

"Nobody told me about a new member. We vet participants. Please bring in a portfolio of your work."

Um, my portfolio. "Sorry. I don't have one." I scooped up my materials and jammed them into a backpack. As I turned to leave, the tall lady with a kindly smile took pity on me.

"Hi, I'm Leigh. That's a lovely pin you're wearing," she said.

"Thanks," I replied. "I just finished it."

Amie's head swiveled, and her eyes fixed upon the pin. "You make jewelry?"

"I dabble at it," I admitted, "but I'd starve if I had to live off the proceeds."

Helena, the third of the trio, fastened a Velcro splint around her wrist. "We'd all lose a few pounds if we depended on art for income." She turned to Leigh, "Now there's an idea—a new bestseller, *The Watercolor Diet*."

"What do you do for a living?" Amie continued her interrogation, albeit with a kinder tone.

"I'm a graphologist, a handwriting analyst."

That did it. Amie scrawled her signature on a piece of paper and handed it to me.

I glanced at it. "Sorry, I'd need more than a signature. I take my work as seriously as you do." I headed for the door, but Amie was not to be denied.

"C'mon, just a few words. What should I write?"

OK, I could do this. I'd been the flaky entertainment at enough inane parties to give quick, mostly nice profiles with an occasional barb thrown in so people didn't think I was shoveling smoke. "Write, 'The quick red fox jumps over the lazy brown dog.'"

Amie wrote the sentence and pushed the paper toward me.

"You have a big heart, but you don't like to show it, and, well, you're a bit stubborn and outspoken."

Leigh, the tall one, giggled but was silenced when Amie shoved the paper toward her.

"What's that sentence again, dear?" Leigh asked.

"Oh, for heaven's sake, turn up your ears," Helena chided.

Leigh fumbled with a hearing aid that squeaked when she pushed it into her ear. "Sorry."

I repeated the sentence and watched her make languid loops in a forward slanting pattern. I didn't need to examine it. I knew I'd find a gentle soul with a vivid imagination. I threw in "diffident" to round it out.

So, on to Helena who had already written her sentence and signed and underscored her signature.

"Well, actually, this handwriting is . . . just plain outrageous."

Helena hooted and they let me stay for curiosity value. Although I wasn't paying full fare at the movies myself, Amie dubbed me their "spring duckling." She was known for malaprops and mixed metaphors.

□   □   □

This morning's class had begun with Amie's instruction: "Today we'll paint in the style of Georgia O'Keefe." For reference, she'd brought an illustrated book about the artist and a collection of postcards.

Right. O'Keefe. Orgasmic flowers. While Leigh arranged a still-life setup of calla lilies, Amie and Helena argued about the legalization of marijuana, a conversation that mutated into a heated interchange about alternative surgical interventions for incontinence.

I half listened while leafing through the book. My anxiety level ratcheted up a few notches. I forced myself to take in long, slow breaths to lessen the tightness growing in my chest. I didn't have a snowball's chance of completing this exercise. Discouraged, I spread out the postcards of O'Keefe's flowers. *Yes!* I snagged her rendition of calla lilies and returned to my seat.

Talk dwindled as we concentrated on painting. At eleven-thirty we posted our work on the sideboard.

After a few moments of contemplation, Amie began. "Cat's is the only one that looks like an O'Keefe."

It was true. Their personal artistic visions were well developed, while I, unfettered by training, had created the best copy.

Leigh studied my picture and cocked her head. "All it needs is a black dog."

"Did O'Keefe paint animals?" I asked.

Helena groaned and Amie covered her mouth.

"No, no, dear. An artist named Bonnard coined the term," Leigh explained. "The 'black dog' is something incongruous the artist inserts deliberately to catch the viewer's interest. Something that doesn't belong—like that daub of color Helena added where none was called for." Leigh pointed to a touch of orange in Helena's painting that made the dominant blues pop forward.

After the critique we packed up and ate lunch down the hall. The old ladies talked about raising money for a dream cruise of the Greek Isles.

"Remember, we've also agreed to clear out Charley's house

while she's in the hospital," said Helena.

Leigh explained that Charley was an artist who had been a member of the group until recently when she moved into a life-care facility. "In this market, she didn't expect her house to sell so quickly. Now she's in the hospital, and the buyers want to move in."

I didn't inquire about Charley's health problems, because the question would most likely prompt a tale of epic proportions.

"There's an enormous amount of stuff in that house," groaned Amie.

"A lesson for all of us to downsize," said Helena.

"Maybe we could hold a yard sale," suggested Leigh.

"*Estate* sale, if you want to ask decent prices," corrected Helena.

Amie was quiet for a moment. "Remember when we volunteered for the PBS station's fundraising auction? And a month later, we cleaned up at the post-auction auction?"

"Uh huh. I still have a load of junk I bought that I've never used," said Helena.

"How does it work?" I asked.

Leigh explained, "After the fundraiser, the station holds a sale for the volunteers to clear out surplus inventory that never made it into the auction. In the first period, items are seventy percent of the asking price. Then, after a gong sounds, items are reduced to half price. When the gong sounds again, the remaining items are readied for the silent auction."

"So, if you really want something, you pay seventy percent. Undecided, you wait until it goes for half, and, if you're willing to gamble, you hold out for the silent auction," I paraphrased.

"That's it," Leigh said. "Everyone gets a number. You write your number plus a bid on a tag attached to the item. Every bid must increase by at least some pre-determined amount—a dollar, ten dollars, or, for special items $100 or $500 dollars.

"It's amazing. People end up hauling away all manner of things they never would have purchased at a yard sale."

"How about holding the sale in Charley's three-car garage?" Helena suggested. "We can sell her stuff and throw in items of our own."

"Do you think she'd mind?" asked Leigh.

"She's in no position to object," Amie said with a grim downturn of her mouth.

□ □ □

During the following week, I studied O'Keefe's paintings in an art book I borrowed from the library. I also found an analysis of O'Keefe's handwriting in one of my graphology books. To get an understanding of the artist's personality, I traced over the samples of her script a few times. Amazing how well that works.

When I painted the lilies a second time, the rendering was freer although still true to the original composition. In the spirit of a thumbnail sketch, I included an arrow indicating the light source, and drew in a few perspective lines. For my black dog, I daubed a trace of magenta into the predominantly white flower, and then, just for fun, I added a few handwritten notes on the sketch ("in the style of" O'Keefe's writing, of course) mentioning the location, Ghost Ranch, New Mexico.

At the beginning of the next class, I showed the ladies what I'd done.

"It's better, dear," murmured Leigh, noting the black dog accent. Amie smiled and patted me on the shoulder. "It looks like the real McCabe."

"McCoy," Helena corrected. She gave the picture a cursory glance. "Not half bad."

Well, hot damn, I made it over the median.

"Speaking of names, is Cat short for Cathleen?" Leigh asked, to change the subject.

"Catherine," I mumbled, put off by their dismissal of my picture. Amie chuckled. "We're the old cats."

"With your mouth, you're Siamese," said Helena. She turned to

Leigh. "And you're a Persian without the squashed-in face."

"And you?" asked Leigh preening a bit.

"What breed do you think I am, Cat?" Helena asked, deflecting the question.

"Domestic short hair."

Helena let out her signature hoot. "Alley cat, of course. How about you?"

"I'm feeling more like a black dog right now."

They laughed and began the organ recital, the weekly litany of blood drawn, tests endured, and parts replaced, removed or rearranged.

As we left, I tossed the study into the trash.

□   □   □

A group of early birds waited outside Charley's garage a half hour before the sale began the following Saturday. I handed out numbers from a roll of movie tickets while Amie explained the format.

The dealers grumbled because they couldn't make an early killing and run to the next sale. A few peppered Amie with questions and left when she wouldn't relent on the rules.

"We may have made a big mistake," worried Leigh watching them leave.

"Too late now," muttered Helena.

Amie eyed one of the dealers who stayed to view the pickings. "Here comes a wolf in cheap clothing."

Helena whispered, "More like a shark."

Leigh giggled. "Looks like Flipper with that upturned nose."

Comparing that obese bowling pin of a man with his moist lips, small unblinking eyes, and honker of a nose to a cute dolphin was a kindness, but that was Leigh's nature.

He cruised the room with the graceful economy of motion peculiar to heavy people, scanning the tables, and fingering a few items in passing. He jumped the queue at the jewelry table by wedging his protruding gut between two women. He snagged a silver charm bracelet they were considering and backed away before they could object.

I watched him pause before the artwork stacked against the back wall of the garage. Paging through the paintings, he shook his head, rejecting picture after picture.

Amie walked around the room smiling, whispering, "Caper diem," holding the gong overhead to remind buyers that the current period could end at any second.

To our surprise, sales were brisk as risk-averse shoppers paid full price for prized items. Flipper stood in line to buy the silver bracelet.

"Not going for the art collection?" I asked him at checkout.

"You must be kidding," he snorted. "For five thousand dollars? I don't recognize any of the artists' names. Frankly, I wouldn't pay half price for them."

Amie overheard his remark. She straightened to her full five foot two and approached. "Allow us to introduce ourselves. Leigh, Helena and I are all signature members of the American Water—"

"No offense, girls," Flipper interrupted, "but I wouldn't hang *any* of those pictures on my wall." He turned his back on her and withdrew his wallet to pay. Amie's face flared to alizarin crimson. Leigh pulled her away before she made a scene.

During the second period the crowd thinned considerably and sales slowed to a trickle. After what seemed like an eternity, Amie hit the gong.

About twenty-five stalwarts milled about as the silent auction got underway. Those with special interest in an item watched covertly to see who else was bidding on it. When they thought their competition wasn't watching, they swooped in and raised the bid.

I have to admit, I got caught up bidding on a charming antique wall clock. After half an hour, I was confident I was the sole bidder. I'd get it for twenty-five dollars! I checked the bid sheet from time to time as I ventured farther afield searching for other bargains.

When I returned after ten minutes, someone had sniped me.

I upped the bid by five dollars and watched for my competition. I pegged her the fourth time she raised the bid. She knew I'd made her and looked directly at me with a smile. I finger waved. We stalked each other, pretending nonchalance through two more bid cycles.

"How's it going?" Amie asked. She looked at the bid sheet in my hand and laughed. "Good luck!" She marched off waving the gong overhead.

I looked at the sheet. Good grief! What was I thinking? Or not thinking? The last bid was over the original asking price and way more than I could afford. I walked away, shaken by how easily I'd been suckered.

A cluster of people crowded in front of the art collection at the back of the garage where Amie was holding forth in low tones to a woman next to her. I was surprised to see that Flipper had returned and was circling the group, tilting his head toward the conversation.

Curious, I walked to the table and picked up the art collection bid sheet. Bidding had begun at $100 with minimum increments of $100. After an initial flurry, the original number of bidders had whittled down from nine to two. The high bid stood at $900, a far cry from the earlier asking price of $5,000. Better than zero, although I could tell by the old cats' long faces that they weren't happy.

"What's happening? I thought this was a silent auction," I asked the lady next to me.

"A local artist had a question about the O'Keefe sketch."

I slid past Leigh into the group behind Amie. I was a head taller, and could easily see over her. I gasped. My little seven-by-five inch O'Keefe sketch was propped in front against the larger pictures. It looked great, but then, everything looks better matted and framed. A small, elderly woman with a cane winced slightly as she stepped forward to look more closely at the painting.

I pushed my way to the front. "What's the idea?" I asked Amie.

"Shhhhh!" she responded.

Heads turned.

"But you can't sell that." I reached for my picture.

Amie latched onto my arm with a falcon's grip and tapped the lady with the cane on the shoulder. "Charlotte, I'd like you to meet a new member of our art group, Cat. Cat, this is Charlotte Jameson. Mrs. Jameson is another signature member of the American Watercolor Society."

Mrs. Jameson switched the cane to her left hand to shake hands. A wide smile wreathed her face accenting merry eyes that made her look as if she were about to laugh. "I was admiring that picture and wondering if it could be authentic," she said.

Jeeze! I shook my head. "I shouldn't think so. A representative from Sotheby's took all the *really* valuable antiques and famous artists' pictures. Evidently they didn't think it was genuine."

"But, it's smaller. I didn't see it the first time through. It's possible that the appraiser didn't either."

"Could it be a workshop demonstration?" asked Amie, frowning at me.

"If so, O'Keefe would have signed it for the participant," I countered. "No, I think it's a copy. A good copy, but a copy nonetheless."

Helena stepped forward. "You're either suggesting that we don't know art or that we're misrepresenting this picture." She lowered her head and stared at me with raised eyebrows. "I assure you, we know art. We've told Mrs. Jameson we can't attest to the provenance of this painting."

"Providence?" I asked.

Helena rolled her eyes heavenward. "I rest my case."

I backed away only to bump into the soft expanse of Flipper's belly.

"Watch where you're going," he grunted. He blimped me aside on his way to the bid sheet where he entered $1,000. I smiled and relaxed. I wouldn't mind if that bloviating hunk of blubber won my picture.

But as soon as he walked away, Mrs. Jameson limped to the table. She wrote her ID number and $1,100.

Damnation. Much as I admired the old cats, I couldn't let this kindly woman be snookered.

"Mrs. Jameson, may I have a word?" I pulled her aside. In a low voice that I hoped the circling Flipper couldn't overhear, I swore the picture was a fake.

"How can you be so sure?" she asked. "What are your art credentials?" She was polite, but her eyes scanned the crowd for Flipper.

"Well, actually, I'm a beginner," I stammered.

Amie's talon sank into my arm a second time as she insinuated herself between us. "Cat is a novice who was placed in our class. . . *by mistake,*" she announced in a stage whisper that could be heard in Buffalo.

That stung. Might as well tell the whole story. "The picture is the result of an exercise we did in class. We were painting 'in the style of O'Keefe.'"

"Uh huh," Flip's nasal voice behind me challenged. "Sure you were. You're a rank beginner, and you painted a convincing O'Keefe study in a class?" Flip turned to me. "Why are you so all-fired determined to discourage us? "

"Because it's my picture!"

He sauntered to the table and upped the bid to $1,500.

"Mrs. Jameson" I whispered, "I *copied* a postcard. Amie, tell her. You know it's true," I pleaded.

Amie shook her head. "Cat, this is embarrassing. Pull yourself together." She exchanged a glance with Mrs. Jameson, shrugged, cast her hands in the air, and walked away. Mrs. Jameson entered $1,800 on the bid sheet

Before the ink could dry, Flipper wrote in his ID. He looked at me. "Clever ploy, sweetie, but it won't wash. If you want the picture, you'll just have to bid like the rest of us." He offered an unctuous smile and jumped the bid to $2,000.

What could I say to make Mrs. Jameson believe me? In the art world, I was a fish out of soup, as Amie would say. But I do know about handwriting. I dashed to the hallway and retrieved the handwriting book from my backpack. When I returned, I glanced at the bid sheet: $3,000 with Mrs. Jameson in the lead.

I took her aside again. "I can prove that the writing isn't O'Keefe's. I'm a handwriting expert." I opened the book to the author's analysis of O'Keefe's handwriting. "Look at the difference in the distance between the letters on the painting compared to O'Keefe's writing in the book." I pointed out the discrepancy. Although Mrs. Jameson seemed to follow my argument, she was more interested in tracking Flipper as he cruised the room.

"And here, see the wider spaces between both words and lines? We can measure these traits as well as a host of others." Mrs. Jameson's attention lagged. "Notice how this script has lead-in strokes, taller *t* stems, and upper loops that—" I closed the book as a shadow darkened the page.

"Doing a little research, ladies? I should have known you two were working together." Flipper wrested the book from my hand. "Let me see." He opened to my bookmark and studied the text for a moment. He glanced from the book to the painting and back again, comparing the handwriting.

"Pretty convincing." He handed the book back to me, walked to the table and bumped the bid to $4,000.

Mrs. Jameson limped to the table and looked at the bid sheet for a long moment, then shook her head and backed away. Phew! For a minute, I thought she'd win. *Come on, Amie. Ring that gong!*

Flip circled twice to make sure he still had the high bid and then directed his attention to an oriental rug.

I turned aside to console Mrs. Jameson, but she was gone. For someone in pain and dependent on a cane, the woman moved with amazing speed. She grabbed the sheet and wrote as fast as she could.

Flipper forgot all of his mother's exhortations about being kind to old ladies. He lunged and snatched the paper, causing Mrs. Jameson's pen to smear on the last digit of her $4,500 bid.

"Hey!" she objected.

He ignored her and entered $5,500.

Mrs. Jameson's face flared red. She pounded her cane on Flip's shoe.

"Owwww!" Flip let go of the sheet and hopped about, more surprised than hurt.

Amie paraded by with the omnipresent gong. "Last call. Just seconds to go!" she cried.

Helena scooped the bid sheet from the floor and handed it to Mrs. Jameson. She smiled and wrote $6,000 with a triumphant flourish.

Flipper reached over her shoulder and ripped the sheet from her hand. He held it high over his head while he scrawled $7,000.

"Put it down! Not fair!"

Flipper laughed, dangling the sheet just out of reach.

"Amie! Help!" Mrs. Jameson raised her cane to strike.

BONG!

Flipper pumped his fist in the air. "Better luck next time, old girl."

Mrs. Jameson lowered her cane and threw her pen to the floor.

"Best take this with me," said Flipper with a smile, tucking the picture under his arm. "I'll bring the van around for the others," he called to Amie as he left the garage.

In flash of motion from my left, Amie flew at me. I raised my arm to protect my face as she enclosed me in a warm hug. "You were magnificent!"

Mouth agape, I watched Mrs. Jameson, Amie, Helena, and Leigh try their level best to execute a group high five.

Mrs. Jameson approached me with a wide smile. "Hi. I'm Charley. I've heard so much about you."

She noticed my confusion. "Charley, short for Charlotte. My

father wanted a boy," she laughed.

"But . . . you're in the hospital."

"Yup. Hip replacement."

The penny dropped. "Why didn't anyone tell me?" I demanded.

"Forgive us, dear, but we couldn't," Leigh explained. "You were our black dog."

△ △ △

Katherine Fast *aka Kat is on her eighth or ninth life focusing on fiction writing, watercolor and handwriting analysis. Her short stories have been published in Level Best anthologies and "The Bonus," published by NEWN, won a flash fiction award. She's now doing her level best as an editor. She and her husband live in Massachusetts with a big Boss dog and two spoiled cats.*

Cold-Blooded Killer

Tom Sweeney

Prison guards have a bad rap. Sure, some of the guys are a little hard-nosed, but nothing like the mean-spirited and sadistic bullies you see in the movies. Most of us are just regular guys. We treat the prisoners decently, commiserate with those who claim they're innocent—pretty much all of them—and joke with those so inclined. For most of us guards, violence is distasteful. We don't take pleasure in hurting anyone, and killing someone is the most distasteful thing of all.

That's why I hate execution days. My part in an execution is planned, staged and performed to a schedule. Cold blooded. I can't even claim heat of the moment. Most of the murderers we house committed crimes of passion, killing during emotional duress and often more deeply regretted than the public could ever believe.

There are very few truly cold-blooded killers in this world. Vecciorello is one of them, and Willie and I would soon be escorting her to the execution chamber.

For now, Willie and I waited in the Guards' Lounge, staring at each other without speaking. The gray Formica tabletop between us reflected the color of Willie's face, and probably mine, too. Every few seconds he'd sigh, or I'd sigh, or one or the other of us would look up at the round, institution-style clock hanging on the olive green wall opposite the room's single door. Usually we played cards and listened to the radio, but executions upset us, me more than Willie. We knew time would pass quicker if we followed our routine, but our hearts weren't in it.

Normally I work the exercise yard. I like being outdoors, and the prisoners all behave better in the fresh, open air. We joke, we laugh. I referee arm wrestling and chin up contests. I enjoy being a prison guard.

The job I had to do today had nothing to do with being a prison guard. It was listed in my personnel jacket under "Other Duties as Assigned." I had been assigned this other duty three times now, and each time I hated myself afterwards. Never again. I'll call in sick from now on if I have to.

The door hinges squawked and we both jumped. Jerry Neville, the warden's assistant, poked his head into the room. Execution Day left its ugly mark on him, too. Jerry looks a lot like Jack Nicholson, and normally, when he stuck his head into a room, he put on that crazed face that Nicholson did in *The Shining*. You know the one, where Nicholson's character Jack Torrance rips a hole in the locked door with an axe, sticks a wildly insane face through the hole, and says, "Honey, I'm home." Today, Execution Day, Jerry looked serious, somber, thoughtful. The effect was somehow scarier than Jack Torrance trying to murder his wife. Redrum, indeed.

Neville cleared his throat. "Time to get Vecciorello," he said. He stared a moment, opened his mouth as if to say something else, then shook his head and left. He was lucky—his part was done.

Willie and I scraped our folding metal chairs back across the worn linoleum and stood. We left the dingy, green room to walk side by side down a dingy, gray corridor. Normally this corridor was heavily traveled by guards and staff. Today it was empty. "Why do we have to get her?" Willie said. "Why doesn't Neville just fetch her himself?"

"'Cause we're the guards and it's supposed to be our job. Besides, would you get near Vecciorello if you didn't have to?"

"Not me! Not that cold fish." He shivered. "More like a machine than a fish. Those eyes—hollow, like there's nothing behind 'em.''

"There isn't. People who have emotions don't kill other people in cold blood." This wasn't a topic I wanted to pursue, so I stepped out and walked ahead of him a few paces.

At the end of the hallway, in front of the heavy steel door of the transfer lock, I stopped to wait for Willie to catch up. Just as he arrived, I heard the door on the other side of the lock clang shut. I stepped back and the inner door swung open. A faint whiff of metal and machine oil escaped from the lock. Andrea Vecciorello stood between her uniformed escorts, looking bored.

Vecciorello was tall, close to six feet, lean and muscular, wearing the hard angles of her face like a badge. She stepped from between the other guards, who merely shrugged at me and Willie.

"Ready?" she asked us.

Willie stiffened beside me. "Yeah, I'm ready. How 'bout you?"

I put a hand on his arm before he did something stupid. "Easy, man. It's just a job we have to do. Keep it that way and we'll be fine."

Vecciorello snorted and strode past us, and when we scrambled to catch up, she turned suddenly and said, "Boo!"

Willie jumped back and she laughed, more with condescension than humor. "Not funny," I said.

She laughed again, and walked down the hallway with a measured and steady gait, certainly more steadily than either me or Willie. We escorted her into the outer chamber and sat down, relieved. Our job was done for now, though the worst part of mine loomed ahead.

Willie and I stared at the wall, trying not to think, while the warden took care of the preliminaries. Suddenly I realized that no one was speaking. It must be almost time. I looked up at the large, round clock. One minute to ten. I couldn't take my eyes off the second hand jerking its way slowly past the twelve at the top. Click, pause. Click, pause. Click, pause. God! I clenched my teeth and forced my eyes to look away.

The damn thing was twin to the clock in the guard's room. Same clock as I had in grade school. And high school. Big and round, with that damn, slowly jerking second hand, slowly clicking out the seconds, causing time to drag.

This waiting for the execution was like waiting for class to end, just like when I was back in algebra. I remember turning away from that clock, forcing myself not to look for ten minutes, twenty minutes, until it seemed that class had to be running over. Then finally, when I couldn't stand it any longer, when I was sure the teacher had droned on for an hour, I'd look back at the clock and see that only seventeen seconds had passed.

I looked up at the execution clock again. Fifteen seconds had passed.

I looked over at Willie. He stared at the wall, eyes still unfocused. His lips moved soundlessly, either praying or cursing—I had no idea which.

Then, suddenly, it was ten seconds to go. My eyes shot to the red clemency phone in front of the warden, then darted back to the clock. The silence was total, the air so thick with it I could barely breathe. Five seconds. Four . . . three . . . two . . . one. Ten o'clock.

As if tied to a puppeteer's strings, all heads turned in unison, all eyes in the room focused on the red clemency phone. No one really expected it to ring, and it didn't. The unseen puppeteer twitched his string and everyone's head swiveled to face the warden. He sighed and nodded to me.

I hated this part the most. I had to activate the Executioner's Light that would glow inside the chamber, signaling the executioner to turn on the juice. Thus I initiated the execution, and in a way was as much a killer as Vecciorello.

I took a deep breath and flipped the switch. Through the Chamber's glass partition, the red Execution Light came to life, a single, bloody accusing eye.

Nothing happened at first. Then Vecciorello stepped over to the large switch and jerked it down with a single, quick yank. Tiny sparks arced across the contacts as current flowed to the electric chair and through the body of the condemned murderer strapped to it.

The lights dimmed and justice was served.

But . . . Did I just see Vecciorello's face fade into a moment of rapture? Just for a moment? No, probably not. Cold-blooded, she is. Killing is just a job to her.

Still . . .

△   △   △

Tom Sweeney *lives and writes in Portsmouth, New Hampshire. His short stories have appeared in magazines* (Ellery Queen Mystery Magazine, Analog Science Fiction, Woman's World) *and anthologies* (Mystery Street, Mammoth Book of Legal Thrillers, Fedora: Private Eyes and Tough Guys). *His stories have been short listed for the Shamus Award and Pushcart Prize. He is currently working on a novel.*

Endgame

Woody Hanstein

The letter from the law firm came on Wednesday along with a bill from the hospital for the $800 I still owed after breaking my collarbone helping Cheryl Peterson string Christmas lights in the teacher's lounge. I took the mail upstairs, fed Socrates and opened a beer. Then I drank half of it while I studied the envelope. My divorce had been final for over a year, so there was no reason for a lawyer to be bothering me now.

The return address on the envelope said BAKER & QUINN, Attorneys at Law in letters raised so high I could have made them out with my eyes closed. Below the firm's name was an 8th floor address in the new bank building on the waterfront downtown.

"Here goes nothing," I said to the cat, and I opened the letter. I read it twice to myself, and because Socrates looked interested, once more out loud to him.

> *Dear Mr. Grant,*
>
> *I am the Personal Representative of the estate of Edward Lewinsky. At the time of Mr. Lewinsky's death on February 14, 2010 he left a will that leaves certain small items of personal property to you. Please call my office to schedule an appointment so these things can be distributed.*
> *Very truly yours,*
> *Margaret Blackwell, Esq.*

I drank some more beer and wondered what Ed Lewinsky could have left me. I'd known him only a year and knew he had a son who was an air traffic controller somewhere out in the Midwest. Ed moved into the apartment directly across the hall soon after my divorce became final and my ex-wife moved to Burlington with her kickboxing instructor.

One Saturday morning soon after Ed arrived, I helped him upstairs with his groceries. His apartment was the mirror image of mine, just more sparsely furnished. The living room was empty except for a worn overstuffed chair in the corner wedged between a standup lamp and a small bookcase half-filled with books, and in the very center of the room, an old fashioned wooden card table and a lone kitchen chair. On the table was a chessboard with only a few pieces on it and an open book of chess problems.

"You play?" the old man asked after he caught me eyeballing the two-knight endgame he was working on. He was thin and about my height, and even though he had to be pushing eighty he still had posture a drill instructor would have envied. On that day, like every other one, he wore a white short sleeve button-down shirt with a skinny black necktie and khaki pants, and perched on his curved beak of a nose were wire-rimmed eyeglasses with lenses as thick as ashtrays. The old man's pale, skinny arms stuck out of those white sleeves like pipe cleaners, and they were speckled with age spots the color of new pennies.

I told Ed I had played a little chess in my day, and he smiled like he'd just won the lottery. Then, before I had a chance to object, he was bringing out a second chair from the kitchen and setting all thirty-two carved wooden pieces back on the board so we could get down to business.

Ed Lewinsky and I played three games of chess that first Saturday, and before long we had settled into a routine that lasted right up until his death. On Monday and Thursday evenings I'd come over at six o'clock with takeout Chinese from the restaurant across the park, and we'd eat it with chopsticks and play chess until nine. We were pretty evenly matched although our styles of play couldn't have been more different. Ed's chess, even when he was playing white, was cautious and controlled and all about consolidating any small advantage without gamble or sacrifice. Mine was more aggressive and reckless. Ed was serious about his chess, but while we played we talked—sometimes about chess because Ed had such a passion for the game and its history—but we also spoke of other things: the news of the day or the cruising sailboat I someday hoped to own or about his work as a code breaker for the CIA back in the 1950s.

If Ed Lewinsky had other visitors besides me, I never saw them in the entire year he lived across the hall. I could tell that our regular visits meant a lot to him, and even though he was fifty years my senior, they made my life richer too. I was saddened beyond words when he'd told me just after Thanksgiving of his illness and how far along it was and of his decision to spend his last days at his apartment and not in a hospital. Those last few weeks a home nurse stopped in four times a day, but until the very end we still kept to our schedule, the chess, if anything, becoming more important to both of us.

I learned of Ed's death early one Sunday morning in February from the Filipino nurse who came in on weekends. There was no memorial service I ever learned of and my efforts to find his son on the Internet were unsuccessful. A week or so after Ed died, two moving men came early one Saturday morning and within twenty minutes had boxed up or broken down the little he had and loaded it all into the small truck they'd left double-parked in front of the building.

I missed playing chess with Ed and I missed his kind and gentle manner, but life does go on and before long a pretty redhead with a little girl moved into the apartment across the hall, and soon after that winter eased its way into spring. To fill the void I even joined a chess club that met on Wednesday nights at the public library, but it somehow wasn't the same and after a few weeks I stopped going and took to riding my bike after dinner in the lengthening daylight.

I put down the letter from Ed Lewinsky's lawyer and finished my beer. Then I made myself some eggs and went out for a bike ride, and when I got home I graded some papers and went to bed.

□   □   □

Between classes the next day I called Attorney Blackwell's office and made an appointment to go in after school the day after that.

"But please don't get your hopes up," the lawyer said before she hung up. "It's just a few things."

I drove to school in the rain on Friday morning and taught calculus and geometry to six classes of teenagers with more important things on their minds than mathematics. When the last bell rang at two o'clock, I drove into Portland and killed an hour at the used bookstore across from the fish market. I bought a book about living on a canal barge in the south of France because it was something that had always intrigued me, and then I headed over to the bank building and rode an empty elevator up to the law offices of Baker & Quinn.

I stood in the lawyers' waiting room admiring the view of the harbor until a trim middle-aged woman in a tan suit came out and introduced herself as Margaret Blackwell. We shook hands and I followed her back to a corner office with a view even more expansive than the one I'd just left. She sat down behind a solid mahogany desk and slid a two-page document in my direction. I took a seat across from her and began to feel greedy for even coming.

"This is a copy of Mr. Lewinsky's will," she said. "You'll see that his estate is rather small. He's left a Fidelity mutual fund account worth around $5,800 and all of his furniture to the Salvation Army. This box of items he's left to you."

She bent down beside her chair and picked up a cardboard box that she set on the desk in front of her. I could see Ed's chessboard on top of it and, taped to it, a legal-sized envelope marked in black marker PERSONAL AND CONFIDENTIAL. Attorney Blackwell slid the box across the desk towards me.

"I just filed Mr. Lewinsky's will on Monday down at the probate court," she said. "I'll need to hang on to the funds in his retirement account for a few months to make sure there are no claims made against his estate. But the items he's left you wouldn't mean anything to potential creditors, so you can have them now."

I took the chessboard out of the box and then a blue velvet bag that I knew contained Ed's chess set. I opened the drawstring and pulled out a black rook.

"It looks like a nice set," Margaret Blackwell said.

"It is," I said. "I'll take good care of it."

"He said that you would. He really thought quite a lot of you."

"I thought he had a son," I said.

"He did." She shook her head. "They were estranged."

I put the chess piece back in the bag and set it on top of the chessboard. The rest of the box contained the twenty or thirty books that had filled Ed's small living room bookcase—all of them about chess and most of them quite old and worn. Besides the books, contained in a smaller red cloth bag, was the old chess clock that Ed pulled out during those rare times when our matches got serious. The clock was a simple one, but it was beautifully made and had matching oval shaped clock faces that I had admired more than once.

"So what do I do now?" I asked.

Margaret Blackwell wrote the date on a piece of paper and handed it across the desk to me. "Just sign this receipt and you'll be almost all set to go."

"Almost?"

"Just how well did you know Mr. Lewinsky?" she said.

"Why do you ask?"

"Because I had a visit on Wednesday from an FBI agent with a search warrant," she said.

"Because of Ed?"

"It seems so," she said. "Do you know what he did before he retired?"

"He worked at a bank, I think. Down in Boston."

"First Bank of Boston. He was head of security until they let him go in 1990. Apparently he sued them for age discrimination and lost."

"I never knew that," I said.

"I knew nothing of it either, until Agent Wilkinson came by. He was hoping to find the $222,000 he says Mr. Lewinsky stole from First Bank of Boston shortly after losing his lawsuit."

"Ed Lewinsky? He had to be kidding."

"He was quite serious, I assure you. Mr. Lewinsky's salary was $74,000 a year and at his trial he testified that he planned on working three more years before he was terminated. The FBI thinks he stole the money because a jury wouldn't give it to him."

"Just because the math works out? Just because three times 74 equals 222?"

"That was part of it. Agent Wilkinson said there was a glitch in the computer program the bank was using, and the thief could have stolen millions if he had wanted."

I realized I was shaking my head, still unable to accept the notion that the old man I knew had been some kind of master criminal. "So why did the FBI show up now?" I asked. "Can they still prosecute a crime that old?"

"No, the statute of limitations on the theft ran out long ago. But apparently, the FBI has set up some kind of task force to try to recover proceeds from unsolved crimes. One of their computers picked up Ed's name from the probate court filing, so Agent Wilkinson came visiting with that warrant."

"How did he react to finding just that small Fidelity account and Ed's chess set?"

"I'd say he was rather disappointed," Margaret Blackwell said. "But he did seem interested in Mr. Lewinsky's note to you."

I looked down at the envelope attached to the chessboard and saw that it had been cut open on one end and then taped closed. I peeled off the tape and removed two sheets of paper and smoothed them out on the desk. The top sheet was a handwritten letter from Ed. It had been written in a thin, shaky hand on unlined paper and was dated February 12, 2010, just two days before he died.

> *Dear Paul,*
>
> *By now you will have received my chess things from my attorney. Getting to know you this past year has given my life great meaning. I don't know what you will hear about me after my death, but I hope you know that I am an honorable man who would never have taken anything I was not entitled to.*
>
> *I know that neither making decisions nor taking chances come easily for you, but I hope you can get some enjoyment from my old chess things. Your openings have always been strong— it's your endgame that needs work. So for a change, why not try to live like you play. Like a famous man once said—nothing ventured, nothing gained!*
>
> *Your friend,*
>
> *Edward R. Lewinsky*
>
> *P.S. Attached is a collection of games I think you'll find interesting.*

The second sheet was also written in Ed Lewinsky's old, spidery hand. On a single sheet of yellow legal paper he had made a list with a blue felt tipped marker of ten famous chess matches. For each entry he had listed the year, the location and the names of the two grandmasters who were involved. I studied the sheet for several minutes and then folded it along with Ed's letter and put them back in the envelope.

"Agent Wilkinson thinks it's some kind of code," Margaret Blackwell said. "He's left the originals, but he's taken copies of both of those documents Mr. Lewinsky's left you. He thinks those ten games are somehow a clue to the whereabouts of the money Mr. Lewinsky stole."

"How? Does he think there's a number to some Swiss bank account imbedded in the moves of a hundred-year-old chess match?"

Margaret Blackwell laughed. "I think it sounds foolish, too, but you still should probably expect a visit from Agent Wilkinson."

I thanked her for the warning and rode the elevator down eight floors and found my car and drove home with my new chess collection sitting on the passenger seat beside me. I carried Ed Lewinsky's box upstairs, fed the cat and made a grilled cheese sandwich. Then I set the chess set up on the table in front of my living room window. I poured some good scotch into a glass and sat down on the couch and began to look through the box of books Ed had left me.

They were all about chess. They covered openings and endgames and the best recorded matches in the careers of great Grandmasters, nearly all of them long dead. Some of the books had pages marked by paperclips or thin strips of paper, and many had seen better days. I ate my grilled cheese as I thumbed through the books, and then I poured some more scotch and put the Red Sox on the television. A couple of innings later I shut the game off, unable to concentrate on anything beside the notion that the kind man I knew had possibly been a thief.

Finally I took out Ed Lewinsky's list of chess matches and went on the Internet and printed off all forty-one moves of the first one he'd noted—the final game Bobby Fischer played against Boris Spassky in Reykjavik, Iceland in 1972. I moved Ed's chess set to my coffee table along with his chess clock. Then the cat and I spent the next two hours recreating that famous game, but if a clue to Ed's lost fortune was buried anywhere in it I wasn't going to be the man who found it. In the end, just like years ago in Reykjavik, Fischer's Queen's Gambit was successful, and then the cat and I called it a night.

I lay awake in bed for a long time, but I didn't sleep. There in the dark I thought about Ed Lewinsky and especially about the advice contained in the note he wrote me right before he died. I hadn't needed Ed to tell me about my fear of commitment—I wasn't even thirty years old but was already more cautious than an old man. I had been afraid to take the job I was offered that past fall teaching in New Zealand or to sail to Bermuda with Harry Crenshaw and his brother back in July or even to ask out the pretty redhead who lived across the hall.

Saturday morning finally came and I showered and shaved and drank two cups of coffee while I continued to ponder my timidity and the paradox of my chess-playing relationship with Ed Lewinsky. The entire time I knew him, on a chessboard he wouldn't risk a pawn to draw out my pieces, but it was just possible that in real life he had done something ridiculously bold. I, on the other hand, in Ed's living room could fearlessly sacrifice piece after piece for just the chance of a counterattack, but knew that the closest I'd ever come to a life on a canal barge in France was the used book of photographs I'd bought the day before.

It was a beautiful May day, and I was getting ready to go out on my bike when my apartment intercom buzzed. I hit the button and asked who was there.

"My name is Barry Wilkinson," the voice from the front door said. "I'm with the FBI. If you'd let me come up I'd like to speak with you for a minute."

I hit the button on the intercom, and in a minute he was standing at my opened front door trying his best to look around me into the apartment. He was a little over six feet tall, and although he was carrying around a few extra pounds, none of it looked soft. He wore a dark suit and had a head of short, bristly grey hair and a round, weathered face.

"I assume you know why I'm here?" he said.

"I suppose so, but if Ed Lewinsky was a bank robber, you wouldn't know it by me."

"You mind if I come in? It really won't take long."

There was no point in delaying things, so I opened the door the rest of the way and invited him inside. He walked into my living room and spent a while studying the view of the park out my third floor window. Then he walked over to the chess set and reached down to center a pawn more exactly on its square. He picked the chess clock up from the coffee table and pressed the brass button atop one of the two clocks and you could hear it begin to tick. After watching the clock face for a few seconds he depressed the button again and set the clock back down.

"I'm more of a poker man, myself," he said.

"Chess isn't for everybody."

"It seems your friend Mr. Lewinsky liked it quite a bit. Would you mind telling me anything he ever mentioned about First Bank of Boston?"

"I knew he worked there, but that's it. He never said a word about getting fired or suing them or certainly about stealing any of the bank's money. Personally, I think you're all wrong about Ed."

"About the theft? Not a chance. And just between us girls, I can't even blame him. From what I could tell when I first looked into this back in 1993, your friend got screwed big-time when they fired him. And to make it even worse, at his trial it sure looked like those bankers lied about it. But whether he got screwed or not, I still couldn't stand by and let him walk away with $222,000."

"Then why didn't you arrest him?"

"Because he was too smart. He'd set up an account in a false name at a bank in Harrisburg, Pennsylvania, and had the money wired there from Boston. We had an agent there the next day, but the money had already been withdrawn and we spent the next six weeks looking for someone the teller described as a 200-pound Chinaman."

"So let's say you're right. What makes you think that in twenty years he didn't spend it all?"

"Because we've had our eye on him. Not all the time, but enough to know that he didn't go through that much dough living as modestly as he did." Agent Wilkinson picked up Ed's list of chess games that had been sitting beneath the chess clock. "I've got a copy of this from the lawyer," he said. "There's an agent of ours out in Spokane who's some kind of chess Jedi master, and in his spare time he's going through these matches move by move. So why don't you save us the time if you find anything out? There's a clue somewhere in all this, I can promise you that."

"Look, I've already told you what I know. Now I'm going for a bike ride."

Wilkinson looked me up and down and shook his head. "Well, I guess I'll be seeing you," he said. Then he put a business card down on my coffee table and headed out the door.

I took my bike out and rode fifty miles out to McCaw Point. As I looked out over the bay I thought of Ed Lewinsky, and I was suddenly curious to get a better look at those matches he had listed for me. I took the ride home as hard as I could pedal and when I got there I took a long, hot shower and then sat down with a beer in front of Ed's chess set and my laptop computer. I spent a couple of hours researching the next four games on Ed's list, but none of them taught me anything.

The next match listed was a game played in 1927 between Alexander Alekhine and Jose Raul Capablanca in Buenos Aires. I found several articles on the Internet describing how the two chess giants had battled through thirty-four grueling matches until Alekhine finally wrestled the world chess championship from the rival he had never before beaten. I was getting ready to play out the match on my new chessboard when the photograph on my computer screen caught my eye. In it, both men sat hunched over their pieces, deep scowls of thought etched on their faces and, there at the edge of the board, stood a chess clock with the same, graceful oval shaped faces as the one on my coffee table right next to my empty beer bottle.

I picked up Ed's chess clock and looked at it with new eyes. I turned it over, and admired the well-worn, green felt on the clock's bottom, and then for the first time I read the fading label affixed to the clock's back. It was about the size of a driver's license, and although the typeset print on the label had badly faded, I could still make out the name of the Zurich clock company and the year 1921 and then several lines of German almost too small to read. There was something else on the label also: two faded signatures, both so faint after eighty years that I wouldn't have noticed them if I hadn't been looking so carefully. Both had been written in a flowing script, and they said Alexander Alekhine and JR Capablanca.

I looked back and forth from that photo on my computer screen to Ed Lewinsky's clock for a long time. Then I spent a half-hour on the Internet looking for a reputable dealer in chess antiques. I settled on a company in New York City and dialed the phone number I'd found online. A man answered, and after I'd asked him my question, he transferred me to a woman with a strong French accent. I repeated the question for her twice, and then she put me on hold for so long I was beginning to wonder if she'd hung up. When she came back on the line her voice was filled with excitement, and she gave me the news I'd expected to hear.

She told me that the clock signed by Alekhine and Capablanca had been purchased back in 1994 by an unknown buyer from a dealer in Holmes Chapel, England. She also told me that the market in chess-mad Russia had skyrocketed for anything related to the revered Russian grandmasters. At auction in Moscow, under the right circumstances, she believed the clock would fetch at least $500,000 and possibly much more. She also told me that for a fee of twenty percent her company could arrange the authentication and transport of the clock to Moscow and make sure it was sold in the safest and most advantageous way possible.

I looked down at the clock and at FBI Agent Wilkinson's card sitting next to it. Then I asked the woman if her business was open on Sundays. "To see that clock we would be," she said, and I made arrangements to meet her the next day at noon.

I tore up Agent Wilkinson's card and put it in the trashcan under the sink. Then I put a change of clothes in a gym bag along with the chess clock, wrapped carefully in the softest sweatshirt I owned. I filled up Socrates's bowl with dry cat food and topped off his water and locked my apartment door behind me. I stood there in the hallway for a minute, and then I knocked on what once had been Ed Lewinsky's door.

The pretty redhead opened it and smiled when she saw me.

"I have to take a little trip this weekend," I said. "But I was wondering when I get back if you might be interested in having dinner?"

"That would be nice," she said.

△   △   △

Woody Hanstein *is a trial lawyer in Farmington, Maine where he also teaches college law classes and coaches rugby. He is the author of six mysteries and a number of short stories and is the founder of the Smiling Goat Precision Juggling Corps.*

The Red Door

Peggy McFarland

Aloud knock disrupted his thoughts. Shamus yelled, "Cheri! Can you get that?" before he remembered she'd left him. He couldn't get used to it.

Or maybe it was just denial. She left me. She left me. He tried the words in his mind, didn't dare hear them out loud. Not yet.

He reread the last few paragraphs of his novel about a down-on-his-luck writer losing the love of his life, and needing to move on. Into a new world . . .

Shamus sighed. The next line vanished.

Outside his window, a full clothesline partially obscured the overflowing dumpster in the alley. A sleeve's flutter revealed a discarded treadmill. Cheri had loved her treadmill. He missed the whirring of the motor, the slight cha-cha of the belt, her spurts of off-key singing between gasps.

Shamus leaned his head against the cool pane. Cheri would say, "Work, then write. Writing not pay bills." Cheri, who never used contractions. Cheri, who slipped into her Mandarin accent when she felt angry. He looked down at that forlorn treadmill, hating it, a reminder of his loss.

He was on the verge. Why hadn't she understood? His writing provided something—almost two-thou so far this year.

So his credits appeared at e-zines rather than print publications, but he was making headway. A "Shamus O'Shaunessey" link appeared first from a Google search. Didn't Cheri realize what progress that was? His writing would provide.

In time.

Knock, knock.

"Just a *minute!*"

He truly did not want to see anyone. Unless it was Cheri. She'd left everything behind.

Maybe she wanted to retrieve her things. He had loved to tease her, called everything in the apartment "mine." Lips drawn taut, vein pulsing under her mocha temple, dark eyes glowering between almond slits, she would say "ours." He guessed he'd won that one in the end.

Even if she only came to glare at him, he would welcome her. Yes, an angry Cheri was better than no Cheri at all.

He glanced at the picture of Cheri hanging above the unmade daybed. Cheri smiled, her pointy chin atop his messy hair. He rushed to the front door.

A trash bag by the entrance tripped him. "Cheri? That you?"

He checked the peephole within the solid white panel. No one.

Shamus leaned against the door. He wanted her back. She used to argue he did not fill her needs. What had she needed?

He could list them: Attention, Conversation, Help with finances, Help with chores, Intimacy." He looked at his feet. Take out the trash.

No, he didn't want to dwell on Cheri and her lists. He didn't want to dwell on the void. His manuscript waited on the screen. Without Cheri's support, he'd have to finish it quickly, get it out of his head, onto the "page" and find a job.

Knock, knock.

Shamus whipped open the front door. No one stood in the hall. No hum from the elevator, its doors shut. The fichus tree at the corner stood still, no fronds trembling to indicate a body had rushed past. Shamus slapped his door. Where had the knocks come from? Downstairs, carried through ductwork? He hoped not. Plenty of times, he and Cheri had contributed their share of noise. His gaze flitted left and right, up and down. What had the neighbors heard? Cheri's angry accusations, his whiny justifications. Outbursts punctuated by bangs and thumps.

He wished Cheri were here to fight with him now.

Shamus slammed the door, replaced the chain lock, ignored the trash bags, the cluttered coffee table, the paper-strewn couch. He stopped in the mini-hallway, ignored the bathroom door to the left, the archway to his study on the right. Cheri's cross-stitched "Home Sweet Home" pillow dangled from the master-bedroom door before him. Her body was gone, but Cheri's memory filled this space. Shamus choked back a sob and turned to his study. For now, his bedroom too.

A red door commanded the center of his room.

A free-standing red door. Brass knob glowing from filtered sun rays. The door's shadow darkened his computer.

Shamus remained in the archway and stared at the red door. His pulse quickened, a scream bubbled up his throat. What should he do? A fucking red door in the middle of his study, in his lonely apartment.

Maybe he was hallucinating. He hadn't slept well lately. He couldn't remember sleeping at all. He rubbed his eyes.

Still there.

Knock, knock.

"Who is it?" His voice squeaked. He slammed both hands over his mouth. His rational mind asked how could a hallucination knock. From his vantage point in the archway to his study, the door appeared a divider, cutting his study in two.

Knock, knock.

Shamus ventured one toe over the threshold, pulled it back. Call the authorities, that's what he should do. Who was the fucking authority of appearing doors? If Cheri were here she'd investigate. She was fearless. She'd call him a coward, tell him to write about it. Then she'd snipe about money. "Get paycheck for door story."

Thing was, he could see himself embellishing, meeting up with

Donovan at the pub over pints of Guinness. A funny, self-deprecating story:

"A what?"

"A fuckin' door. Yeah, I couldn't believe it myself—a free-standing, red door in the middle of my room."

"What does Cheri think?"

"Er, yeah, about that . . . she left me."

The story didn't sound so humorous. He'd work on that.

No story until he investigated, explored, studied the goddamn door. Donovan would take Cheri's side, call him a bloody wanker if he didn't at least try the knob. Cheri's voice popped into his head. Complaining that he always needed a push.

Shamus inched forward, sidled along the door's edge, dove for his desk chair. Hinges on the left inside the doorframe, brass knob on his right. He stared at the flat surface of the door. Red. Fire engine red. Christmas berry red. Not blood red—though that could have inspired a more compelling, sinister story. Bright, happy red. So why was he gnawing on his lower lip?

A charcoal lens ringed in gold bulged about a third of the way down from the standing lintel. Where a peephole belonged. Man height. Eyeball height. Shamus stood. Shamus-eyeball height.

He clutched his hair, fisted it into clumps. Think! What does a red door mean?

Cheri decorated their apartment door red every Lunar New Year, something about luck. How had he forgotten that? She forced him to help her clean every inch of their apartment. He teased her. "Sweep away evil spirits? Is Aunt Hong haunting you?" She had play-punched his shoulder and lectured about her cultural traditions, red doors and red envelopes, a time for presents and forgiveness. Was he forgiven for not appreciating Cheri?

His Grandma O'Shaunessey had painted her door red. "To scare the witcheries and wickeds," she'd explained. What was so wicked in his life that a red door took residence in his study?

He snorted. "Warding off rejections?"

The door didn't respond.

It wasn't a holiday and he wasn't visiting Grandma and Cheri wasn't around, but a cheery red door dominated the middle of his room.

Shamus forced his memory, almost chuckled. Killarney's had a red door. When asked why the front door was so fuckin' bright, the owner had said, "You live in bloody America, and you don't know? Red means welcome, so shut the focking door and order up, writer-man."

Welcome? To where? Shamus touched the knob, then let go. He decided to inspect the other side first. He argued with the Cheri-voice, "See? I'm investigating."

The Cheri-voice snorted, before her counterpoint. "You investigate because you too frightened to open."

Damn Cheri. She read him like a book.

On the other side, his room lay as it should: rumpled daybed, nightstand with his alarm clock, the red LED numerals shining steady, the picture of Cheri and him smiling, her eyes squinted, his eyes red points.

The red in his eyes matched the door.

He turned from her picture, noted no knob on this side of the door. He approached the backside of the peephole. Not concave, not convex, just flat, a miniscule window to his workspace. Without thought, he peered through it. He saw a tiny version of his paper-strewn desk, his darkened computer screen. His work so distant, almost insignificant. He shuddered. Cheri would have understood that viewpoint.

Two knocks vibrated against his nose.

Shamus jumped back, heart hammering. He scurried around to the desk side of the door, fell into his chair.

His mind screamed "*No!*" but his trembling hand reached for the knob. Cheri wanted a provider, a protector. Maybe the door was a test. He wanted to pass.

His fingertips brushed the brass. A spark tingled his fingertips. The knob jiggled. Not ready, no sirree, not yet, his mind argued. He jerked back his hand.

Shamus hurried to the kitchenette. He grabbed a wooden chair, raced back to the room and shoved it under the knob. In the movies, that tactic stalled the bad guys, bought the hero time. Shamus didn't feel like a hero. If Cheri were here, she'd have called him a coward as she grasped that handle and yanked.

He swallowed pasty spit. Yes, he was thirsty. Fortify his courage, he rationalized. Shamus rifled through a pile of clothes on the floor, grabbed a tossed sweatshirt and left the room. He glanced at the closed, master bedroom door, flipped his middle finger at the cross-stitched sentiment on his way out of the apartment.

□ □ □

Shamus yanked open the familiar door and allowed the close atmosphere of Killarney's to envelop him. He elbowed his way to the bar, searched the stools for a familiar face.

He raised a hand to wave at Donovan until he realized his buddy snuggled with a woman in the far booth. "Working it," his buddy would say. Shamus turned before Donovan noticed him and instead worked his own way to the bar.

The bartender set a beer before Shamus. He reached for his wallet, opened it to find only a receipt. Shamus started to ask if a credit card would be OK when he heard a disembodied voice say, "No worries." He raised the glass in a mock toast to the bartender's back, chugged back a healthy swallow, and then slammed it onto the oaken surface.

A guy jostled him to get to the bar. Shamus tripped, hit his forehead against the rim of his glass. "Excuse me!" he shouted, but the guy didn't seem to realize he was responsible. Shamus rubbed his head at the flash of pain. If he were drinking with Donovan, the guy wouldn't have gotten away with it. Shamus didn't feel angry; he felt alone.

He glanced back at Donovan's booth. Miss-Right-For-Tonight draped her arm across Donovan's shoulders, her black-tipped fingers stroked his neck. Shamus remembered when Cheri sat next to him, when her red-polished fingertips stroked his neck. Bright, happy, free-standing, cheery-door red. Shamus shook his head, gulped his beer.

A server squeezed between customers and elbowed her way next to Shamus. Shamus got a gorgeous view of her breasts, crowded and crammed above a scooped neckline—was it still a neckline if it fell just above the nipples? Shamus reached for the pen behind his ear. He wanted to use that one in his writing.

As he searched for something to write on, he imagined his face buried in that cleavage. Small-breasted Cheri rarely let him touch her breasts. She said fondling them was not foreplay.

The receipt in his wallet—he could write on that. He tried to think of a suave pick-up line as he reached for his back pocket. With Cheri gone, he could move on to bigger and better breasts. He chuckled. He could touch and taste and sample other women's breasts, or any body part he desired. He wrote that, too.

Shamus folded the paper. "Creations" in bold type topped the receipt. Cheri's favorite restaurant. His creations on the back of her Creations. Providence, he thought. Then he remembered why he had the receipt. Their last fight.

The night he said, "Dinner, my treat." Shamus wanted to celebrate. The editor had suggested minor rewrites for "Confessions," then he would publish the story.

She ordered the Chilean sea bass, Shamus ordered the rib eye. They shared a sparkling wine. Her eyes shone, she apologized for not believing in him. He brushed her words aside—he remembered waving his hand in the air, erasing invisible words between them. She laughed her lilting, almost apologetic laugh. He loved the way Cheri's delicate fingers pinched the glass stem, graceful as she toasted to his success. She leaned across the table, intent on his words. Her silk clad foot caressed his shin under the table. Shamus felt like a god.

The server placed the check between them. With a magnanimous flourish, Shamus opened it, placed his credit card atop the bill and clapped it shut. Cheri's black eyes glittered.

"You say 'my treat.' You pay with our credit card. How is this your treat?" she asked, voice a decibel above a whisper.

Wary of her tone, Shamus tried an endearment. "Sweet cheeks—"

"Do not call me that."

"Er, Cheri, I will get paid. The story is as good as—"

"You said 'paid.' Not 'as good as,' you said 'PAID!'"

Shamus remembered her lips pursed tight, a thin slit underlining her delicate nose, accenting her pointy-chin. He remembered her beautiful almond-shaped eyes appeared charcoal-hard as he explained he would get paid; the check for his story would arrive before the credit card bill. Her words spit and spoiled the space between them. Her deep breath gathered a hurricane wind.

"Nothing is yours until you hold it. Why do you not understand?" Tears tracked Cheri's cheeks. She bolted out of the restaurant.

He remembered thinking he should chase her, hold her, make sure she'd remain his. Instead, he signed for the meal, stuffed the receipt into his wallet, pretended his woman had not made a scene. On the empty sidewalk he watched a taxi turn; its taillights disappeared.

Gently, he shut the apartment door. The whir of the treadmill harmonized with the hum of the refrigerator. Shamus listened for off-key melodies. He heard a discordant sob.

Cheri jogged. Shamus stared from the doorway. She glared at him and hit a button. The belt whirred louder, faster. Shamus hated her for making him feel so . . . diminished. She accused him of needing to be led; he accused her of running away from him. They yelled, shouted hurtful things at each other—

The busty waitress shouted at the bartender to top off the friggin' beers.

Shamus put the receipt back into his wallet, drained his beer. Guinness residue slid down the sides, pooled at the bottom of his empty glass, tiny bubbles growing and popping, thick liquid oozing into a pool. His head hurt. He could use another drink. Maybe Cheri had left Tsing Tao in the fridge back at the apartment. He had no cash; he didn't want another credit card receipt.

He slapped his back pocket, exhaled. If he could submerge into his story, maybe he could tolerate the damn, lonely, red-door-infected apartment. Infested. No, infected. Damn. Words tripped him, too.

□   □   □

Shamus tripped over a trash bag as he entered the apartment. He sniffed, thought he caught the citrusy spice of Cheri's perfume. He glanced at the closed master bedroom door, wishing she slept in their bed, wishing he could cuddle against her petite beauty. No, he wasn't ready to sleep, and definitely not in that bed.

He hoped the red door had disappeared. Even if it remained, he'd write. A story idea was forming, incorporating the lines he jotted down, and door or no door, he had to get it out of his head.

Shadows obscured the daybed. Only the alarm clock numerals broke the darkness on the left side of the room. The right side glowed.

Light seeped from under the red door, burst from the cracks between the door edges and its frame. Light haloed the wooden chair wedged under the knob, the aura gleaming onto his computer, his desk and chair.

He flipped the switch, bathing the room in light, washing away the door's emanations. He cocked his head. A distant car horn, gurgling pipes, his ragged breaths.

Shamus walked to the wooden chair, thinking he'd yank it free. The charcoal lens stared at him. Should he peek?

He leaned over the kitchen chair, laid an ear against the red. No sounds, no knocks. He gazed at the golden ring, the charcoal lens. Same color as Cheri's eyes. Cheri would have peeked by now. He inhaled, blew out his exhale, stared at the peephole.

The lens winked.

Shamus ran from the room screaming. He ran to the front door, intent on escaping from the glowing red door with the winking peephole.

Trash bags tripped him. Shamus' head slammed against the tiled entry. He lay where he landed, cursed the bags, felt tears burn. I can't live like this anymore he thought, flung an arm across his eyes and let his sobs echo.

His head hurt. Shamus wiped his cheeks, rubbed his head. He rolled on his side, stared at the living room, the open kitchen. Dishes filled the sink, spilled onto the counters. Take-out containers littered the table, dirty clothes heaped in odd places.

Shamus struggled to upright, sniffed. Her scent lingered under the stale air, under the moldy food, under the decay. He should clean.

Shamus toed a garbage bag. He didn't remember filling the bags. His last stumble must have split one open. Shamus rubbed his sore head again, gaped at the rip. A swatch of flannel spilled out from the bag.

Shamus recognized his writing shirt.

He tore open the bag, found more of his clothes. He ripped open a second bag, found his toiletries, his papers, a binder with his finished stories. A soft gasp wafted from his study.

"Cheri?"

Shamus staggered to the study. Cheri sat in his desk chair, stared at an open document on his computer screen. His latest manuscript, about a down-on-his-luck writer losing the love of his life, needing to move on. Into a new world. The red door loomed on her left.

"Cheri?"

"I did not mean it to happen. I wanted us to be." Cheri's hands covered her face, sobs shook her petite back.

The fight. Shamus remembered the fight—the fight that began when he used their credit card, when she left the restaurant, when he hadn't held her.

That night, he found her on the treadmill. He yelled at her to support him, to believe in him. A melodic whine blended with the motor's whirring. Cheri's earbuds were in place. She ran faster, ignored him. He yelled louder, yanked the earbuds free. She screamed at him, told him get a real job, dreams do not pay bills. She ran faster, stopped arguing with him.

He strode across their bedroom, pulled the power cord from the outlet. Cheri yelled at him to leave, just go, walk out the door, start a life without her. He told her to leave if she didn't want him. She said. "I pay, I stay."

He grabbed his crotch and shouted, "Sānbā," not sure what he called her, but knew he'd insulted. She screamed a primal cry, threw a bedside lamp. He ducked, she charged. Her fists pummeled his back. He turned and tried to bear hug her still. She twisted within his clutch, wrenched herself free. He grabbed for her but stumbled, tripped over the lamp.

His head slammed into the treadmill base. Cheri screamed. He remembered her face over his, her caress against his cheek, her chant. "I am sorry, so sorry, baby. I am sorry, so sorry." He remembered blinking.

That was the last time he had seen Cheri. Until now.

He knew it was an accident. She loved him. She never left. He was the one not here. He walked to her, touched her.

She did not feel him.

Knock, knock.

Light from behind the red door blanched the room. A red door could ward away evil; it could symbolize forgiveness. There was no evil here. There was nothing to forgive.

Knock, knock.

A check lay on his keyboard, his name as the payee. Cheri leaned back, wiped her eyes, shook her head. Her hair was disheveled, her clothes rumpled. To Shamus, she never looked more beautiful.

She spoke to the computer. "You are good writer. I am so sorry."

Knock, knock.

Sometimes, a red door just meant welcome. He turned the knob. The door swung open, bathed him in light.

△ △ △

Peggy McFarland *lives in Nashua, New Hampshire with her family, and is the general manager of a restaurant in Chelmsford, Massachusetts. Her stories have appeared in numerous online venues as well as in* Shroud Magazine, *and anthologies published by* Absent Willow Review *and* Six Sentences. *She is currently working on a longer story (using the word novel intimidates her). Baby steps.*

Count to Ten

Nancy Gardner

S aints alive, Flo, would you please slow down," Sister Ann calls. "We need to go over our plan."

"Ah, not again, Sister," I says, over my shoulder, as I hotfoot it across Kenmore Square, on my way to a game at Fenway, me with my gut all shivery like when I'm shooting craps.

Then I remember she's the one holding the tickets and pull up short to wait for her and my friend Rose.

They huff up, both breathing hard. Sister Ann wags a finger at me. "What do you do if something upsets you?"

Can't blame her for worrying. After what happened at that there museum. Which wasn't my fault. And, anyhow, that mouthy guard deserved it.

Rose don't say nothing, just looks at me with them sad-sack eyes.

I cave. Feeling like a damned parrot, I says, "Take a coupla big breaths. Count to ten. Don't do nothing I'll be sorry for later."

"That a girl," Sister says, twisting her married-to-the-Big-Guy ring.

"Okay if I'm hoping for a rhubarb?" I can't help asking.

"Rhubarb?"

"Ain't you never heard of a rhubarb? A dustup. Can be between players, between ump and players, even between players and fans."

She raises her eyebrows, like she's praying. "As long as you're not in any rhubarbs."

"No rhubarbs for me," I say. "Now can we get a move on?"

Sister's ready, but not Rose. She sticks one of them crippled hands into that moth-eaten carpetbag she carries every place and pulls out a Yankees baseball cap and crunches it over them once-red curls.

Before I can stop myself I say, "You gotta be kidding, Rose. Ain't I told you a thousand times the Yankees suck?"

"Language," says Sister Ann.

"Oops, sorry Sister, sorry Rose, meant to say they stink." Ain't kidding when I says I'm sorry. Don't like swearing around no nun, specially one who scares up two hard-to-come-by shelter beds, don't jaw-bone us about church, and scrounges up three Sox-Yankees tickets.

We turn onto Yawkey Way and melt into Red Sox Nation, joining the mob of fans. We push past hawkers selling Sox geegaws and past food wagons peddling nose-tickling sausages and such.

"Gate B, ladies," Sister Ann says, pointing to a sign. She heads toward it.

Me and Rose stick close.

"Popcorn," Rose says, her voice all jingly. Rose's a sucker for popcorn.

"Smells great, Rose," I say. What I don't say, is that the smell of the popcorn, the sun warming my face and the jabbering fans puts me in mind of better days. Days when I was heading to a game with my dad.

Rose grabs my arm. "Careful."

I step out of the way of a bunch of badass bruisers cutting us off from Sister Ann as they hustle a big shot through the VIP door.

"Ben Affleck?" I holler across to Sister.

She shakes her head no as she steps back beside us. I wonder what's stuck the I-smell-a-skunk scowl on her face.

I stop wondering 'cause they start herding us through Gate B. Which puts a big old shit-eating grin on my puss. The grin don't last. I get whacked from behind by a skanky brunette in coke-bottle glasses.

"Watch it," she growls, pushing me as she rips through the line.

Like lightning, Sister's whispering in my ear, "Breathe, Flo." She's also got a hold on my shirtsleeve. "One . . . Two . . .Three . . ."

I ain't got no choice but to uncurl my fists.

Over by the park wall, the skank's waving a fistful of dough at a grinning scalper. I'm hoping he robs her blind.

Then the line starts moving, we're inside the gate, and Sister is flashing three tickets at the turnstile guard. But before he'll take the tickets, he slaps his hand up like some traffic cop, right in Rose's face.

"Sorry, but you can't bring that inside," he barks, pointing at her bag. "You'll have to check it."

Rose squeezes her eyes shut, and any fool can see he's scaring her big time.

"Who you think you're talking to, Buster?"

"I'll handle this," Sister Ann says, stepping between us.

I suck air and do the counting thing, all the while fretting that if this keeps up I ain't gonna remember how to handle assholes.

Sister wrestles Rose's bag away. "Remember, Rose, we talked about this. You'll get it back right after the game." She opens it so as Rose can see inside. "Just take the you-know-what."

Rose don't move.

"Rose," Sister snaps.

Rose blinks, pulls something outta her bag and lets Sister hand the bag over to the jerk.

Then, Hallelujah, we're hightailing it inside.

Where Sister Ann backs herself against a wall and motions us to stop. I'm scared she wants me to do the counting thing again.

Instead, Rose says. "For you."

When I see it I go cold. My heart whacks a crazy drumbeat in my chest. Finally I'm able to stretch out a shaky paw and take it. A broke-in catcher's mitt.

For years I been telling Rose how I used to be the go-to catcher on my high school softball team. And not a bad pitcher, neither. Because of my dad's coaching. He never missed a game, and when I'd hit a homer or stop a fly ball, you'da thought he'd bust a gut. One time, another dad called me a loser. Dad socked him.

Maybe my life wouldn'ta gone south if I hadn'ta let him down. It happened one Saturday night. Some no-account loser came after the measly few bucks in dad's hardware store till. The loser had a gun and my dad died, alone, in a pool of his own blood.

Cops never caught the guy. It was my fault cause I shoulda been there to stop the loser or the bullet. Instead, I bagged out so I could party with my friends. Don't even remember the names of them friends.

"Like it?" Rose asks.

I lift the mitt to my nose and sniff the leather. "Like it?" My brain's gone all whirly-giggy. "Hot damn. 'Course I like it." I slip my paw inside and give the mitt a couple of whacks. "Where'd you get it?"

Sister answers for Rose who don't talk much. "Providential, Flo. She found it when she was out on one of her trash can forays. It cleaned up very well, don't you think?"

I nod and can't stop whacking it. "Jeez, Rosie, I shouldn'ta busted your chops about the Yankees," I say, my mood turning bodacious, so bodacious I don't even care I lost my Red Sox cap on my last bender.

Rose trades that lost-lamb look, a look I hate worse than the look of them burns on her hand, for that marshmallow-soft, hide-and-seek smile.

Sister leads us to our seats. They're primo, second tier, first row, right field. Foul ball heaven.

"How the heck did you peg these, Sister?"

"Donated by a good friend of St. Bridget's who wants to remain anonymous."

I wiggle my hefty backside into my too-skinny seat, trying to get comfortable. My two beanpole friends got no such trouble. Still and all I got no complaints.

The humungous TV screen across the field lights up. Sister points to a close-up of some VIP.

I check it out, hoping it's Ben Affleck. But it's just some bald little guy in a suit.

"Who's he?"

"Judge Rushmore. I just read an article about him in the *Globe*."

"What'd it say?"

"He took out a restraining order against his ex, claiming she's dangerous. It's ironic because he's known for his tough pronouncements against women who are victims of domestic abuse." She's twisting that ring again and shaking her head.

"Damn," I mutter.

Music starts up and I forget the judge. A guy in a trooper's uniform trots onto the field and sings "The Star Spangled Banner." Then the players trade places with the trooper.

Everybody leans forward. Soon I'm working up a sweat yelling for the Sox.

They strike out the first three batters. Then the Yankees do the same.

By the third inning I'm parched. Sister must be too. She snags a guy selling hot dogs and cold drinks, asks us what we want.

I order a giant dog and a giant Pepsi. Only thing better woulda been a giant beer and maybe a chaser.

All's Rose orders is a bottle of water, which she nurses like I'd nurse a pint of Jack Daniels.

Me, I scarf down my dog, guzzle the Pepsi.

A couple minutes later, A-Rod steps up to the plate and hits a homer, which sets me to groaning.

But not for long. Matsui steps up and slams a foul. Right at me. Right at my mitt. Which I'm stretching forward, never mind the wise guys all around me, trying to muscle me outta the way.

"Come to Momma, come to Momma," I sing. And snag it!

The wise guy to my left, face painted half blue, half red, tries to knock it out of my glove. I hold on like a bulldog. He lets go. I raise my ball sky-high, soaking up the screams from Rose and Sister, who're on their feet slapping my back.

I whap that ball into my mitt and hear my dad calling, "Go with the fastball, Flo." I slide my fingertips over the seams—into that four-seamer grip he taught me. Thinking of my dad makes me kinda sad though, so I stuff the ball into my pocket and get back to the game, where the Sox are up.

Sister and me join the clapping and chanting. "Let's go, Red Sox, let's go."

Not Rose. She don't make a peep.

When I see she ain't too happy, I'm put in mind of the fact that without that mitt I probably wouldn'ta caught the ball. So when I sees a guy selling popcorn, I know how I can cheer Rose up. Got a bit of moola in my pocket. I scraped it together by picking up empties off the street and turning them in at Ralphie's.

I pull out my wad of ones. "I'm springing, Rose. Popcorn." I wave the guy over and pass him my dough. He leans in with a box. He and Rose freeze.

It ain't hard to see why. The guy's face wears a mean burn scar, a scar his long blond hair and Red Sox cap don't hide.

Rose goes all pasty-faced, but she sucks in air and reaches for the popcorn. He smiles at her, salutes.

"You know him?" I ask.

"Larry. Burn Center," Rose says. She pokes one measly piece of popcorn in her mouth.

My little friend don't say much about her visits to the Burn Center. I know she's got her reasons, and I let it be.

Rose picks at her popcorn and sips at her bottle of water. And the Sox and Yankees stay tied. By the eighth inning, I'm hoarse from shouting. I'm also sure that any minute the Sox will pull ahead. But all that Pepsi I drunk puts me in a bind.

"Gotta pee," I whisper to Sister, who don't take her eyes off the field.

"Go with her, Rose," Sister says. "I'll watch the seats." We both know she's sending Rose along so's I keep to the straight and narrow.

We pass the food court, and I'm hauling ass so fast I ain't even tempted by the beer smells coming my way. Finally, I see the sign for the can. And lose Rose.

I turn and see her standing ten feet back, like some ice statue. Staring at that popcorn guy, Larry.

"Come on, Rose." I call

She just shakes her head, points her water bottle Larry's way. Maybe she wants to see how his burns is doing. She got hers years ago, in a God-awful fire that killed her hubby and her little kid. That fire's what messed Rose up. Left her easy to break. Not like me and my shit. With me, it's all my own fault.

I can't wait no more. I squeeze into the smelly can and wait in the friggin' line. By the time I'm done and back outside, Rose ain't waiting.

Out on the field, the fans is singing "Sweet Caroline" and I wanna get back. But first I gotta find Rose.

I scoot up and down the food court looking for her. Then, wham, I'm hit from behind. I stumble, turn, and damned if it ain't the broad with the coke-bottle glasses. Only now she's sporting a Sox cap and, around her neck, she's wearing a popcorn tray. Like before, she don't say sorry, just grunts and rushes past.

"Asshole," I call.

She looks over her shoulder. "Toothless hag."

I get a gander at the eyes behind them monster glasses. They give me the willies. They're cold, stone dead. Like some dead fish from Fulton's Fish Market.

And the bitch called me toothless. I ain't toothless just 'cause I'm missing one front tooth.

I spot Rose standing off to the side, near a hallway, flapping her arms like some sad little sparrow that can't fly.

I race over. "Rosie, you hurt?"

She don't answer, just grabs me, leads me down the hallway, to a door at the end with a sign saying, "Employees Only."

Inside it's a cleaning closet. Only it's none too clean, what with napkins and empty popcorn boxes and popcorn rolled across the concrete floor. But that ain't the worst of it. Rose's friend, Larry, lies in the middle, blond hair spread around him like a halo, a little pool of blood turning the halo red. Don't see his popcorn tray neither.

"Hit. Gun," Rose says, lifting her arm and smashing it down like a hammer. "Took tray."

"That bitch had a gun?" I ask, knowing, just knowing, that Rose's talking about Fish Eyes. "Did she hurt you?"

Rose wags her head no. "Hid." She acts out how she hid behind the open door. Then she rushes back to Larry and kneels beside him, pours some of her water on a napkin, wipes blood from behind his ear. "Needs help," she says, looking up at me.

"I'm on it," I say, and whirl into the hallway, race back out to the food court.

"Over here. Someone's hurt," I call to the security guard across the way. He's hanging out in front of the Luis Tiant Cuban sandwich counter.

He looks over at me like I got two heads.

"Ya deaf? Guy needs help."

He slow-walks over. "What's the problem?"

"Man down there. He's hurt bad." I point. "Ain't kidding," I say, and give him a little shove.

I think he's gonna shove me back, but instead he must get it, get that I ain't kidding. He books it to the closet, cell phone to his kisser.

Larry's gonna get help, but I ain't feeling better. Keep thinking about that bitch and how she hit him with that gun. How she mighta hurt Rose. And what's she got a gun for anyhow? She planning to pop some poor slob?

Then I remember Sister's plan. I breathe and count to ten. Count to ten and haul ass in the direction I last seen Fish Eyes. When I sees her slipping through a door, I give it some hustle.

On the other side of the door, I'm under the stands, along with ten, maybe twelve, noisy food sellers who're stuffing popcorn and Coke and what-all into their trays.

Fish-Eyes ain't stuffing. She's swerving past them and taking to some stairs.

I hoof it behind her as fast as I can, groaning when a stitch stabs my side. I curse myself and my hard-living days, and have to stop to catch my breath. I lose sight of her as she beats it round a landing.

Pushing myself forward, I take them stairs two at a time. When I reach the landing, I swerve left, where she's tiptoeing down stairs leading to the best seats in the house, right behind home plate. Big Shot Land.

Nobody's watching Fish Eyes. They're too busy watching the Sox uniform who's out on the field, stealing second base.

"Focus, Flo," I mutter, and force myself to forget the field.

What Fish Eyes is doing scares the bejeezus out of me. She's creeping towards the front row. Where Ben Affleck or the judge and some other VIPs sit.

Everybody's too busy hooting and hollering and slurping beers to pay attention to no pretend-popcorn seller.

As she slips down the second row, she's fiddling with something shiny, something metal, something she's lifting like slow molasses outta the tray. A snub-nosed revolver.

The world slows down like I'm swimming through Jello. Fish Eyes is gonna get off a shot before Ben or whoever she's after's got a chance.

I shout but the crowd drowns me out.

She's sliding that pistol down by her leg.

Me, I'm sliding my hand down my pocket.

Her eyes don't leave the front row.

Mine don't leave her while my fingers curl around a smooth, hard idea.

I grope for the seams and settle across them in a perfect four-seamer setup. I'm not hearing nothing, not smelling nothing, not seeing nothing. Nothing but Fish Eyes.

Then the world speeds up.

She's edging sideways faster and lifting the revolver. "You cheating bastard," she yells.

"Now," I tell myself, winding up, stepping forward, heaving.

Heaving and missing.

My ball whizzes past Fish Eyes, hits the arm of a guy sitting to the right of the judge, flies into the netting, whips back against the steps. "Damn," I mutter.

Still and all my pitch ain't a total waste. The guy it hits, he's one of the bodyguards, and that whack from my fastball sends him whirling round. Whirling in time to knock the gun outta Fish Eyes' hand.

Then there's them other bodyguards who're now scrambling across the judge and lunging for Fish Eyes.

Before she can blink, she's on the ground and screaming like a banshee.

Some drunks nearby must think it's a game, 'cause they decide to join the fun. Popcorn and beer fly.

Fish Eyes is outta commission, but I got me another problem. I ain't leaving without my ball. It's somewhere's underneath that there rhubarb.

I get on my hands and knees and crawl down the aisle to where I last seen it. My fingers squish through soggy popcorn and stale beer. A big sandal steps on my hand, but I stifle a yelp and keep crawling. I see the ball. I ignore my soggy knees, crawl faster and grab it.

Who cares if the ball's sticky? So's the rest of me. I stuff it back in my pocket and crawl up them steps, knees touching a soft lump. A lump that stops me. A soggy old Red Sox cap. "Thank you, Lord," I whisper, stifling a chuckle as I clap it on my head.

At the top of the stairs, I do a quick scan. No one's looking my way. Too busy watching the goings-on in the Big Shot's section. I brush myself off as best I can, start whistling 'cause of what a fine day it's turning out to be. Until I remember Rose. The fat grin on my face takes a hike.

As I clomp down the back stairs, cops push past me. I hustle back to Rose, who's standing near the hallway again, watching EMTs wheel away a stretcher.

"Larry gonna be okay?"

She nods. "Ambulance. Hospital." She puts her hands together like she's praying a thank you.

If Rose thinks he'll be okay, then he'll be right as rain 'cause Rose used to be a nurse. Before the fire.

"Damn fine. Now we better haul ass back to Sister and the game." We race for our seats.

"Where have you two been?" Sister asks, looking all pinched and worried. "There's been an assassination attempt on Judge Rushmore. Someone said it was his ex-wife. He's okay, but I've been worried sick about you both."

"Helped. Larry." Rose says.

"Yeah, Sister, that friend of Rose had an accident and we had to get him some help. He's gonna be okay, though."

"Anything to do with the assassination attempt?" Sister asks.

Rose shakes her head.

"Thank heaven," Sister says. "And you, Flo, you kept to our plan?"

I suck in a breath and count to ten. "Right-o, Sister. Ain't done nothing I'm sorry for."

"Good. Very good. Let's see if we can enjoy the rest of the game in peace."

Rose slips past Sister to her seat. I try to follow.

Sister stops me. "What's that smell? And where did you get that

hat?"

"Found it," I says.

"You found it?" Her eyebrows pinch together.

"Lying in a puddle of beer." I give her a little whiff of my breath. "Guess that's why nobody wanted it."

She squints. "You're sure?"

I cross my heart. "Trust me, Sister. I'm telling you the God's honest truth. I found it in a puddle of beer."

She lets me pass.

Squeezing by, I see it's the top of the ninth, see the score's tied. I wiggle into my seat. Beside me, Rose gets out her half-full box of popcorn, stuffs a handful in her mouth. I'm really glad she's seeming happy. It don't happen too often. Still and all, it's the Sox I'm pulling for when I turn my cap inside out and rub my ball for luck.

△ △ △

Nancy Gardner *has had her short stories published in magazines, anthologies and online. Currently she's working on a mystery set in Salem, Massachusetts and featuring a modern Salem witch who uses her ability to walk into other people's dreams to unmask a murderer.*

All that Glitters

Kate Flora

Sometimes she just had to get out of the office. That's just how it was. Ex-military and six years with the Marshal's Service, Gracie was trained to conform. She could walk the walk and talk the talk, knot her tie and shine her shoes with the best of them. She knew shit from Shinola and she could pick the bad guy out of a crowd like nobody's business. But once in a while, the urge to misbehave overtook her. Little stuff, like wanting to slam a jelly donut up against a wall full of wanted posters or put a fart cushion on some uptight asshole's chair. Draw her gun at an inappropriate time and caress the barrel like it was someone's precious dick. Stuff that could escalate if she didn't tamp it down.

When it got so bad she was itching like the guy in the Elvis song, she'd leave the office, come out here to the park, and sit on a bench. Brick wall behind her to cover her back. And the whole roiling mass of humanity before her, doing its awkward human things. Spring drew people to the park like a picnic drew ants. Drew them in exuberant hordes, people who'd peeled down and were displaying swaths of bare skin to the sun's warmth.

The snoring wino on the next bench, newspaper over his face, bubbled like a hookah. Last week, the snoring wino had been an undercover cop. Gracie had made him in a nano, giving him a running commentary on all the bad acts he was missing because of the newspaper, while he'd studiously ignored her.

Overhead, trilling birds signaled their desire to mate. Part of her own itch, she thought, was a desire to mate. Mate with an unsuitable person. Cross lines. Break rules.

Gracie didn't like people that much, but she enjoyed watching them. Sometimes she'd practice. Study them quickly, then look away and describe them. Clothes, appearance, distinguishing characteristics, anything unusual about their gait, the way they carried themselves. Other times, she'd just watch. Right now she was watching the well-to-do matron on the other side of the fountain who stood out from the crowd because she was wearing so many clothes. Navy St. John Santana knit. Coach shoes and matching bag. Multi-colored hair, the kind of processing that took hours to achieve glossy and natural. Everything about her said money, comfort, security—except the way she walked.

The woman walked like someone who'd recently had a beating. A pretty bad one, too, the kind that made you carry yourself like a fragile vessel. Made the little muscles in your face tense, your neck go stringy from holding your head up. Those clothes were a clue, too. Long sleeves and a high collar on a warm spring day, when everyone around her had rolls of jiggly white fat on display, like thick white bread waiting to be toasted.

The woman wasn't there for pleasure. She scanned the park like she was looking for something. Someone. And then, as she turned so she was facing Gracie, the droop went out of her shoulders. She came striding across the cobbles around the fountain like a heat-seeking missile. Closing the space with purposeful steps straight toward Gracie, then dropping down onto the bench beside her carefully, like something might break.

She was a small woman, more clothes than substance, though a close-up view disclosed that the boxy knit hid a Barbie figure. Large, high breasts and tiny everything else. How did the old joke go? Guy says to his buddy, "Hey, you oughta see my new girlfriend. 44 inch chest, 23 inch waist, 34 inch hips." The buddy says, "What does she do?" "Well," the guy says, "with a little help, she can sit up."

Gracie hauled her attention back to analyzing her new companion. The woman had once been gorgeous, and still was very pretty. Diamond studs glittered in neat pink earlobes. The flawless make-up didn't quite conceal old bruises. The woman sat a moment without speaking, and then, without actually looking at Gracie, she said, "I need your help."

"I don't know you," Gracie said.

"You look like someone who knows her way around," the woman said. "Someone who doesn't back down. Who knows how to get things done."

A reasonable assessment. The woman had a wonderful voice, rich and full of undernotes, marred by her hesitant way of speaking. Gracie, who sang herself, thought she might be a singer. Be or had been. There was something about the appearance and attitude that suggested domesticity. A domestic relationship with someone who wanted all the control and held all the cards.

Gracie was intrigued. Usually, she held the cards and knew what was supposed to happen. This had all the elements of a surprise. So instead of the brusque brush-off she usually gave strangers, she sat back and waited.

"My husband wants a divorce," the woman said.

"You don't?" Gracie asked. She had no patience for men who beat on women, little for women who let themselves be beaten, though she often understood why women did.

The woman shook her head.

"Even though he beats you?"

"What I would like," the woman said, eyes lowered and hands clasped as for confession, "is for him to die in a horrible, excruciating way." It was exhaled on a sigh, the harsh words at odds with that richly musical voice. As Gracie shifted, she added, "but that's not what I wanted to talk to you about."

"You don't know me," Gracie repeated, "and I don't know you.

You don't look like someone who normally approaches strangers. So what's this about? Why me?"

The woman fingered an earring, the beautiful diamond flashing in the sunlight. "I've seen you here before. You look . . . I don't know . . . commanding. Capable. You study the park like you see everything and everyone, but nobody bothers you. Ever." As though she knew Gracie's next question, she pointed at the tall white office building across the park. "My therapist's office is on the seventh floor. That third window in from the end, that's his waiting room. Sometimes I watch you while I'm waiting."

She twisted the earring again, followed by some handwringing made difficult by the oversized purse in her lap.

"I have to go," Gracie said. She was sorry for the woman, but this dithering pushed her aggravation buttons, and anyway, she didn't like the idea of being watched.

"I'm annoying you," the woman said. "I'm sorry. Harold says I'm the most irritating woman on the face of the earth. It's just . . . you see . . . that I need some help."

"I can see that."

"No. You can't see. I mean, I can imagine how you'd think you see. Or, after what I've said, that you think you know what I mean. But that's not it."

Harold was right. This battered, dithery woman was extremely aggravating. If it weren't that her dislike for men who beat on helpless women outweighed her contempt for helpless women, she would have been long gone. "What do you mean?"

A massive diamond flashed in the sun as the nervous hands twisted. Where one sleeve had crept up, the woman's wrist was bruised purple. "I want someone to rob my house."

Jesus! A referral to a tough lawyer, a pep talk with the bastard husband, strategies for safety planning and escape, all that Gracie might be able to help with, but not this. She stood. "You've got the wrong person," she said. "I'm a government employee. This probably isn't the best part of town to recruit criminals." She pointed toward her office. "That's the federal building."

Of course, there were plenty of bad guys in and out of that building. But she wasn't going to suggest this woman recruit one of them. You had to pick your bad guys, and that was a fine art. One even a pro could get wrong.

"Not a real robbery," the woman said, standing too. "Just some assistance in collecting what is rightfully mine. Harold says he wants a divorce." She let it go a beat. "What he really wants is to get rid of me and keep everything we own. I'm a possession, like all the rest, only I'm one he doesn't want anymore. I thought that if our things, my things, got stolen, Harold could collect the insurance, and then maybe he'd divorce me instead of killing me."

The things people said to strangers.

"I can't help you with that."

Gracie studied the woman's face for signs of deception, for all the clues and cues she'd been taught to recognize. For the ones she'd known practically since she could walk. Not just who was lying, and how big the lie, but when someone was going to explode. Going to hit her. When the nice man was being nice because he was really a nasty man. When to lie low, when to push back. She saw desperation. She saw hope. And something else. A sense that the woman understood her. That before their choices diverged and this woman let herself become someone's Barbie doll while Grace got tough, they had walked some of the same paths.

"Forgive my bad manners, please, and how badly I'm doing this," the woman said. "My name is Bambi Forbes. Barbara Forbes. I'm a trophy wife whose husband, Harold, wants to trade her in on a newer model."

"Harold Forbes the auto dealer?"

"Harold Forbes the Auto KING," Bambi corrected. "Harold's first wife died under mysterious circumstances, and he was never charged. I'm beginning to fear I will share the same fate."

"Then why don't you just leave?"

Bambi's head came up, and suddenly Gracie was staring into a pair of startling eyes, a perfect emerald green with dark rings around the irises. "Why do you think?"

Gracie stared at the people in the park, going about their business just as they had a few minutes ago, oblivious to the small drama that was unfolding on Gracie's bench. She answered her own question. "Because people don't leave Harold Forbes. He leaves them? He's— what did Bush used to say?—the decider."

"Exactly. He controls all the money. All our assets. The only thing I have is my jewelry, which is very valuable. He won't let me take that if I go."

"It's not worth it to you to leave that behind, if it means you're free and you're safe?"

"You think that would be right? That he should toss me out on the sidewalk like a broken chair after he's had the best twenty years of my life?" The words burst out. "Even if it were worth it, there's still the divorce. The dealing. He doesn't want any of that. He just wants me gone. There's the bimbo, you see. And this bimbo is pregnant. And Harold, he's nearly sixty now, and thinking about mortality, is hot to make this kid legitimate."

"But not so hot that he'll pay you to go?"

The glittering green eyes stared at Gracie, the black pupils seeming to dilate as Bambi spoke. "You know how guys like Harold become auto kings? Being tight with every goddamned buck." The refined mask had slipped a little, and a tough, if beaten down, street kid peeked out at Gracie. "Every buck. So to answer your question, even if I leave all that behind, there is no 'free and safe,' there's just oh dearie me, my beloved Bambi has abandoned me, terribly sad missing persons case, police please take notice, followed by promptly marrying the woman who comforted him in his grief."

"If he doesn't divorce you, how's he going to marry the bimbo? It takes years for a missing person case to be resolved."

Bambi tossed off a humorless laugh. "Someone whose penmanship bears a remarkable resemblance to mine will sign all the necessary papers before I 'disappear.'"

"You leave a 'in case of my disappearance' letter with your lawyer?" Gracie asked.

"As if anyone ever paid attention to those. And anyway, the Auto KING can talk his way out of anything. He's a car salesman, you know." The narrow shoulders rose and fell, the augmented chest stayed fixed and perky. "So yeah, I guess I could try to just slip quietly away. But I hate to let him win like that, you know? And it might not be enough for him."

"Let me think about it," Gracie said. "Can we meet tomorrow?"

The green eyes swam with tears, surprising Gracie. Bambi was a piece of work, that was for sure. Or several different pieces of work, loosely stitched together. Which was something Gracie needed to think about, too. Anything could be a setup. A fraud. A test of character or loyalty. The Marshal's office wasn't such a straight-arrow place as TV writers made it seem. Tommy Lee Jones characters were thin on the ground. It was more like little territorial nests of rats that liked to steal shiny things from each other. Gracie was a shiny thing, though she bore some bits of tarnish.

"Tomorrow. High noon." She gave directions to a different bench in a different park. Without waiting for a response, she stood and walked away.

□ □ □

She was supposed to stay away from Billy. Her rule. Office rule. Rule of common sense. But there was that itch. And a need for a dark, smoky place and a good Manhattan and Billy across the table. Besides, she needed to talk to him about the bank thing. That was legitimate, something the higher-ups wanted. So she called him, and as the sun sank slowly in the west, tinting the mountains with gorgeous crepuscular colors, Gracie slipped into a little black something and her favorite Manolos and went downtown to one of the few places quiet enough for a conversation.

Billy was late, which he reliably was, and she had time to take a few laps across the surface of her drink—straight up, three cherries—before he was standing there, radiating sex in a way that few men could. Ladies do love outlaws. Every female eye in the restaurant followed him with a hungry longing.

"Hey, Squirt," he said, "you clean up good," and slid into the booth across from her.

They talked about scoping out the bank that seemed like the next best target for the Genteel Bandit robbery, like AUSA Laura Bower wanted. Details, timing, issues, precautions. Contact info. Billy wanting to know what the US attorney's office was offering in return for his cooperation. Gracie getting a little uncomfortable at Billy's delight. He'd been arrested for robbing banks. He was supposed to act repentant.

They talked about their younger sibs. His Irish twin, Jack, her Patrick. Gracie ordered steak, rare, a retro lettuce wedge. Billy fish and sweet potato fries. He ordered a second martini, Gracie another Manhattan.

Sometimes she didn't know what she was going to do until she did it. This was one of those times. Halfway through her second drink, having vetted Bambi that afternoon on the government's dollar and now reasonably sure it wasn't a setup, she found herself telling him about Bambi's dilemma. He had some ideas that matched her own. Get invited to the house. Leave surveillance cameras, equipment was never a problem for Billy. Use that video to plan an opp. They might be on opposite sides of the law, but they'd been raised together, and shared something of a larcenous soul.

She was just slightly tilting to starboard when they left the place, leaning more heavily than necessary on Billy's arm, maybe just to show all those swooning girls who was leaving with the prize. But Billy had no intention of saying goodnight any time soon. Billy, her former foster brother, the bane of her existence growing up. The man who'd reappeared on her radar screen as a bad guy while she'd become the girl in the white hat. The bank robber she was supervising, getting his help catching a bigger fish in return for a pass on his crimes. The man who knew how to push her buttons in all the right ways, just as, years ago, he could push them in all the wrong ones.

Four hours later, her itch well scratched, and most every inch of her whisker-burned, he slipped away like a thief in the night—which is exactly what he was—and she snuggled into her covers to get a smattering of sleep before she had to shower him off, put on one of her expensive, boring suits, and head back to the office.

For once, when Dirkk Postman came in looking smug from nailing the AUSA, Gracie wouldn't be jealous. Postman was a pretty thing, but he was way too uptight for a woman who loved outlaws.

□ □ □

Bambi was restless, apprehensive, and moving even more slowly than the day before. When Gracie described their plan—the being invited for a drink part, not the installing hidden cameras part—Bambi was unsure. There was no trace of the angry woman who wasn't going to go quietly that Gracie had seen the day before. This one was pretty much beaten into submission.

"So you've changed your mind?" Gracie said. "You're going to let him toss you out like yesterday's trash, leaving you with nothing? You're going to sign the divorce papers and slink away?"

Gracie wasn't sure why she cared, except that someone needed to help this woman find her spine, and she had an unfortunate predilection for rescuing people. It came from having to fight so hard to protect Patrick, her sweet, feckless, dreamy little brother, from Billy and Jack and her "loving" foster parents. She wanted to shake Bambi and ask what had happened to yesterday's determination. But she knew where it had gone. Auto King's fist had knocked it out.

"We've got to act soon," she said, "so what evening this week is good to invite me and my dear friend for drinks?"

"Harold doesn't like . . . "

"Look," Gracie said. "You came to me with this. And if you think he might harm you, you don't have time to waste, right? I can help you leave or I can help you leave with something to fund a new start. Your choice."

When Bambi didn't respond, she moved on. "You never have people over?"

"Oh, of course. All the time. Harold's friends. We . . ."

"So we'll come when Harold's friends are coming and just blend ourselves right in."

"Tonight." Bambi put her hands over her mouth, like a naughty child trying to call back her words.

"What time, and what are we wearing?"

"Seven," Bambi said, her shoulders drooping, as though the burden of this, never mind that she'd asked for it, was too much to bear. "Cocktails."

"And I'm your friend from where?" Gracie asked. "Gym? Yoga? Book group?" When Bambi only goggled at her, she said, "Never mind. We met when I gave a talk on women and personal safety." Something she'd done that could be verified. "You keep your jewelry in a safe?"

"The best pieces. In the bedroom closet. The rest is in my dresser. Harold has things, too. In a box on his dresser. Watches, rings, cuff-links."

"And the combination is?"

Bambi shrugged.

"Jesus!" Gracie said. "How could you let him—" But that wasn't productive. "You have a security system. What's the code?"

For a moment, the woman hesitated, like she didn't know that, either. Then, fumbling, she unclasped her purse, and handed Gracie a crumpled sheet of paper. A list of numbers, codes, locations. All the internal motion sensors and security cameras. Location of the motion-activated outside lights. A floor plan of the house. Made, crumpled and thrown away, then retrieved. So Bambi wasn't totally beaten down yet.

"Good," Gracie said, tucking it away. "What else do I need to know?"

□ □ □

It was parody of a cocktail party. Overdressed, jewel-encrusted people with sprayed-on tans and bright white teeth trying to impress each other while getting too drunk too fast. It didn't take much to make conversation, either, Gracie found. Just ask anyone a question about himself, and he was off and running, delivering a dull life story right into her cleavage, like a little mike in there was recording every word. The Auto King himself deigned to deliver a lengthy monologue on the nature of his success to her breasts, while Bambi took Billy and some others on a "tour" of the house.

The food was served by an attractive, if blowsy young woman with waist-length dark hair and a belly just beginning to push at the buttons of her uniform. By staring daggers at both Bambi and Gracie, and spending more time lounging in sluttish attitudes than in service, she made it abundantly clear that she was the candidate for the third Mrs. Auto King.

What a sleaze, Gracie thought. Getting his bimbo to serve at his party. Rubbing it in his wife's face while putting his new honey in her place. It made her want to drop caviar on the white sofa and hoisin sauce on the white carpet. Actually, it made her want to practice "interrogation methods" involving sensitive body parts on the man. But she was a professional and an adult, and there was more than one way to skin a King.

Two hours in, the company was so drunk Gracie thought she and Billy could have broken into the safe and cleaned out the house without waiting for everyone to leave.

By the time she got him out of there, Billy was glowing with larcenous joy. "Those people, Gracie," he said, as she slid behind the wheel. "It would be like shooting fish in a barrel."

"No shooting. No fish. This is all about helping a poor lady retrieve what is rightfully hers. That's all. You're supposed to be walking the straight and narrow, remember?"

"You're no fun."

"Life is not about having fun, William Bradford Shaughnessy, and you know it."

"Your life isn't about having fun, Gracie."

Somehow, both of them found a way to make that evening fun.

□ □ □

The night their home was burgled, Harold "Auto King" Forbes and his wife Barbara were attending a fund-raiser for the opera. Barbara Forbes wore an elegant long-sleeved, high-necked gown of black lace over taffeta to cover her newest bruises. US Marshals Grace Christian and Dirkk Postman were having a lengthy dinner with William Shaughnessy, one of their informants, their presence indelibly marked on the public's memory when they had to foil an armed robbery between entrée and dessert.

Gracie enjoyed reading about the burglary in the paper. Police said that the robber was very professional. Power to the home had been cut. None of the neighbors had noticed any strange cars or suspicious individuals, though one recalled seeing a Verizon truck in the neighborhood that evening. There were no footprints, fingerprints, hairs, or fibers. The home was undamaged, and all that appeared to have been taken was Mrs. Forbes' jewelry and Mr. Forbes' watches. The Auto King never mentioned to police the $250,000 that had also been in his safe, nor his unregistered handgun, though crime scene techs detected gunshot residue inside the safe.

A month after the robbery, Barbara Forbes disappeared. Despite her husband's very public hue and cry, her lawyer contacted police with a letter from Mrs. Forbes, urging the police to consider foul play in the event of her disappearance.

Recalling the Auto King's slobbering monologue to her cleavage, Gracie smiled to herself as she slipped the disk with the video of Harold beating Bambi into an envelope and sent it off to the police.

Bambi, her nest egg secured with Gracie's help, had acquired a new identity—also acquired with Gracie's help—and was happily making a new life for herself in south Florida. Her bruised body and spirit were healing, and she was dating a man who worshipped the ground she walked on.

For her part, Gracie never wore it in public, but alone in her apartment, she sometimes liked to strut around wearing nothing but the gorgeous diamond necklace Bambi had given her as a thank you gift. Billy was much more careless about wearing the Auto King's fanciest watch, but that was Billy. And Billy's brother Jack, housebreaker extraordinaire, had $50,000 in cash and a handgun. Who knew? Someday it might come in useful.

Gracie stopped sitting in that park.

△ △ △

Kate Flora's *books include series mysteries, police procedurals, suspense and true crime. Current projects include a true crime and a novel in linked stories. She spent seven years as editor and publisher at Level Best Books. Flora is a founding member of the New England Crime Bake. She teaches writing for Grub Street.* Redemption, *a Joe Burgess mystery, will be published in February.*

Death by Deletion

C.A. Johmann

For the umpteenth time, Leslie, get rid of Caroline," said the gruff voice I knew so well but hated to hear from at times. This was one of those times.

"But . . . but," I stammered into the phone, trying desperately to come up with a reason not to snuff out Caroline that I hadn't used before. Nothing came to mind.

"Do it. Now. It's long overdue," he interrupted my buts.

"But Caroline gave me the idea. She's why we're in this position. I owe her some loyalty, don't I?"

"Like I haven't heard that one before. This is the real world, honey. Caroline is superfluous. She's a loose end. We can't take the risk."

"I'm willing to."

"I'm not." A note of anger had seeped into the gruffness. "I've put a hell of a lot of time and effort into this. I'm not taking any chances."

"What if I just make her disappear, vanish, like witness protection?" Even I heard the begging in my voice and was disgusted.

"What's with you and Caroline?" Did I hear a softer note in his voice? "It's not like you haven't done this before. Remember Eddie? And Janice?" he reminded me rather gently under the circumstances.

"I know, I know. It's just that Caroline . . ."

"Don't go there. Listen. No more excuses, no more delays, no nothing except get the job done." His voice grew hard again. "This isn't a request, you know. They want it done and done soon or the deal's off. Is that what you want?"

"No," said a small voice I barely recognized as my own. "I want the deal. How much time do I have?"

"Forty-eight hours. Thursday at noon."

"What? I need more time to figure things out."

"Thursday. Noon."

"That's impossible."

"You don't do it by then, I will, but it won't be pretty."

"Oh, god. OK, OK, I'll try," I moaned and hung up. Forty-eight hours to plan, to plot. Shit. I poured a rum and diet Coke, and drank deeply.

□　□　□

Second drink gone. Better get started. I turned on the computer and brought up the document. Click: Edit. Click: Find. Type: Grove Street Cemetery. Yep. There she was—seventy-ish, tall and slender with a regal bearing. Unknown, unnamed as yet.

That day, like every other before, she entered the Grove Street entrance precisely at 1:00 p.m., turned left, then right onto Cedar passing Eli Whitney's and Noah Webster's graves. But that day, unlike any other, she witnessed a murder and, fortunately for me, ran. The police never identified Caroline, but I came to know her well.

I blocked the relevant text, cut and pasted it into a new file for notes, and switched back to the original document. Click: Edit. Click: Find. Type: Caroline. Cut and Paste. And so on until the bitter end. Some revisions. A little food, a little sleep, lots of coffee. More revisions. More food, more sleep, more coffee. A final read through. That'll work.

Thursday: 11:52 a.m.

Click: Send.

Bye Caroline. Damn all literary agents and publishers.

△ △ △

C. A. Johmann, *Ph.D., is a research biologist turned science reporter, turned pharmaceutical R&D manager, turned children's author of seven non-fiction books, among them the award-winning* The Lewis & Clark Expedition. *This is her first short story, her first mystery, and her first fiction for adults. A former director of the Rochester (NY) Children's Book Festival, Johmann lives in Connecticut.*

Nameless

Cheryl Marceau

"What the hell is that smell?" The door to Room 117 was barely ajar but the odor struck Belanger like a cudgel. He and his partner had been dispatched to the Mountainaire Motel just after 1:00 p.m.—checkout time. The place had been a fixture in town for decades, still displaying a huge fifties-vintage neon sign facing Main Street. It was the kind of dump the flatlanders never stayed in, unless every other motel was full for fifty miles around.

□   □   □

She put down the scissors. It took longer than she'd expected but it was finally done. The last piece of clothing was tucked into the bag. Nothing too flashy—she didn't want to stand out. There was no way they'd be able to track her this way, even if some snoop managed to get a look at her things. It wasn't impossible—she knew what they were capable of. On impulse, she took a small velvet-covered jewelry box from the top dresser drawer and wedged it into her bag.

□   □   □

Belanger stepped into the room and waited for his eyes to adjust to the dark. "God, it's bad. Hey, open that window, will ya?"

Gaffney gave him a look Belanger hadn't seen since he was a rookie. "You gettin' soft?" Gaffney said. "Not like you haven't been around bodies before."

"Jesus!" Belanger answered. "You know I have, you sonofabitch. This one's gawd-awful, though. What the hell is that damn smell?"

Gaffney sniffed the air. "Maybe there is somethin' different. I know it from somewhere, though."

□   □   □

She hadn't dared to tip her hand by drawing down the accounts. As quietly as possible, she'd accumulated some cash over the past couple of weeks. It wouldn't be enough but it would have to do for now. She'd find a way to manage. The credit cards and IDs were already sitting somewhere in a landfill.

Now, standing at the door, she felt a jolt of anguish knowing she would never be able to return. She dug her fingernails into the palms of her hands. What was done, was done.

Fear pushed her off the spot where she stood and kept pushing until the apartment door was locked behind her. As she walked away from the building, she threw the key into a storm drain. No going back.

□   □   □

Belanger scanned the room. One double bed, a small table with two Naugahyde-covered armchairs, a built-in bedside shelf with a big ceramic table lamp and a phone. He pulled open the frayed curtains to let in more light. Another lamp sat on the dresser, and next to it, a small velvet box and the motel key. Past the dresser was an alcove that served as a closet, where a large black suitcase had been placed on the luggage rack. Clothing strayed from under the top of the bag. The bathroom wasn't visible from the door.

The woman sprawled on the bed, her left arm dangling over the side next to the wall. Belanger guessed she was in her late twenties, maybe early thirties. She appeared to have fallen—passed out, at first glance. Gaffney moved closer but Belanger decided he could see just fine from where he stood. The woman had red hair, the artificial shade that came from a drugstore bottle, with a hint of dark brown at the roots. Her hair fanned around her head in garish contrast to the purple and pink cabbage rose pattern of the tatty bedspread. She wore a black satin robe, belted but splayed open. Belanger noticed lacy black panties beneath the edge of the robe. He caught a glint of an earring where the woman's hair fell away from her face. It looked like she might have been expecting someone. There were no obvious signs of forced entry at the door or window, although the state cops would still have to go over every inch of the room. Freakin' shame, Belanger thought. Pretty girl like that.

□ □ □

She waited with the others for the bus. The ticket agent had looked at her like she was stupid when she'd said she wanted to go north. "Where exactly, lady?" the agent had asked. She got out of the line and stood to one side to study the schedule, then returned to the window and asked for a ticket to one of the towns on the route. It was a big enough place that she'd heard of it. Easier to fade into the crowds there, and it would give her a day or two to figure out where to go next. It was also a place where she had no ties. No one would think to follow her there. She prayed she was right.

The ride was tense. She found a seat toward the middle of the bus, next to a man wearing a bandanna around his dreadlocks and listening to music on headphones. He seemed indifferent to her presence. She was reassured by this, but still every muscle in her body clenched each time someone in front of her got up to walk to the lavatory in the back.

□ □ □

"What d'ya think?" Gaffney said. "Natural causes? Maybe she had a medical condition."

"Did anyone hear or see anything?"

"Dispatcher didn't say—just said the call came in from the motel. I guess Dee found her."

"Kinda late for tourists. It's gettin' to be hunting season," Belanger said. "How come no cars in the parking lot?"

"Don't know if our Jane Doe had a car or not. Dee lives a couple streets over. Probably walks to work. If there was anyone else here last night, we'll have to track 'em down."

The officers walked around to look. One car was parked behind the building, facing a vacant lot and the mountains beyond. It had New Hampshire plates and was definitely not a rental, at least not from one of the national companies. Could have been a Rent-a-Wreck, Belanger thought. Could also belong to the desk clerk. We'll have to check.

There was no one in the lobby, although the coffee maker was switched on and the coffee smelled scorched. Belanger guessed that it sat untouched all day, every day. Any guest with half a brain and a couple of dollars in their pocket would go to the Dunkin' Donuts before they'd drink that sludge. He looked in the wastebasket to see if there were any used cups, just in case. The trash was empty, as he'd expected.

□   □   □

Ninety-three dollars. That was all. It wasn't enough. The woman grabbed her jewelry case from the nightstand and looked inside although she knew what she would find. Nothing remained but the sapphire and diamond earrings, and those she could never sell. She quivered, fighting tears. Crying never helped, she thought. She had to stay focused.

She dropped onto the bed and felt it shimmy. The room in the B and B was decorated in Victorian-style kitsch, with a high-posted bed that she thought had probably come from someone's attic where it should have stayed. The waitress at the coffee shop had recommended this place. The woman found it stifling. At least no one had bothered her here.

The aroma of food reached her, coffee and bacon and toast. Her stomach heaved, whether from nausea or hunger she couldn't tell. She arranged a heather gray cashmere sweater into precise folds and placed it on top of the clothing already packed in the large black, wheeled suitcase she'd hoisted onto the bed. Might as well get my money's worth, she thought. I'll get breakfast before I go. Breakfast and then what? She'd been traveling for days now—had lost track of how long it had been. She didn't know where she was going or what she would do when she got there. Don't think about it—just keep moving, she told herself. You know what will happen if they find you.

□   □   □

"It doesn't look like murder, does it?" Belanger asked. It wouldn't be the first killing in Whitinsville, but it would still be unusual if you didn't count bar fights that got out of control. There had been a few suspicious hunting accidents over the years but nothing that they could prove was manslaughter, much less murder.

"No, but . . . I don't see pills, no blood, nothing. I'd say it was natural causes, maybe suicide except I don't get how just yet. And why would you pick a place like this to die if you were gonna do that?"

"You mean this motel?" Belanger looked around in distaste.

"Yeah, and a jerkwater town like this. She's not local. You want to off yourself, there are plenty of ways to do it. Why here?"

"Maybe she didn't. Coulda been natural causes."

"Looks kinda young for that," Gaffney said. "Check out those legs. She sorta looks like one of those women with their own personal trainer. Doesn't seem like someone who'd die young."

□   □   □

Three places were set at the breakfast table. She had begun to hope that she would be gone before the other guests got up, when a couple in their forties came in and sat at the other two places across from her.

"Mornin'," the husband said, offering a beefy hand. The couple wore jeans and matching polo shirts. She studied them looking for a hint that they might not be what they seemed.

"Isn't this the sweetest little place?" the wife asked. "Our room is so cute. The book was right. I always trust their advice," she said, tapping the guidebook she'd placed on the table. "We've never had a bad experience with them. I can't wait to get out and look around. Are you staying here long?"

"Not really," the woman replied. She considered leaving before the food was brought out. These people seemed fine but she wasn't sure. She couldn't risk giving anything away.

"Just passing through?" the husband asked. "What a shame you can't stop and enjoy it."

☐   ☐   ☐

The officers looked more closely around the room. The furniture was intact, nothing broken, no sign of a struggle. Belanger wouldn't have been surprised if there had been. He'd only been on the force a few years but he'd seen plenty. Mostly it was domestic stuff. There was a lot of that up here. Leaf-peeping tourists took pictures of the fiery foliage and the pretty town commons, but he knew how ugly it could get away from the sightseeing spots. Lots of guys drank their paychecks and blamed everybody else when the rent was overdue or there was no more money for beer. They struck out at whoever was handiest—and who wouldn't or couldn't strike back. This didn't look like that. He wasn't sure what it did look like.

☐   ☐   ☐

The Concord Trailways bus pulled to the curb in front of the Irving gas station, and the driver came down the stairs to take her bag. "You ladies don't believe in traveling light, do you?" he joked, and lifted the bag into the bus's cargo compartment. "Go on up, I'll catch you in a minute."

She found a seat in the back of the nearly empty bus, bending her head low as she walked down the aisle. The driver reboarded and looked around a moment until he spotted her. He came back to her seat and stood over her grinning. "Had trouble finding a seat in this crowd, huh?" She cringed at his booming voice. "Where to?" he continued.

"How far can I go for thirty dollars?" she asked softly in reply. His look of pity suggested he knew her story. She wanted to wipe that look off his face. He had no idea. "So how far could I go for that?"

"The fare to Whitinsville is twenty-seven dollars and forty cents.

If you're short of money you might be able to find work there. Although it's kinda the end of the season. Nice town, though, Whitinsville."

She handed him a twenty and eight faded soft single bills. He took the cash and wrote out a ticket on a small pad. "Here," he said, handing over the ticket and her change. "If you want to take a nap, I'll give you a shout when we get there."

She didn't tell him that she'd stopped sleeping a long time ago.

□   □   □

Belanger looked over the clothes. Gaffney was right. Not a single label. Chrissake, she even cut them out of her bras. He fingered the softness of the gray sweater. "She didn't get this at Wal-Mart."

"You think? You see anything at all with a label, tag, something?"

"She didn't miss a thing. Real thorough."

"Better leave this for the Staties. Come on, we'll talk to Dee."

□   □   □

She was surprised it looked so much like the postcards. These were real mountains. She thought the only mountains like this were out West. She leaned her head against the window and stared at the scenery as the bus headed north. The emptiness of the landscape took her by surprise as well, reflecting her own emptiness. There was also a growing fear that in leaving the cities and crowds, she had brought the world in on her. The fewer people she saw, the more exposed she felt. There was no place to hide up here.

She wished there was some way to stop. The B and B owner in that last town had been nice to her. It felt good to be able to talk to someone once in a while, let her guard down some. It felt good to forget the fear.

□   □   □

Dee Watkins' cart was parked on the sidewalk outside Room 102. "Morning," Belanger called out before he walked in the open door. He didn't want to startle her.

The girl straightened from her work when the police entered the room. Gaffney elbowed Belanger as a flash of cleavage showed. Jeez,

Belanger thought, she's his own kid's best friend. Dee looked like she'd been crying, her makeup smeared and her nose red.

"It was awful," the girl said, before they had a chance to ask her anything. "I just saw her lying there, you know, and I thought maybe she was still asleep. I mean, I knocked on the door real hard but there was no answer so I let myself in. There she was. It was gross." Dee sniffled and wiped her eyes. "It was j-just awful." She started to cry in earnest.

"Did you touch anything in the room?" Gaffney asked.

"No, Mr. Gaffney. Just the doorknob. I got out of there as fast as I could. If I'd of stayed in there another minute, I'd of thrown up all over the place."

"Was the room locked when you got there?" Belanger said.

"Just the door. Not the chain."

"Could someone lock that without a key, like if they were leaving?"

"'Course they could. Just twist that little button on the knob."

□ □ □

"Whitinsville," the driver sang out as he came to a stop in a parking lot in the middle of the town. The building directly in front of the bus looked like an old mill. A visitor information sign was posted on the door.

"Miss? This is the place. Now you just go into the visitor center there, and I bet they can help you find a nice place to stay and a bite to eat."

She watched him watching her in the rearview mirror. She pulled on her coat and grabbed her purse, then made her way to the front, avoiding looking directly at the handful of other passengers who watched her.

As the driver pulled her bag out of the luggage bin, she fumbled with her purse. Would he expect a tip? She couldn't spare anything now. On the other hand, it might be better to tip him. She couldn't afford to buy his silence but perhaps she could buy a little goodwill.

She pulled two more faded singles from her wallet and offered them to him.

"I can't, miss, company policy—but thanks all the same. Now don't you go looking so sad. You'll do fine." He smiled at her, climbed back into his bus, and drove away.

She hadn't realized she'd looked as forlorn as she felt. She rejected the visitor center, instead rolling her suitcase to the sidewalk and looking up and down the street. It was the kind of town you'd see in an old movie. There was a motel not far to the left. On the first block to the right were a drugstore, a diner, and a bar that advertised karaoke on Friday nights and fifty-cent draft beer on Wednesdays. A little further down were a hardware store and a burger drive-in. Just across the street she saw a gift shop, a pizza place, a laundromat, and two churches. I wonder what day it is, she thought. Could I go to confession?

□ □ □

"Let's take another look before the Staties get here," Belanger said.

"Trying to show off, huh? Think it's worth getting your chops busted?" Gaffney asked.

"Nah, I just want to see what we can see."

They crossed the motel parking lot back to Room 117, gravel crunching underfoot. "It'd be hard to sneak around here," Belanger said. "Somebody would hear you."

"Not if you were asleep. It isn't that loud." Gaffney opened the door. "Go on in."

Belanger didn't know what he was looking for, but he wanted to find something.

□ □ □

"Sure, we have rooms. I can give you the President's View room on the end—king bed, two windows including one that looks out at part of Mount Washington, and a nice little refrigerator and microwave. It's real popular."

"I need something . . . inexpensive. What's your cheapest room?"

the woman asked. She knew she looked like she could afford better. She had afforded better, not so long ago. Until now she'd hardly known this kind of place existed. But that was history.

The older woman behind the knotty pine counter reached behind to the rack of keys. "How about Room 117? I'll give it to you for the off-season rate. That doesn't really start for a couple of weeks, but it always gets slow here after Columbus Day."

"How much?"

"Forty-six ninety-nine, plus tax. Call it an even fifty."

She felt her breathing seize. That would leave her only fifteen dollars and change. The reality was crushing. What now? Turning her attention back to the desk clerk, she answered, "Do you have anything cheaper, anything at all?" She hated sounding pathetic, like she was begging, and she could tell she had by the other woman's reaction. She nodded and handed over fifty dollars, and felt the room spin as she did.

□   □   □

Gaffney flipped his notepad shut. "Look, I don't know about you but I don't see anything here. I'm going out to the car to wait for the state guys. I'll make a couple calls in the meantime—see if I can track down that bus driver."

Belanger nodded. Dee told them she had been across the street having lunch in the pizza place when the woman arrived the day before, and had seen her get off the bus. This fact seemed strange by itself. No one ever took the Trailways bus to Whitinsville unless they were visiting someone. Tourists drove or arrived with tour groups. This woman didn't look like the type to travel by bus. Nothing about her made sense.

The smell especially bothered him. It didn't belong here. Just like this princess didn't belong here. Belanger studied her without touching, just looked at her and tried to imagine what she'd been like alive. In spite of the cheap dye job, everything about her looked expensive.

Gaffney stuck his head in. "Dispatch found the bus driver. I've got his cell number. I'm going to give him a call."

"Sure," Belanger answered, not really focused on his partner.

"Something else, too. Fred Voss walked over a minute ago and stopped to shoot the shit. You know Fred. There's nothing he won't stick his nose into." Gaffney laughed. "Anyway he says he saw some woman last night, around five-thirty, walking down the street. Kinda nice-looking, didn't recognize her. Must have been from away. Fred knows everyone north of the Notch. Last Fred saw of her, she was going into the True Value."

Belanger pondered this information. It had to have been the woman in the motel room. What would she have wanted in the hardware store?

□   □   □

The afternoon hours were the hardest. It didn't matter where she was. She didn't want to risk leaving her room, but those long hours of self-imposed captivity were the worst. It was then that her mind roamed wild and tormented her. She reacted to every rumble, every whine, every laugh. She knew she couldn't keep running like this forever.

The woman paced, trying hard not to notice the reek of mildew from the bathroom or look too closely at the threadbare bedspread. She found herself imagining what might have transpired on that bedspread over the years. It was too disgusting to think about.

□   □   □

There was nothing more to see. He'd looked in and under the dresser drawers—carefully, avoiding leaving fingerprints. This close to the border, smuggling dope wasn't unheard of. He ran his hand along the little shelf above the hangers in the closet.

Belanger was about to concede defeat. He hadn't looked closely at the bathroom before. What the hell, he thought, it can't hurt.

□   □   □

She hadn't expected to fall asleep. She was just so damned tired.

The sound of someone walking across the gravel parking lot jolted her awake. She listened with every bit of concentration she could muster. Her pulse thudded in her head, and she thought she would be sick.

She held her breath unconsciously as she checked the peephole in the door. There was no one in sight but that could mean nothing. She might have been seen. Anyone on the bus could have given her away.

What to do now? There was nothing between here and the border. Besides, she didn't have a passport. No way to get over the border. Nowhere else that she could go.

The light was golden—late afternoon, she guessed. Reflexively she glanced at her watch, remembering too late that it was gone.

She started crying. Time to stop running.

☐   ☐   ☐

"Whatcha got?" Gaffney asked.

Belanger stood just inside the tiny bathroom. There were spatters of vomit on the floor around the toilet. "Remember Fred was saying he saw some woman go into the True Value? She must have bought this there." He grasped an empty green plastic jug using a scrap of tissue. "Looks like it fell in the corner. Didn't see it at first for the shower curtain. Bag was in the trash." He pointed at a brown paper bag with the hardware store logo, tossed in the wastebasket.

☐   ☐   ☐

She choked and gasped. No! Her head reeled. Tears streaked down her face. Her stomach heaved in great rolling waves. Her body contorted in a spasm. Oh God—I can't, dear God in heaven not this—

☐   ☐   ☐

Gaffney grabbed the jug and pointed at the label. "Malathion—bug juice! That's what stinks so bad! My wife uses it in the garden. What the hell is it doing here?" He went back to the bed, leaned over the woman's face and sniffed. "Goddamn if she didn't drink the frickin' shit. Must be how she killed herself."

"No damn way." Belanger grabbed the jug from Gaffney and

waved the empty jug under his partner's nose. "Take a whiff."

Gaffney snorted and gasped.

"Could you stand a good long drink of this?" Belanger said. "The bottle's empty. You know damn well somebody couldn't have drunk this on their own. Doesn't figure that she'd buy it and dump it down the drain. Somebody must have been here. They must have poured it down her throat."

"Staties'll get prints, check it out, but there's nothing says anyone else was here. Look around—not a thing outta place, nothing broken, no sign anyone broke in. She must've done it herself," Gaffney said.

"How in the name of God almighty could she drink enough of that shit to kill her?" Belanger asked, convinced that he'd been right. His gut told him all along this had to be murder.

□ □ □

Days later, Belanger hadn't stopped thinking about the Jane Doe. The New Hampshire Medical Examiner and the state cops had done their work. The case was closed. It was time to put the whole thing out of his mind, but he couldn't help himself.

He still believed it was murder, had to be. There was just no other way it could have happened. You don't cut all the labels out of your clothes and run from who knows where just to drink bug poison in a hick town in the north woods. She'd been running from who knew what danger.

After all that, they got to her anyway.

△ △ △

Cheryl Marceau *is a human resources executive at a technology company in the Boston area. Her first short story, "Unleashed," appeared in* Thin Ice. *She is also working on her first novel, a historical mystery. When not exploring the back roads and ice cream stands of New England, she and her husband live in Arlington, Massachusetts.*

Skye Farm Standoff

Ruth M. McCarty

Win MacLeod wiped the sweat off his forehead with the sleeve of his blue-plaid flannel shirt before setting up another log. He'd been splitting wood since dawn and still couldn't control the anger that he'd gone to bed with the evening before.

Cassie was going to leave him. She'd announced it right at the dinner table as if she was telling him about some new recipe or dress pattern she'd found.

Jesus, they'd been together since high school. He brought the ax down—sending wood flying in every direction. The physical act helped keep his rage in control while adding to the cords he'd sell in the fall.

He took off his shirt, sat down on the stump he'd been using to split the wood, and took a cool drink of water from the old pail he'd filled from the spring. His hand shook as he drank from the ladle.

Today was Sunday. Cassie would normally be getting ready for the eight o'clock Mass at St. Anthony's Church on Main Street about now. He looked toward the house and saw her moving about the kitchen. So she was up.

Cassie was going to leave him, but not for another man. She wanted him to sell his farm—the farm that had been in his family since 1719 when his Scottish ancestors had come to New Hampshire and settled in Ashgill. For almost three-hundred years, a MacLeod had lived on and worked this land. The original Skye Farm, named for the Isle of Skye that they'd hailed from, had close to three hundred acres, and now it was down to twenty-five, with half of that hills. He knew he could easily work it for another seven years and then turn it over to their son, Ian. Ian would surely be ready to come back home by then.

Win dipped his shirt in the leftover water and washed the rest of the sweat from his face. He couldn't let her leave. He threw down his shirt and strode to the side door. He scraped his boots, leaving them on, and marched into the kitchen.

Cassie stood at the sink filling the coffee pot from the tap. He noticed her back stiffen as she heard him enter. "Morning, Cassie," he said.

She didn't turn to look at him, but she did mumble something that sounded like "Morning." He watched as she poured the water into the coffee machine. She added a paper filter and a few scoops of ground coffee before pushing the start button. Win looked at the clock. It was dang close to eight o'clock and she was still in her bathrobe and slippers.

"Ain't you going to church?" he asked.

She turned and looked at him for the first time since he'd come in to the house. Her eyes were puffy, like she'd been crying all night. He guessed maybe she had, but he couldn't rightly tell as he'd fallen into a deep sleep after their fight last night.

"I'm not going this morning," she said.

"Are you sick?"

"Sick? Am I sick? Yes, I'm sick," she yelled. A bitter laugh escaped from her throat. "Sick of doing the same things, the same way, every single damn day."

Win had hoped that she'd reconsidered leaving after he'd argued his side last night, but it looked like she was still aiming to fight. He had to make her see. "It'll only be seven more years, Cassie. Then Ian will come back, take over."

"He's not coming back! Don't you get it, Win? He doesn't want this life, doesn't want to spend all day working—slaving—and for what? Food on our table and a tax bill the size of Texas?"

Win crossed the kitchen in two strides. Cassie held her ground, not even flinching as he stopped inches from her. His arm muscles ached as he tried to control the anger flowing through them. He kept his voice steady and said, "Make me some breakfast."

Cassie stormed over to the refrigerator and he sat at the table in silence.

She made his usual Sunday morning feast—eggs and toast and crisp bacon and fixed his coffee with milk and three sugars, the way he liked it. He grunted, "Thanks" as she placed them before him. He dunked the toast in the runny yolks, enjoyed the crisp bacon and washed it down with a sip of the coffee.

"You gonna go to the ten o'clock Mass?" Win asked.

Cassie still stood. "I told you I'm not going today. I'm going to pack my things."

Win saw the determination in her eyes. "What things? You giving more stuff to that consignment shop?"

Cassie closed her eyes—shook her head at him. "My clothes. I'm going to pack my clothes, Win. I told you last night. I'm not staying."

"And I told you last night you're not going anywhere." He pushed the unfinished plate back and stood. He headed for the back door and pulled both sets of car keys off the rack. "I'll be fixing the fence down by the river."

He heard Cassie yelling, "You can't make me stay. I'll call Ian. He'll help me!"

Let her call Ian. Won't do her much good.

□   □   □

Cassie hadn't thought it would be this hard. She'd gotten up her nerve and called a real estate agent two weeks earlier and he'd come to the farm when Win had driven to Massachusetts to look at two new horses he'd been planning to buy.

"Believe it or not, Ashgill is a hot property right now. Developers are falling all over themselves buying up the land before the next boom. You could subdivide, make a good amount of money, and still have enough of a farm to make a good living."

She thought Win would be thrilled to know what the land was worth but when she told him last night, he went into a rage. There was no way he was selling. He wanted them to struggle for seven more years and for what? To celebrate 300 years of the same family owning this godforsaken piece of land?

Win didn't give a care how she felt. All he cared about was passing down the land to Ian. And all Ian wanted was never to set foot on it again.

She hurried to dress, then went to the attic to take down the two ancient suitcases she'd brought with her when she'd married Win. So old they didn't even have wheels. Cassie didn't know why she'd kept them. What did they need suitcases for, anyways? They never went anywhere. When you owned a farm, it owned you.

Cassie opened her drawers. She had plenty of jeans, sweaters and undergarments. She packed the first suitcase with them. Then she went to the tiny closet that she and Win shared. He had two good suits—a brown one for meeting with the bank loan officer and a black one for funerals. Thankfully, he hadn't worn the black one in a long time. Cassie had the dress she'd worn to Ian's graduation from college and a two-piece suit she'd kept for funerals. She folded them carefully with tissue paper and placed them in the other suitcase. She'd need the suit to go on job interviews. At least she hoped she'd be asked to one. She'd talked with a temporary agency over in Londonderry who said they would help her find a job. She had taken typing in high school and had learned how to operate the laptop Ian had helped her buy so she could communicate with him while he was in school. Ian lived in Cambridge, Massachusetts now, with a girl named India, and they both had good jobs. Cassie knew Ian was never coming home.

□ □ □

Win finished fixing the fence and packed up the tools just as his stomach growled. He was mighty hungry and wondered as he headed back to the house if Cassie would have come out of her snit long enough to make him a decent meal. He just didn't get her. She had everything she needed right here on the farm—a roof over her head, food in her belly and sex almost as good as their high school days. No, better than their high school days. What did they know about sex then, anyways? And, she didn't have to worry about getting pregnant anymore after Ian.

She wasn't really leaving him, was she?

□   □   □

Cassie finished packing long before the noon hour. She'd tucked the two hundred fifty-seven dollars she'd managed to hide from Win into the side pocket of the suitcase that held her jeans. It wasn't easy to accumulate that much money from the Grade B eggs she sold at the local farm stand. It really didn't amount to much, only enough to pay one week's room and board and the security deposit needed on the rooming house she'd read about in the *Londonderry Times*. A nonsmoking residence for women, it read. She'd like that, at least until she could find a job, then she'd find an apartment or such.

Cassie knew better than to expect any alimony payments or financial support from Win. The farm barely broke even and anything left over went to feed the livestock, repair the equipment or pay the utilities so they'd have heat and light in the winter months.

She felt a pang of guilt when she thought about Win trying to do it all. How would he be able to cook, clean, and feed the chickens?

She was really leaving him, wasn't she?

□   □   □

Win took his muddied boots off at the door. No sense in getting Cassie all riled up anymore than she was. He had to give it to her; she did keep a clean house. 'Course it was only her and him since Ian left. How hard could that be?

"Cassie?" he called as he entered the kitchen. She was nowhere in sight. He listened for sounds of her in the house and felt a little ping of relief as he heard the wheel on the clothesline creak as she pushed it along.

He supposed he should fix that old dryer she'd been complaining about, but he guessed he'd be able to put it off until next fall. Why run up the electric bill when the sheets smelled so fine from drying outdoors?

Win glanced at the stove and the pot of something simmering on the back left burner that sure smelled like last night's stew. He glanced at the table, set for one, and shrugged his shoulders. The stew smelled mighty good and it always tasted better the second time around. He had to give her that too; she knew how to fill a man's belly with the food the good Lord gave them.

He really couldn't let her leave.

□   □   □

Cassie heard the screen door slam as Win came in for lunch and kept on hanging the third load of the morning on the clothesline. She knew she complained a lot about Win not fixing the dryer, but she knew he'd take a half a year of Sundays before he'd fix it if she didn't. Of course, she'd never let on how relaxing hanging out freshly washed clothes could be, and that they smelled so good when she took them in at the day's end. Sometimes she'd be pulling loads in at dusk— while watching the springtime sun set over the barn. Amazing red skies or dark brooding storm clouds, Skye Farm lived up to its name.

Could she really leave this?

□   □   □

Win ate in silence. Cassie had left out the last few slices of bread she'd made the morning before. He'd spread fresh butter over them, dunking them in the savory gravy of the stew. He was a meat and potatoes man, and savored them along with the carrots, onions and Bisquick dumplings Cassie had added to the stew.

He wondered if Cassie had called Ian on the phone or contacted him on that darned e-mail thing Ian had set up for her.

He never understood what had possessed Ian to move to Massachusetts. To Cambridge of all places, where you couldn't find a parking place to save your life and had to take your life in your hands if you wanted to cross the street! How could Ian leave the quiet beauty of Skye Farm for the noise of the city?

And why the hell did Cassie want to leave too?

□   □   □

Cassie heard the back door slam as she came into the kitchen. She frowned at the stew spilled on her stove and the dishes left on the table and mumbled, "The least the bastard could do is run his plate under the water so I don't have to spend the day scraping dried stew off it."

She picked up the portable phone and dialed Ian's number. After four rings, the answering machine picked up. "Hey! It's Ian," her son's voice said, and then a female voice said, "And India," then together, "We can't come to the phone right now—you know the drill, leave a number."

Cassie hung up. She hated leaving messages on anybody's answering machine. What if they were home and listening? What would she say that didn't sound frumpy? And what if they were making love like she and Win used to do on Sunday afternoons?

They hadn't done that in a long time. Not in the afternoons and sometimes not for several nights in a row. When they'd first married, they did it every day and sometimes more than once. Sometimes even in the barn or out in the field under the beechwood tree.

That was before her miscarriages, before Ian, before this damned farm became a full time job.

She would call Ian's cell phone in the morning to let him know what she was doing. He'd help her set up in Londonderry when she found a place.

But she needed to leave today. She took out her sewing box, felt around under the many colored threads, and found the spare key to the Ford F-150 that she hidden there after one of their fights. She took her birth certificate, Social Security card, and the little jewelry she had and put them in the faux leather case that came with the laptop. She'd drive to Londonderry and worry about how Win was going to get the truck later.

He really couldn't stop her, could he?

□   □   □

Win was at a loss. He wasn't quite sure what to do with himself. He'd spotted a sickly looking fox prowling around the property last week and decided he'd blow off some steam by tracking it now before it got into the henhouse. He thought about telling Cassie where he'd be, but decided to let her wonder.

□   □   □

Cassie had everything ready to go. She hadn't seen hide nor hair of Win since morning, though she knew he'd been in to eat. He could be anywhere on the farm. She did remember him saying he had some fences to fix, so maybe that's what he was doing. It was now or never. She slung her pocketbook and laptop case over her shoulder, then picked up a suitcase in each hand. She looked around the bedroom— at the bed they'd shared for so long and wondered if she was doing the right thing. Maybe, just maybe, Win would miss her and not because she wasn't there to do the mindless everyday chores.

Maybe he'd come after her.

□   □   □

Win came whistling into the yard between the house and the barn. He'd found the fox. Took it out with just one shot. It was sick so it was a good thing he got it. He'd call Ed McAuliffe at the animal control office in the morning to let him know.

As he walked toward the barn, he noticed the door was open. He thought he closed it before he headed out. The sound of the Ford engine turning over confused him. He had the keys in his pocket. He took them out and sure enough, he had both sets. Was someone hot-wiring the truck?

He raced for the barn—shaking the gun in the air while yelling for Cassie. She'd call the police.

□　　□　　□

Cassie put the truck in reverse and started backing up. Looked in the rearview mirror and nearly died when she spotted Win running at her with his shotgun in his hand. Good Lord, he was going to stop her.

She gunned it, hoping Win would move out of the way. She felt the thud as the bed backed into him. "Oh, God, what have I done?"

Cassie put the truck in park. Slowly opened the door. Win sat in the dust, his gun nowhere in sight. He was laughing.

"What the hell's so funny?"

"The look on your face." Tears from laughter were running down his face now. "I thought someone was hot-wiring the truck."

"And what's so funny about that?"

"I guess I must have looked like a crazy man coming at you with a gun and calling your name."

"You did scare the living daylights out of me. Are you hurt?"

"No, Cassie. I moved out of the way and hit the truck with the butt of my gun."

"You stupid bastard," Cassie yelled. "I thought I killed you."

"Where were you going?" Win got up, all signs of laughter gone in an instant.

"Nowhere. Just checking to see if that old key I found in the junk drawer fit anywhere." Cassie prayed Win wouldn't look in the cab and see her suitcases.

"Cassie, you going to go to church next week?" Win asked.

Cassie nodded. "Yes, Win. I'm going to the eight o'clock. Just like I always do." She didn't add she'd be going to confession, too— for that one split second of joy she'd felt as she gunned the truck.

△ △ △

Ruth M. McCarty's *short mysteries have appeared in all of Level Best Books' anthologies. She received honorable mention in* Alfred Hitchcock Mystery Magazine, NEWN *and mysteryauthors.com for her flash fiction and won the 2009 Derringer for Best Flash Story for "No Flowers for Stacey" published in* Deadfall: Crime Stories by New England Writers.

Ambush

John Bubar

The threat, or more accurately, what Speck Gagnon thought of as the threat-of-a-threat, came ready-to-wear in the midst of a typical Wednesday. The morning began with the usual cup of instant coffee and peanut butter on toast, followed by a hair-of-the-dog beer. As Wednesday was Speck's grocery shopping day, he watched the local morning show to catch the weather. He'd be out a good part of the day after all, and had another beer while waiting for the traffic to settle down out on US Route One.

He walked out of his trailer promptly at ten o'clock, but before starting his pickup, he had a new ritual to perform. Pulling a white plastic jug of brake fluid out from behind the bench seat of his F-100, Speck topped off the master brake cylinder. He had a leak somewhere, discovered a month ago. Maybe in the lines, maybe in the master cylinder itself, maybe both, but with a little care he could nurse the old girl into town and back. Satisfied with his work, he put a beer in the cup holder and pulled himself into the cab.

Easing out his driveway, he joined the dirt road that would lead him to the highway. Between second and third gear Speck popped the top on the beer and sipped what had foamed onto the top of the can while he steered with one knee and shifted into fourth. He smiled at the thought of nursing his truck and nursing his beer at the same time.

Shopping completed, he rewarded himself with another beer at the Viking Bar and Grill then drove over to the Vet Center to yank the chains of a couple of buddies who had the misfortune of being Marines. His jarhead friends loved to see him. Speck could tell, because whenever he came through the door, they'd hunch over their checkerboard and pretend they didn't see him. Then it would be his job to take a shot at their beloved Corps. Last week, standing over their game of checkers, he'd asked, "Do you know the easiest way to kill a Marine?"

"Ain't no easy way, asshole," Antoine said, looking up and pushing his glasses back into place. He'd lost half an ear in a firefight at Khe Sanh, and his glasses were forever slipping down his face.

"Yeah, asshole." Sam spent a fair amount of time repeating what Antoine said. They were both dry drunks, but Sam had really fried himself.

"Throw some sand on a brick wall and tell him to hit the beach," Speck said.

He watched them tsk-tsk and roll their eyes like it was the first time they'd heard it. Then they jumped up, shook his hand and got up close to him, smelling his breath, which was as close as these pussies got to a real drink anymore. He wondered if they were going to try and save him again today—get him into a program.

Instead, they wanted to fight the war they were too old for. The one splashed across the front page every day. Their solution, by way of a two-minute lecture delivered by Antoine and approved of by a nodding Sam, was a version of kill'em all and let God sort'em out. Speck wanted to ask how many free-fire zones they'd seen in Vietnam, thought better of it and made to leave, but they weren't done with him.

"You better look out, airborne," Antoine said.

Speck paused at the take-care note in Antoine's voice. "Why's that?"

"A gang's been rousting trailers out in the willywhacks where you live. It was in the paper."

"There was this old lady," Sam chimed in. "Ambulance takes her away in the middle of the night. She dies three days later. Her boy goes to clean out her place and finds her front door busted in. Her shit spread everywhere. Only two miles from you."

"Then there's the old guy beyond you. They busted down his door and cleaned him out while he was in Florida visiting his daughter." Antoine again. They were taking turns with him, had probably practiced their lines all morning.

"It was in the paper today—maybe half a dozen trailers. Cops want you to keep your lights on—TV too, when you leave—make it look like you're home. Like any of us can afford the electricity. You be careful, soldier. You need a Marine to guard you, you just let us know." Sam delivered his lines with that I'm-a-Marine-and-I've-got-you-surrounded look.

"They're punk kids," Antoine said. "But dangerous if they get behind you so you cover your tail out there. Stealing old people's stuff. They're not worth spit. Couldn't have carried our water when we were their age."

"Yeah," Sam echoed. "Couldn't have carried our water."

Speck left with his usual good-bye, flashing them both middle fingers, his hands dancing above his head. They loved that. It made them feel young again. Reminded them of when someone used to care enough about them to publicly tell them to go fuck themselves.

Going home that day, Speck noticed the brakes were fading bad, worse than he'd expected, and he wondered if it was a sign of worse times to come. Work with the signs, his father had taught him, don't fight them, anticipate. He'd been thinking of his father lately as the anniversary of his death approached and began to bang some ideas around about what he could do if some punks tried to break in, wanting to take what little he had.

The following Wednesday the brakes failed as Speck slowed to merge with the oncoming traffic speeding north along US Route One. It wasn't the spongy responsiveness he had worked around for the past week; the fading, but not quite failing, he had hoped would last five more days, until his social security check arrived, and he could afford to get them at least partially fixed. If he couldn't get them repaired today, he'd have to leave his truck at the garage. Without a truck in the dooryard, he thought, my place will look deserted. He wondered if this too was a sign, like his father used to talk about, of puzzle pieces falling into place.

Finishing the last of his beer, he tossed the can into a drawstring bag he kept in the passenger side foot-well just for that purpose and was rewarded with a scratchy aluminum-scraping-aluminum sound as it joined its empty siblings. It was only his third beer of the morning, and he felt the satisfaction of smoothly double clutching down into first gear and coasting to a stop against the berm behind Jorganson's Garage.

He loved this old truck. One of Ford's finest, only 287,000 miles and not much rust that you could see. The worst of the visible rust had been taken care of three years before when he'd replaced the right front fender with a blue one salvaged off a junker. He hadn't bothered to get it painted white to match the rest of the truck. It's what's inside that counts, he told anyone who joked about the interesting color scheme. Anymore, the blue fender reminded him of those days when he would discover he was wearing mismatched socks. There was always something, he thought, tugging at what little money a man had. Today it was brakes, not rust, and he would have to convince Shorty to extend him a little credit.

Everyone knew Shorty LeRoux, the owner of Jorganson's Garage. The hyperactive, crew-cut little Frenchman with an intuitive sense for cars and people had retired from the Army at thirty-nine and returned home determined to work the rest of his life only for himself. The Army had taught him the importance of reconnaissance and he quickly learned that while his French ancestors had settled in northern Maine long before the Swedes arrived, the Swedes had the money. He had watched the major Scandinavian holidays celebrated with the same passion as the American ones, and knew from his quick inventory of their parking lots that the Lutheran churches were full of the prosperous every Sunday morning.

To name his fledging business "LeRoux's Garage" was out of the question. He had picked Jorganson out of the phone book and painted the sign himself. Years later, he still worked on the Saabs and Volvos of those Swedes, who, in the early days, had brought in their cars to be serviced by someone named Jorganson, and had left, pleased with work delivered on time and at a reasonable price by someone named LeRoux. Shorty catered to the Swedes, who were unfazed by his high hourly rates, appreciated his professional work, and paid promptly. But there were never enough of them, so he had of necessity developed another set of clients.

Speck was one of those. He found Shorty working under the hood of a red Saab convertible. The Saab's owner, a florid-faced man in his thirties with thinning blond hair, paced in Shorty's office.

"My brakes finally shit the bed, Shorty." Speck kept a respectful distance, careful not to be caught standing over the smaller man. "The old girl's out back. Master cylinder out of a junker is all it'll take. Can't imagine anything else. I can give you fifty now and the rest the first of the month."

"I saw you lug it in." Shorty didn't bother to look at him. "It's a four-hundred-dollar job. There's nothing that old in a junkyard anymore. Twenty-year-old F-100s get crushed up right away, so I'll have to get rebuilt parts. We both know you need to replace those rusted brake lines too. I'll need the money up front. I don't want to have to come out to your place like I did before." He said the last part quietly as he lowered the hood of the Saab.

"That was a tough time. For Christ's sake, Shorty, it was Christmas. I had to send something to my kid. Give a fellow vet a break, will ya?"

"Don't yell," Shorty glanced into his office as he slid into the driver's seat. "I'll get you back on the road for three twenty-five, but you show up with the money. I'm not bullshitting about the rebuilt parts. I get the money and you'll be on your way in twenty-four hours. You can leave your pickup here until then, but not more than a couple weeks or I'm charging you for parking." Then quieter still, "And don't ever play the vet card again. It's not becoming." The Saab started smoothly.

Embarrassed, Speck gave it up. I should have paid him for that muffler in December, he thought, and avoided his banging on my trailer door the first week in February.

"All right, I'll be here in five days. Count on it, but I've got to go for groceries to get me through. If that car's ready to go, maybe your customer can give me a ride into town?" But Shorty had already gotten close enough to smell Speck's breath.

He'd walked a half-mile, a dozen cars ignoring his outstretched thumb, before he was picked up by Smitty Carlson, who had recognized him from the bar at the VFW.

"Looks like you need a ride, son." Smitty was in his eighties. Calling a man in his sixties "son" was a routine adoption for him. "Warm day for the end of June. Sure don't envy those boys in Iraq fighting in that heat."

"Heat or cold, fighting a war is all hot work. I appreciate the ride, Smitty. I lost the brakes on my truck today." Speck had given Smitty his hoped-for response and settled back to listen once again to an old man's memory of a winter spent retreating down the Korean peninsula. The Chinese had just ambushed Task Force Drysdale on the road to Hagaru-ri when the red Saab convertible overtook them. Rich kid in an expensive car, and what had he ever done to earn the free country he was speeding through? Speck interrupted Smitty's story to say that kids today couldn't have carried Smitty's water, spoiled as they were.

Smitty dropped him in the Shop & Save parking lot in the middle of town. Speck hesitated a moment before saying thanks in hopes that Smitty would offer to stick around and give him a ride back home, but Smitty didn't offer and Speck wouldn't ask. Asking would have felt like playing the vet card.

The Viking Bar and Grill was across the street and a beer was calling. He hated to pay bar prices, but he needed a quiet place to sit and get his head around his grocery list before he went shopping. Considering his food options, he drank a couple of two-dollar drafts. Fifteen minutes later, he threw four ones on the bar and emerged back into the summer sunlight.

He would only be five or six days without transportation but, just to be on the safe side, he bought two cases of beer. There was a good sale on Old Milwaukee. He picked up canned tuna for his dinners, peanut butter for his lunches, two loaves of bread and a pound of coffee. When Speck remembered that the cab ride home would cost him sixteen dollars, he put the bread and the coffee back. He could eat the tuna and peanut butter right out of the container and recycle the one-time-used coffee grounds he kept in a can against just this kind of tight-money day. He didn't want to spend himself down to nothing.

His trailer was eight miles from town, six miles of tarred road and two miles of dirt, and was set on a sliver of land bordering a ten-acre spruce swamp he had inherited from his father. Forty feet long, his Fair Winds mobile home was more than big enough. It was jacked up on blocks and he had salvaged some plywood from a building site one night to make a skirting for it. In the winters he cut spruce boughs and stacked them against the plywood. He liked the look of the place in winter. The cabdriver turned down his offer of a couple of warm beers for the ride back to town and had been smart enough not wait around for a tip. With the groceries put away, Speck went outside, found his rake under the trailer, and went to work.

The first night was the toughest. In hopes that it would help him sleep all afternoon, he drank a little more than usual after the raking was done. The punks wouldn't show on the first night of an empty driveway, but his plan was to sleep during the days and be awake all night, so he had to get his body used to that schedule. He tossed and turned the afternoon away, waking up to the alarm he had set for an hour after sunset, drinking a beer and eating a can of tuna fish in the dark. This night was a training night, a time to think about what he might have forgotten, a time to rehearse. He added light to the bathroom with a second night-light and took the bulb out of the refrigerator, so if he needed a beer in the night, the light wouldn't give him away when he opened the door.

They were creatures of habit, these punks, so he figured they'd bust down his front door like they had all the others, which would put them in the kitchen-TV room where they'd rummage about looking for booze. Then they'd search the closets in the narrow hallway that led to the other rooms, throwing all the clothes on the floor looking for money, then follow the hallway to the bathroom to look for pills, and then spill into the bedroom where he'd be waiting, sitting in the corner farthest from them, a full clip in a forty-five, sitting on half-cock with the safety off. They'd be backlit, perfect targets as their eyes adjusted from the nightlights in the bathroom to the sudden darkness of the bedroom.

His father danced into his mind. What great days they had shared in the woods. His old man had taught him to read the signs of the animals, to understand how they used the terrain to conceal themselves, and how to drive a wounded animal, but never corner him.

"Any animal, hurt and in a corner, will do the unexpected, the unpredictable. Always make them think they have a chance." He'd delivered that advice on Speck's fifteenth birthday, pausing halfway through his bottle of Jim Beam. Then he'd laughed at himself, snorted really, his familiar sadness disappearing for a moment, and had offered the bottle to his son.

Speck's mother had railed at his father for years to stop his drinking and traipsing through the woods, and join her in embracing Jesus as his savior. Speck was fourteen when she took off for Nashville with a man from her church, leaving a note that said she'd send for him. A bus ticket arrived a year later. He tore it up. He couldn't leave his father drunk and out of work.

On the day he passed his draft physical for the Army, in the July after he graduated high school, Speck's father cooked him his favorite dinner of peas, fresh from their garden, and trout, caught that afternoon. The next morning the sheriff arrived to tell him there had been an accident. His father had been found dead, tangled around a rail fence he had tried to negotiate at night with a loaded gun that had accidently discharged beneath his chin. They needed next-of-kin to identify the body. The sheriff had been careful with him, but the warden had pointed to the half-empty bourbon bottle and the flashlight they'd found beside the rifle, as if to say the poacher with the drinking problem had got what he deserved.

In his grief Speck had challenged all of them, screamed at them really, to tell him why it made sense that a man who could walk up to any deer he wanted during the day would choose to hunt at night under a light. He still had a clear image of that grim-faced old sheriff grabbing him by the shoulders, holding him at arms-length for a moment, and then telling him to let his father rest in peace.

The second night was easier. Sleep had come during the day. He hadn't taken on so much beer when he was awake and had put down quite a charge of peanut butter at lunch, then a nap, and tuna once again after sunset. Sitting in the dark sipping a beer, he ran his nose along the barrel of the Lieutenant's gun, smelling what was left of the gun oil he had used to clean it two weeks before. The Lieutenant hadn't needed his forty-five when Speck had finally gotten to him, so he'd thrown it in his pack, smuggled it home, and kept it clean. He'd scrubbed the Lieutenant's blood off it with his toothbrush. For the first few years he was back, he'd take the gun into the woods every June 13th, stalk a deer, and dry fire on it. His then-wife never understood him, but, like his father, he had found the woods to be a spiritual place—an Army chaplain had taught him the meaning of that word—and Speck thought that not killing something was a reasonable way to mourn the Lieutenant. He should have been walking point that day. He would have seen the signs that the Iowa boy had missed. After Speck's wife left him and took his daughter with her, he stopped going into the woods and contented himself with giving the weapon a good cleaning every June.

Between one and three in the morning he heard more traffic noise than his dirt road deserved for that time of night. It felt like a drive-by recon.

By the third night he was getting into rhythm. The pillow he'd put behind him the night before made the corner a lot more comfortable, and he'd found an old dark green blanket to throw over his white legs. It was a cool June and he'd been cold sitting on the floor in a black tee shirt and a pair of dark plaid boxers his daughter had sent him for Christmas. He'd sent her a card in return with the longest letter he'd ever written. Come full circle, he thought as he sipped a beer, my mother gave me underwear for Christmas.

There was a close-in recon at midnight. Remember the first rule of ambush, he told himself, let them come to you. He flashed on the memory of that day he had spoken up and told the Lieutenant, "Sir, with respect, your ambush plan doesn't suit the terrain." For the first time in his life, men stood silent and listened to what he had to say. "If we make them think we're only above them, they'll scramble down hill, scared and wounded maybe, toward that little stream. Then they'll wait to see if we follow, which we do making a lot of noise, and they'll decide to set up an ambush for us on the other side of the stream. Only the other half of the platoon will already be there, waiting to catch them in the open water."

A week later the Lieutenant started calling him the Ambush Master, Alpha Mike for short. All the guys called him Mikie, the first grown-up nickname he'd ever had. It felt good remembering those times, sitting there in the darkness with a gun, listening to his new enemy stumbling around outside.

They were circling the trailer, stepping on the small branches he'd raked up outside his bedroom window, so as to tell him right where they were, his hedge against a sudden decision on their part to gain access somewhere other than the front door. Two, maybe three of them, and noisy. Occasionally murmuring. A little yelp when one of them tripped over a cement block he had covered with spruce boughs. Punks, he thought, as he opened another beer and listened to a car start up in the distance. Carry his water? They couldn't even find his water.

At first light, he looked out his kitchen window at a patch of dirt he'd raked smooth, and studied the footprints the enemy had left behind. Only two, he decided, one his size, maybe bigger, and a smaller one. A punk in training. He carried out his regimen of sleep, punctuated by used coffee, beer, peanut butter and tuna, and was wide-awake at sunset. They'd come tonight. All the signs pointed to it.

Shortly after midnight he heard a car roll into his driveway. He looked at his watch. 0037. No attack just before dawn for these two. They wanted a lot of darkness in front of them. He heard them circling the trailer again, still stepping on the branches but avoiding the cement block this time. Then some loud knocks on the door. A check against their recon. Five heartbeats later the window in his door exploded—safety glass—a sticky explosion. They had a crowbar, or maybe a baseball bat, but some sort of deadly weapon. He saw deflected light up the hallway. One of them had a flashlight.

"Just beer and a peanut butter jar with a spoon stuck in it. Maybe the old fart spends his money on drugs." It was a young man's voice followed by a murmured response.

Come here, boys. You're only little vandals, he thought. Not like the big Vandals or the Goths or the Huns who knew war all their lives. High school—sophomore year—Mr. Berkley—World History— Speck had been only thirty months from pulling a trigger in Vietnam.

They didn't bother with the closets. They went right to the bathroom, but it was empty. He'd made sure of that. He wanted them to hurry out of the light and into the darkness.

"Maybe he keeps his pills in the bedroom." He was surprised to hear a girl's voice. "And in his bedroom . . ." She let the words linger, holding their promise.

The last girl in his bedroom had hardly been a girl. Skinny. Blonde, mostly. Younger than him, but looked older. She had sat down beside him at the bar, back when he was holding a job and could afford to drink in bars, and had watched him limp off to the men's room. When he came back she'd asked, "What happened to you?"

So he told her Jimmy McCauley's story—two AK-47 rounds in the left hip. It was more romantic than arthritis. She'd followed him home so she'd be sure to have a ride in the morning, telling him she didn't trust the reliability of any truck with a funky blue fender. If she noticed that his wound hadn't left any scars, she never mentioned it. When she awoke the next morning, she found him angled up in this same corner, holding the Lieutenant's gun, pretending to be asleep. She left quick enough.

He had thought about the woman since, but only to wonder if she would be his last one ever. It was a girl that killed Billy Peters one day on patrol. She came out of a hooch, shot him in the face, and tried to run. Girls will kill you too, the Lieutenant always told them.

The boy led the way, a baseball bat in his right hand, a small flashlight in his left pointed at the floor. The girl hung back a little. Come on, come on, Speck thought, I need you both in here facing me. He saw her framed in the light reflected from the bathroom— nineteen, twenty maybe, shoulder length hair—the same age his daughter was when she had reached out to call him for the first time. The boy pointed his flashlight toward the top of the dresser. Nothing there. And he began to scan the room with it. She was like that Vietnamese girl who wouldn't run away from him the week after Billy died. No matter what he did she just kept walking toward him and he had to light her up. The Lieutenant and the Chaplain told him he'd done the right thing, but why hadn't she run? Just run?

He wasn't sure he'd said it aloud. Had his cotton mouth crippled such a simple word? He said it again, "Run."

She screamed, "Tony, Jesus, Tony. Run!" and took off down the hall, but the boy had other ideas. He pointed the flashlight in the direction of the voice, saw an old man in a blanket on the floor pointing back at him, and swung one-handed with the bat.

It was a near thing. The light blinded him and Speck felt the swish of the bat as it passed by his face, but he fired a round where the boy had to be and heard a grunt. Then the flashlight tipped and fell and he got an image of the boy against the bedroom wall in time to get off another round, aiming center mass, just like he'd been trained. He hammered back to half-cock and waited. His ears were ringing, but he could hear a gurgling sound and smell the blood. The car in the driveway started and then was gone. The gurgling stopped.

He waited patiently for five minutes. His father had taught him patience. Then he fired off the rest of the clip around the bedroom, as if he'd panicked, and tossed the empty gun on the bed. It was time to call 911. He found the boy lying in the doorway. Blood had soaked the shag carpet and he had to wade through it to get to the phone in the kitchen. Beer first or call first, he asked himself. Beer first. The cops will see the bloody tracks, refrigerator then the phone, but he knew they'd understand once they checked his record and saw the DUIs.

The 911 operator was more of a problem than he had imagined she would be. "They broke in," he said over and over, "I shot one of them. Come quick," and hung up. She had called back to verify the address and to keep him on the line, but he'd said, "Yes, yes. Come quick," and hung up, then left the phone off the hook. The first beer had gone down fast and he was opening the second one when he felt his feet stinging. He hadn't noticed walking through the busted glass on the way to the refrigerator, but he must have. Some of the smaller pieces had penetrated the skin, so he sat down and brushed what he could off the bottom of his feet, getting his hands bloody in the process.

It was a two-beer wait until he heard the first sirens, plenty of time to practice his most important line. The one he'd heard on that TV show about the cops and the lawyers. He'd watched that rerun a dozen times. But sitting there with a beer in his hand and his feet sticking to the kitchen linoleum, he still couldn't decide which word he wanted to come down hard on:

I was AFRAID for my life.

I was afraid for MY life.

I was afraid for my LIFE.

△ △ △

John Bubar: *After thirty-six years as a pilot in both military and civilian aviation, John found his way back to school and is currently a candidate for an MFA in Writing at the University of New Hampshire.*

Her Wish

J.A.Hennrikus

Making Elizabeth that promise had seemed like a safe bet. After all, the doctor had given her even odds. Considering the sheer force of her personality, I figured the odds moved up to the 80th percentile. Plus she'd caught me off guard. When she begged me for the favor, I never dreamed it would involve breaking her husband out of jail.

We were unlikely friends in many ways. When we walked down the street together, Elizabeth complained we looked like the number ten. I was tall and thin with short hair, tailored clothes in shades of black and grey. Elizabeth called me a cranky Yankee. She was short, round with long, curly hair and a tendency towards flowing garments in bright jewel tones. A transplanted Texan, she talked a lot, and could turn a phrase like no one else. She shocked me with her brazenness, made me laugh with her commentary and humbled me with her praise. With her, nothing was said or done in half measure. She was amusing, challenging and exhausting. Our friendship was along the dinner-after-class or lunch-at-Bertucci's lines, not Thanksgiving dinner or help-me-move. Nonetheless, I considered her my friend.

We signed up for a seminar on Jane Austen, looking forward to our Mr. Darcy hot flashes. When she missed the first *Pride and Prejudice* class I was concerned, but she emailed that she had an infection and the antibiotics had wiped her out. The second class came and went. No Elizabeth. I emailed and called. And called her again. Finally she called back—from the hospital. It wasn't an infection after all; it was inflammatory breast cancer.

The Internet can be a blessing because of the wealth of information readily available, but also a curse because the bad news isn't broken gently. The statistics on inflammatory breast cancer were frightening. I was still processing facts when Elizabeth's email arrived. "We still on for Thursday? They sprung me yesterday, and I have a hankering for pasta puttanesca."

By Thursday I was a wreck, unsure what to say or how to say it, desperately afraid I would collapse in tears when I saw her. "Just let her talk," advised my closest friend Mary, who had battled her share of health issues. "Don't pretend everything's OK, 'cause it isn't. But don't cry and make her feel bad. She's the one who's sick."

I tried to put a happy face on, to little success.

"Jesus, you look like someone died already." Elizabeth cackled at her own joke. I barely cracked a smile.

"Elizabeth, I'm so sorry. This sucks." It was the best I could do given Mary's "don't cry" rule. I reached across the table and put my hand on hers. She turned her palm up and squeezed.

"It does. But I've got a great doctor, and he tells me he has a lot of tricks up his sleeve. I am not going to die."

I believed her. Partly because I wanted to, but mostly because I figured no cancer had a chance against Elizabeth. And so she started her battle: two rounds of chemo, a mastectomy then radiation.

On the second Thursday of September, a month before her surgery, I spotted her in the back booth before I entered the restaurant, so bright was her fuchsia turban.

"Nice scarf," I said as I sat down. "You look good, Elizabeth," I lied. The waiter arrived with seltzer with lemon and smiled at us both. Some people had bartenders who knew their drink of preference. We had Henry, the cute waiter at Bertucci's.

"And what can I get you ladies today?"

"You know what I want, big boy." Elizabeth's bad Mae West

imitation made us all laugh.

Henry and I started our weekly dance, "Try the special"—"No, I really shouldn't"—"OK, I will." The flash on Elizabeth's left hand caught me off guard. I handed my menu back to Henry and openly stared at Elizabeth's finger.

"That's a pretty band. Is it your mother's ring?" It looked too new, but I didn't know how else to bring the subject up.

"No. I, well, I got married last weekend."

"Married?" Elizabeth had never mentioned anyone special. She'd lamented about the dearth of eligible men in Boston, hadn't she? Or maybe she'd married a woman? Did she think I couldn't deal with that?

"Married?" I said again. "Who is the lucky . . . person?"

"His name is Juan Carlos."

One mystery solved. I searched the memory banks but nothing came to mind. "Juan Carlos? Have you known him long?"

"Nineteen years."

"Nineteen *years*?"

She nodded.

"Elizabeth, I feel like an idiot, but I can't remember you mentioning Juan Carlos."

"That's because I haven't. You're the first person who's noticed the ring."

"I'm fairly observant."

"And methodical. You're the most methodical person I know."

Was that a good or bad thing? "And Juan Carlos is?"

"In prison."

"OK." Cranky Yankees do not pry, despite the stakes. "Elizabeth, you can tell me what you want. I'm happy to listen. But if you'd rather not . . ."

"If I'd rather not, I wouldn't have worn the ring." She took a slow sip of her soda and then a deep breath. "OK, here goes. Did I ever tell you about my save-the-world youth, when I was a social worker?"

I nodded. Elizabeth had a colorful job history, eventually finding professional happiness as the administrative assistant in a college dean's office. "The salary isn't bad, the benefits are good, and the classes are free," she'd say.

"I met Juan Carlos when he was on work release. He was young, sexy and charming. We became friends. And later, more than friends. I've visited him every Sunday for the past nineteen years. Didn't you find it weird that I was never able to come to your brunches?"

"I just thought you didn't want to."

"I did want to, but I can only visit Juan Carlos on Sundays. I've missed a lot of brunches over the years."

"What did he do?" I had a suspicion, since nineteen years is a long time to be in jail, but her answer still startled me.

"Murder."

"Murder?"

"Yeah, first degree. I'm not going to pretend he didn't do it, he did. He was young, barely spoke English, got caught up in a rough crowd. Someone threatened him. Things escalated. He killed the guy. He didn't kill the guy's friend, who ID'd him at the trial. He had a public defender, got convicted of first degree murder without the possibility of parole."

She spoke for a long while about the journey of their friendship. I didn't interrupt or ask questions. "He's changed. He's a spiritual man now, so far from the man they convicted," she said.

"I'd assume so, otherwise you wouldn't spend every Sunday with him."

"Thanks, Amy. It means a lot . . . whew, I feel better. A few people know about Juan Carlos, not many."

I looked at my friend and realized the turban wasn't the only thing glowing. "Congratulations, Elizabeth. I'm not going to pretend that I condone murder, but you seem really happy, and that's good. So congratulations."

"Thanks."

"So how did all of this happen?"

"I asked him to marry me."

"You asked him?"

"Yes. I've been getting things set up for while I'm in the hospital. You know, lining up cat sitters, stopping the mail. It occurred to me that if something happens, and nothing is going to happen, but *if* something does happen the only way they'll let him visit me is if we're married—and if I'm dying."

"Which you're not going to do."

"Absolutely not. But . . ."

"Better to be prepared."

"Spoken like a true Yankee."

It was the closest we'd come to discussing the elephant in the room. The moment passed, and we ordered dessert.

□ □ □

Two weeks before the surgery, she told me about the lesion on her brain.

"It's no big deal, just some extra radiation. I figure that once all this is done, between the chemicals and the radiation, I damned well better have some freakin' super powers."

I smiled, but couldn't laugh. "Shit, Elizabeth."

"Shit." She took a long sip of diet soda, her final vice. "Amy, I have a favor to ask you. It's kind of big."

"What?"

"If they let Juan Carlos come visit me in the hospital, I want you to help him escape."

"What?"

"Just hear me out. I was just thinking that if he comes to visit me, that means things aren't going well. I want something good to come from all of this. So I was thinking that you could come up with a plan—"

"A plan? Me? What are you—?"

"I've put some money away, in a shoebox in the trunk of my car. I want you to take it for him. And figure out how to make it happen."

"Elizabeth, I can't."

"Amy, you have to. I'm begging you. I'd do it myself, but I can't seem to think straight these days. You always think straight. Just come up with a plan."

I've always been a good girl. I only dared skip a half-day of high school and I couldn't take the guilt so I got my father to write me a note. I've never had a speeding ticket, and parking tickets go less than a week unpaid. I recycle. Small children and animals love me. I wouldn't consider myself the first choice for planning a jailbreak, but Elizabeth was right—I am methodical. I also had faith Elizabeth would win her battle so there would never be a need for this "plan." If it gave her peace of mind, who was I to say no?

"OK."

"Really?"

"Really."

"How long will it take?"

"How long?"

"Will you have something by lunch next week?"

"I don't know, Elizabeth."

"'Cause I'll be in the hospital the week after. And I'd like some time to react to it beforehand."

"I'll have something by next week."

□ □ □

I telephoned Mary on my way back to the office and told her what I'd agreed to do.

"I'll help," Mary said.

"You'll help?" I asked.

"Sure, why not? Listen, Amy, she needs something to hold on to. And this is it. It's a little nuts, but it's what she wants. Obviously she thinks a lot of you. Didn't you say that you were one of the first people she told about her wedding?"

"She still hasn't told some of her closest friends. I'm not sure why she told me."

"It's because you are a stoic Yankee. It's one of your best traits."

"Thanks."

"And you don't judge, at least not on the outside. And mainly not on the inside. Plus, as you've said, you have a different kind of friendship. Plus it makes you a less likely suspect if we do spring him."

"Jerk."

"Think of it as a logic problem: something Elizabeth can think about while she recuperates. I know it's been bothering you that you can't do anything to help her. Now you can. Figure this out. Give it your all. And as I said, I'll help. It would be fun to plan the perfect crime."

□   □   □

I needed help. Who else to call? Even though I considered it an intellectual exercise, I was fairly certain most people would frown on participating. But I'd need some assistance at the hospital.

"Call Ray," Mary suggested.

"Ray?" Ray and I had worked together for a number of years. He and Mary had crossed paths at my holiday open houses, hitting it off despite their age difference.

"Yes, he'd be great at this."

She was right. Ray disdained authority just enough to like the idea, but could pull off a professional demeanor when necessary. As Mary predicted, Ray was into it. Or she was good at spinning the request. Or both.

"When does Elizabeth want the plan?" Ray asked.

"Thursday," I said.

"Cool. I'll get you some notes ASAP. Do we get code names?"

Not code names, but the plan needed a name. "If I refer to the JC plan enough, people will just assume that I found religion," Ray said.

Not if they've known you for more than five minutes, I thought.

□   □   □

The four of us had dinner at my house the next week. I laid out the broad outline and timetable. Ray and Mary presented their logistics research, and described their part in the escape. The depth of detail we had was phenomenal. Mary explained our plan to distract the guards. Once they were out, Ray would have a bicycle waiting for Juan Carlos at the delivery entrance and they would ride a short distance to his best friend's cousin's car.

"A bike?" It was the first time doubt crept into Elizabeth's voice.

"A bike." Ray sounded confident and Mary nodded in support. "A car would have to go by a guard of some sort, probably be caught on videotape. A bike can be snuck up beside the building. The car will be waiting on another street."

Elizabeth shuffled through the papers. No one spoke. It seemed like a good plan to me, but what did I know?

"Elizabeth, if there's something you think we missed . . ."

"No, I think you got it all." She looked at each one of us, tears rolling down her face and a beautiful smile plastered across her mouth. "Thanks, guys. This is so great. I know we'll never need to use it, but just in case. Just in case." She cleared her throat. "Just in case . . . take him to JP Licks first thing, OK, Ray?"

"JP Licks?"

"Yeah, he loves their Cow Tracks ice cream. I bring it with me every Sunday, but it's always half melted. And it's in a cup, I know he'd prefer a cone."

Bless Ray, he never missed a beat. "JP Licks it is, then it's the wide open road."

"Where will you take him?"

Ray shook his head. "Better you don't know all the details, Elizabeth."

Surprisingly, she agreed.

□   □   □

At first it looked like the plan was going to be a forgotten footnote in Elizabeth's life. Then they found one spot, then another. I'd visit every few days, watching her deteriorate as she submitted to progressively more aggressive and experimental treatments. Only two things escaped her decline—the will to live and her mind. Finally, around Valentine's Day, her doctor and social worker gently suggested she get her affairs in order. Juan Carlos's visit would be scheduled. Elizabeth asked to see Ray and Mary.

It was difficult for her to speak more than a few words now, so Mary took Elizabeth's hand. "Ray and I will be ready."

□　□　□

When I was a young girl my mother had a two-cookie rule, although my sister and I desperately tried to find ways to subvert the two-cookies-a-day limit by looting the cookie jar. My sister hatched a plan: she'd climb onto the counter, maneuver the heavy glass jar out of the corner so it cleared the upper cabinets, remove the lid, take the cookies and put the jar back. My only assignments were to hum or sing to mask the sound of the lid hitting the side of the jar and to grab the cookies.

I hummed the whole time, never changing pitch or missing a note. But when my sister's steady hand began to lift the lid, I panicked and went silent. The jar clinked, our mother yelled and my sister didn't talk to me for three days. We tried the plan twice more. Same results. Despite the best laid plans, I panicked.

□　□　□

Mary drove me to the hospital on the nights when I visited Elizabeth. Mary would say, "I'm going to check in with that cute nurse, Harry," and wink. Elizabeth would respond with a shadow of her wonderful smile and a weak thumbs-up.

Thursday was the day. It was Mary who told me after she got the call from Harry.

"From Harry?"

"Yeah, you know, Harry. The night nurse."

"I know who Harry is, Mary. Why would he call you?"

"To let me know about Juan Carlos's ETA. He doesn't know exactly when, but he knows the window of time . . . What's wrong, Amy?"

I told her the humming story. By the time I was done we were parked in front of my apartment building. Mary flipped her phone open and punched one button. "Ray, Mary. I'm coming over. We've got to come up with plan B. Amy is afraid she'll clutch. And I'm afraid she's right."

Mary and I watched Juan Carlos enter the waiting room accompanied by two guards. No shackles or chains, but the guards wore uniforms and were armed. Juan Carlos wore the prison uniform of a blue shirt and jeans. No one seemed to notice. Mary moved down the hall. I stopped breathing and panicked as I looked toward the elevators. A few minutes later, I saw the guards leave the room with Mary and walk toward the nurses' station. She smiled and laughed, expertly manipulating them so their backs were to the door. Harry, who had stayed beyond his shift, walked over to talk to them. Behind her back Mary flashed the signal, three fluttering fingers and an OK sign. I stood and walked toward the exit, pretending to look for a cigarette, as if going out for a smoke. I opened the door and took a big deep breath of the February air. It cut into my lungs.

I walked to the corner of the building. Ray leaned against the wall, a bike in each hand. I aimed my phone and took a couple of pictures. I wanted to show Elizabeth proof of our success.

"Game on?" Ray asked.

I nodded and walked down the ramp of the parking garage toward the bus stop where we would pretend to wait. Finally I saw them: two figures in gray hoodies barreling down the side of the building on bikes. I was so surprised I almost forgot the phone, but I snapped a few quick pictures before they turned the corner. The next bus arrived within minutes, and I got on and headed toward JP Licks.

A couple of days later I brought an unopened letter with a Texas postmark to the hospital. Elizabeth removed the oxygen mask aiding her struggle to breathe. "Open it," she said.

The words were brief:

> *Rest well, my darling. I am safe.*
> *Your devoted husband, Juan Carlos*

"I have something else for you," I said, holding the photo up for her to see. She grabbed it, peering at the image of Juan Carlos in a 2007 World Champions Red Sox hat, gray hoodie, winter jacket and jeans holding a large ice cream cone in front of the original JP Licks in Jamaica Plain. She clasped it to her heart.

"Thank you," she whispered, smiling one last time.

Elizabeth died the next night.

□　□　□

I waited as pockets of people milled around, waiting for their visit to begin. Mary had offered to come along, but I had to do this on my own. When he approached, I stood and offered my hand. "It's nice to meet you, Juan Carlos."

"Amy, a pleasure. I am pleased that I can thank you in person for the kindness you showed my sweet Elizabeth."

"She was my friend . . ." I couldn't go on. I clumsily handed him the package. "Here are some condolence cards, some of her books and the picture we gave Elizabeth. They've all been approved for you to keep."

"And she believed—?"

"She did. I think so, anyway."

"It is a good photo."

"Yes, Ray did a great job of it. The hat was a nice touch, wasn't it? Shows that it isn't an old picture of you. I don't know if she noticed the detail, but it was a nice touch."

"I would have believed that I was there myself, if I didn't know better."

"The guards were good sports, allowing us take the picture in front of the white wall. Made it easier to scan it into the computer. And Harry was great, pretending to be you."

There was little more to say. "Goodbye, Juan Carlos. I am so sorry for your loss."

"A loss for all of us. Thank you, and your friends. You made my Elizabeth very happy those final days."

"I only wish we could have, really. I think Ray would have . . ."

Juan Carlos shook his head and smiled. "Is that ice cream?" he asked, pointing to the bag on the table.

I'd almost forgotten. The ice cream was packed in extra ice to delay melting. I took the cup out of the bag and slid it across the table. "I also brought you a cone. Elizabeth said that you liked cones."

△ △ △

J.A. Hennrikus *is the Executive Director of StageSource. Last fall her story "Tag, You're Dead" was published in* Thin Ice: Crime Stories by New England Writers. *She tweets under @JulieHennrikus, and group blogs on nhwn.wordpress.com. She wrestles with illusions of athleticism, is an avid theater goer and a proud member of Red Sox nation. Her website is jahennrikus.com.*

The Lesson

Pat Remick

A tiny black spot on plain white paper.

More like a speck, really. No bigger than a pencil tip. Right in the middle.

Each day for the past week, the same style No. 10 white envelope had been delivered to his apartment, his name and address written in tightly controlled cursive with a black pen. No return address. A Manchester, New Hampshire, postmark beside the American flag stamp.

Until today, each innocuous envelope addressed to "Mr. Richard 'Dick' Springfield" had contained a blank piece of paper.

The dot surprised him.

He supposed the envelopes were a prank by one of his sixth-grade male students, who were all hormones and jockeying for attention with behavior skirting the edge of bad. It was early in the school year, but each day at Norman Rockwell Middle School produced a new twist on the old theme of trying to impress girls and all of it was juvenile.

The girls in class rarely gave him problems, but took advantage of any opportunity to tattle on their male counterparts. He was surprised they hadn't alerted him to this plot. The rumor mill was uncharacteristically silent.

It wouldn't be difficult to locate his home address; it was listed in the phone book. But most of his eleven- and twelve-year-old students lacked the attention span to follow through on any project, never mind systematically mailing a succession of identically addressed envelopes. Richard didn't recognize the handwriting, but one of his students could have persuaded someone to address them in exchange for something as trivial as a stick of gum.

It was an infantile attempt to irritate him. He'd ignore it.

□ □ □

"All right, students, settle down," he said the following Monday morning.

"What did you do this weekend, Mr. Springfield?" Johnny Franklin schmoozed with all of his teachers, hoping they'd be more lenient at the end of the grading period. It usually worked.

"I corrected papers. Did any of you do anything more fun than that over the weekend, like try to play a joke on someone, maybe a teacher?"

A few students looked at him curiously, others laughed. None looked guilty. An excited murmur arose as the children began sharing their weekend activities. Two girls in the back were giggling and one, Molly Dinardo, returned his stern look with a radiant smile.

"OK, that's enough. Take out your books, ladies and gentlemen."

Another white envelope was waiting that evening, tucked between the credit card offers and the electric bill. Richard forced himself to delay opening it until he was inside his apartment. In case the perpetrator was watching, he didn't want to appear annoyed at the practical joke.

He unfolded the sheet of paper and saw a small perfectly round black dot. It looked like it was made with a black pen. He compared it to the spot from the previous day. Somewhat larger, but not by much. A very odd game, he shrugged.

He doubted the source was a co-worker. The older women treated him like a favorite nephew and the younger ones saw him as a big brother. There were no spurned lovers among his colleagues; he knew better than to risk problems at work over a romantic relationship gone bad. There were so few men on the staff that all of them were on good terms and grateful for male colleagues.

The only faculty member who knew anything about his personal life was his best friend Brandon O'Brien, the school's Phys Ed teacher. Their friendly rivalry often included practical jokes but the dot campaign didn't seem like Brandon's style. Richard dialed his cell phone anyway. "OK, jerk, you win. This dot thing is annoying. You can stop now."

"What the hell are you talking about?" Brandon said.

"Are you sending me letters with black dots on them? I really need to know."

"I already told you I screwed around with your computer last week and I'll admit to the fake vomit on your car seat. But I haven't sent any dots, although maybe I should if it freaks you out like this."

Richard told him about the unsigned correspondence.

"That's weird. Think it's a student? That Billy Tully is a piece of work," Brandon said.

"This seems a little advanced for Billy. What if it's someone on the staff?"

"Nah, everyone loves you, which quite frankly I'm tired of hearing. How about a parent?"

Richard didn't think so. He worked hard to make sure everyone, students and parents alike, left his classroom on friendly terms.

"Maybe you pissed off one of your neighbors by coming in at all hours with all your women," Brandon laughed.

"Doubt it. They're always saying they envy my social life."

"Then my money's on someone you dated. Didn't Shakespeare say 'There's no wrath like a woman scorned'?"

"The saying is 'Hell hath no fury like a woman scorned.' It's not Shakespeare; it's from a play called *The Mourning Bride* by William Congreve—well after Shakespeare's time. The actual quote is 'Heaven has no rage like love to hatred turned, Nor hell a fury like a woman scorned.'"

"Thanks for the literature lesson, Mr. English Teacher. I teach Phys Ed, for chrissakes. All I'm saying is maybe your pen pal is on that rejects list of yours, which I do appreciate you sharing with me, by the way. Sure saves me a lot of time in the dating pool."

Richard took his beer onto the balcony. He used his shirt to clean his wire-rimmed glasses and surveyed the parking lot. There didn't appear to be any vehicles that didn't belong.

At least he wasn't being stalked by some ex-girlfriend. He ended all relationships on civil terms, convincing the women his issues, not theirs, rendered him incapable of making a commitment. They were so grateful to hear "It's not your fault, really" that they never sought elaboration.

Although Richard kept a "Losers List" of women he deemed unworthy of a second date, the beautiful bartender he recently began seeing wasn't one of them. When he asked Cassie later that evening if she knew anything about his mysterious letters, she looked perplexed. "Is it some kind of bizarre secret code?" she asked before leaning in for a kiss.

□   □   □

Thursday and Friday brought progressively larger dots. Richard estimated that at this rate, it would be weeks before he received a dot large enough to cover the paper, if that was the ultimate goal. Or perhaps the final communication might be a blank piece of paper and the series would begin again. Richard felt foolish even thinking about it.

The mail was delivered early on Saturday and Richard's euphoria at finally besting Brandon in their Saturday morning tennis game evaporated when he saw the envelope. It contained another dot, again slightly larger than the day before.

He added the sheet to the pile. If this continued, the police would need the letters and envelopes to charge someone with harassment. Perhaps the authorities could trace the handwriting; they did that sort of thing on television all the time. He decided to purchase plastic gloves later to handle the evidence without interfering with fingerprints.

Cassie was working Saturday night at The Sleeping Dog Bar and Grille and he didn't want to spend the evening alone in his apartment. Brandon didn't answer when he called to invite him to share a few beers at her bar. None of his other drinking buddies were available either, so he opted to stay home and call Cassie during her break.

Richard powered up his laptop. The welcome page photograph of his sixth-grade homeroom class had been replaced with the dancing words "hey, butt-face." Somehow Brandon had gotten into Richard's laptop again.

He restored the original photo, checked email and updated his Facebook page before trying to reach Cassie during her break. When she didn't answer, he left a message. A bottle of bourbon was his companion while he spent the rest of the evening trolling dating websites to see what he was missing. He was surprised Cassie hadn't returned his call. It must have been a busy night at the bar.

Richard's head ached the next morning from too much alcohol and too little sleep. He headed for the corner store to buy some orange juice to clear the fog. It was not until he put the carton and a Sunday newspaper on the counter that he noticed Cassie's smiling face beneath the headline: "Local Woman Dies after Rock Thrown from I-93 Overpass."

Richard's knees buckled. He gripped the counter and felt his heart lurch into his throat. "My God," he moaned.

"Mister, are you all right?" the clerk asked. "Should I call 911?"

Richard waved him off. "I just need to sit down." He released his grip on the counter and slipped onto the floor. He was afraid to read the news story, but had to know what happened. The report said a car driven by Cassie Parker, 25, careened off the road into a tree after a large rock smashed through her windshield while she was en route to her job at a local bar.

Now he knew why she hadn't answered her cell phone.

Dazed, he stumbled the six blocks to The Sleeping Dog. The manager and two employees were setting up for Sunday brunch. "Everyone is pretty broken up about this, especially since the cops don't think it's an accident," the manager said.

Richard gasped. "What do you mean?"

"They have a witness who saw one person, maybe two, on the overpass about 15 minutes before Cassie drove under it. The cops think if it had been random, the person would have run out onto the overpass, dropped the rock and booked it. They think someone was waiting for her car."

"Jesus, why?"

"That's what they're trying to figure out. Who'd want to kill her?"

Richard shook his head and thanked the manager. He needed to get back home to think. He wasn't sure what to do next. He didn't know her family and the only friends he'd met worked at the bar. He had nothing to add to their inquiry, but the authorities no doubt would question him once they learned he dated Cassie. Neither his principal nor the School Board would appreciate his involvement in a messy police investigation. Better to stay out of it as long as possible. But he had to talk to someone. He dialed Brandon.

"Hey butt-face, I saw you called last night," Brandon yelled into the phone. "I guess I didn't have service. So, did you figure out who's sending your dots?"

"No, but you remember that girl I was dating from The Sleeping Dog? She was killed in a car wreck last night. And the cops don't think it was an accident. They said someone threw a rock off the overpass."

"Oh, shit, really? I'm sorry, man. What kind of world is it when someone gets their kicks from dropping rocks on cars? Cripes, I hope it wasn't a kid from school."

Richard spent the rest of the day in a daze. He tried to concentrate on his lesson plans but fell asleep, only to dream about Cassie being chased by dots and one of them falling from the sky as she reached for her cell phone to answer his call.

□   □   □

Richard wanted to call in sick, but decided it would be best to stay under the radar and follow his normal schedule. His homeroom class seemed to sense his dark mood and settled down quickly.

Even Johnny Franklin was quiet. Molly Dinardo was his only absence, but the room was so hushed that it did not seem possible that there were eighteen children in it. For the first time in his teaching career, Richard couldn't wait for the day to end.

He rushed home to some comfort from Jim Beam. But first he had to face his mailbox. Inside were several advertisements, more credit card offers and the familiar white envelope. He put on a pair of plastic gloves and after some fumbling, managed to open it.

Instead of a dot, there was a crudely drawn bull's eye.

The prank had progressed from silly to sinister. If the bull's eye meant he was a target, what was he being targeted for? Someone was messing with his mind.

He poured a large glass of bourbon and sat down on his black leather couch, studying the bull's eye between gulps. What if the bull's eye meant the sender had hit a target? Richard's breath quickened and his stomach lurched. Maybe Cassie was the target and the killer was bragging about it. Whoever dropped the rock off the overpass could be the same person sending the dots, meaning the prank had turned criminal.

It also meant Cassie died because of him.

He had to go to the police. But Richard envisioned how his report would look in the newspaper: "An officer took a report from a man who said he had been receiving black dots in the mail. Richard Springfield, 31, claimed he did not know who was sending the dots or why."

People would think he was nuts. Better to see what the next day's mail brought. In the meantime, he needed a diversion. He turned on his laptop. The class picture was gone, replaced this time by a scrolling message: "Mr. Springfield is a Dick."

□ □ □

His homeroom seemed more rambunctious than usual on Tuesday morning and Richard had a difficult time concentrating. He couldn't bring Cassie back, but maybe he could establish whether one of his students was using the U.S Postal Service to harass him.

"All right, class. Today we are going to learn how to address professional letters and envelopes without using a computer. Take out your pens."

He handed each student a blank No. 10 envelope and watched their reactions. Most looked bored, but a few seemed curious. When he handed one to Molly, she blushed and said, "I like your Dr. Seuss tie, Mr. Springfield."

"Thank you. A special lady friend gave it to me," he told her.

Molly looked devastated. He suspected it was because she had a crush on him. It was not uncommon for sixth-grade girls to become infatuated with male teachers. He smiled and turned his attention to the rest of the class.

"The Post Office must be able to read the address to deliver your letter. So use your best penmanship to write my name on the center of the envelope. On the line below it, add my street address and apartment number."

He walked up and down the rows of desks as they worked. Not one envelope was addressed to "Mr. Richard 'Dick' Springfield."

Hands shot up. "What if we don't know your address?" Johnny asked.

"Make one up," he said, glancing at each student's envelope as he walked quickly through the room. No one had written his correct mailing address, either.

It appeared his tormentor was not in this class, but he or she might be in another of his English classes. He would need to repeat the exercise in all of them. He also could not ignore the possibility that any student devious enough to cause Cassie to hit a tree also would be smart enough to figure out the reason for the assignment and write something different. Although he had a difficult time believing one of his students was a killer, he intended to take the envelopes home to compare them to the anonymous envelopes.

During a break between classes, he checked his email and found an unusually cryptic message from George Shaines, his principal, saying, "See me during your lunch period." His first impulse was to march into George's office and demand to know why he was being summoned. But if his fear was unfounded that the police had contacted the school about his connection to Cassie, overreacting might tip off George that something was amiss. Richard finally understood the trepidation his students felt when they were called to the principal's office.

When Richard knocked on his open door, George did not smile. "Close the door behind you," he said.

Richard sat opposite the principal's desk as George pushed a pile of magazines toward him. "Take a look."

There were copies of *Playboy*, *Penthouse*, *Hustler*, *Maxim*, a magazine featuring extremely "big-breasted women" with the acronym *BBW* as its title, and an assortment of hard-core pornographic publications.

"Who did you confiscate these from? Was it Billy Tully?" Richard said.

"No. These have been arriving in the office with your name on them. They were so disgusting that my secretary kept them in her desk until I returned from my conference. Why did you have these sent here? I'm disappointed you showed such poor judgment, Richard."

"Surely you don't believe these belong to me. Besides, I prefer smaller breasts."

George ignored his attempt at humor. "Your name is on the label."

"I didn't order any of these but if I had, I'm not an idiot. I would have had them sent to my apartment. Someone's trying to make me lose my job."

George listened without expression while Richard told him about the letters. "What did the police say?" George asked.

"I haven't reported it. I was afraid they'd think I'm crazy. But this is going too far. Someone's out to get me. You have to believe me."

George glared at him. "I suggest you contact the police immediately. And get rid of this filth. I don't want you embarrassing my school."

Richard slammed the door on his way out and stuffed the magazines into an empty backpack he retrieved from his classroom. He was heading for the faculty parking lot when he saw Brandon.

"Hey, jerk. Thanks for getting me in trouble about the girlie magazines. And quit screwing around with my laptop."

Brandon's mouth dropped. "I don't know what the hell you're talking about. I think those dots have gone to your brain." He stomped off.

If Brandon was telling the truth, someone else—a student or maybe the person sending the dots—had accessed his computer and ordered the magazines. His password wasn't difficult to figure out. He would change it after he dealt with the magazines.

Richard closed his car windows so no one could hear him use his cell phone to cancel the unordered subscriptions. The magazine representatives assured him the problem would be resolved immediately—until he reached *BBW*. "The order is signed by a 'Mr. Richard 'Dick' Springfield' so maybe you did order it," the representative said.

Richard persuaded him to fax a copy of the order so he could check the signature. Richard rushed to the office to grab it before the fax finished inching out of the machine and into the hands of the nosey staff. The familiar handwriting proved his tormentor had moved from mail to magazines. What was next?

It was eerily quiet when he returned to his classroom. A few students spoke in whispers but most avoided looking at him. Richard checked his desk. Nothing seemed out of place, although his laptop might have been moved. It contained his lesson plans and he had repeatedly warned his students not to touch it or the school computer he used for everything else.

"Mr. Springfield, is it true you got called to the principal's office?" Johnny asked.

Richard frowned. "I met with Principal Shaines, but I'd hardly describe it as being called to his office."

"Are you going to get fired? Some of the teachers said you were in big trouble," Molly said.

"Everything's fine. Get out your books, ladies and gentlemen."

◻   ◻   ◻

His apartment mailbox was jammed with at least a dozen obscene magazines. They were mixed in with dozens of envelopes from credit card companies with firm pieces of plastic inside. Apparently his tormentor also was applying for credit cards in his name. In the middle of the heap was the dreaded plain white No. 10 envelope.

Richard donned plastic gloves and compared it to the handful of envelopes he'd brought home from his classes. There were no matches. He ripped open the new envelope. Inside was a sheet of paper with a black dot slightly larger than the one preceding the bull's eye. The pattern had resumed. Richard was unsure whether to feel relieved, or concerned about how it would end. He didn't want to wait any longer to find out.

Richard dialed the Police Department's non-emergency number and asked to speak to a detective. When the receptionist asked the reason for his call, he told her he was being harassed. She promised someone would return his call within the hour.

He turned on his laptop, but he felt too unnerved to work on his lesson plans. He checked his email but needed a better distraction. He trolled through his favorite Internet dating sites, checking for new entries to see if he knew any of the women seeking love via the

World Wide Web and how many he'd previously dismissed. There were several in each category tonight.

The sites were helpful in screening potential dates. Richard looked first for an intriguing photo and then hoped the woman listed "erotica" as a turn-on because it signaled she was willing to share more than dinner. He'd study the profile information for clues to locate her but make it appear their meeting was happenstance.

He found Cassie when she listed the nearby Sleeping Dog as her favorite restaurant. He never expected to see her behind the bar.

When he couldn't track down a candidate, he resorted to going through the dating service to flirt online under an invented user name (his latest was BigDickie123). If things went well, he invited the woman to meet him at a bar in another town. He arrived early and waited near the entrance so he could slip out unnoticed if the woman didn't look as good as her photo. It also earned her a spot on his "Losers List."

□   □   □

One of his rejects, a hairdresser with the pseudonym SuzieQ69, had a new photograph online tonight. She still looked hot and he knew she was willing. He'd left her in a bar when he saw she was too young and trashy-looking to be seen in public with someone like him. After all, he was a schoolteacher with a reputation to protect. SuzieQ69 had sent him a pretty nasty email through the dating service after he stood her up, but he ignored it like all the others and set up a new user name. After seeing her latest photo tonight, perhaps he should reconsider. He wanted to take a closer look at the newest prospects first. It might help relieve his anxiety.

Three hours later, Richard was still awaiting a callback. He telephoned the Police Department again.

"Sorry, Mr. Springfield. The detectives are tied up investigating a fatal accident. The first one available will contact you."

Richard turned on television news. The local anchor looked grim as he announced a school principal was killed after losing control of his vehicle on his way home from a School Board meeting. Footage of the demolished SUV filled the screen as the newscaster reported Principal George Shaines had died near the spot where bartender Cassie Parker crashed the week before.

Richard stared at the television long after the news ended. First Cassie, now George. It had to be more than a coincidence. Were they dead because of him?

He had to talk to the authorities. Richard telephoned the Police Department a third time. "Listen, I really need to talk to a detective about the Shaines and Parker murders," he said.

He was quickly connected to a Detective Katzenberg, who urged him to come down to the station as soon as possible. Richard brought the anonymous correspondence, his students' envelopes, and his laptop.

He was ushered into a small windowless room. Katzenberg closed the door. "I hope you don't mind but I want to give us some privacy," he said.

Richard told Katzenberg about the letters, unwanted magazine subscriptions and the credit cards he never ordered. He showed the detective the envelopes and unsigned sheets of paper, along with his students' envelopes. "Can you get fingerprints from these?" Richard asked.

"It would be easier and faster if you could identify the handwriting. Does it look familiar?"

"No, and it doesn't seem to match my students' writing. I don't think it's one of my kids, but I could be wrong. Can a handwriting expert prove that?" Richard asked.

"We don't have one here but that's something we can consider later. One of our evidence technicians will take a look at the materials you brought after you sign a receipt and provide your laptop password."

Minutes later, Richard handed everything to the young woman. She disappeared and so did Katzenberg's smile. "Now tell me about

Miss Parker and Mr. Shaines," he said.

When Richard was done, the detective removed his glasses and rubbed his eyes. Finally he said, "Is there anything else you want to say?"

"That's all I know."

"Where were you on the nights that Miss Parker and Mr. Shaines were killed?"

"At home, why?"

"Can anyone verify your alibi?"

Richard was stunned. "Alibi? Am I a suspect?"

"Well, you're the only one who's said Principal Shaines was killed after a boulder was thrown off the overpass. We haven't released those details and his secretary claims you two had a pretty heated argument yesterday. Is that true?"

"Yes, I mean, no. The news reports said George went off the road near where Cassie was killed. I just assumed that something was thrown off the overpass."

Katzenberg smiled. "Haven't you heard the expression that assuming makes an ass out of you and me? I'm no ass, Mr. Springfield."

"Do I need a lawyer, Detective?"

"You could call an attorney and talk to me later, or you can talk to me now. Your choice."

Richard telephoned Brandon instead. "The cops think I killed Cassie and George, too. Get me a lawyer, and fast."

"You better not be joking, asshole."

Richard sighed. "I wish I were. Please call someone. Now."

There were several attorneys in the school's parent population and despite the late hour, Charles Ivins, Esquire, was at Richard's side within forty-five minutes. He advised the detective not to question Richard further unless he planned to charge the teacher with a crime.

"Mr. Springfield claimed he had something to share about the murders of Cassie Parker and George Shaines. He came here voluntarily," Katzenberg said.

"If you're not going to charge him, we're leaving now— voluntarily."

□ □ □

The first thing Richard did when he got home was leave a message on the school's answering machine that he needed to take a personal day. He finally fell asleep about six a.m. Four hours later, his new attorney called. The police had been to the school and the news wasn't good.

"They found some disturbing things on the school computer. The Internet history shows you searched through several years' worth of news articles about people being killed by objects thrown off bridges and overpasses."

Richard was speechless. His tormentor had not only killed Cassie and George, he had used Richard's classroom computer to find out how to do it.

"It wasn't me. Someone figured out my password."

"They believe you killed the principal because he confronted you about what you were doing on the school computer. They also checked your laptop. They contend it shows you visited all kinds of dating sites and stalked Cassie Parker. They're going to charge you with murdering both of them."

Richard couldn't believe this was happening. A single tiny spot of black ink had ballooned into murder charges and blown his life apart. His teaching career was over. His reputation and credit were ruined. He could be facing life in prison for two murders he didn't commit.

And he still didn't know why.

□ □ □

Brandon was his only visitor. Richard felt humiliated in his baggy orange jumpsuit behind the Plexiglas that separated them, but Brandon didn't seem to notice.

"I ran into one of our old students outside the courthouse the other day," Brandon told him. "Remember Susan Quinlan? Mousy little thing, real quiet. She had a crush on you, I think."

Richard nodded. Susan had been in his first class nine years earlier. "What was she doing at the courthouse?"

"I don't know. But she's all grown up, very blonde and really stacked. I feel like a dirty old man saying this about a former student, but she's hot. I think she said she's a hairdresser, or something, in Bedford. I was too busy looking at her boobs to pay attention."

Richard stared at his friend. It sounded like Brandon was describing the woman he knew as SusieQ69. Was it possible that Richard hadn't recognized his former student?"

"She asked me to give you a message," Brandon continued. "She said she wants you to know she's not a loser anymore. Tell you what, my friend, that's an understatement."

Richard's mind raced. Had she found out about the "Losers List" on his laptop?

"And she was with one of the girls in your homeroom, that Molly Dinardo. Did you know they're stepsisters and very close? Molly gave me something for you. She said it might cheer you up."

Richard watched as Brandon opened the No. 10 envelope addressed to "Mr. Richard 'Dick' Springfield" and unfolded the sheet of paper inside.

"Oh, isn't that cute?" Brandon laughed as he held the paper up to the Plexiglas.

Looking back at Richard was a hand-drawn smiley face.

It was surrounded by hundreds of tiny black dots.

△   △   △

Pat Remick *is an award-winning short story author and veteran journalist, and has co-authored two non-fiction books. She won the 2007 Al Blanchard Crime Fiction Award and her stories have appeared in previous Level Best Books anthologies. A member of Sisters in Crime and Mystery Writers of America, Pat is working on a novel. Her web site is www.PatRemick.com.*

Boxed

Daniel Moses Luft

The voice on the other end of the phone said one word: "Now," and then clicked off.

"'Bout time," Skinner whispered to no one as he folded the phone shut. He pulled a plastic bag out of his duffel and gathered up all his takeout trash from his trip to the Mexican place around the corner. He cracked the door open, slipped out of his tiny, dark closet and dumped the food into the hallway trash. When he returned he reached in the duffel again, pulled out a semi-automatic pistol, stuffed it into the pocket of his coat and pulled the duffel over his shoulder. He looked up and down the halls as he walked down three flights of stairs and onto the street where he was happy to breath chilly, wet, springtime air again.

Skinner had been living in the utility closet for three days, watching with binoculars through an old dryer vent. He'd been studying the couple on the other side of Beacon Street. He'd watched them fight, make up, cheat on each other, do lines of coke together and separately then go back to fighting. He had been stuck in an unused closet of a Boston University dorm, still as a statue and only going into the hall to sneak out of the building for food or to use the bathroom late at night.

Outside, in early evening, he walked through the alley behind the dorm to the university parking lot, over a short chain link fence and through the Cambodian restaurant's parking lot to Beacon Street. He slipped his hands into his coat and felt the rounded corners of the semi-automatic in his right hand, the single key to a rental car in the other. He stopped to open the door to his Honda minivan with tinted windows. He tossed his duffel along with his phone onto the passenger side without looking and pulled a box of vinyl gloves from under the seat. He took two and replaced the box underneath. He checked the meter but didn't add any change.

He gave no pretense of hesitation as he crossed the two lanes of Beacon, two sets of railroad tracks, then over another two lanes of traffic. This put him in front of the brownstone he'd been watching.

After he slipped on the vinyl gloves he tried the back door. It was one of the places he couldn't see from the closet but he had checked it late every night. The door was locked like he expected but it had a cheap lock on it. Skinner gave three kicks and the knob fell off.

He slipped into the dark, back hallway but he could see a sliver of light under the kitchen door. He crept along the floor and listened at the door for nearly a minute before he slowly turned the knob.

The kitchen was empty and clean the way he had seen the cleaning lady leave it an hour earlier. The room even smelled new and looked like the kind of gut rehab that had happened all over Boston for a full ten years and then had abruptly stopped. Skinner liked new construction. It meant flimsy locks that pulled apart and lightweight hollow doors that didn't squeak on their shiny new hinges.

He passed through the kitchen and headed up the stairway that led to the master bedroom on the third floor. Skinner had seen the wife leave moments before his phone call and knew that she would be gone for the night. The husband would be upstairs in the shower. The guy liked to take long showers before he left for the night. He always came home late and usually stumbling drunk. Skinner wondered why anyone would bother putting a hit on the guy. He was eventually going to fall onto the train tracks or get run over by a car or fall asleep in some snow bank. But the contract had called for a break-in, a robbery and a body at home.

He padded up the stairs as quietly as possible even though he heard the water running in the shower. The bedroom was messy with clothes on the floor. Skinner held his ear against the door before he quickly turned the fake brass knob to the bathroom and flung open the door. He was surprised that there was no one behind the sliding glass door and the shower was empty. The water was running straight into the drain.

He felt a chill of confusion for a moment before he turned around to see the man he had come to kill standing naked and flabby with a revolver in one hand and a magazine in the other. He had black hair and wore a goatee that was surrounded by a fat face that threatened to swallow the beard. He was actually pretty hairy all over, Skinner realized.

"What are you doing here?"

"I just came in here looking for money."

"If you wanted that you'd have waited until I finished my shower and left. Who sent you?"

"What? No one sent me."

"Don't even try to look surprised. Why don't you just put the gun down and you and I will have a little talk."

"Talk?"

"Yeah, I might let you live if you tell me who sent you."

Skinner thought about this for a moment. The fat guy had him. The revolver was too close to miss him while Skinner's semi-automatic was still pointed into the bathroom. Skinner looked at the gun in the other man's hand and then at the gut rolling over the other man's junk.

"I'm putting the gun down."

"Let it slide out of your palm slowly, hold onto it with your thumb and forefinger."

Skinner did this.

"Now turn around and drop it on the floor between us. Good.

Now, put your hands up. Don't move. You move—I'll kill you."

The flabby man tossed the porn magazine onto his bed then slowly lurched toward Skinner. The revolver was close enough to touch him but the man kept it a few inches away from him. He patted Skinner's coat pockets with his fat empty hand and felt for another gun that wasn't there. Then he moved his hand over to Skinner's shirt like he'd done this sort of thing before.

"I don't have anything else on me."

"If that's true you would be stupid. You don't look too stupid to me so I'm going to check."

Skinner's eyes darted away from the gun to the doorway where he saw motion.

"And I'm not stupid either. You want me to look over my shoulder, punk?"

"What's going on, Lou?" Lou's wife said as she entered the room.

Lou turned his head for a second then back at Skinner.

"Why are you back so fast?"

"I forgot my wallet. What is going on?"

"What's it look like is going on? I've got some guy here who wants to fuckin' off me for some reason or another."

"What do you want me to do?"

"I don't know. Maybe call your father."

"OK, I'll go downstairs."

"No, wait. Stay here. Check this guy."

"What do you mean?"

"I mean check him for weapons."

"Is that a porn magazine on the bed?"

"Just shut up about that. Never mind it and see if he's got a gun on him."

"You mean like frisk him? I don't want to touch him."

"Why not?" I seen you do it to some guy last week."

"No, you didn't."

"Yes, I did, at that new place in Allston, on Brighton Ave. What's it called? Tavern something."

"Did you follow me?"

"Of course I followed you. I saw the guy buy you shots. I saw you feel him up like you were some whore from Chelsea."

Skinner stopped sweating and began looking at the two of them. He could not believe that they would sit there and bicker while he was in the room. The guy hadn't even had his wife grab the gun off the floor. Skinner knew that if the argument continued, he might be able to reach down and grab it.

"You know I've never even set foot in Chelsea, Lou."

"It's just a comparison. Now get down on your knees and check this guy out to make sure he doesn't have anything on him. You know how to get on your knees, don't you?"

"Not fair, Lou."

"Just let it go and do it."

The woman stared at Skinner for a moment before she approached him. Skinner kept his eyes on the naked man with the gun. When she was very close, close enough for him to smell both her perfume and her breath mints, she dropped her fur off her shoulders onto the carpet and stretched out her arms. She moved her manicured fingers slowly over Skinner's body, more like a caress than a frisk.

"All right, just do it," Lou said.

"That's the way Lou talks when he's in the mood," she said to Skinner.

"No jokes," Lou said. "Just hurry up."

"Yup, that's my husband."

She moved her hands off his shirt and onto his pants. The pressure of her hands increased. She was taking her time and showing off to her husband, which really bothered Skinner. He silently admitted to himself that, given a different time or place, he might find her hands very exciting.

"You find anything?"

"I think I found something I like a lot."

"Just shut up about that."

"I don't know, Lou, it's tough. His body's so different from yours. He's got so many muscles and contours."

Her hands were all over him, front and back. Lou was naked in front of him. Skinner kept his eyes on the gun.

"You liking that, punk? You like my wife feeling you up?"

Skinner stared at the gun.

"Answer me, punk."

"What? No, I don't like it."

"You saying my wife ain't hot? Like she can't get you up? I think you're being fuckin' rude. Bust into my place, let my wife feel you up and not even say she's hot."

Shit, Skinner thought. I really don't want to think about her now or if she's hot.

"I'm not saying that either."

"Well, my wife is hot."

"I believe you."

"Look at her."

"What?"

"Just look at her. Do it!"

Skinner jerked his head to see the woman on her knees next to him. She was very attractive, young too, with expensively styled brown hair, high cheekbones and dark brown eyes. But she wasn't what he expected after he'd looked at her through the binoculars for three days. She had harsh, sharp features, just short of mean, thin lips that were used to pursing in anger and frustration. He brown eyes were seductive but Skinner couldn't read any expression on her face at all.

"She's hot, isn't she?"

"Yeah, she's hot."

"What was that? Louder."

"Yes, she's hot. A knockout."

"And you're a good-looking guy. Aren't you?"

"I don't know. Maybe."

"Well, you are good looking. The kind of guy she likes for a while but she keeps coming back to an ugly, fat bastard like me."

I wish I'd brought the long-range rifle, Skinner thought. I wish I'd shot them both yesterday from that little closet in the dorm across the street. I wish I were on the pike driving home right now. Christ, I even wish I were in that closet again, getting found by campus security.

Her hands slid down the back of Skinner's legs to where he kept the knife taped to his ankle. Her hand paused for a second and then slid back up. Skinner tried to keep his eyes on the gun and the fat naked man who held it. He didn't try to understand the woman's intentions.

"He clean?"

"Yeah, Lou. He's clean."

She stood up and grabbed her fur off the floor.

Skinner wondered how he could possibly cause a distraction that would let him pull up his pant leg and grab hold of the knife.

"Thanks, babe."

"No problem honey." She sneered down at the magazine on the bed as she opened the armoire on the other side of the room and hung up the fur.

"So mister shitty intruder," Lou said to Skinner. "I guess that proves that you are dumb. You must've got by on those good looks so far. Now tell me who sent you."

Skinner began to sweat again. He tried to think of some long-winded line of bullshit he could hand this guy while he waited for a moment to get the knife. "Like I told you before, I just came in for the money."

"You're no thief. You don't even sound like you come from around here."

"Boston's a cosmopolitan area."

"Not even a little funny. Some guys might try to joke their way out of this. But you're just not funny. You're dumb and you're not funny."

"Actually, honey?" the woman said as she walked back to her husband.

"Yeah, what is it?"

She wrapped her arm around the man's furry chest and hugged him. She leaned in toward his ear like she was going to kiss him but she whispered: "He's got a knife."

"What?"

The man turned his head to face his wife as she smiled at him.

Skinner grabbed the fat hand with the gun in it and pointed it at the ceiling. Then he began kicking the naked man in the balls and the stomach and the knees. Skinner realized that the fat guy wasn't so dumb either. His face was red with pain but he didn't scream or fire his weapon. Instead, he tried to regain his balance and wrench his gun away from Skinner as he shoved his wife away from him. Eventually he fell to his knees. Skinner kicked him in the face and broke his nose. Blood fell out of his smashed nostrils and he was squirming down on his knees.

It was then that Skinner realized that the man was reaching his other hand down on the floor, grasping for the discarded semi-automatic. Skinner gave another kick to the flabby gut and let go of the hand with the revolver. The naked men fell on his naked ass and pointed his gun where Skinner had recently stood but he couldn't see through the blood and didn't realize that Skinner was lying on the floor in front of him.

Skinner grabbed his automatic and the two men shot at the same time. The fat man's revolver fired into the plaster. Skinner's semi-automatic fired into the fat man's hairy chest. The naked man didn't fire a second time.

When he stood up Skinner looked around in silence. The thin woman was sitting on the bed looking down at her dead husband.

"You work fast," she said as she reached into her bag and pulled out a cigarette.

Skinner kept his automatic pointed at her.

"There's blood on your blouse."

"I felt it hit. I knew it would. That's why I put the fur away."

"So who was that guy?"

"A big bastard."

"I know that but was he somebody important? Someone who's going to get special treatment by the police?"

"He used to be someone special."

She was unbuttoning her blouse. Skinner watched her and she watched her dead husband. She slipped the blouse off her shoulders and it looked like she had tattoos all over her ribs and stomach. Then Skinner realized that the marks were bruises.

"He was good at it," she said. "Knew how not to let it show."

"Sorry."

She looked up at him and gave a faint laugh. "Nothing for you to worry about. There's five thousand in a plastic bag in the freezer. Take it."

"I've been paid."

"I know." She looked at him for the first time since the shots were fired. She smiled and her face looked brighter than it had before. "Take it anyway." She reached into her dresser and pulled out a new blouse. "If you promise to take this with you."

She handed Skinner the stained shirt she had just removed.

"Why did he want you to call your father?"

"I don't feel like talking anymore. You can read his obit."

"Fine."

"Don't look for it tomorrow. I'm not reporting it now. I'm going out again and I'm not coming back until after the *Globe* and *Herald* are past deadline."

Skinner stopped in the kitchen and found the plastic baggie full of $100 bills. He shoved it in his coat pocket and walked outside toward his car. He gave a final glance across the street to the building he had lived in for three days. The windows were lit up now and the sky was dark. The tiny dryer vent he had looked through with his binoculars was still dark.

△ △ △

Daniel Moses Luft *has written numerous book reviews for* Mystery Scene *magazine and mostlyfiction.com and was formerly a copy editor for Sovlit.com. Excluding a few quotations he made up for his college newspaper, "Boxed" is his first fiction publication.*

The Rose Collection

Louisa Clerici

I've never seen the ocean. Sometimes I wonder what it would be like to stand before such a great body of water that you couldn't see to the other side. There must be a feeling of wanting to step in, immerse yourself in all that vastness. To connect with something so powerful that it appears to go on forever.

That's the whole trouble with living in Cooper, Indiana. You can see the other side of everything. I can stand at my kitchen door and see Gladys Cosgrove hanging personal whites on the line in her backyard. I can sit in the parlor rocker by the window and watch the Cosgrove twins, Brady and Peeker, ride their bikes back and forth on the street, back and forth till I'm hypnotized.

I've counted the chickens at Hemingway's Farm. I've driven to the town limits and just sat by the interstate calmly waiting for a car to go by. Sometimes on a hot July day, sitting on the front porch just swatting the flies away, it feels like my life is passing by me with nothing caught up in the moments to show for it.

I try to keep occupied. I prepare a hearty breakfast for my husband Frank every morning at 5:00 a.m. Two eggs over light, just the way he likes 'em, crispy bacon but not dry. Two thick slices of wheat toast lightly buttered and slathered with my own strawberry jam. Coffee, dark and smooth and rich, three and a half cups exactly. Two cups for Frank. One cup for me with my morning toast and a half cup to have later, after Frank leaves for work and I can sit by the window and sip, breathe in the scent of wisteria and listen to the roosters sing.

And there's always busy work. Dusting the crystal vases on the mantle, rearranging the tiny Hummels Frank's mother left him, three little figurines. I like the little lady holding the bunch of flowers the best. Her yellow hair is neatly tied back with a brown kerchief. Her face is looking up with eyes that are smiling, as if she just knows something good is going to happen today. Frank's mother Gertrude Peckham loved her Hummels. She used to say to me, "Laura, you need a hobby. There's more to life then work, work and work. You need to collect something. It makes me all happy inside picking out each one, adding to my collection. You see, look here, they're all signed and numbered on the bottom. Isn't that just great!"

I think I first got the idea when Mrs. Constance Butler died a few years ago. She had been the oldest person in town, ninety-five on her last birthday. I used to visit her because it was the kindly thing to do, but I liked it. Her bright blue eyes always looked at me as if she really saw me. I complimented her one day on the small fancy brooch she wore on her starched and ironed ivory blouse. It was all sparkly with a pale gold intricate rose. She said it was a pin made in the forties by someone called Haskell. She treasured it because it was the last present her husband had given to her before he passed away. What a surprise when after her funeral, her lawyer Mr. Bernard told me she had left me the pin, put it in her will, he said.

The next week he handed me the small black velvet box and a light went off in my head. I decided to visit the Cooper Public Library. Turns out they had two books on collecting antique jewelry and could order more if I needed them. I did. I got all into it. Found out the difference between a Jensen and a Marvella necklace. Learned all about quality and began to spend time on the library computer searching the Internet for pieces I could purchase.

Frank almost shit when I told him I wanted to drive all the way to Cumberland, Indiana that summer because they had a massive flea market there where I might find some jewelry for my new collection. He said, "Now Laura, you're taking this too far. Isn't it enough you spend all that time at the library? Who'll make my dinner if you go to Cumberland?"

It didn't matter. Frank died in his sleep two weeks later and I went to Cumberland all by myself. I got an old mildew-smelling room at the Three Crossings Motel on Route 9 for one night and spent the better part of two days walking in the heat between old folding tables filled and overflowing with "stuff." It was amazing; everything imaginable could be bought there, old Sinatra records, cracked and chipped china plates with floral patterns, books and tools and even Hummels. And I finally found my first piece, a delicate platinum iris pin from the fifties with a tiny cut-crystal stone in the center of the flower. I was so happy!

When I got back to Cooper I was so exhausted from the trip, it felt like I slept for the next two days. Then I went to Frank's grave and brought a yellow rose from our garden. I told him all about everything. The way that sleazy man with the black lacquered hair tried to sell me some cheap chain-store jewelry. As if I didn't know better. The way I hunted through tarnished silver chains and plastic rings. How I met Mrs. Isabel Layton who'd owned a stall at the Cumberland Flea Market for nine years. She loved jewelry and had once visited Tiffany's in New York City. I held up my iris pin in the sunlight and shiny facets flashed to the outer corners of the graveyard.

That first trip to Cumberland was just the beginning. I studied hard all winter; some weeks I felt like I lived at the library. I scouted websites trying to learn more about what dealers were offering for sale. I was determined to have what would someday be a perfect collection.

I was so busy with my new passion that sometimes I wondered how I ever managed to have anything else in my life, but I did. My neighbor Gladys introduced me to her widowed cousin Philip Abbott, and we were married the following winter. I wore the platinum iris on my off-white wool suit for the ceremony. Philip didn't really understand my hobby but he tolerated it. That spring we had only been married for four months and Philip said he had to put his foot down. We just didn't have the money to squander on a foolish trip to Cumberland.

But I ended up going by myself on Memorial Day weekend. Even Gladys said I should, I needed to get away, begin healing after the horrible tragedy. She said if I didn't, pictures of Philip tumbling down the steep cellar stairs and breaking his head open might haunt me forever.

My second visit to Cumberland was wonderful. I stayed an extra day. Isabel Layton showed me a handsome Emmons brooch made in 1949. It was a circular swirl of green stones with a gold vine of tiny pearls dripping from the center. I was desperate for it.

When I got back from my trip I had a feeling of satisfaction I'd never known before. I spent the rest of that summer trying to get more jewelry knowledge. Cooper's nice librarian Abigail Spencer ordered books for me to read and I often took them over to Hope Valley Cemetery to visit Philip. I always brought him a pink rose from the garden and I stretched out on the grass and read him whole paragraphs from *Fifty Years of Collectible Fashion Jewelry*.

I spent so much time at the library that Abigail sometimes made coffee and we sat behind her desk and I told her stories about famous jewelry that had been commissioned in the 40s and 50s by Hollywood starlets and wealthy debutantes. I always wore one of my three pieces; the platinum iris, the pearl brooch, or Constance's rose. Abigail would finger the polished gems and tiny beadwork and we would ooh and aah together. Sometimes we would invite Theodore Brum to join us. He was always at the library working on his genealogy charts, a project he started after his wife died and he hoped he'd finish and give to his grandchildren that Christmas. I liked Theodore, he was a real gentleman, and he had a lot of patience for a man. He would sit sipping his coffee for hours and listen to my stories, in no hurry to go anywhere.

Theodore and I were married in January on a frosty cold winter morning. I wore a simple ice-blue dress with a dainty Florenza necklace that Theodore had given me as a wedding present. He had ordered it from an auction house with Abigail's help and it was lovely, delicate filigree metalwork with hand-painted porcelain pastel flowers, a work of art. I felt all happy inside walking down the chapel aisle.

All that winter I prepared for my now annual trip to Cumberland. I had begun exchanging letters with Isabel Layton. She spent winters in New York City with her sister and every few weeks I received one from her. I would sit in my parlor rocker and devour each line. The pages were filled with stories about the jewelry shows she had gone to and news about new purchases she had made and would be available at her business in the flea market that summer.

I couldn't wait. Thinking about Cumberland filled me with excitement. The thrill of never knowing what you might find. A search for treasure that was always a surprise. Theodore didn't like to travel but decided to come with me, so I booked a room at the Three Crossings. The motel was the only place to stay in town and I had gotten used to it, actually felt nostalgic about its cheap old rooms.

The week before we were to leave Theodore's two grandchildren informed him they would be coming for a visit. They had been sorry they hadn't made it to our wedding and wanted to meet me and see their grandfather. My husband couldn't believe I wouldn't cancel my trip. I told him it was fine with me if he stayed home and spent the week with them but I was going to Cumberland.

Theodore was so upset. "But they want to meet you." He frowned and insisted I cancel.

Who would think that husband number three would be so impossible. But husbands aren't numbered like figurines and who's counting anyway.

I couldn't rest that night. Theodore went to bed and I sat in my rocker, crying softly into the tassels of a golden pillow. I had to go to Cumberland. I had no choice.

I finally fell asleep in the chair, only waking when the Cosgrove twins started batting a ball around at 6 a.m. in their front yard. God! Gladys never could control those boys. I opened the front door and yelled at them. I should have known better, that never worked in the past. Instead they started riding their bikes back and forth between our houses.

I went down the hall to the bedroom thinking maybe if I lay down I could manage another twenty minutes or so of zzz's. I felt exhausted. I found Theodore still snoring loudly, not bothered at all by the sounds of Brady and Peeker riding by our open bedroom window. Of course, he had no trouble resting. He was looking forward to seeing his grandkids. He wasn't going to miss the trip we looked forward to all year. The yellow pillow was still wet with my tears from the night before as I sat down on the bed next to Theodore, for what would be the last time.

The Doctor was surprised; he wasn't sure why Theodore must have stopped breathing sometime in the early morning hours. Theodore had been in excellent health for a man in his 70s. But these things happen.

I really enjoyed meeting his grandchildren at the funeral. It was nice getting to know them for a few days before I left for Cumberland. I gave them the genealogy report that Theodore had just finished. I knew it would be a last gift they would keep and enjoy and pass on eventually to their children. The three of us went to their grandfather's grave and I placed a white rose on Theodore's stone.

The night before I was to leave for Cumberland I started packing. I closed all the open windows in the house just to make sure I wouldn't forget in the morning. I knew the next few days would be stormy.
I woke up early, excited and happy and so I was almost dressed when the sheriff came. He waited while I grabbed a sweater and found my Haskell rose pin on the mantel where I'd left it the night before. I

fingered the Hummel lady in passing, wondered who I should leave the figurines to. Maybe Peeker Cosgrove. Yes, I think definitely Peeker. After all, collections are meant to live on, in someone else's house, on the vast mantle of someone else's life. I stepped outside and it's funny, I almost thought I could smell the ocean.

△ △ △

Louisa Clerici's *short stories and poetry have been published in literary anthologies and magazines including* The Istanbul Literary Review, Carolina Woman Magazine, City Lights, Off the Coast, Shore Voices, Bagels with the Bards *and* The Shine Journal. *Louisa is the host of DreamSpeak, a popular venue for writers in downtown Plymouth, Massachusetts and has just finished her first novel.*

Sweet Hitchhiker

Steve Liskow

PJ Gaines wears a Tigers cap and a man's shirt that gapes open over her bikini top, and under her cut-offs, her bathing suit is giving her a world-class wedgie. Declan Austin has a towel folded under her butt so she doesn't soak his leather seat.

"My parents are still seriously screwed up about my sister," she says.

"I'll bet." Even with the car windows open, Deck smells of tanning butter, his body the rich brown of a worn baseball glove. "Are they getting anywhere on that?"

PJ's fists knot in her lap. "The cops just keep asking the same questions, over and over. Yes, she liked to hitch, everyone knew that. Yes, she and Tom broke up. Yes, she called me when she had car trouble, but I was charging my phone and didn't find her voicemail until two hours later."

PJ keeps her voice steady. "No, I don't know anyone who wanted to hurt her."

Last week, hikers found her twin sister CJ in a shallow grave off Higgins Road, twelve days after she disappeared. Nineteen years old. In high school, the sisters swam the last two legs of the 1500-meter relay until their senior year when PJ popped an eardrum going off the high board. She lost her swimming scholarship and about half the hearing in her right ear, but she was still the class salutatorian.

Deck's eyes flicker toward PJ's belly-button ring. "They have any ideas?"

"Well, they think she hitched a ride and the guy killed her. But that's as far as they've got."

They found CJ's Saturn parked in the lifeguard's space at Indian Lake, five miles from the grave. Both front tires had punctures.

PJ swallows the bile in her throat. "They know where Tom Janssen was for twelve hours before and after she disappeared, too, and it wasn't anywhere near her."

She feels Deck's eyes on her belly button ring again and pulls her shirt closed. When he turns west, the sun warms her face through the windshield.

"It could have been some weirdo just passing through." Deck shifts his aviator sunglasses off his own Tigers cap and onto his nose, white with zinc oxide. "I mean, maybe the guy looked at how she was dressed . . ."

"She'd been at the beach." PJ hates people talking that way about her sister. "She was going to be an elementary teacher, for Christ's sake."

"C'mon, Peej, even I talked to her about it a couple of times. Lots of little kids around, they look up to the lifeguards. They shouldn't see a girl falling out of her top."

"She wore something over it, Deck. Just like I do. Well, most of the time." PJ can't be a lifeguard anymore, not with her bad ear. But she's still going to be a teacher, too. She and CJ used to talk about that, how they might end up in the same school. People who didn't know them wouldn't even guess they were sisters, CJ with her blonde hair and blue eyes, PJ with hair and eyes like acorns. CJ was four minutes older and an inch taller. And a "C" cup.

"You're looking at my ring again." PJ sees Deck's hands tighten on the steering wheel. "We got our belly buttons pierced together, got the same rings. Pop was pissed, but Mom thought it was cute."

"Your dad wanted to ground you both." The sun glints off Deck's shades, big silver triangles. "But it was just before the senior prom and you'd already bought your dresses."

"And you rented the limo."

"Yeah."

Deck follows the double yellow line around the patch of woods. A highway sign warns about deer crossing.

The beads of water have dried on PJ's legs, and she's got goose bumps. She digs into her tote for her cell phone. "Funny, isn't it. Tom taking me, you taking CJ. Then she dumps you for him."

Deck slows down for an SUV with a driver who seems to be reading a map.

"I half expected you to call me when she did that." PJ checks her inbox. Empty. "It's really nice of you to give me a lift like this. I couldn't believe it, my spare flat, too."

Deck passes the SUV. Kansas plates, definitely a tourist. "I'm glad I got to you instead of some stranger. I mean, that's the same thing that happened to CJ."

"I know. It freaked me a little." The bars on PJ's phone disappear in the tall trees and she puts it back in her tote. "Maybe she screamed and the guy panicked."

"Huh?" Deck's eyes flicker to the right, where Dotty Blair walks on their side of the road, legs tan as toast, big orange headlights. Jealousy bubbles in PJ's stomach.

"Why he killed her."

Deck's shades jerk back to the road. "That's sick, Peej."

"Well, the son of a bitch buried her. Why do you suppose he'd do that?"

"So nobody'd find her." Deck clears his throat. "Have they found her navel ring?"

"They think the bastard took it as a souvenir." PJ's fingers choke her towel. "She said some guy came onto her a few days before."

"Who?"

"I don't know. She didn't seem too upset about it. Well, it happened a lot, you said so yourself. The way she dressed."

Deck turns on the radio, then turns it off again.

"My sister liked attention," PJ says. "And she was built for it, wasn't she?"

"You're pretty, too, PJ."

"Not like her." The sunlight flickers through the trees and across Deck's shades. "It was like she couldn't get away from it. She said it was like death and taxes."

Deck's tanned fists are big as meatloaves squeezing the steering wheel.

PJ takes off her cap and lets the wind blow through her short hair. "Nobody's ever felt that way about me."

"I like you, Peej."

"Like. Yeah."

She looks back, but there's not another car in sight.

"Everyone knew CJ liked to hitch." When Deck's voice slows down, the car does the same. "Remember what they put under her yearbook picture? 'Thumbelina.' That's what everyone called her."

He scrolls through radio stations again. "But that means the guy who killed her knows her, and that means we know him, too. That's creepy."

"Yeah." PJ puts her cap back on. "You were pretty pissed off when she dumped you for Tom."

"I got over it."

"I was disappointed when you didn't call me up after that. Symmetry, right?" PJ points to a path between birch trees. "Pull in here. I want to show you something."

Rocks and fallen limbs turn the ground into a jagged maze. Deck crawls along, the car rocking like they're riding out a storm on Lake Huron.

"She broke up with Tom, too." PJ watches the trees glide closer to the car. "Just before . . ."

"How come?" Deck rests his shades on the bill of his cap again and frowns at the obstacle course beyond the windshield.

"She got a phone call saying he was seeing Dotty Blair. He said it wasn't true, but she didn't believe him." PJ squints as the last beam of sunlight slices between tree trunks. "She told me she should have found out who called her first. Well, that was CJ, too, wasn't it? Shoot from the lip."

Deck's eyes peer over the hood for the path of least resistance. "That means someone who knows her, too. Did the cops try to trace the call?"

"Whoever killed her took her purse." PJ feels her voice fade like the bars on her phone. "Her cell, her keys." Shadows from the trees turn Deck's face into a mask. "Her purse wasn't with her body."

The trees look tall enough to reach heaven. Higgins Road, where they found CJ, lies less than a mile beyond them.

"She was naked, wasn't she?" Deck says. "When they found her? The sicko took her clothes and her . . . belly button ring."

"Yeah." PJ catches him looking at her stomach again, still flat and firm. She still swims, but now they won't let her be a lifeguard. "You think he kept them as trophies? Is he going to try this again?"

"Christ, Peej." Deck's voice is gravel. "Don't think about things like that. You'll make yourself crazy."

"I can't think about anything else, Deck." PJ takes off her shades. "You were the first guy who . . . maybe the only. I don't know if she and Tom . . ."

"Probably." His voice becomes a growl.

"She still cared about you, Deck. She was thinking of calling you up again." PJ feels her voice wobble and looks out at the trees.

"No idea who called her about Tom? He and Tom ought to be top of the cops' list."

PJ drops her sunglasses back in her tote. "Tom was at that party when she disappeared."

"I know. I was, too." Deck peers through the windshield. "What do you want to show me, Peej? There's nothing here but trees and rocks. We go any farther, I'm not sure I'll be able to get back out."

"Just a little more." Up ahead, she sees the mound that conceals a cave she never knew existed until a few months ago. She's lived around here all her life.

"How come you never asked me out after Tom dumped me?" Her voice feels thin as smoke.

"I like you, Peej. But we're too close. It'd be too weird."

"You went out with my sister."

"CJ was different." Deck kills the ignition and the car feels cramped. "She never felt like anyone's sister. She was always more of a . . . I don't know . . . a girlfriend, not a good friend."

"That doesn't make any sense, Deck." PJ realizes there's a tree only inches from her door so she can't open it.

"Your mom and dad brought you and Ceej to the beach the day we met, remember? You were, what, nine?"

"You told us you were a lifeguard." She smiles at the memory. "We knew you were too young."

"Next year I was, though."

"Yeah." The tanning butter smell fills the car, sickly sweet like dying flowers. "You were so proud of that, the youngest lifeguard on the beach."

"Shit, I showed you how to dive, how to do the backstroke . . ."

PJ touches her ear. "If I'd remembered what you taught me, I wouldn't have gone into the water wrong, messed up my ear."

"You were a better swimmer than she was, PJ."

"She swam anchor."

"But you gave her the lead, swimming third leg. A couple of times, she couldn't have held on without those extra lengths. You were both so beautiful, the water shiny like diamonds on your body. On your suit, so tight."

PJ fights to get the words out. "So why her and not me, Deck?"

Mosquitoes whine into the car and Deck pushes the button to raise the windows.

"Why would you ask her out, but not me?" Tears burn PJ's eyes.

"How come you made love to her, but not to me? You just said I'm pretty, too."

"I told you. It was . . . is . . . different with you." She feels his voice go faster, chasing a guy's version of truth. "Besides, Tom must have . . . um, didn't he?"

"But I loved you. I wanted you to be first. I wanted you to be there for me, too."

"I am here for you, Peej. Shoot, I came and picked you up when you called, didn't I? When you had a flat tire too."

"You did." PJ's hands choke the Coppertone bottle in her tote. "Just like with CJ."

"What?" Deck's forehead wrinkles. "Wait a minute."

"I'm surprised the cops didn't talk to you long ago."

"They did. But Kenny threw that party, remember?"

He rests his right arm across the back of the seat and it looks big enough to crush the life out of her.

"You said you were there, too." PJ wishes she could see his eyes more clearly through the shadows. "But it was late afternoon, lots of beer, everyone wasted. Nobody even saw you slip away to pick her up."

"Whoa, PJ. Where are you going with this?"

"Her clothes are in that cave up there, aren't they, Deck? And I'll bet her navel ring is in your pocket so you can play with it when you get lonely, am I right?"

Deck's bulk fills the car, twice her size. "That's really sick."

"You killed her, Deck. I loved you, and you killed my sister."

"No way."

"The cops will believe me when I tell them, though."

Her hand fumbles in her tote bag again: the damp towel, her phone, her sunglasses, then her fingers find their prey. "That's what she told me that day, the guy who was bugging her, but I misunderstood because she said it into my bad ear. Death and Taxes."

"Huh?"

"My bad ear. Deaf after that damn dive. She said 'Declan Texas,' like she always called you, instead of Austin. Remember, from when we were learning the state capitals?"

"That was years ago, PJ."

"But I'll tell the cops I just remembered it."

He reaches for the ignition, but she closes her hand over the keys.

"You stuck that screwdriver into her tires." Her voice feels like metal. "Then you offered to give her a ride and brought her here."

His hand squeezes hers and she almost stops. She watches his face understand.

"PJ, you took her phone because your number was on it, didn't you?"

The smell of tanning butter fills her head. Metal again, like blood. "My sister, my twin, and you killed her. Then you buried her and let the animals eat her."

"You're out of your frigging mind." His fists clench, then his eyes widen. "Wait a minute. How do you know it was a screwdriver that—"

She jams it into his chest. He tries to grab the handle, but she rises up on her knees and holds on with both hands, driving the point deeper until her arms are slick with blood and he sags against the door. She hooks his bloody hand into the top of her bikini and yanks down. His blood paints her shirt and breasts.

She watches his eyes lose their luster, his chest stop moving, his last breath bubble between his lips. His left fist clutches her top.

"I loved you." She doesn't even recognize her own voice.

She moves her sister's belly button ring from her pocket to his and dumps the contents of the glove compartment on the floor. That tree blocks her from opening her door, so it's a good thing she left CJ's clothes in the cave yesterday.

She finds her cell phone in her tote and dials 911.

△   △   △

Steve Liskow *has published stories in the last five* Level Best *collections, and "Hot Sugar Blues" will appear in* Vengeance, *an MWA anthology edited by Lee Child, next spring.* The Whammer Jammers, *his thriller about roller derby, will be published before year's end. He lives in Connecticut with his wife Barbara and two rescued cats. www.steveliskow.com.*

Sisters in Black

Mary E. Stibal

My mother was a smart, caring, and elegant woman, but above all else, she was forgiving.

As for me, I don't have a forgiving bone in my body.

The day of her funeral about two hundred mourners had gathered at the Cathedral of the Holy Cross in Boston's South End for the service. Her five sisters who still lived in Manhattan were there of course, all of them in black, with flowing silk scarves. But they always dressed in black, even for weddings. My mother told me years ago that's what sophisticated New Yorkers wear.

I met her sisters on the sidewalk, and we cried and hugged and hugged again as we watched her casket carried up the steps of the cathedral. Inside, the sonorous organ music was majestic I suppose, if one is into weeping.

Five minutes after the service began my mother's ex-husband Victor showed up.

I hadn't seen him for two years. I told him I'd kill him if I ever saw him again. And so here "again" was.

I thought he was still in prison.

At that moment my gun was tucked under the front seat of my car. There were a couple of reasons why I didn't run across the street and grab it, not least of which this was my mother's funeral after all. The second was the two hundred eyewitnesses part.

My mother used to say, early in my career, "Just because you're

221

with the government doesn't mean you need to 'waltz around' everywhere with a loaded weapon."

I thought I did.

Victor slid into the pew right behind me.

"This is a private funeral," I hissed. "So please leave."

The priest, reciting the words from the Mass for the Dead, looked up. And then went back to his text.

"She would have wanted me to come," whispered Victor.

I said, out loud this time, "She would not!"

The priest stopped mid-sentence and stared. My mother's sisters sitting in the pew across from me looked over as well, and after a long ten seconds the service continued. But I kept my eyes on the bronze coffin less than ten feet away, wishing my mother would somehow throw open the lid and step out, saying something funny like she always did. She was dressed in black of course. I'd seen to that.

Another thing to know about my mother was that she was religious. I know she said the rosary for Victor every morning up until the day she died.

And here I was at her funeral, just itching to kill him.

My mother never said as much, but I knew she wasn't thrilled twenty years ago when I went to work for the DEA. I think she would have rather I'd been a starving actress, or a penniless dancer on off-Broadway. Wearing black of course, not the earth tones I favored.

"I'm not sure I like the idea of a gun-toting daughter," she'd said my first weekend home after I'd joined the agency (she really did talk like that). Although to be honest I think she would have liked my gun better if it had been a sleek, stainless steel derringer rather than my heavy, bulky Glock. Like I said, she was from Manhattan.

The organ launched into another dirge, and Victor sang along with the choir. He was off-key.

I don't know why my mother married Victor. My father had been dead for ten years by then, but she could have picked someone else. Someone who wasn't associated with Organized Crime, not that she had the slightest clue. Victor was a wealthy lawyer, handsome and charming, with a big house in Newton and a place on Martha's Vineyard. I do know for sure she was stunned when he was indicted for conspiracy to murder, with racketeering and money laundering numbers two and three on the long list. Although the state's evidence against him and his clients was significant, Victor refused to say anything, other than to take the Fifth. Over and over.

And so my mother left him.

Since they were still legally married she couldn't testify against Victor, but that didn't stop his associates from sending a team of goons one night to rough her up. By the end she had a concussion, a broken arm, a black eye, and a cut on her forehead that "all really doesn't hurt as much as you would think," she'd told me in the emergency room at Mass General.

Victor was out on bail at that point, and after I took my mother back to my place in the Seaport District I went to his apartment in the Back Bay. That's when I brought up the "I'll kill you" part.

There was a lengthy trial which made Boston headlines for months, and after a mistrial there was a re-trial with the charges greatly reduced, but it was Victor, not his clients, who went to prison. Their divorce was finalized shortly after he was incarcerated, but my mother was never the same. Two years and three months later she died, the cause of death listed as heart failure, but it should have read heartbreak.

When the priest got to the "kiss of peace" part of her funeral mass I walked across the aisle, caressing her coffin as I passed, to kiss my mother's sisters on each cheek. We ignored our streaming tears.

Victor could kiss himself.

At the end of the service I walked behind the casket, and following me, in a swirl of black were her sisters, holding hands. Shay, the oldest, reached in front and grabbed mine. How sweet I thought, and held it fiercely. Outside we went down the cathedral steps, all together in a row towards the black, swanky hearse.

Victor walked around us off to the side just as a nondescript beige car pulled up behind the hearse, a Toyota I think but I couldn't swear to it. I do remember the back passenger window was rolled down. All of which I told the police about twenty times.

There was a quick burst of gunfire from the car, and I knew right away it was a shotgun. Victor was on the last step when he crumpled to the sidewalk, his bloody head just fifteen feet from the hearse. The car peeled off and we all stopped dead. Within minutes an ambulance blared up, and then wave after wave of screaming police cars swarmed in. There was chaos for over an hour.

Towards the end Detective Lieutenant Amick of the State Police blasted in, all very "law and order" in her blue and gold braid uniform and tall boots. I'd known Donia for years, and she told me Victor's murder was probably a mob hit. Just two days before, according to her informants, there'd been a flood of anonymous tips on the street that Victor had decided to testify against his clients. All of them. A welcome surprise for the DA, very bad news for his clients.

My mother's burial service was delayed until that afternoon, since everyone had to give a lengthy statement. So it was well after 3:30 p.m. before we gathered under the quiet, green tent over her grave in Brookline. As my mother's casket was lowered into the sad ground that windy afternoon, each of her sisters threw a red rose on her coffin.

Then, they all looked at each other and smiled, their black scarves billowing around their necks.

And that's when I knew.

The next day I went to Saks and bought a slim black dress and a long, black silk scarf. Very sophisticated, I thought.

△   △   △

Mary E. Stibal *lives in Boston's Seaport District, has published in* Yankee Magazine. *This story marks her third appearance in a Level Best Books anthology. She grew up in Iowa and has five sisters, to whom this story is dedicated. She says that while they don't necessarily dress in black, they are all firm believers in good, old-fashioned retribution.*

The Fallen

Joe Ricker

A cross the alley, Rick and Alice began to fight. Their son Benny scrambled through the apartment for his mittens and coat and hat and let himself out of the apartment. *Motherfucker* was the only word Jeremy could make out through the telephoto lens on his camera. He snapped away catching various poses of their lips as they projected the invective toward each other. It wouldn't take long for Rick to drop her with a right hook. Jeremy'd seen that half a dozen times already.

For two weeks he'd been watching them, and it wouldn't have been different from any other drug investigation except the captain kept him on surveillance no matter how much evidence he collected against Rick Stallings. Buyers went to Rick, and Jeremy took their pictures. They were an indiscriminate mix of people whose likeness was their desire. Base-heads arrived with their infected gums and their money crumpled and dirty, frat-boys with cashmere-cotton blend sweaters and the crisp straight bills they'd received from the ATM, blue collar guys on payday so they could stay up and get the most out of their drinking time, hookers in need of making the most out of their working hours, and meticulous housewives who would have run out of energy by noon without it. They all knocked on the door with their reasons and needs. They all made their contributions to that social dynamic. They all gave Jeremy a reason other than his divorce to be stuck in that crummy, third-floor apartment.

The apartment was on the back end of the building and overlooked a dead end alley that businesses had used for deliveries. There were no businesses at that end of town anymore. Even the bustle of rats had diminished to a few struggling survivors. The apartments were all the same—shitty carpet stained with piss, vomit, and blood, and the walls dropped strips of paint from corroding sheetrock. There was the constant sound of running water and crying and screaming. Jeremy snapped a few more shots of Rick and Alice then put the camera down.

A bottle of whiskey sat within arms-reach, unopened. He'd quit drinking to save his marriage, but Mally left anyway, without a goodbye, a note, nothing; only her small footprints filled with falling snow leading up to the street by the time he'd gotten home. He'd walked through the empty house with the one-month sobriety chip he'd just received and a wallet-size card that had the Serenity Prayer on one side and a poem about footprints on the other. "The times when you have seen only one set of footprints in the sand, are when I carried you." Jeremy thought about the card, whispered, "Bullshit," and lifted the camera. Footprints began where angels dropped you, if you landed on your feet, the weight of you unwanted, your prayers a burden on the ear of God.

Rick and Alice circled around the small wooden table. Rick had pulled his shirt open. Jeremy put the camera to his eye. The lens brought the eagle tattoo on Rick's chest into focus—poorly done and faded on his left pec. Alice was wearing a white t-shirt and light blue panties. Her thighs flexed as she moved toward Rick on the balls of her feet. She had bony shoulders and thin arms—her fingers delicate and long. She looked good, Jeremy thought—as sleek and elegant as the stainless steel paring knife she was holding. Jeremy wished she'd sink it in Rick's neck or get lucky and poke through a rib. Alice threw the knife at Rick. He swatted it away. She went to the refrigerator and pulled the revolver from the top of it. Rick moved slowly with his arms out.

Jeremy put the camera down again. He didn't want any evidence against Alice if she decided to dump a round or two into Rick's chest. They stood for a moment until Alice began to cry and Rick pulled the gun from her hand and the two hugged. Jeremy put on some jeans and sat in the corner of the apartment on a milk crate. He put on his boots and secured them with duct tape after the laces broke. The tread had been worn flat, and the leather was soft, like a moccasin. Jeremy tore the few pages of notes from the pad on the counter, folded them around the camera's memory card and stuffed them into his back pocket. The last gulp of coffee was cold and he spit it into the sink. He put on a long john shirt, a black hooded sweatshirt, a thigh-length black leather jacket, a black beanie and gloves.

Metal chattered against metal as Jeremy made his way down the ladder of the fire escape to the alley below. His exhaled breaths chugged through the rungs as he descended. Benny, Alice's kid, was circling on his bicycle until his back tire caught a patch of ice and the bike kicked out from under him. The boy toppled to the pavement at Jeremy's feet and quickly recovered.

"Sorry, mister," the boy said and jerked his bike upright by the handlebars.

Jeremy rubbed the end of his nose with two of his fingers, adjusting it to the cold. He studied the kid's face wondering how old he would be before black eyes and split lips would start appearing—when the boy got bigger, maybe, harder for Rick to handle—when the boy wouldn't just take it anymore. Jeremy pulled his jacket tighter and made his way to the end of the alley. The gray-and-brown brick multiple story buildings stood around him. Clouds hovered low in the sky, rippled like corrugated roofs. Snow, dirty with car exhaust and sand, clung to the base of the sidewalks and buildings. The streets were narrow, even more so with the mounds of snow pushed to the side by plow trucks and left there so the city could impose parking bans and spend the night towing.

O'Connor's, the corner store, was two blocks down on the right.

He stopped there every morning for a cup of coffee on his way to the park. O'Connor scratched his neck and sighed more than anyone really had to when Jeremy pulled change from his pocket coin by coin to pay for the coffee. O'Connor got his knees broken by a scar-faced Irishman after a bad bet on the '85 Super Bowl. He hobbled around with a cane on the rare occasions he wasn't nested behind the counter.

"Coffee'd be cheaper if you made it at home," O'Connor said to Jeremy.

"Then I'd have no place to get rid of all this extra change."

"You could take it up the hill and give it to the panhandlers."

"They don't sell coffee." Jeremy smiled.

O'Connor shook his head and swept the change from the counter into his palm.

□   □   □

Jeremy waited for the captain behind the high school at Grant Field. The remaining faculty made their way to the staff parking lot. Some of them lit cigarettes as they fled school property. Wind rolled a wave of glistening white over the snow-covered field. Jeremy dumped the rest of his coffee when the captain arrived. The captain remained wrapped in his wool pea coat, a tan scarf wrapped tightly around his neck, and his hands and fingers gloved in calfskin despite the heat in the vehicle. His hair was gray, even the well-manicured goatee. His eyes were bright and focused because he slept at night.

"The snaps were good yesterday," The captain said after Jeremy closed the passenger side door.

"The part where Rick Stallings smacked his kid around?"

"We're not here for that, Jeremy."

"This doesn't feel right. I've taken more pictures than an Asian tourist. How long am I going to be on this?"

"Stallings has slipped through our fingers twice. I'm not taking another chance of him being acquitted."

"You didn't have this kind of evidence last time."

"If I remember right, the last time you made a bust a bartender testified that you were drunk when you made the arrest."

Jeremy pulled his hat lower over his ears. "I've been sober three months."

"Let's keep it that way. You been to any meetings?"

"What, and miss an eight-round amateur bout with Stallings and his wife?"

"Don't get fucking smart with me. You're lucky you're still a cop."

Jeremy fished the memory card from his pocket and placed it on the seat between him and the captain. "I'd better get back."

The captain spoke when Jeremy pulled on the door handle. "Hang on, kid. I didn't mean to be so hard on you. Just keep doing what you're doing. This will all be over soon."

Jeremy smirked. "You mean, eventually."

He climbed from the captain's car and followed his footprints from the day before across the field, a single unwavering set through the snow. He stopped to look back only when he'd reached the other side, before he scrambled up the banking. The captain's car was already gone.

Jeremy walked by his childhood home. New families had moved in, grown, and left. He walked down to the sandpit, where his father had driven the car that night—where Jeremy had escaped from the car over the bits of broken glass from the window he'd shattered with his hands—where his father's life ended in the front seat of the car with pills and carbon monoxide while his mother's body lay in the trunk.

Benny sat in his room on a plastic lined mattress coloring the outside edges of his coloring book around the figures that had been colored before Jeremy got there to watch Rick. The crayons were worn down and Benny made his choice of color by the smell of them—held them to his nose and sniffed then tossed the unwanted back into the small plastic baggie. Benny turned through the pages of his coloring book—each page colored to the edges. He climbed off the bed and pushed his dresser away from the wall and started a mural. He'd chosen a forest green crayon and drew a tree—the shape of a cookie-cutter Christmas tree. After he finished off the green crayon, he moved to a red one and began to color circles at the tips of the pointed branches.

Rick moved through the apartment and Benny pushed the dresser back and leapt to his bed. The blood vessels swelled on Rick's neck until they were throbbing, and more swelled and branched out on his forehead as if something crawled beneath his skin, and his expression was pain and not anger. Benny pushed himself against the headboard and flinched when Rick snatched the coloring book and rolled it up. But that was all that Benny did in the way of defending himself. When Rick went to thwacking Benny with the book, Benny rolled to his stomach and relaxed, whimpering into his bag of crayons and wetting the peeled paper with tears. Rick tossed the coloring book next to Benny where it unraveled like the wings of a spine-injured bird. Benny sat up after a moment and dug through the crayons. He took what was left of the black one and went back to the mural behind the dresser. He slashed through the tree with angry strokes until the crayon was gone.

Alice tugged on Benny's arm the next morning on their way down to the bus stop. Jeremy hung back a block and watched the boy slap his lunch box off the back of his leg. His backpack was puffed out with air and looked far too large for the small boy. In his other hand, Benny carried the plastic baggie full of used, paper-pulled crayons.

On surveillance, the worst acts are never the reason for watching. The acts of abuse, rape, sometimes even murder were ancillary to the purpose. The victims were significant only when they served their purpose, when they provided what was needed. Sometimes, rapists and abusers and murderers were sent to prison. There they paid their debt to society, while the victims remained vulnerable and scavenging for justice or hope or faith. And God judged the wicked, giving value to their life while the victims served only a purpose for that judgment.

That evening Benny sat on his bed holding the revolver in his palms. He aimed it ahead of him with both hands wrapped around the grip, his head sunk between his shoulders to look down the sight and his elbows out. Benny straightened up and looked down at the revolver again. He swung the gun around him taking aim at different points of the room. Benny grew more confident with the weight of the gun and stood on the bed. He attempted to spin it on his finger. Jeremy could feel the muscle fibers between his ribs tighten. The gun fell to the mattress. Jeremy put the camera down. Benny retrieved the gun and made another attempt.

The gunshot popped, muffled by the walls and the window of Benny's room. His small body pushed against the tension of the glass for a quick moment before it quit on him and let him fall. The fabric of his clothing bloated with the air forcing between the threads. His eyes were closed and the shocked expression remained on Benny's face as he moved through the air, his body limp as it drifted down. Glass sang against the ground like the song of wind chimes from a gentle breeze. A muted thump—one quick, hideous sigh rose through the alley when the boy hit, sending a cloud of snow dust curling and billowing around his body, rising half the distance that he had fallen.

Alice burst into Benny's room. She braced herself against the wooden frame of the broken window. The remaining shards of glass cut into her flesh as she screamed down the alley for her son— reaching out as if she were lunging for his hand to save him. Her reach caught only the brisk wind against the cuts on her palms.

Only the people moving by on the sidewalks stopped to peer into the alley. In the windows of other apartments, where there was movement and where Jeremy was positive that they'd heard, he waited to see the curtains flutter, but nothing.

Jeremy slipped down to the floor gazing at the chaotic scars on his hands, like worms crawling over the pavement after rain. He leaned against the cabinet of the sink long after the ambulance had come and spurt its spinning lights through his window, after the various voices of the crowd had twined themselves into an inconsiderate whine, after the beeps and static crackles of communication devices had slipped into the night to report other tragedies.

□ □ □

"This shouldn't have happened," Jeremy said. He stared through the windshield of the captain's car—his lips parted slightly, a dark, empty look in his eyes.

The captain turned the heater dial down. The air blowing in the car diminished. "Jeremy, this was a horrible tragedy. Nobody could have seen this coming."

"If we'd busted Stallings a week ago, we wouldn't have had to see it coming."

"No. We're not superheroes. We can't prevent the death of every innocent person out there. Rick's going to meet with his suppliers. Focus on that, Jeremy. You make this case and your previous debacle will be ancient history. I promise this will be over soon."

Jeremy looked down to the scars on his hands. "Like everything else," he said.

"Should I be concerned about you?"

"In what way?"

"I'm concerned about how this affects you. I can't risk blowing this operation."

"You'll get Rick Stallings, captain. Don't lose any sleep."

□ □ □

Rick and Alice didn't fight for three days. People arrived with their needs, to receive and scurry away to feed their own tragedies, to meet the conformity of their own agendas. They passed their money into Rick's hands and he rewarded them with the treasures they so desperately sought. Jeremy clenched the still unopened bottle of whiskey he'd kept on the counter next to his notes and his camera and the binoculars, waiting for whatever was going to happen.

On the day of the funeral, Rick moved through the apartment gathering money from his various hiding places. He loaded money into a duffel bag from the crisper drawer in the refrigerator, the top shelf of the cupboard, and from beneath a loose floorboard in his closet. Alice came from the shower wrapped in a towel and sat next to the black dress she had laid across her bed. Her hair was wet, matted together, and heavy on her shoulders. She rested the back of her bandaged hands on her thighs and stared blankly through the doorway of her bedroom. Alice's body trembled while she dressed.

The funeral was held in a large cathedral church—the parking lot as grand in size but nearly empty. Jeremy waited for the stragglers smoking near the entrance to go inside before following them. The pews sprawled beneath the large space of the church. Benny's casket was displayed beyond the pews small enough to require only four pallbearers, and in the grand space of the church it seemed ridiculed because of its tininess.

He fought his urge to weep until he made it home and opened the bottle. Then, after he'd lifted it and smelled the relief it had promised in whispers since he'd stopped drinking, the urge was gone. Jeremy licked his dry lips and put the bottle down. He posted himself over the sink and waited, looking through the alley at Alice and her bandaged palms pressing against her eyes.

□   □   □

Rick opened the door for his suppliers, and despite their black apparel and hats pulled low over their foreheads, Jeremy could tell they were cops—Evans and Kittredge. Jeremy sighed, and the duties the captain had given him made more sense. He'd fucked up his last bust, and the captain had given him a chance to make sure this bust was righteous. Jeremy punched the button of the camera until his knuckle cramped and he switched to using his middle finger. When he filled the memory card, he quickly replaced it and snapped away again.

Six pictures into the new card, when Rick Stallings cut a small hole in the bag of blow to test the quality, Kittredge left the apartment.

What the hell? Jeremy thought. Before an answer came to him, Evans slipped a small, silenced .32 from inside his jacket and put the barrel in Rick's face. Evans shot twice, and went into the hallway. The camera fell from Jeremy's hands and clunked in the sink. Evans moved into the bedroom where Alice sat on the bed and shot her twice before she could see anything more than a flash in her peripheral vision.

Jeremy chambered a round into his Glock as he pounded down the fire escape. When his boots hit the pavement, a shadow spun from beneath the metal stairs. Another hit struck Jeremy's gut then his arm. Jeremy dropped his firearm and gasped for air as he went to the ground. Kittredge tossed the pipe he'd swung into a dumpster and scooped up the pistol Jeremy was reaching for. The hollow thumps of his heart droned through his chest.

Evans came into the alley before Jeremy could catch his breath. The two of them dragged him to a dumpster and pushed him against the brick. Their breaths twisted together and rose into the night as they stood above him. The streetlight at the end of the alley shone over their backs and shoulders and shadowed their faces. When they started on him each punch brought a still frame memory of the things he'd seen—the heated metal coat hangers charring lines into the flesh of an infant's face, the father opening the door to his twelve-year-old daughter's room in trade for a fifteen-minute fix, the bubbles subsiding in a tub of water where a mother held her child because it wouldn't stop crying. They couldn't hit him enough for his memories to run out. He'd been a spectator, a participant in the creation of victims. Jeremy savored the pain in his bones from where they'd hit him. It had been a long time since he'd been hit like that—a long time since he had curled into a ball and prayed for God to stop the hitting, but there was no begging and Jeremy took what they had to give him until everything went numb and dark.

When Jeremy came to, he could tell he'd been in the car for a while. Kittredge was asleep against the window in the seat in front of him. Evans stared over the wheel like he was fitting the car into a tight space. The person next to him cracked the seal on a liquor bottle. Jeremy knew that sound—relief. He straightened himself the best he could against the ache in his temples and looked over at the captain.

"Take a drink, Jeremy," he said, holding out a pint of Senator's Club.

A flash of heat burned in Jeremy's gut. He remembered the stoic look of his father the night he drove them to the sandpit. The captain, despite his stoic look, shared a seat with comfort, and Jeremy had finally made sense of it all.

"Good pay day, Captain?" Jeremy asked.

"Just drink the fucking booze, kid."

Jeremy took the bottle. "Where are we?"

"The County," Evans said.

"Interesting."

Evans leaned back in his seat. "Not as interesting as the murders you committed."

"I didn't kill anyone."

The captain sparked a match and lit a cigarette. "You killed yourself a long time ago, kid."

Jeremy turned his head from the captain and tipped the bottle. When he finished his drink he sucked the taste from his teeth. "My fingerprints are all over the surveillance equipment. Smart move, Captain. This wasn't even a sanctioned investigation, was it?"

The captain blew smoke over Evans' shoulder.

"Why me?" Jeremy asked.

"Convenience, Jeremy. Plausibility. Simplicity. Choose whatever reason you want."

Eventually, the car slowed and stopped at a gated road. Kittredge got out and opened the gate. When Evans pulled past, Kittredge closed it. He crossed behind the car and got in, squeezing his hands together for warmth.

Farther down the road they stopped and Kittredge pulled Jeremy from the back seat. The moon lit the hard, packed snow on the road.

The white gleamed in the light until it faded into darkness ahead where the road curved out of sight or simply ended. The other men climbed from the car, Evans eager to put him down. The captain fanned his jacket open and worked the buttons closed. Evans pulled his throw-away piece from his ankle holster—a dingy snub nose revolver like the one Benny had become a victim to, nothing special or significant, only something to serve its purpose.

"Any last words?" Evans asked and waited for Jeremy to respond. When he didn't, he motioned Jeremy forward with a tilt of his head.

Douglas firs shaded the ground from the light of the moon on each side of the road. Jeremy stepped beneath the darkness of the tree branches hearing his footsteps pack the snow. Ahead of him, the darkness slashed through the trees—nothing, peace. With his first couple of steps he thought of the sheet of plywood that covered Benny's window, the bull's eye his death had left on the ground. He continued to walk. With each step he felt increasingly lighter. When spring came, his footprints would melt away. There would be no indication that he had walked. It would be as if he had fallen there in the spot where the bullets roared through the cold air and brought him down.

△ △ △

Joe Ricker *received his B.A. in English from Ole Miss and his MFA from Goddard College in 2009. During that time he worked as a cab driver, innkeeper, bartender, and sales consultant. He has been published in* The Hangover, Thuglit, Rose and Thorn Journal, *and* Fifth Estate *magazines. "The Fallen" is his third publication with Level Best Books.*

Clamming Up

Dashiell Crowe

The rain came down sideways as the Logan Airport Express crossed the Cape Cod Canal, taking me off Cape for the first time in more years than I cared to count. At least it wasn't snow. Somewhere over Utah or Idaho or some other state a hard-assed female PI from Nobtucket had no frigging business in, where giant irrigation systems carve round discs of green on the semi-arid plains 35,000 feet below, a rising sun teased in a brief, blood-red appearance. It vanished in jet wash at 650 mph.

The rain followed us across the country, pinging harder than nails against the fuselage as the landing gear shuttered out of the belly of our plane. I caught only a fleeting glimpse of Mount Hood, looming like St. Helens' big bad brother over P-town west—Portland, Oregon. I had no business in Portland. I was headed to the coast to follow up on a more than probable insurance fraud Commonwealth Bay Casualty & Assurance would pay me big bucks to prove. Two million rode on the outcome—10% for me if I saved them the rest. Who couldn't use a quick two hundred grand?

Myron Fishbaum, the little schmuck who ran the Nobtucket Insurance and Real Estate Agency and had sold the liability policy, told me about President City, Oregon before I left. "Not much different from Nobtucket, Massachusetts—crowded in summer, dead in the winter—except for the casino."

Which gave me a brilliant idea.

I'd kill two birds with one bullet—prove poor, crippled, accident victim Jason Blodgett could get up out of his fancy electric wheelchair and dance the fandango; and get a feel for how the natives (meaning the year-round citizens of the city, not the Native Americans running the joint) felt about a casino in their midst.

I fast-talked Quentin Sears, President of the Nobtucket Chamber of Commerce, into backing my idea. The Wampanoags had been sniffing around for a location ever since they'd gained Federal tribal recognition. It looked more and more like Beacon Hill would approve casinos somewhere in the Commonwealth. The Nobtucket Chamber needed evidence, something more than cold statistics, on how a casino might affect their quaint little beach resort town. The chamber was footing the bill for my trip (economy class all the way), which meant I could afford to take Myron's case on contingency. I sure hoped old Blodgett was up to a little jig. I had my cameras ready.

As soon as I told the rental car agent off the airport I was headed over the coastal range to President City, he upgraded my economy car to a gas guzzling 4x4 SUV.

"Lucky for you we have one on the lot. Four by four or chains, and we don't allow chains on our rentals," the guy told me as I declined all the extra coverages and signed my life away on the credit card screen. "Oregon Department of Transportation requires it to travel through a snow zone. Don't want any latter-day Donner Parties." He laughed at his own humor.

I gave him my you-gotta-be-kidding-me eyebrow raise.

"Big fines if you get caught in a two-wheel drive without chains in your trunk." He handed me the keys and a map of Portland. "Have a nice day, Ms. Yeats."

It rained all the way over the mountains and down the other side. It rained on the coast highway as I threaded my way through a surprising line of traffic from the superstore shopping plaza and the turnoff to the casino to the fleabag Quentin Sears' secretary had booked over the Internet from the Cape. The place was at the opposite end of town.

Highway 101 through this long, narrow city had all the charm of Route 28 in South Yarmouth—motels, hotels and blocks of low-slung stores obscuring any glimpse of the sea only yards away to the west. The beginning of steep, timbered mountains loomed to the east.

Seagulls and crows dive-bombed each other in and out of a dense coastal fog as thick as my Yankee accent, as I pulled into the Economy Inn Cabins, Trailer Park and Family Campground. The night clerk—a woman about ten years my senior, with grey streaks frosting her black hair and trifocals fit for Mr. Magoo—signed me in. She took down the plate number and, seeing the rental agency sticker on the rear window, demanded payment in full in advance for the three nights I'd reserved.

"Standard operating procedure," she told me once the credit had cleared. "We don't get the highest class of people, no offense."

"None taken," I said. No point in pissing her off. I'm sure I fit right into her image of a fly-by-night about to stiff her for whatever I could. I'd purposely dressed in my oldest, most comfortable clothes for traveling—faded Roebucks jeans, a flannel shirt softened to threadbare in the wash, scuffed Boondockers and a worn leather Harley Davidson jacket. I'd replace the jacket with a windbreaker when I stalked Mr. Blodgett. Too conspicuous.

She handed me the key to cabin eight and recommended a place called Clem's Clam Shack for the best clam chowder I'd ever taste, bar none. I wasn't about to argue, not 'til I tasted whatever these West Coasters passed off for chowder. At least, she assured me, they made it with cream, not tomato.

I pulled out the map of President City I'd picked up at the IGA and asked the clerk where I could find Division Avenue, the street where Mr. Blodgett had last been seen motoring his wheelchair up the middle of the road.

She circled the motel and the street and drew a line to Clem's. They were both in easy walking distance and the street was only two blocks from the beach.

"How's the casino treating you?" I asked as I refolded the map and zipped it into the inside pocket of my jacket.

If she'd had little antennae—couldn't tell through the rat's nest of hair on her head—they would have shot right up straight. "Whaddaya mean?"

I shrugged. "You know, it help business any?"

She returned my shrug. "Not so's you'd notice. Few more people up that end of town in the winter maybe. You a gambler?"

"Me?" I pointed to my chest, shook my head. "Not really."

She gave a knowing nod. "My recommendation—leave your credit card in the car."

Cabin eight—one small room and a bath with shower, no tub—contained a bed sans headboard, an ancient wooden luggage rack, one straight-back wooden chair, no closet, no clothes hooks, and one towel I wouldn't let a stray cat take a piss on. Whatever art had once covered the lauan panel walls had left only screw holes.

I pulled back the big flower print bedspread, careful to avoid touching the ubiquitous stains. Underneath, a thin waffle-weave blanket covered greyish linens, once white. It smelled of mold and old sex. I gave the bed a thorough spray of extra strength RAID I'd picked up at the IGA, then pulled out the Navy poncho liner I carry in my duffel and covered the bed. I'd add the fleece blanket and pillow I'd bought at the airport before sacking out for the night.

I walked to Clem's in the rain, catching a break in the suppertime crowd for what turned out to be, if not the best chowder I'd ever eaten—and you have to go some to beat The Blue Whale or the old Backside Saloon—at least in the top ten. And that's saying something coming from this old Cape Codder.

By the time I got back to cabin eight, the smell of RAID had dissipated to a whiff on entering. It was no stronger than the smell of the cigar clamped between the teeth of the large gentleman in an oversized, rumpled suit sitting in my only chair.

He puffed and exhaled a grey ring. "Evening, Ms. Yeats."

I kept my hand on the doorknob, ready to fling the door shut and run for the SUV, wishing I'd somehow managed to smuggle my piece past the TSA at Logan. "Don't think I've had the pleasure," I said in a voice surprisingly calm and not at all in synch with the fluttery palpitations of my heart.

His thick lips rose in what he must have thought was a smile. "You can call me just Joe."

"What's your pleasure, Just Joe?"

His upper lip twitched, but he hid it well. "Understand you're a gambler."

"You're misinformed."

One bushy black eyebrow twitched with his upper lip. "Don't believe I am." He leaned back on two legs until the chair back hit the lauan wall. He puffed and blew out a series of smoke rings.

"Just for grins and giggles, suppose that I were."

All four legs hit the floor. "You're in the wrong section of town for the casino."

I nodded.

"Yet you're asking about it."

"Just making conversation with the desk clerk."

He nodded.

"What's it to you?"

"That was my next question," he said.

I shrugged. "Like I said, just passing the time while the woman checked me in."

"Her name's Flo."

"While Flo checked me in."

He grunted.

"You mind telling me who you are, beyond Just Joe?"

His right hand made a move toward his jacket.

My muscles tensed for a spring out the door.

He sensed my mood. He held his hand palm out like a traffic cop and used left thumb and forefinger to peel his left lapel off his chest. The fob, stuck inside his shirt's breast pocket, carried a silver shield. "President City PD. Vice."

My muscles relaxed. My teeth unclenched. I laughed.

"You think that's funny?"

"Hilarious."

His teeth chomped right through the stump of his cigar. It fell into his lap.

He jumped up, brushing wildly at the embers melting the threads of polyester to his crotch. "Son of a bitch."

I doused the towel in the sink and handed it to him. He took it without a word and scrubbed himself down.

"You know, we're in the same line of work," I said as he handed me back the towel.

His eyebrows went up.

I did the delicate opening of the jacket trick and pulled out my license. "Dalmatia Yeats, Private Investigations. Confidential. Trustworthy. Thorough." I handed him a card.

"And a bit out of your territory, not to mention not licensed here." His finger flicked the card. "You working?"

I nodded.

"Somebody sent you all the way across the country?" His back went up. "'Cause we got plenty a local talent."

I shrugged. "They needed somebody nobody knew. Our subject seems to have made the local guy."

"You carrying?"

I shook my head. "I flew."

He nodded. "Not like the old days."

"Roger that."

"Ex-. . .?"

"Navy," I said. "Master-at-Arms."

He pocketed the card, held out his hand. "Marine Recon."

I whistled. "Semper Fi."

That got a genuine smile.

He had a good handshake, strong but not overpowering. We both let go at the same time.

"Mind telling me why you're here, Ms. Yeats?"

"Dal."

"Strange name, Dalmatia."

"Stranger parents."

He nodded.

I told him half the reason I'd come to President City. Over a six pack of beer and a pint of Johnny Walker Red, he gave me more information about the ins and outs of housing a Native American casino than I could have gleaned on my own in three months. I made notes.

"You ever seen this guy?" I handed him two pictures of Jason Blodgett, one before the accident on Nobtucket's main street that left him wheelchair bound, one after. He'd aged twenty years in twelve months.

He fingered the second photo. "Moved in with his daughter. They live down near the beach in an old shack. Not far from here."

I nodded.

"Of course. Why else are you staying in this dump."

I nodded.

"Traffic division's always pulling him over in that damned chair—won't stay on the sidewalk."

"Anybody ever see him out of it?"

"Drugs or booze?"

"The chair. I don't care if he drinks himself blind. Commonwealth Bay's not insuring his liver."

He flicked the photo against his thumb. "Suspect fraud, do they?"

I nodded.

He shook his head. "Can't speak to that one. Your Commonwealth Bay hear something?"

"Scuttlebutt has him dancing the fandango."

Joe laughed. "I don't think so. We're not much into the fandango around here."

"You know much about him?"

"Some. Hard to miss a man like that. They say he comes from money. Lost a bundle in the crash. He's squeaking by on some kind of disability. His daughter's getting married sometime soon. Saw the announcement in the paper."

"You read the society section?"

He smiled. "Good detail work, sitting watching the wedding gifts while the wedding party's off celebrating. We watch all the announcements."

I nodded. "You wouldn't have any objection to my setting up a surveillance. I've only got three days."

"Not much time to catch someone, if he's catchable."

"It's the right three days."

"Scuttlebutt?"

I nodded.

He rose and walked toward the cabin door. "Knock yourself out. I'll let the rest of the—"

"Do me a favor, not a word to anyone else."

He thought a moment. I could see the gears turning. They stopped and he gave me a salute. "You got it. Three days. Good hunting." And he disappeared into the fog out the door.

□ □ □

I slept 'til noon, waking with half the cotton in Georgia in my mouth and the vague sensation of things crawling over my skin. I stood in the shower letting the water run until the hot ran cold.

I spent the afternoon in the library using their files and the Internet. In the evening I laid my plans.

The next day I set up my surveillance on a rise on the ocean side of Jason Blodgett's house. It was a small shingle-and-shake affair with one of those caps over the metal chimney that looks like a Spanish Conquistador's helmet.

Jason spent the morning on the back deck in his wheelchair, never once giving a single indication he might rise up like a phoenix. His daughter, a dowdy thing in misshapen sweats and a frown, flowed in and out of the house catering to his every whim. I would have slit my goddamn throat.

A breeze came up in the afternoon and he powered himself inside. I shivered in the weeds with my binoculars trained on the house, trying to see inside the windows. The sun glinting off the water reflected off the glass, sending back nothing but copper color and glare. When it set, I headed back to Clem's for another try at their chowder. I wasn't disappointed.

The third day—Sunday—dawned overcast and chilly. At least it wasn't raining—yet. I set up my surveillance on the hill above the small white church where Melissa Blodgett was scheduled to marry a bearded biker named Morgan Frump. He arrived on his Harley in a morning coat and jeans, his sidecar festooned with streamers and spray painted JUST MARRIED in neon pink.

She must have been desperate.

I understood why.

Jason Blodgett escorted his daughter into the church in his wheelchair. She wore white—a surprise given the size of her belly.

The church had set up a small tent outside for the reception. The guests piled in and I trained my paparazzi-style zoom lens on the dance floor.

As the band struck up a tune I couldn't say that I recognized— perhaps through no fault of my own—the bride took to the floor. Jason followed in his wheelchair. Then, with an effort that seemed more than human, his ham-sized hands pushed against the arms of the chair and he rose, until he stood—wobbling.

Like the Frankenstein monster, he took a step, then another. He placed his hands on his daughter's shoulders and he danced. It was hardly the fandango.

I got my pictures.

□   □   □

I checked out of cabin eight at nine the next morning. I made two stops before I left President City. One was at Clem's.

It rained all the way to the airport and half way home.

It was raining at Logan when we landed. It turned to snow half way to the Cape Cod Canal.

I checked in with Quentin Sears first thing the next morning. There'd be no bonus from the Chamber, but I'd known that up front. From Quentin's reaction, there'd be no casino anywhere near Nobtucket, if the Chamber had anything to say about it.

I waited until just before lunch to go see Myron Fishbaum in his cramped office behind the town hall.

"You get what we wanted?" he asked before I could sit down.

I sat. "Answer me something first."

Myron gave me the Fishbaum eye. It wasn't pleasant.

"Was Commonwealth Bay part of the insurance default bailout?"

Myron looked annoyed. "Why?"

"Was it?"

"Just about every insurance company was. Everybody knows that."

"But was Commonwealth Bay?"

"We're small potatoes. We lay off our risk on the big boys. Our partners weren't any better, or worse, than anyone else."

"And Jason Blodgett lost his shirt in that default."

"Could have." Myron shrugged. "Not my problem. He should have diversified."

He'd answered my question in his roundabout way, shading and slicing the truth.

"What has this got to do with his claim?"

"Nothing," I lied. "Just curious."

"And . . . ?"

"Sorry to tell you, the man's a cripple. Lots of pictures. Not the one you want."

All the air seemed to go out of Myron.

"But I did get a chance to talk to your Mr. Blodgett."

Myron almost jumped out of his chair.

"He had no idea who I was."

Myron relaxed, a bit.

"My guess, he'd settle for half, if you pay up now."

"Half. A million dollars?"

"Better than two."

"And I suppose you'll expect your ten per cent of the million."

"Of course. That was our deal. Ten percent of whatever I saved you."

I left him mulling it over and headed for the Blue Whale to test out their chowder.

□ □ □

Two weeks later I got a card from Mrs. Frump. It was a picture postcard of the honeymoon couple with Mickey at Disneyland. The message on the back read: "Dad got his due. Thanks."

Took six months and two lawyers to get my hundred grand out of Commonwealth Bay.

△ △ △

Dashiell Crowe, *a native Cape Codder and inveterate snoop, finds intrigue in every nook and cranny of the five villages of Nobtucket, from which he draws his characters and stories. Dashiell loves a good mystery, especially one where justice is not held hostage to the letter of the law. Dashiell hangs out at www.nobtucket.com and at www.DashiellCrowe.com.*

A Fortune To Be Had

Sharon Daynard

Meg Proctor waited until she heard the front door close before letting out a squeal of delight from inside the tiny dining room she'd commandeered for a Tea Room. Over the course of two months, she'd made more money than she had in a year working in community theatre and as a bank teller combined.

What started as a meager investment in a fortuneteller's license, a bolt of black velvet fabric, a few props from a second-hand shop, and a dozen candles with the intent to hone her improv skills and maybe turn a profit in the process, snowballed into a gold mine. Every palm she read, spirit she channeled, and tarot card she dealt, was dead-on. Heads nodded, cheeks flushed, and tears flowed as she whispered what only her clients and the dead could possibly know. Die-hard skeptics didn't know what to make of her. Believers heralded her as gifted and unparalleled, booking enough return sessions and private soirées to convince her to quit both her jobs. Meg Proctor was the hottest thing to hit Salem since the witch trials and thanks to Steve Jobs, she was going to make a fortune.

She danced into the foyer-waiting room and waved a fan of cash at her husband, Nate, before tucking it deep into her peasant-style top. "Two hundred and fifty dollars," she practically giggled.

"For dryer lint?" he asked, with a roll of his eyes.

"Two hundred for a cosmic poultice and a fifty-dollar tip for me. Tack that onto the fifty we got upfront for the old prune's reading and we just scored three hundred dollars from Mrs. Eleanor Danbury Fitzgerald-Finch of the Beacon Hill Fitzgerald-Finchs." She pursed her lips and turned up the tip of her nose with her index finger.

"You'd better light one of your cure-all candles and pray the old prune's nephew, Ellsworth Danbury the Third of the Boylston Street Law Offices of Danbury, Wincham, and Douglas, doesn't get wind of his aunt's spendthrift ways. You can't tell a rich old broad her house is haunted, sell her some dryer lint, and not expect it to come back and bite us in the ass." He pulled up the law firm's webpage on his iPhone and angled it toward her. "Nothing like a cease and desist order to put the kibosh on a get-rich-quick scheme."

"It's not my fault someone whispered in my ear about a former owner who blew his brains out in the study," she purred, nuzzling up to him. "Eleanor isn't going to be a problem. Old ladies adore me."

"Do me a favor and ease up on the hard-sell with the old dames," he said, switching to a game of Scrabble on the iPhone. "Most of them are living one Social Security check to the next. It's bad karma."

"Whatever." She shrugged off the notion with a sigh. "Did you ever dream selling fortunes would be this easy?"

"So far," Nate mumbled, dragging the S, C, and A tiles across the screen to form the word SCAM. "One of these times, I'm not going to find anything to whisper." He curled his index and middle fingers into air quotes around the word whisper. "And then what?"

"I'm an actor, I'll improvise. I'll throw out a few general statements, wait for one to register a hit with the client, and let them fill in the blanks." She leaned down and added a P to the word. "But if you do your job eavesdropping and engaging them in conversation, I won't have to resort to cold readings. If they pay with a check, you look up the town they live in. If they hand you a credit or debit card, you tell them you're having trouble running it through the machine and ask if they had a problem the last time they used it and where that might have been. You comment on the scarf they're wearing, the car they pulled up in, or their perfume. A few hits on Google, a little whisper in my ear, and ta-da!" She tapped the earpiece hidden beneath the black beaded shawl draped about her head and shoulders. "Madame Zielinska knows all."

"What Madame Zielinska doesn't know is when to stop," he grumbled. "It's just a matter of time before someone either comes back here looking for their money or runs to the cops. Two hundred dollars for dryer lint, are you insane?"

"Cosmic poultice," she corrected, adjusting the gold lamé turban on his head. "I did my homework before we ever started this venture. Two hundred dollars is well within the bounds of what the others are charging. Not so low the client thinks it's junk and not so high they run to the cops if and when they figure out it is. Besides, it's all in fun, Nate."

"You think this is fun?" He gestured to his outfit. "You've got me dressed up like Lawrence of Arabia goes Goth—black pants, black shirt, black tie and a bonnet straight out of *La Cage aux Folles*. It was fun five weeks ago when it wasn't about the money. What you're running now is a con."

"You're looking at this all wrong, baby." She offered a pout as she ran a red lacquered nail along his jawbone. "I tell people what they want to hear, what they need to hear. They're better off without the jerk that dumped them. There's a job offer on the horizon. Dear sweet dead dad is smiling down at them from the great beyond. Half the people that walk through that door are desperate for entertainment. The other half are desperate for absolution. We provide both. Desperation comes with a price, Nate, and in Madame Zielinska's Tea Room it can run as much as three hundred dollars."

□ □ □

Biddy and Patience Pendergast made their way along the brick walkway, sidestepping seasonal swarms of witches, vampires, freaks, and fairies. They stopped outside a less-than-stately Victorian with a freshly painted plaque above its doorbell.

MADAME ZIELINSKA'S TEA ROOM
Readings By Appointment Only

"Madame Zielinska, my rosy red behind. Suzie Swindle is more like it," Biddy sneered. "I guarantee you tomorrow morning that sign'll come down faster than a pair of panties on prom night."

Patience flushed a deep crimson. "Please, Biddy. You promised to be open-minded. Like Papa always said, if you can't say something nice about someone—"

"It's probably because they're wearing a court-ordered ankle bracelet," Biddy finished her sister's sentence.

"Papa never said anything of the sort." Patience adjusted the pillbox hat on her head, smoothed the bodice of her floral printed rayon dress, and jabbed the doorbell with a white-gloved index finger.

"How would you know?" Biddy argued. "I'm three years older than you. Do you have any idea how many conversations I might have had with Papa in those three formative years? Hundreds, maybe thousands, of father-firstborn chitchats, and I distinctly remember many a night Papa tucking me into bed after I recited my prayers, kissing me on the forehead, and warning me about heathen fortune tellers wearing court-ordered ankle bracelets, just before he turned my light out."

"Court-ordered ankle bracelets didn't exist eighty-four years ago." She jabbed the doorbell a second, third, and forth time.

"Court-ordered ankle bracelets, chain gang shackles, inmate leg irons, they're all the same thing," Biddy shot back as a man dressed completely in black except for a gold turban, holding a bright orange bowl filled with candy opened the door. "Our condolences on the passing of your camel, Aladdin," she muttered, scanning him from head to toe.

He looked at the two elderly women dressed in their Sunday best and let out a muted sigh. "Do you have an appointment?" He pointed to the plaque.

Biddy reached deep into the bowl and dropped a handful of candy into her purse as she brushed past him into the foyer. "If Madame Zielinska were any kind of a psychic, she'd know we were coming."

Patience mouthed the words "I'm so sorry" and offered a smile to the man as she followed her sister.

"Raking in the big bucks, are you?" Biddy asked, scanning the foyer. Eight empty folding chairs lined its walls and a battered mahogany podium, that looked like it had been salvaged from the local landfill, stood sentinel at the inner doorway. Black velvet drapes obscured the windows and twinkling strands of miniature clear Christmas lights zigzagged along the black painted ceiling.

"The place smells like nine cats and one litter box," she muttered, taking a seat beneath a large oval mirror rimmed with black silk roses.

"Madame Zielinska is in meditation," the man declared from the podium. "I'll announce you shortly."

"That would be splendid," Patience all but gushed.

"Simply splendid," Biddy mocked.

"Isn't this fun, Biddy?" Patience asked. "We haven't been on an adventure in years."

"An adventure? Are you really going to call throwing away good money on riffraff an adventure? We could have had an adventure back home in good old Portsmouth, New Hampshire, but no, you had to whine until I drove you all the way down to the Witch City on Halloween of all days."

"But that crumpled pack of Salems we found in the attic . . .? It had to be Marla's. Papa didn't smoke. The Universe was leading us here."

"The Universe," Biddy scoffed. "It was a GPS and it would have been nice if the damned thing could have mentioned that pothole before we hit it. Do you have any idea how much a new tire and a hubcap are going to cost? At least two hundred bucks."

"It's all part of a greater plan," Patience reminded with a pat to her sister's knee.

"Greater plan, my Aunt Millie's bloomers," Biddy groused, noticing a stuffed raven perched on the podium. "Texting the Grim Reaper for decorating tips?" she asked the man.

"A few pastel throw pillows would brighten the room right up," Patience offered with a scrunch of her nose.

The man rolled his eyes and held the iPhone out to them. "Playing Scrabble."

"Biddy has one of those cell phones," Patience said. "She's very high-tech. Biddy even has a computer and a VCR."

"Amazing," the man mumbled.

"Are you a computer person?" Patience asked him.

"Used to be," he answered, "until I got laid-off a couple of years ago."

"A couple of years ago, you poor thing." Patience shook her head. "At least your wife's doing well."

The man looked up from his game to Patience as the inference sunk in.

"I'm sorry," Patience apologized. "I noticed the new Rolex and you're still wearing a wedding band. Jewelry is one of the things people part with first when money's tight."

"She's doing good, real good," the man answered before returning to his game.

"Of course she is," Biddy mumbled. "She's the one running this con."

"Biddy, please," Patience cautioned. "We're doing this for Papa. His soul can't rest until—"

"Papa's soul has been resting just fine all these years."

"How can it knowing this doesn't belong with us?" Patience pulled a ring from her purse. "The emerald alone has to be two and a half carats and I counted sixty-eight small diamonds about the stone and down along the band. It was Marla's engagement ring."

Biddy ripped the ring from Patience's hand and held it tight in her fist. "Are you insane bringing this here?" She looked from her sister to the man. He appeared too engrossed in his game of Scrabble to have heard the exchange.

"I thought if Madame Zielinska held it she might be able to glean a bit of information from it or contact Marla's spirit. It's called psychometry," Patience whispered.

"We don't even know if these stones are real." Biddy checked to see if the man was still preoccupied before swiping the ring across the mirror above their seats. Her jaw dropped at the scar left in its wake. Settling back into her chair, she signaled her sister to keep quiet.

"I told you it was real," Patience whispered.

"Fine, it's real. But there's nothing that says it belonged to Marla."

"Of course there is," Patience said. "The initials MAK and DPH are etched inside the band. Marla Adelaide Kroft and that monster Douglas Preston Hennessey. We've had nothing but bad luck since we found it in the attic. First the hot water heater had to be replaced and then the washing machine. Last week it was the microwave. The cat's gone missing and—"

"Keep your voice down," Biddy warned. "The King of the Gypsies over there is listening to every word we say."

"Madame Zielinska won't be able to help us if you don't have an open mind about all of this."

"An open mind," Biddy sneered, dropping the ring into her purse. "An open wallet is more like it. Hey, Aladdin," she called to the man. "How much is this fiasco going to cost us?"

"Readings start at fifty dollars," he answered, looking up.

"Fifty dollars!" Biddy barked. "For a buck ninety-nine I can buy a Ouija board at a five and dime and commune with the dead to my heart's content."

"It's not costing us anything. It's Papa's money." Patience dipped into her purse and retrieved a yellowed envelope. "Fifty dollars," she announced, pulling a single crisp bill from it.

The man put down his iPhone, held up a marker, and motioned Patience to bring the bill to him. With two quick dashes he marked it with an X. A scowl crossed his face as he looked at Patience and announced, "It's counterfeit."

"Counterfeit," she almost choked on the word. "It can't be."

He held up the bill and pointed to the black X. "Yellow is okay. Black is counterfeit."

"Oh, Papa," Patience sighed, looking up at the ceiling. "First that ring and now this. What next, a moonshine still in the potting shed?"

"Ixnay on the ingray," Biddy hissed.

"Your Papa was into counterfeiting, was he?" the man asked.

"He was not," Patience's voice raised a decibel or two higher than acceptable in friendly conversation. "Our father was a reverend, The Reverend Ephraim Pendergast."

"Reverend or not, counterfeit detector pens don't lie." He handed her back the fifty.

"And according to Detective Lance Lennon of the Portsmouth PD Bunco Squad, they don't work on bills printed before 1959," Biddy shot at him. "What's the year on that?" she asked Patience.

"1957." She handed the bill back to the man without looking at it. "That's why I picked this particular fortune telling parlor. 1957 Providence Way. It was kismet."

"Welcome to Madame Zielinska's Tea Room," a woman's voice echoed from inside the house. "Please, join me."

□   □   □

"Patience is such a lovely name." Madame Zielinska smiled, dipping her head slightly as she greeted her guest. She turned her attention to Biddy and murmured the same.

"No it's not," Biddy groused. "It was a riot when I was four. At eighty-four it's a given." Madam Zielinska's head dipped a bit more; her smile broadened a bit more.

"Prove to Biddy you're a real psychic," Patience urged. "Pull her name out of the cosmos and she'll stop this juvenile behavior.

It'll be easy for you. There isn't a single one of our dead relatives that doesn't know Biddy's given name." She turned to her sister and screwed her face into a knot.

"Go ahead, wow me," Biddy egged her on. "I'll even give you hint. It ain't short for Biddeford."

Madame Zielinska lit the candle in front of her, closed her eyes and took in a deep breath. She lifted her hands above her head and swayed her upper body as she hummed.

"Look, Gypsy Rose Lee, I didn't drive forty-five miles down here in a twenty-year-old Corolla held together with duct tape and bubblegum just to play Name That Tune," Biddy snipped.

A grin teased at the woman's face before expanding into a full blown smile. She opened her eyes, dropped her hands to the table and revealed, "Obedience Victorine Pendergast, born November 27, 1927 to Camille Dubois Pendergast and Ephraim Mason Pendergast." Patience let out a gasp. Biddy snorted. "And her charming sister Patience Genevieve Pendergast, born June 1, 1931. Your parents are in this room with us."

"They are not," Biddy groaned. "They're buried at Calvary Cemetery in Portsmouth."

"Your mother passed over when you were twelve and Patience only nine," Madame Zielinska went on. "The Reverend joined his bride on July 18, 1988. He's telling me it was an accident."

"For the love of Pete," Biddy sneered. "He drove his car off the Kancamagus Highway during a rain storm. It was in all the papers. What color was the car he was driving? Better yet, how many miles were on it and what was the license plate number?"

"I can only relay what those who have passed over tell me."

"What was our father wearing the day he died?" Biddy pressed. "What color shirt did we bury him in? Who was our mother's maid of honor? What was her favorite flower? Go ahead ask them. After all these years, they must be dying to chat."

"Enough, Biddy," Patience reprimanded. "You're giving off

negative energy."

"We all have auras," the fortuneteller said with a smile. "Yours is a lovely shade of rose, Patience. You're sensitive, artistic, and compassionate. And yours, Biddy—"

"Is shit-brown," Biddy grumbled.

"There's a darkness about the two of you," the fortuneteller went on.

"Bet it's that shitty aura of mine," Biddy leaned over and whispered to Patience.

"I see the letter M and the color green, emerald green."

"Yes!" Patience practically came out of her seat.

"This is ridiculous," Biddy groused. "She was listening in on our conversation the whole time we were in the waiting room."

"That's not true." Patience shook her head. "She knew your name was Obedience. We never mentioned that in the waiting room. She knew our birthdates and Mother's name. She even knew the day Papa died and—"

"Another woman is trying to get through," Madame Zielinska spoke in a whisper. "I can't make out her name. Carla or Darla maybe?"

"Marla!" Patience was on the edge of her seat. "Her name is Marla."

"She's sobbing. She's telling me there's a cursed object in your possession. A ring."

"Marla's engagement ring," Patience gasped.

"The man who gave it to her was from a wealthy family in Maine."

"Bangor," Patience nodded. "He was a skunk and a womanizer."

"Until the curse is lifted, there will be no peace for either of you."

"I told you," Patience shot a look at Biddy. "We're cursed."

"Well, lucky for us we wandered into Madame Zielinska's One Stop Shopping for the Damned." Biddy rolled her eyes. "How many blessed candles is it going to take to rid the curse?" she asked the fortuneteller. "One this week, two the next? A year from now we'll still be coming back here listening to this malarkey and lighting candles while you pocket every penny we have. It's a damn shame no one from the afterlife bothered to tell you we're broke. Bankrupt, busted, shit out of luck and cash."

"I prefer to think of it as temporarily insolvent." Patience flushed a deep scarlet. "When we found Papa's keepsake box in the attic with Marla's ring and a fifty dollar bill, I took it as a sign. I thought it was going bring us good fortune."

"Well, the joke was on us, Patience," Biddy cackled, retrieving the ring from her purse. "All this got us was a busted tire and another bill we can't pay." She held the ring up, twisted it ever so slightly and watched as the glow of the candle played off the stones and flickered in the fortuneteller's eyes.

"Please, we've come all this way," Patience pleaded. "There must be something you can do about the curse. Can't you see we're desperate? We'll send you a few dollars every month—"

"We will not." Biddy dropped the ring back into her purse.

"But the curse and Papa's soul . . ." Patience's eyes welled up.

"We're leaving. Now, Patience."

A single tear ran down Patience's withered cheek as she turned to the fortuneteller and begged, "Please, help us."

"Your father wants you to leave the ring with me," Madame Zielinska said.

"He does not," Biddy countered. "Patience, we're leaving."

"I'll donate my services to lift the curse and return the ring to Marla's heirs," the fortuneteller continued.

"That's very generous of you." Patience dabbed the corners of her eyes with a white-gloved finger.

"No, it's not," Biddy snapped at her sister. "We're taking that ring to a pawn shop, getting the tire fixed, and going home."

"And . . ." Madame Zielinska smiled. "Your father has asked that

I pay you two hundred dollars for your trouble."

"Did you hear that, Biddy? That'll pay for a new tire."

Biddy jutted her jaw from side to side, looked at her sister, and back to the fortuneteller. "I don't think you heard my father right. He said ten thousand."

"Biddy!"

She shot a glare at Patience. "Do you have any idea how much that ring might be worth?"

"It doesn't matter. This isn't about money, Biddy. It's about doing what's right."

"Ten thousand dollars," Biddy repeated the price to the fortuneteller.

"I'm sorry, but that's not poss—"

"We'll take three hundred," Patience blurted out.

"Three hundred dollars!" Biddy screeched at her sister.

"Three hundred dollars it is." Madame Zielinska blew out the candle, dropped her head, and shrouded a smirk behind her black scarf.

"And we want it all in twenties," Patience added, steering Biddy out of the room. "Folks look at you cross-eyed when you hand them a fifty."

"Ladies." Nate Proctor smiled as he handed Patience the money. "Five hundred dollars in twenties," he said, shooting a glare at his wife. "We wouldn't want your father thinking anyone was taken advantage of."

"Bless you." Patience hugged him. "God bless both of you."

"Five hundred friggin' dollars," Biddy grumbled under her breath. "Oh, someone's been taken advantage of all right." She pulled the ring from her purse and held it tight in her fist for a second or two before relinquishing it to the fortuneteller.

"I hope that ring is cursed," Biddy muttered her sentiments to the Universe as she and Patience walked out the door and down the walkway.

"Amateurs," Meg Proctor whispered to her husband as she slipped the ring on her finger.

◻ ◻ ◻

Biddy Pendergast waited until she heard the front door lock engage before letting out a squeal of delight. "It never gets old, does it?" she giggled, pulling the emerald ring from her purse.

"Amateurs." Patience shook her head as she fanned through the twenties. "Next stop Mrs. Rita's Psychic Readings, 93 Grant Ave." She pulled a yellowed envelope from her purse and checked the $50 bill inside. "The last two digits in the serial number are 93 and good old Ulysses S. Grant is staring straight up at me from the front of the bill. Why, sister, I do believe it's kismet."

"How many more of those costume jewelry rings and phony fifties do we have?" Biddy asked as she clicked the remote starter to a late-model Mercedes parked two doors down.

"Enough to make us a fortune."

△ △ △

Sharon Daynard *has crossed paths with a serial killer, testified before grand juries, and taken lie detector tests. Her short stories have appeared in magazines and anthologies in both the US and Canada. She is a member of the New England chapter of Sisters in Crime.* www.sadaynard.com

The Armies of the Night

Janice Law

Vivian heard the children's voices and stopped, her hands poised over the sink where she was washing the last of the breakfast dishes, neglected in the morning rush. House tidied, some calls made, some orders taken. Ever since the company's skin care products had been shown to deter bugs, spring was a big sale time. Good thing, too, with two children and health insurance and town taxes coming again all too soon.

That was why she'd come back. The house was free and clear and big enough, and, as her friend Roberta said, Vivian could work the e-representative business from anywhere with a fast connection. True. So there was no reason, no logical reason to stay away.

A good building. That was what the realtor had said, for yes, Vivian had considered selling it. Had intended to sell it. A good sound foundation, roof okay, kitchen—but there the realtor, a chunky woman with a good haircut and expensive shoes, had paused. "Needs updating. Really a complete renovation."

Vivian agreed that the appliances were ancient. "Everything works," she said, but hesitantly, for even now, after so many years and a life of her own, it was hard to see the house clearly when every room vibrated with the pressure of memory.

"Listen, put in new cabinets, granite counters, a good hardwood floor, and you'd add $30,000 to the asking price easy." The realtor had a way of widening her shiny blue eyes with any mention of money.

"It would be expensive," Vivian said. "It might cost me that much out of pocket to have the work done."

"To get top dollar," the agent began.

Vivian didn't hear the rest of her spiel. She had no money to upgrade the house, and it would have to sell as is. And why wouldn't it? The land was good, five acres with trees and a small pond. The house was sound and could be made beautiful.

Vivian took a deep breath and focused on the dishes. It had just been bad luck that the real estate bubble burst when it did. A few months more and the house would have been in the hands of someone keen on new floors, modern counters, stainless steel appliances, and other accoutrements of chic housing, while Vivian and the children decamped for somewhere far away, because she could work from home as long as she had a fast Internet connection.

Instead, here they were in the rambling old farmhouse with the good framework and the isolated location. To be sure, there were neighbors now. On winter evenings, Vivian could see the lights of the Utleys and the Savics glimmering through the trees, and if she wasn't mistaken, those were the two younger Morse boys playing with David and Matt. The pond was a real magnet, along with the tree house and the tire swing, which was so old and outdated as to be a novelty.

Her boys loved the place. Loved the stairs, loved the attic with the heavy beams and the little roof window. Loved the screen porch with the yellow light, loved "the woods," the acre or so of oaks and maples.

"A paradise," Roberta had said when she visited. Roberta was a college friend, tall and lanky with red hair and what Vivian had always thought of as a sexy pout. "You never said you grew up in Eden."

Vivian had realized that she had never mentioned anything at all about the house or her family. Perhaps that meant she and Roberta were not quite as good friends as she had thought. "Oh, you know how it is," she'd said. "When you're growing up, you can't wait to get away to the bright lights."

"And then you come back and see the possibilities," Roberta said, casting a covetous eye on the siding—wide and old fashioned with courses of shingles up top. A brute to paint.

"It could be done up—but I'm glad I didn't with the market."

Roberta, who loved decorating and had a grasp of design, was horrified. "Oh, you couldn't sell it!"

Standing at the sink, Vivian wondered about that. Was it is one thing to inherit but another thing to sell? She shook her head at this nonsense, rinsed off the dishes, and dried her hands. Imagination was her enemy; she'd learned that early, and, unbidden, she heard her father's voice in some neglected corner of her memory saying, "Vivian has such an imagination. A vivid imagination for Vivian," in a tone of voice that left no doubt that this was undesirable. Very. And until she returned to the house, she'd done a good job of keeping stray thoughts at bay.

A lifetime of training, she might say, but just the same she kept looking out the window and straining her ears. With children, too much noise was bad, but too little was worse. Was it good or bad that they loved the house? How they had taken to the place.

She'd tried at first to keep them from the wood; there were snakes, she said. But then the boys visited the state forest where a naturalist showed them snakes and let them touch them. The ranger taught them about the only two dangerous ones, the copperhead and the rattler, and told them how the latter was endangered, all information that they related to her with high excitement.

Now they had built a fort in the woods, and any time she needed to find them, Vivian had to go down the path past the barn, dark and smelling of dust and old hay just as it always had. Amazing how smells linger. No surprise her father's cigarette smoke had permeated the walls, but that the smell of a barn should linger was unexpected.

She never went into it. She'd made the tour with the realtor, seen the stalls, the hayloft, heard it described as a "wonderful horse property," and gotten herself back out into the sunshine. Naturally, the boys, with the special perversity of her offspring, loved the barn, too. She'd vetoed a pony, but now they were agitating to join the 4-H and have a steer or a pig. "Or chickens? Couldn't we at least have chickens?"

Sooner or later Vivian knew that something alive and demanding would arrive to inhabit the barn. She'd have to supervise and be in and out with the electrician, for surely the wiring was unsafe, or with the plumber, because she couldn't remember if there was running water or just the old hand pump. Then she'd be inside, half blinded by the combination of the glare from the big double doors and the shadows that fell from the loft. Remembering.

You can look into such a barn and not know what you're seeing. You see shapes, silhouettes, outlines that might be something or might be nothing, and you scream at an old rug or a bundled-up tarp, because, "Vivian has such an imagination." You sniff the air—ah, mistake. The eye, so quick, can be fooled, but the nose, that more primitive organ, detects all and forgets nothing. Never. She thought that was when her father started to talk about her imagination in a negative way.

Her eye caught a blond patch—a towhead, David her oldest, leading the way across the little meadow beside the pond. David was the leader, a boy with imagination, the devisor of games and designer of strange and probably dangerous constructions. What was that glint? What was he up to now? A shovel. She'd have to be sure he returned that to the garden.

They'd be digging somewhere; that was the latest thing, and Vivian gave a little shiver. She'd gotten a shock a week or so ago when she came across David burying a turkey leg, part of a carcass she'd been saving for soup stock. She'd given a little cry and then had to hide her distress and pretend interest, because David had wanted to see if it would get maggots and how it would change and whether they could detect it later with Jimbo, who was the Savic's spaniel.

Vivian thought that possibly her father had been right after all, that she was cursed with too much imagination. Her fears were foolish, really, and without foundation. The boys' excavations were just the latest craze, the product of too many TV crime shows. They liked *CSI* and *Bones* and something else with lots of letters. They were fascinated by the computers, by the images of fingerprints, by the revelations of blood, by easy answers. All unwholesome, Vivian thought. Even a steer might be better.

But they liked finding out. They were entranced, she saw, by secrets uncovered, by crimes come to light, by the mastery of science and the almighty computer. David's current hope, if she remembered correctly, was the discovery of an Indian burial ground.

"Native American burial ground," Matt had corrected. Matt was ten, less imaginative, more precise. David would borrow the garden tools or some of her dad's old saws; Matt was the hope of having them returned.

He was carrying something, too, she realized, and she stepped from the window to the screen door and looked out. He had the pickax, and Vivian caught her breath. It was surely her dad's and where had the boys unearthed that from? Somewhere in the barn? Or from the shed, the little lean-to that adjoined the garage?

"A separate garage!" Roberta had said. "You're so lucky. I hate these new houses with the garage stuck onto the front of the house and all you see are those immense run up doors."

She'd insisted on seeing the interior. "And is this a closet?"

"Leads to the shed," Vivian said, and mumbled something about the old days and a long ago pony. "Before my time."

Roberta had tried the door just the same and was a bit put out that it was locked. Roberta was big on useable space. "You don't know what you have here!"

Vivian thought she did but said nothing. She'd been glad the door was locked and content to leave it that way. It had always been locked when she was a child. Always. Though at this thought, Vivian paused. Was that right? Or had Mother used it for some of her preserves? Had she? Maybe it was only after she left that the shed was locked, because her dad liked to keep his tools clean and tidy and "away from small hands." Maybe so.

Now, years later, the wood around the hasp had probably rotted or the boys had levered it open; they'd found a cat's paw a few weeks earlier and had amused themselves prying nails out of some old timbers. She could foresee anything closed would soon be opened, and small hands would help themselves to whatever had been locked up and laid away.

I should never have come, Vivian thought, I should never have brought the boys here. But that was just nerves and imagination. Everything had just been imagination—imagination and grief, grief for her mother, grief at her father's transformation, grief at the unexpected revelations of an overactive imagination.

Mother's loss was the start, though Vivian thought "loss" was not the right word. Mother had vanished, abandoning her and her father to gloom and anger. Her father drank a lot, while Vivian obsessively awaited letters, a phone call, a strange car in the drive with Mother at the wheel. She'd been hysterical, then angry, then depressed, and then, as she reached the queasy shores of adolescence, uneasy, deeply, deeply uneasy.

This was bad mental ground, and the reason she had started saving money like a mad thing at sixteen, forswearing the cosmetics and records and new clothes her friends favored. She hid every penny in a punky beam in the attic and bided her time, though on the surface, things were better. In some ways.

Her father was gone a lot at night. At first she'd been frightened by the shadows in the old house and wanted him home. She disliked the black night beyond the yellow arc carved by the porch light, and the late headlights sweeping across her window disturbed her sleep.

The next day, her father would be quiet and tired, with no outbursts of temper and nothing much to say. On those mornings, Vivian knew she would be asked nothing, though she was sometimes aware of his watching her closely.

Children do like to pose awkward questions, so she must have asked at some point, before asking anything became impossible. "I have to work. I need to put food on the table." That's what he'd said, although even at eight, the year Mother disappeared, Vivian had known that was a lie. Father worked at the feed store that opened at 7:30 a.m. and closed by 5:00 p.m. Everyone in town knew that.

"Late deliveries," he'd say if she heard something in the hall and came to the top of the stairs. Then he was out the door, though the grandfather clock in the hall chimed eleven or even twelve, and no one delivered to Henderson's Feed and Farm Supply at those hours.

So it must have been around the same time, when Vivian was eight or nine or ten, that the shed was locked, and it was not long after that she started to avoid the barn, where the car stopped on those nights when there were "late deliveries" at the feed store. She knew that, because she'd wake to the lights, white then red, and the sound of the car idling. In warm weather, she'd hear the scrape and rattle of the barn door, and various thoughts that lived in the shadows behind her bureau would seep into her mind.

The woods came next on places to avoid. "You keep the hell out of there," her father said. "You get bitten by a snake or cut on that old barbed wire you'll need a tetanus shot." He must have been trying to take out some of the wire and the old posts, because one day he had some bad scratches, and later Vivian noticed that there was fresh dug dirt up under the trees.

Had she said something about the fence? Vivian didn't know. She remembered him giving her what she thought of as an evil look. "You play in the front yard," he said. But who was she to play with? Vivian avoided having other children home. Dirty and smelling of smoke, the house was not as it should have been. It was all too evident that her mother was gone, that things were amiss. Anyone could tell that, and some people talked about it, too.

Vivian must have been seventeen when she finally asked. Not long before she took her savings and as much cash as she could collect from the house and accepted the oldest Parkhust boy's offer of a lift to the train station. She had grown tall, and with walking everywhere and working in the garden and at the diner, she was a sturdy girl, who could take care of herself. Vivian had to laugh in retrospect. She'd managed all right, with her eyes half shut. Wise child.

But one night—was it night? Vivian rather thought so, one night then, when Father was drinking. It struck Vivian that he had drunk a lot after Mother disappeared though not so much during the period of the "night deliveries." What did that mean?

He'd been sitting glum at the table with a six-pack and a bottle of Jack Daniels. "Where do you go?" she asked, just like that, as if they discussed everything all the time and half the property was not taboo for her and perhaps—though she had not thought of it until just this minute—half taboo for him, too, for he never entered her room and never came by the pond.

"Go? What do you mean, go?" Too drunk then, to natter on about the erratic schedules of the feed companies.

"When you go out? At night?" Even remembering it, Vivian felt sweat running down her spine.

He poured some more whiskey, and Vivian thought he was not going to answer. She waited. Her life with Father had taught her patience.

"I'm fighting the Armies of the Night," he said.

She had known in that moment that she had to leave—and soon. She never looked back. She cultivated forgetfulness, found work, and made new friends. She met Peter, her husband, a great piece of good luck that lasted until a drunk driver crossed the median on the Sawmill and smashed head on into his car, leaving her a widow with two small boys and the need for a cheap roof over her head.

So here she was at the old kitchen sink with a ton weight of memories and bad nerves, working on forgetfulness and the suppression of imagination, while her children—but here she stopped, alert maternal ears picking up on a different note. "Mom! Mom!"

Injury? A tumble into the pond? Some disaster?

"Look what we've found!"

She stepped onto the porch, at once relieved and wary, as they came running down the path past the barn. Shovel and pick discarded, shirts flying. What would it be this time? A captive frog to be explained and released? Turkey feathers, suitable for a headdress? A bit of an old plow or harness? Really, as her friend Roberta had said, "This is a wonderful place for children."

"We've found it," David yelled. "We've found the burial place!" He had something in his hand, a bone, brownish and old looking, but not that old. That's what stuck in Vivian's mind, just that idea, not that old.

"There's more!" Matt shouted. Matt, who was accurate and unimaginative. "There's more!"

Neither of them noticed her face turn white. "An old horse," she said. "A deer."

But they were not fooled and neither was she. She remembered her first aid training. The bone was a femur and it was too heavy for a deer, too light for a horse.

"I found a rib," said the youngest Morris boy. And he held it up.

"A soldier of the Army of the Night," Vivian said without thinking. Then she looked at their eager faces and thought of their future and took a deep breath. Her father had darkened her life but he would not damage theirs. Not if she could help it.

"We must put them back," she said. "If it's a burial ground. We must cover them over and leave them in peace. Because they were warriors."

The boys' excited faces turned solemn. There was a moment's hesitation, as the temptation of a souvenir for show and tell at school was slowly overcome by the solemnity of disturbing fighting men. "You can leave some turkey feathers," Vivian said. "As a peace offering for disturbing them."

"The Native Americans would have used tobacco," said Matt.

"And we have some!" cried David. "I know where they are!" He wheeled away followed by the others. To the shed, Vivian saw, where, yes, they had discovered a cache of her father's cigarettes. Ancient Chesterfields.

It was so apt it almost made her laugh, but she controlled herself; she'd had plenty of practice. "That will do nicely," she said as she walked with them down the field. "Those cigarettes will be exactly right."

△ △ △

Janice Law's *novel,* The Big Payoff, *was nominated for an Edgar®️ award. Her recent novels are* The Lost Diaries of Iris Weed, *and* Voices. *Her short stories have appeared in* The Best American Mystery Stories, The World's Finest Mystery and Crime Stories, Alfred Hitchcock's Fifty Years of Crime and Suspense, Riptide, Still Waters, *and* Paraspheres. *She and her husband live in Hampton, Connecticut.*

In the Rip

Barbara Ross

P hil broke up with me on New Year's morning as if propelled by the force of some terrible resolution. I was crushed.

Truth? I wasn't in love with Phil. But when I looked into the future, I'd always seen *me* breaking up with *him*. "I'm sorry, Phil," I would say, "but you knew it couldn't last." Sometimes I would add, "I've found somebody else. I suggest you do, too."

Then Phil broke up with me. He'd been thinking about it for some time he informed me, during a rather heated conversation carried on while he threw his things in a Gristedes bag and headed out the door. He thought it was kinder to tell me after the holidays. May I never again be the victim of such kindness.

Because what really hurt was the knowledge that while I was going about my life, buying Christmas gifts, making reservations for New Year's Eve, thinking everything was fine, Phil was living a completely different reality. I was picturing a perfect New York City New Year's morning with Bloody Marys and bagels fresh from the deli, and Phil was planning his exit. It was as if there was a rip in the time-space continuum and Phil and I were operating on completely separate planes.

□ □ □

So the disappointing Phil was gone and I was alone. At least I had my job. Or so I thought.

I'd worked at Drucker/Feingold since I'd first come to New York. Dickie Drucker and Stewie Feingold had been best friends in high school, and when I started, they were still giddy from realizing their dream of opening an ad agency. The job posting I answered described Drucker/Feingold as a "boutique," but in those early days it was more like a card table set up on the sidewalk. They hired me as their administrative assistant. I was as excited as they were. It was my first job.

You could tell what must have attracted Dickie and Stewie to each other back in high school. They were the two shortest men I'd ever seen. Dickie was regular-person short, a very short, normal man. Stewie was tinier still. Perfectly formed, even handsome, but at least half a foot shy of five feet. I towered over them, though I'm just average height. I could've taken both of them out in a single tackle.

Dickie was the word man; Stewie did the visuals. Their campaigns were fresh and the clients loved them. They were also the two most disorganized people I'd ever met. Pretty soon, I started maintaining the project schedules, herding the free-lancers, even managing the clients who called me knowing they wouldn't get anything out of Dickie or Stewie. They did the creative work. I kept the office humming.

Last summer, after five years, I'd finally convinced them I was doing too many important things to be making coffee. So we hired Melanie. Dickie and Stewie loved her instantly. I frankly didn't get it, but she was the best of the bad lot we interviewed and I reluctantly went along.

Melanie seemed an odd hire for us because she was so tall. Our agency was in a neighborhood where we saw plenty of models. Sometimes on the street Melanie was mistaken for one. I could tell she liked it. But where models were all angles and skeletons, Melanie was boneless. She was like one of those rag dolls some clueless relative buys you at a crafts fair, a doll that can't stand up or even sit, and you wonder, what the heck am I supposed to do with this stupid thing? Even Melanie's face, with its round, perfectly symmetrical features, was as soft as pudding.

Melanie wasn't the ambitious girl I'd been. She was content to answer the phone, send faxes and spend all her in-between time playing games on her computer while simultaneously texting with her friends.

OMG! Did you see how blitzed SP was at the party????

LOL! And her dress was fug

So fug!

And so on all day long. I tried to point out some ways she could be useful, but she wasn't interested, and I soon gave up. Not that she was bad company. We shared the open reception area outside Stewie and Dickie's office. We were all pretty happy. I thought we would go on that way forever. Except we didn't.

In November, Amalgamated Magnacorp bought Frodicker Industries which manufactured and distributed Clamay Refreshenating Face Cream, our little firm's largest account. In December, word came that Amalgamated Magna would be moving all Frodicker's accounts to their own giant agency. The economy was terrible and the advertising business especially so, but I didn't worry much about it. I thought, worst case, we might have to let Melanie go, and I'd once again be cursing at the fax machine. I'd answered phones before, and I could do it again.

Instead, on January 2, one scant day after the unsatisfactory Phil had taken a buzzsaw to my ego, Dickie and Stewie called me into their office to tell me they were letting me go.

"But you can't run the place without me!"

"Well," Dickie answered with a sad smile, "we're going to have to try."

"What about Melanie? She's only been here six months and she spends half her time playing computer solitaire."

"Melanie doesn't make enough. We have to make a deeper cut."

"We're thinking she can take on some of your duties." It was the first thing Stewie said during the meeting, and it was, without a doubt, the unkindest cut of all.

I stood up, on the edge of a panic attack. "Don't expect me to train her," I managed to wheeze before I lost the ability to speak.

"Of course not," Dickie replied. I could tell he felt bad. "You're to go immediately. You'll want to focus on getting something new. We'll give you great references, of course."

I turned around, squared my shoulders and walked out, out of Dickie and Stewie's office, out through the reception area where Melanie didn't look up from an intense game of Free Cell. I was into the hallway, then the elevator, and then on the street before I lost it. And before I realized I was freezing. I'd grabbed my handbag off my desk on the way out, but my coat, with my apartment key in the pocket, was still back at the office.

I hesitated for a moment before I decided the hell with it. I wasn't going crawling back, undoing my dramatic exit. I could shiver my way home and Miguel the quasi-doorman, quasi-security guard at my building could let me into my apartment. There was another key sitting on the table by the door where the unworthy Phil had left it just the day before.

□   □   □

So I found myself the next morning, puffy-eyed and headachy, in front of my computer going through the job boards. I didn't feel like looking for work, but my outrageous Manhattan rent was due in four short weeks. In addition, in hindsight, I'd perhaps over-gifted at Christmas. And I'd utterly wasted the money on the dress I'd bought for New Year's Eve with the unfulfilling Phil who knew, even when I was wearing it, that we were breaking up. Phil who knew, even when I was *buying* the dress, that we were breaking up. Phil, phhhft.

By noon I was hungry. The refrigerator was almost empty. I hardly ever ate lunch at home. At least I hardly ever used to. I was about to go out and grab something, when my eye fell on the tomato juice and vodka unused on New Year's Day. Tomato juice, celery, horseradish, these things are good for you, right? So I stirred up the Bloody Mary mix, poured in a little vodka and went back to my desk.

I intended to update my resume, but as I sat in front of my screen, drinking my lunch, I began to wonder what was going on at the office. You don't go someplace every workday for five years and stop thinking about it in one day, do you? Dickie and Stewie had an important meeting at that very moment with a prospect who could make up a lot of the Frodicker shortfall. Had they remembered to go? They never looked at their schedules and the languid Melanie wouldn't have reminded them.

Bah! What did I care?

I got up and fixed another Bloody. Actually, it was just tomato juice and vodka this time, because all that mixing was a pain. I went back to my desk and got to thinking about my office email. Nobody would have thought to shut it off, or change the password or even forward the mail to one of the other accounts. Clients might be waiting for answers to their messages. So I signed on from home, something I'd done more than a thousand times before, an act as natural as walking.

There weren't many new messages. Just a few after-the-holidays sales notices and a forwarded joke from a college friend. I wouldn't have expected much mail on the Wednesday of a short holiday week, but the lack of any clues to what was going on at the office and my overriding curiosity drove me further.

I'd had access to Dickie and Stewie's email accounts from the beginning. That was how I replied to client messages and read emails to them while they were stuck in traffic. Of course, those duties had been Melanie's since July. I hadn't opened Dickie or Stewie's email in a long time, but neither had changed his password in the five years I'd known him. I decided to see what was up. I signed on to Stewie's account.

Loverman. It was there in the subject line in the bold print that indicated it was unread. What an astonishing title. Loverman. But even more astonishing was the sender. Melanie. Melanie?

I didn't hesitate. I opened it.

> *Loverman,*
>
> *I know you're at that important meeting, but I miss you. I can't wait until this evening, to feel your lips on my breasts and have Big Stewie deep inside me.*

Big Stewie! That had to be an optical illusion based on the size of the rest of Stewie.

> *When you read this, imagine my tongue doing that thing you love.*
> *Xxxoxxoxo*
> *Mel*
> *P.S. I took Big Butt's chair. It's nicer looking and more comfortable than mine. I just hope it hasn't been ruined by her ginormous ass!*

I think I actually gasped. I don't think I'd ever gasped before in my life. And then I sat and stared at the email for twenty minutes.

It was the third bad thing in the string of threes, the final, backbreaking straw. First the break-up with the frustrating Phil, then the loss of my job and finally—

Stewie and Melanie.

Melanie and Stewie.

Doing it.

OMG.

Imagining Stewie on top was impossible. The sexual dimorphism was just too great, like stick insects mating, the tiny male practically invisible atop the female. Like a fighter jet landing on an aircraft carrier. I could only picture Melanie on top, sitting astride both Stewies, Big and Small, her limp, rag doll legs hanging over both sides of the bed, feet pooling on the floor.

Of course Dickie knew. There wasn't a thought that entered Stewie's head Dickie didn't know about. My eyes teared up as I pictured the three of them, swanning around the office, sharing a secret and laughing at the size of my bottom. I thought for a moment my head might explode.

But it didn't. I went to the kitchenette and fixed myself another Bloody Mary. This time I left out the tomato juice entirely. I mean really, what was the point? I poured the vodka over some ice, went back to my computer and stared some more.

I realized I wasn't the only victim here. I wasn't even the most aggrieved.

Dickie was a bachelor, but Stewie had a wife. The diminutive, the perfect, Marie-Claire. From Paris. It was as if Stewie had to go all the way to France to find someone as tiny and perfectly proportioned as he was. Marie-Claire was always perfectly coiffed, perfectly manicured and dressed in tiny, perfectly-tailored clothes. Marie-Claire, whose feet were so small she had her fashionable high heels custom made.

Just as I had been, Marie-Claire was living on the wrong side of the time-space continuum. She had a right to know about this. I clicked Forward. I knew her email address at the small wine import company where she worked from years of sending her Stewie's travel itineraries. It popped into the address line the minute I began to type. I hit Send.

I instantly regretted it. Damn! I should have removed the P.S. There was no reason to have inaccurate descriptions of my rear end rocketing around the Internet.

Oh, well. I deleted the forwarded message from Sent mail and marked the original document as unread so it would still show up in Stewie's email in the same bold type. **Loverman.**

I went back to the job boards and tried writing a cover letter.

Dear Sir or Madam:

I am looking for an advertising agency that doesn't practice
deceit, where colleagues don't keep secrets from one
another and no one makes hurtful comments about the size
of other people's posteriors

If you are such a place, I am your girl.

Fortunately, I passed out before I could press Send again.

□　　□　　□

I was awakened in the morning by the persistent ringing of the phone. My stomach heaved. During the night someone had stuck a knife in my head just behind my left eye. The ringing stopped, then started again. I finally answered on the third round.

Melanie. The part of my brain that wasn't about to split open registered distress.

"Slow down," I commanded, though talking made me wince.

"Stewie's in the hospital. He's hurt. Really bad. Dickie's with him. I don't know what to do." The sound of sobbing traveled through the line.

"I'll be there as soon as I can."

I arrived at the office after I'd showered then puked then showered again. Melanie was hysterical. Her skinny, Gumby-butt was parked in my chair.

"What happened?" I shouted above the piteous wailing.

Melanie gulped air. "He fell down the cellar steps."

"Jeezus. How bad is it?"

"Lots of things are broken." The waterworks started again.

"Okay. Get a grip." Of course, she didn't know that I knew why she was so upset. She didn't know I'd collided with that bit of reality. "Let's get busy. Cancel everything for both of them for today and tomorrow. Clear Stewie's calendar for next week and let clients with deadlines know they won't be getting anything."

Melanie picked up the phone and started to punch numbers, but then put her head on the desk and sobbed. I made all the calls.

"What exactly did Dickie say happened?" I asked Melanie for the eleventh time. She was all cried out for the moment and a little more coherent.

"Dickie said they keep Pierre's leash hanging on a peg beside the cellar stairs." Marie-Claire, the teacup-sized person, had a teacup poodle she treated like a human baby. "Dickie thinks Stewie was going to walk Pierre, reached for the leash, lost his balance and fell down the stairs."

"Did Stewie come back to the office after the meeting yesterday?" I asked as casually as possible.

"He was supposed to work late," Melanie sniffed. *Of course, that's what they called it.* "But then the meeting ran over and he had to take care of the dog, so he went straight home." Melanie dissolved again.

As Melanie talked, the vague, guilty feeling that had followed me all morning coalesced, and I remembered the forwarded email. My hangover-tummy turned to a cold pit of dread. What had I done?

I was seized by a compulsion to see the email, to revisit the scene of the crime. "Excuse me," I shouted over the din. "I have to, uhm—" Fortunately, the need to say anything else was drowned out by Melanie's crying. I fast-walked into Dickie and Stewie's office, closed the door and locked it. My stomach was trying to climb up my throat.

I flipped on Stewie's computer and went straight to his mail. Loverman. Where was it? Where was it?

Loverman wasn't there. In boldface or any other face. I checked the Recently Deleted folder. It was empty.

I couldn't catch my breath. Where had the email gone? Had Stewie deleted it? It seemed so unlikely. Had he checked his email as soon as he got home while Pierre desperately crossed his matchstick legs, waiting for his walk? Stewie wasn't a compulsive email checker. He always had to be reminded.

Maybe Stewie had been home all evening, working and checking his mail, and had fallen down the stairs when he was taking Pierre for a later walk? Maybe Stewie and Marie-Claire had such a terrific fight about the email, he was distracted and didn't watch what he was doing?

Or maybe it was even worse. I pictured Stewie, cellar door open, reaching for the leash, unsuspecting and tragically uninformed, then Marie-Claire storming through the back door, hurtling her tiny body toward him and shoving him down the stairs, all accompanied by the frenzied yip, yip, yip of Pierre.

Or perhaps Melanie didn't have the story straight and something else entirely had caused Stewie's injuries.

Like Marie-Claire had backed over him with her car.

Oh. Please. No.

The phone rang. I jumped a mile.

"Thank God you're there." It was Dickie.

"I came to help Melanie. We canceled all your meetings—"

"Listen to me." I heard the catch in his voice. "Stewie is dead."

Seconds ticked by while he tried not to weep and I tried not to scream.

"Dickie, I am so sorry." So much sorrier than you know. "What happened?"

"He hit his head on the way down. His skull was fractured. He didn't regain consciousness. There was never much hope." Dickie paused to collect himself. "I dread telling Melanie."

"I'll tell her."

"She might take it badly."

Ya think? Dickie and I were on the same side of the time-space continuum on this one. He just didn't know it. I wasn't feeling very charitably toward Melanie, but she deserved to be told in person. "I'll tell her."

"Okay. The funeral is tomorrow."

"Tomorrow! Why?"

"Tradition," Dickie intoned, Tevye-like.

"But Stewie wasn't that observant and Marie-Claire isn't even–"

"Tradition," Dickie repeated, and I backed off. What business was it of mine? Except perhaps I was the reason Stewie was dead.

"Dickie, was Marie-Claire home when it happened?"

"She's been in Paris with her family since Christmas. I went over to Stewie's house this morning because he wasn't answering his phone." Dickie sounded like he was going to lose it. "I'm picking Marie-Claire up at JFK tonight."

☐ ☐ ☐

Melanie took the news as badly as predicted. I led her to a bar and filled her with alcohol until I decided her roommates must be home. I turned her over to them, but not before she made me promise to take her to the funeral.

The funeral. Stewie was dead. I trudged toward my empty apartment.

Poor Marie-Claire. Of course, I was relieved she hadn't killed him. Dickie said when he told her Stewie was hurt badly, but alive, she'd fainted dead away. He had to call again later to tell her Stewie was dead. She got on the next plane. I physically ached for Marie-Claire, streaking across the cold, night sky.

My forwarded message was going to make a horrible situation worse. I had a dim hope that on vacation, Marie-Claire hadn't read her work email. I had to delete that message. Of course, it was going to be a lot harder to break into Marie-Claire's email than Stewie's. My only opportunity would be tomorrow when we returned to their house after the funeral.

What a mess I'd made of things. I shivered in my lonely apartment, longing for someone, anyone, even the unsatisfying Phil, to put his arms around me and tell me it would be okay.

☐ ☐ ☐

I drove Melanie to the funeral the next day in a rental car. Dickie was already up front in the synagogue with Marie-Claire. She wore a tiny, perfectly tailored black coat and a hat that obscured most of her face. She didn't react to Melanie when we entered, so my hopes that she hadn't read her email soared.

The service was mercifully short, punctuated by Dickie's heart-rending eulogy. Dickie is a brilliant writer, I've always said. Everyone was moved. Melanie wept so loudly people stared.

At the burial, Melanie clung to me for support, wrapping her body around me like a python. Dickie shot me increasingly pleading looks from across the grave, but Melanie's arms were wound so tightly around my neck that when I tried to ask her to calm down, no sound came out beyond a low gurgle.

Mercifully, Melanie asked me to drop her at the train station before I went back to Stewie's.

□   □   □

When I finally got to the house, it was crowded with mourners. Dickie introduced me to Leslie, Marie-Claire's best friend from work, then moved away to greet others.

"Where's Marie-Claire?" I asked.

"Upstairs, lying down. Poor thing, she's been through a terrible shock."

"Was she doing any work while she was in France? You know, like checking her email?" If Leslie thought the question odd, she didn't show it.

"She better not have. I told her absolutely not to. We've been so busy, the poor thing needed a break. And now, I really hope she took one, because she's going to need all her strength, coming home to this. She's taking it so hard," Leslie inclined her head toward the stairs. "I think the guilt makes it worse."

"Guilt!" Leslie stared at my reaction, so I dialed it down. "What would Marie-Claire feel guilty about?"

"Maybe not guilt, but the what ifs, you know. She was supposed to come back the day of the accident. She'd changed her flight so she could be home before Stewie and surprise him. But that evening she called me to say she decided to stay in Paris a few more days. I'm sure she's thinking, if only she'd been here. She might have seen him one last time. Or, she might have found him sooner, so he wouldn't have been there all night. She might even have walked Pierre and the accident would never have happened. You know how the mind works."

I did know how the mind worked. Poor Marie-Claire. I had to get to a computer.

I circled the first floor and found a home office. It was crowded with people watching a slide show playing on the computer monitor of Stewie in happier times. Damn. I'd never be able to sneak onto Marie-Claire's email from here.

I looked around. The room was all bright colors and sharp angles. Posters from Drucker/Feingold's ad campaigns hung on the walls. This office was Stewie's. There had to be three, maybe four bedrooms upstairs. There was space for another study. I had another chance.

I crept up the stairs. If anyone asked, I would say I was looking for a bathroom. Four closed doors led off a small hallway. Marie-Claire was behind one of them, but which one? I took a deep breath then opened the door on my left. Bathroom. Not helpful, though I was relieved it wasn't Marie-Claire's bedroom. I gave the door on my right a gentle shove. The room was given over entirely to Marie-Claire's clothes, racks and racks of sophisticated outfits that would fit a child and shelves full of fairy shoes.

Two doors left. I put my ear to one. Nothing. Then the other. I couldn't hear anything in there, either. I have to try, I told myself. If there's any chance to delete that email, I have to take it. I chose a door and pushed.

A study. A desk with a monitor and keyboard on it, two chairs, a bookcase. A feminine mauve on the walls. A calendar from the wine company where Marie-Claire worked. Bingo.

Closing the door gently behind me, I tiptoed to the desk and fired up the computer. I waited for the screen to paint itself and clicked on the desktop icon for the email system. I was momentarily flummoxed when a password box came up, but there was really only one choice. I typed PIERRE and the program opened before me.

There were screens and screens of unread email. Titles all mercifully boldface. Marie-Claire hadn't checked her work email while she was in Paris. My heart soared. I was going to get away with this. I raced through the titles.

It wasn't there.

How could it not be? I scoured the list twice more. I searched on the word Loverman. I sorted by subject, then by sender, then went back to sorting by date and hunted through the entire awful Loverman day, feeling more desperate with every pass. How could this be happening again?

I was so focused, so intent, I didn't hear the sound in the hallway. The door flew open. Marie-Claire stood there, a sleep mask pushed up on her forehead, Pierre cradled in one arm. He growled a tinny soprano growl.

"Ah," she said, "eets you."

I stared at her, unable to catch my breath. My mind searched frantically for something to say, some explanation. "I was just checking—" I let it hang there, hoping she'd fill in the blank with the obvious like—"my email."

Or, would she fill in the blank with, "that message I forwarded about your dead husband's affair?" I jabbed the icon to turn off the computer.

Marie-Claire floated across the room and perched on the chair across from the desk, Pierre still in her arms. Her eyes were bright, too bright. With what? Exhaustion? Grief? Guilt?

"I'm sorry for your loss," I said to fill the silence.

"And I for yours."

"Stewie was a good boss." And he had been, right up until the moment he gave my job to Melanie.

"And a good husband," Marie-Claire responded. Did she have similar caveats?

Her expression was attentive, as if she had many questions. I was sure she did. I had questions myself. Had she read the forwarded email? Did she know about Stewie and Melanie? I thought the police might be interested in the answers. They might even check to see if Marie-Claire had arrived home the afternoon of Stewie's "accident" and flown back to Paris that night. It was certainly possible, given the time zones and what Leslie had told me about Marie-Claire's plans to surprise Stewie. Surprise!

That would bring everyone's reality crashing together.

Or would it?

What if I made these terrible accusations and they turned out to be false? What if Marie-Claire didn't know anything about Stewie's affair? What if the horrible Loverman email, mistaken for a Viagra ad, was caught harmlessly in her office spam filter? Then Marie-Claire could go on believing Stewie was a faithful husband for the rest of her life. And I could forgive myself for what I'd done.

There it was again. That rip in the time-space continuum. I had my version, but what was Marie-Claire's reality?

I found, to my shock, I didn't want to know. It was better to be able to hold onto the hope that she hadn't seen the email, than to know for certain that she had.

The computer whirred to a stop. The room grew even quieter. I got up from behind the desk. "I have to go." I hugged Marie-Claire awkwardly, drawing a malevolent stare from the discommoded Pierre.

She returned my embrace. "You are a true friend. Sank you."

Oh God, here we go again. Had she read the email? Did she know that I'd forwarded it? Who else, really, could it have been? Was she thanking me for telling her the truth about Stewie and Melanie?

Or for keeping quiet about all I knew? Or was she simply thanking me for my courtesy over the years, my loyalty to her husband?

Marie-Claire released me and I walked away quickly, anxious to escape. I'd reached the landing when she called after me.

"Zey were wrong, you know—"

They who? Wrong about what? Dickie and Stewie were wrong to fire me? Melanie and Stewie were wrong to have sex?

The voice in my head screamed—*I don't want to know. I don't want to know. I don't want to know.*

"—your derriere—eet ees not so beeg."

△   △   △

Barbara Ross' *first mystery novel* The Death of an Ambitious Woman, *featuring Police Chief Ruth Murphy, was published in August 2010. In addition to her novel writing, Barbara is one of the co-editor/co-publishers of Level Best Books. Barbara and her husband divide their time between Somerville, Massachusetts and Boothbay Harbor, Maine.*

Repose

Mark Ammons

To know someone—*really* know him—you have to catch
his face in repose.
Take that, you bastard!
And that!
And that . . .
Ah, there . . . Now I know you.

△　△　△

Mark Ammons *is a Medford, Massachusetts-based, former stage director, producer, and screenwriter/script doctor. He teaches contemporary drama and directs the MFA Graduates' New York City Showcas for the Boston Conservatory. His story, "The Catch," in* Still Waters *won the Robert L. Fish Memorial Award for best first mystery and was also nominated for an Edgar® award, the first time a story has been simultaneously recognized in both arenas.*

Best New England Crime Stories

Dead Calm

edited by
Mark Ammons, Katherine Fast,
Barbara Ross & Leslie Wheeler

Please send me ___copies @ $15.95 per copy _____
Postage & handling ($3 per book) _____

Total $_____

Please make your check payable to Level Best Books.
To pay by credit card or PayPal, or to learn about other
Level Best anthologies, please visit our website at
www.levelbestbooks.com.

Send book(s) to:

Name _____

Address_____

City/State/Zip _____

Email _____

Level Best Books
411A Highland Avenue #371
Somerville, Massachusetts 02144

information can be obtained at www.ICGtesting.com
the USA
59110112

00009B/10/P

9 780983 878001